DOOMSDAY PASSCODE

Jennifer Wells

ISBN: 979-8330400508

INDEX

PART 1

PASSCODE MYSTERY

CHAPTER 1

The General

Northern Base, The Governor's Residence.

The team, now more familiar with their surroundings, made their way to the residence with no need for a ride from Chu Bai this time. After passing through the security check at the villa district, Svetlana Yevgeniyeva greeted them from afar. Well, not exactly greeted—more like confronted.

She wasn't in her usual Aberrants Bureau uniform today, opting instead for casual summer attire. Crossing her arms, she glared at Cora, her voice dripping with accusation. "Captain, first you steal a starship, then you blow up a lab. What kind of demolition squad is your F777 team supposed to be?"

Cora sheepishly rubbed her hands together. "It was... an accident."

Svetlana, utterly exasperated, didn't hold back, even though she was facing an S7 who could single-handedly take down a Level 5 beast. "I spent three sleepless nights reviewing thousands of files to select that lab! And you—right after the paperwork was completed— you completely wrecked it. How do you explain this?"

"Not... not very well..." Cora's voice trailed off. After a few seconds of awkward silence, she hesitantly asked, "Do you want me to... pay for it?"

The moment the words left her mouth, she immediately clutched her wallet, her big, teary eyes pleading with Svetlana. How much would this cost? They had only just got ahead financially, and now they might have to go back to being broke.

Svetlana couldn't help but laugh at Cora's miserly expression. "No need to pay. I still have some damage coverage left. But could you please try to be more careful next time?"

"Got it. Totally understood." Cora's eyes turned into crescent moons at the news that she wouldn't have to pay.

As the group made their way inside, they encountered Chu Bai, who gave them a curt nod.

In the artificial garden, Dmitri Yevgeniyev was amusing himself with a glass tank in front of him. The old general seemed to be in high spirits as he played with a turtle, flipping it onto its back. The turtle, with considerable effort, slowly extended its head from its shell, struggling to right itself, only for Dmitri to flip it over again.

Without turning around, Dmitri addressed the approaching group. "You're here."

Cora instinctively stood at attention and greeted him properly, "General Yevgeniyev." The others followed suit with their own greetings.

Dmitri waved a hand, signaling that formalities weren't necessary. "I watched the battle footage from Elder Nation. Impressive —calm under pressure, brave, and clever. You're all promising fighters, especially you." He pointed at Cora. "A born warrior. Even the best adjutant I ever had couldn't compare to you."

For someone like Dmitri, who had been forged in the fires of half a century of war, his praise was rare and highly esteemed within the New Pacific Alliance. Cora's cheeks flushed with pride, and she scratched her head, a little embarrassed.

"Chu Bai, you watched the footage too. As an expert in ancient martial arts, what do you think of young Cora here?"

"She's strong," Chu Bai replied bluntly. Cora's combat style was clean and efficient, with no unnecessary moves. Her exceptional physical prowess meant that even to fight techniques, some of her reflexes surpassed his own.

"Which school do you belong to?" Chu Bai asked, unusually talkative.

Cora answered honestly, "Master Zhang. We're from Mount Yue."

Master Zhang had once been a renowned martial arts expert in the Alliance, but he had retired early. Chu Bai, not yet thirty, was unfamiliar with the name. He nodded slightly and didn't pursue the topic further.

Dmitri leisurely rolled up his sleeves and beckoned to Cora. "Cora, since you're here, how about we spar a bit?"

Both being S-rank, Cora thought little of it and readily agreed. "Sure."

Svetlana, however, was alarmed. "Grandfather!"

Chu Bai's expression also shifted, and he stepped forward. "General, that's not advisable."

Dmitri cast a stern glance at them, his imposing aura forcing them to step back. "Why are you panicking? It's just a spar. I'm constantly being told not to do this or that. If I don't move these old bones soon, they'll rust."

The old general was dead set on sparring with the only S7 in the Alliance, and no one could dissuade him. Svetlana huffed in frustration and retreated to the side.

Dmitri then winked slyly at Cora. "Cora, I'm old, and my hand-to-hand skills aren't as good as yours. Mind if I use a bit of Anopower?"

Yuui subtly used her power to whisper to Cora, "Cora, Princess Onyx advises you to be careful. General Yevgeniyev is not a primitive awakened."

In this world, a "primitive awakened" (or similar terms from other civilizations) referred to those who had developed their powers before the apocalypse. Typically, these Aberrants had their abilities significantly boosted by the post-apocalyptic radiation, easily overpowering others of the same rank.

Dmitri, however, had awakened after the apocalypse. Now in his nineties, even as an S-rank, his power couldn't be that high. Cora belatedly realized she had agreed too quickly, but now there was no turning back. She could only mutter, "... Okay."

Dmitri lowered his center of gravity, suddenly launching a knee strike and a straight punch aimed at her throat. His powerful mental force surged, making Cora's legs feel as heavy as lead, immobilizing her. She was slightly surprised—gravity manipulation?

The nearby glass tank wobbled, and the shockwave sent the turtle, still trying to flip over, spinning like a top.

As the fierce punch came dangerously close, Cora gritted her teeth, struggling to lift one leg before delivering a mid-air sidekick! Dmitri's reflexes were sharp, immediately switching to defense, raising his arms to block. Once Cora's momentum subsided, the gravity of Anopower surged again.

The glass tank tipped over, and the disoriented turtle fell to the ground, only to be scooped up by Chu Bai, who casually set it aside.

This time, Cora was prepared. With a grin, she treated it as if she were wearing a few hundred pounds of weights, moving swiftly and jumping toward Dmitri. She delivered an elbow strike aimed at his heart, instinctively following up with an over-the-shoulder throw — only to glimpse Suchat subtly shaking his head in the distance.

Cora quickly caught on and switched to a grappling technique, neutralizing Dmitri's force and nuzzling him backward. Dmitri staggered back a few steps but steadied himself, while Cora also withdrew her hand. In just a few exchanges, she was drenched in sweat, her limbs feeling as if they were encased in cement. Gravity manipulators were indeed tough to deal with.

Dmitri clutched his sore arm, chuckling. "That was invigorating. Did you hold back just now?"

Cora modestly replied, "So did you."

An S-rank gravity manipulator could exert much more than just a few hundred pounds of force.

Dmitri wiped his sweat with a hot towel, casually remarking, "I remember you're an Aether wielder. The sword you brought last time was conjured, wasn't it?"

A lightbulb went off in Cora's head as she instantly grasped the underlying message. She eagerly offered, "Do you like it? I can give it to you."

She glanced around, then reached out toward the toppled glass tank, her palm glowing blue. In a flash, a cold, gleaming Tang sword appeared in her hand. Dmitri hadn't expected her to conjure the sword so quickly, and was silent for a second. "Did you... get that through security?"

The next second, a deafening alarm blared throughout the entire villa: "High-risk weapon detected. Starting Level 1 alert."

Soon, the sound of frantic footsteps filled the air. "An intruder? An assassin? Protect the General!"

Cora silently looked at Chu Bai for help. Chu Bai quietly went to handle the situation.

Not wanting to leave Cora in such an awkward position, Dmitri smiled as he took the sword. "Thoughtful of you. I'll keep the blade."

Onyx coughed lightly, reminding, "Captain, don't forget why you're here."

"Grandfather, now that you've had your fun, you really should take care of yourself," Svetlana scolded, joining in the reminder.

The group returned from the garden to the study, where Onyx got straight to the point. "General, we'd like to ask you about Utopia."

Dmitri Yevgeniyev didn't respond immediately. Instead, he opened a drawer and took out an intricately designed letter that looked like an invitation. When Cora opened it, she discovered it was a pass to Utopia, delivered just two days before the floating city appeared. Damian Blackwood, full of curiosity, asked, "Huh? Grandpa, you qualify for this, right? Why didn't you go up? Everyone else did."

By "everyone else," he was, of course, referring to the privileged classes of Elder Nation.

Given Dmitri's esteemed status and his monumental contributions to the New Pacific Alliance, no one was surprised that he had received a "ticket" to Utopia.

Dmitri slowly shook his head. "Not every governor in the B-District gets this pass. Even for them, the spots are scarce. For ordinary people, it's even more so. In the end, we are all part of a selection process."

"Most voices on the Lucas Network now claim that Utopia's residents have turned their backs on the world, living in luxury while everyone else suffers. But think about it—if someone loses the very foundation they depend on for survival and has to rely on the whims of others, is that really a blessing or a curse?"

Dmitri sighed deeply. "I have little time left. If I went up there, what would happen to the millions of people left here at the Northern Base?" Dmitri was like the anchor that kept Northern Base steady. Even though he rarely appeared in public, as long as he lived, District B10 would remain stable.

"Cora, for the time being, it's best if you and your team stay close to home." Cora was slightly taken aback, sensing another layer of meaning in Dmitri's words.

His old eyes rested on the pass, a sharp glint briefly flashing through them. "No matter what happens to the people up there, I can see that those down here are already growing restless."

Before he could say more, Dmitri's lips suddenly turned pale, and he began coughing violently. Svetlana quickly moved to gently pat his back. Their earlier sparring had taken a toll on him.

Cora suddenly recalled what Rainer Ninnemann had said the night before: "He's only holding on because of his S-rank constitution." Concerned, she asked, "General, we have an A5-level healer. Would you like them to look?"

Her suggestion was a bit out of line, considering that Dmitri, as the highest authority at Northern Base, would naturally have a top-tier medical team at his disposal. It wasn't their place to worry about him.

But Dmitri didn't seem to mind. He slowly caught his breath. "Dr. Franz, correct? From Sycamore in District C40. I visited there when I was younger."

Onyx raised his eyebrows in surprise; it was rare for a governor to remember the names of lower districts. Meanwhile, the 38-year-old Dr. Franz, nicknamed "Old Franz" by his teammates, blushed deeply as they teased him.

Putting on his stethoscope, Dr. Franz focused intently, releasing his mental energy as his expression grew more serious. He didn't immediately offer a treatment plan. Dmitri, understanding, gave him a faint smile. "Getting old means my organs are giving up on me. Sorry to have embarrassed you."

Cora felt her heart sink.

After a long pause, Dr. Franz carefully asked, "General, why haven't you considered replacing your organs with bionic ones?"

With today's advanced technology, high-quality bionic organs were common. As long as the brain wasn't destroyed, almost every part of the body could be replaced—like the mechanical eyes of the Knights of Anna or even the cybernetic eye Punk had during the Felalakas Tournament.

Dmitri's face remained calm. "You're a doctor, so you must know what bionic organs entail, right? It's not worth it just to live a few more years."

Dr. Franz was momentarily speechless.

Yuui and Damian exchanged puzzled looks, while Cora tugged on Onyx's sleeve, signaling the "know-it-all," to step in. Onyx quietly explained, "If an Aberrant replaces their organs with bionic or mechanical ones, it disrupts their original mental energy field, leading to a solidification of their rank. This means... giving up the possibility of a secondary advancement."

Cora's eyes widened slightly as she reflexively glanced at Felix Lucas. No wonder... No wonder he'd rather stay crippled than "stand" again.

The more prideful a person is, the less they can accept being stuck in place. If you can see your limits clearly, every day beyond that becomes a torment. Dmitri was like that, and so was Felix Lucas.

After leaving the villa district, Yuui shared the information he had decrypted earlier using a B-grade terminal.

"General Yevgeniyev is currently at S1 level, but at this rate, he'll soon break through to S2. As for Chu Bai, he's classified as an S5 with a mysterious type of Anopower, though no one has ever seen him use it publicly."

The group marveled at the information before turning their attention to planning their next move. Since they intended to stay nearby and take on local commissions, they had plenty of time to kill.

"Let's go shopping!" Yuui announced, hands on her hips. "We've been in the B-District for so long, and I haven't even explored!"

"I want to go too!" Damian chimed in excitedly.

"You all go ahead; we've got some other things to take care of," Cora replied thoughtfully. "Does everyone have enough money?"

"I've got plenty!" Damian raised his terminal proudly.

"I don't," Felix said matter-of-factly, holding out his hand to ask for some spending money.

Onyx shot him a glance. "Just give him a little."

Fortunately, Cora was generous and transferred a hundred thousand NPA credits to Felix, who walked away quite satisfied.

Once their teammates had left, Cora turned to Onyx, standing on her tiptoes and walking backward with a feline grace—a habit she'd picked up ever since her lynx genes had manifested. "You seem out of it today."

Anyone who'd been tormented by a clingy cat all night wouldn't be in good spirits, either. Onyx rubbed his temples, unwilling to elaborate. "Let's just go buy the flowers."

Cora unhappily extended her claws, about to say something, when she paused, twisting her head. The surroundings fell eerily silent.

"There's an ab-er-rant," she mouthed the words.

Less than two kilometers from the governor's residence, a faint trace of mental energy flashed momentarily under the bright sunlight. If it weren't for their heightened S-rank senses, and if they hadn't been passing by at that exact moment, it would have been easy to miss.

The aberrant hiding in the shadows remained motionless, but the residual mental energy in the air confirmed to both of them—he was nearby.

Onyx closed his eyes, then opened them again, releasing his own mental energy in a sweeping search, but found nothing unusual.

The villa district was certainly under surveillance; if there had been an unknown aberrant, the security would have reacted. Unless... the intruder's Anopower was "invisibility."

He took Cora's terminal and discreetly sent a message: "Unknown aberrant within a two-kilometer radius, estimated level between B and A."

Cora's face turned icy as she slowly unleashed her pressure. The two sides remained locked in a standoff for who knew how long before the invisible aberrant buckled under the strain. His mental energy suddenly surged and shot off in a specific direction.

Cora took off in pursuit, the aberrant darting around the perimeter's high walls before vanishing again. Cora placed a hand on the ground, and brown spots appeared on her skin. The lynx's powerful leap sent her five or six meters into the air, flipping over the wall and closing the distance in an instant!

Suddenly, a mass of pale zombie faces appeared out of thin air, so many that it made her scalp tingle. Each face was crowded with a dozen or more eyes of varying sizes, grotesque and terrifying. They reached out to grab her neck, arms, and legs, trying to hold her down.

The situation would have terrified anyone with slightly less mental fortitude. Cora quickly realized that there was another illusion-type aberrant at play!

She swiped her hand across the wall, summoning a ghostly blue tang sword. With a thunderous sweep, she slashed forward, shattering the illusions in an instant. The opponent's level was clearly not high—likely only a B-rank.

The aberrant staggered out from the pile of zombies, attempting to flee, but Cora swiftly spun around and drove her sword through its chest. His heart shattered, and blood gushed from his mouth as he crumpled to the ground, lifeless.

However, the brief delay allowed the invisible aberrant to slip away again. Cora carefully scanned the area with her mental energy, confirming that he hadn't left but was hiding within a hundred meters.

Onyx's voice came through her earpiece. "Cora, leave one alive and hand him over to Chu Bai."

Cora paused in thought before a sudden idea struck her.

She pulled a speaker out of her spatial storage, set it down carefully on the ground, then took out a pair of specially designed earplugs and inserted them into her ears. Feeling paranoid, she added another pair for good measure before tiptoeing forward to press play.

A strange particle wave emanated from the speaker. Anyone who heard it would feel their nerves unravel, their consciousness fading as if the world were collapsing into nothingness and their insides were rotting away.

If this aberrant had ever been to F191 District, the City of Sin, he would have known that there was something in this world called the "Record of Sins," an artifact that brought endless torment. The speaker in front of him was a changed version, a "Record of Sins Plus," designed by Felix Lucas. It blasted its waves indiscriminately, stronger, more intense, and deadlier than the original.

Thirty seconds later, a thin figure stumbled out from the shadows, clutching his head and wailing in agony. Cora grabbed him and slammed him to the ground. He tried to resist, but Cora quickly dislocated his arms, remembering to keep him alive by holding back some of her strength.

The aberrant on the ground convulsed violently, his pupils dilating rapidly as he teetered on the brink of becoming a mindless zombie—when suddenly, a twisted smile crossed his face. He screamed toward the sky, "Korosu ze!!" ("I'll kill you!!")

As he struggled, his collar loosened, revealing a faint crimson light flashing from his neck—a micro-bomb embedded beneath his skin! Cora's eyes widened in shock as she leaped up into a nearby tree, moving like a cat with its tail on fire, darting to the highest branch.

Boom—!!

A cloud of blood exploded in all directions, raining down like cherry blossoms. The man's head was blown to pieces.

Luckily, she'd moved fast, or she would have been splattered.

Cora gingerly climbed down and lightly kicked the corpse. The aberrant was most definitely dead—no doubt about it. The only living witness was gone. She turned off the speaker, eyeing it curiously. Was this thing really that powerful? Some sort of death anthem? Did it make people commit suicide on the spot? And... Cora scratched her head. Her foreign language skills weren't great, but wasn't the guy's last shout in Delta Island's languages?

CHAPTER 2

BAKA

Chu Bai led a group of Aberrants to the scene.

One of the bodies had its head blown to pieces, and the fingerprints had been deliberately erased, which delayed the collection of biological data. However, the other B-grade illusion-type aberrant was quickly identified, and the person reporting looked grim. "No identity information. They entered the base two days ago."

No identity information meant they were not legitimate residents of the Northern Base. Chu Bai glanced at the reconstructed facial features of the suspect—a plain and unremarkable face, easily forgotten in a crowd.

Onyx snapped a twig, frowning slightly as he disdainfully used it to pry open the collar of the illusion-type aberrant. As expected, a micro-bomb was embedded beneath the skin. Fortunately, Cora's lethal strike had killed him before it could be triggered.

"Did he say anything else?" Onyx tossed the twig aside and pulled out a disinfectant wipe to clean his hands.

"No, just that phrase in Delta Island dialect." Cora was sitting on a tree branch, hugging the speaker with one hand while swinging her legs. The ground below was covered in blood and pieces of flesh—far too messy for someone who loved cleanliness like her. After confirming the target was dead, she had climbed back up.

"Do you remember how it was said?" Onyx didn't hope.

"Sure do." Cora tilted her head, thinking for a second, then cleared her throat and loudly mimicked the man's tone, shouting, "Koroshite yaru!!" ("I'll kill you!!").

Her voice was loud, her tone confident, but the pronunciation...

"Pfft—!!"

The Aberrants on-site tried hard to stifle their laughter. They didn't dare mock an S7-level, but it was almost impossible to hold it in. Stifled snickers reverberated throughout the area.

Every resident in the B-District was required to be proficient in at least three foreign languages before graduating. Because of long-standing grudges, and because a shared language made it easier to trade insults, most people at the Northern Base had studied the Delta Island dialect. This was the first time they had heard such a peculiar "accent."

Cora: What's so funny? I nailed it perfectly!

Onyx's fingers itched; he wanted to pinch her cheeks but restrained himself. He turned to Chu Bai. "These two were death soldiers. They weren't here for us."

If they weren't targeting the F777 team, then they were likely after Dmitri Yevgeniyev.

They had confirmed that they hadn't been followed on their way here. These two were skulking around near the governor's residence, hiding their presence without daring to get too close. With an A-B level, they weren't strong enough for an assassination attempt, so they were probably here to gather intelligence. Unfortunately for them, they ran into Cora.

Chu Bai understood the implication and ordered the bodies to be taken away. "Thank you for your help."

"You don't seem surprised," Onyx observed.

"There have been a lot of 'sparrows' recently." Chu Bai's eyes flashed with a hint of killing intent. Though sparrows couldn't cause significant harm, they were certainly annoying.

"Because 'summer' has arrived," Onyx hinted. When the weather heats, there are always people who get restless.

The scorching sun beat down mercilessly, making everyone sweat profusely.

A year ago, the apocalypse triggered by radiation had descended without warning.

A year later, in the distant north, the S-rank floating city of Utopia had risen, hanging over everyone's heads like the Sword of Damocles.

Dmitri was right—some people couldn't sit still anymore.

Before leaving, Chu Bai looked up at the tree. "That speaker..."

Cora quickly stashed it back in her spatial storage, feigning innocence. "What speaker?" Chu Bai paused for a couple of seconds. "... Just don't use it here again."

Thankfully, the villa district was equipped with high-quality soundproofing, or else the general's desk would already be piled high with complaints from the neighbors. Cora grinned and gave him a thumbs-up, showing that he was a real stand-up guy.

After the others left, Cora gracefully landed on the ground. "Were those two from Delta Island?"

"Not necessarily," Onyx replied. "The grudge between the Northern Base and Delta Island is no secret. Shouting that phrase seemed too deliberate."

The true authority at the Northern Base was Scarlett Holland. If they wanted to gather information, they should have gone to the Aberrants Bureau. Why come to the governor's residence? Dmitri Yevgeniyev was an S-rank. Assassinating him would be nearly impossible. The timing and motivation for these two showing up seemed suspicious, no matter how you looked at it.

It was like they were two insignificant pawns on a chessboard. Then again, perhaps they weren't pawns at all but were simply thrown off course by Cora. Onyx believed that whoever made this move must have had their reasons, but further speculation would have to wait for the next part of their plan to unfold...

"Just now," Cora coughed lightly, her gaze wandering, "wasn't my imitation pretty spot-on?"

Onyx was momentarily taken aback, then chuckled. "Of course it was."

He finally gave in and pinched Cora's cheeks, conveniently forgetting his perfect scores in sixteen languages, and lied through his teeth. "Your Delta Island dialect is better than mine."

Sky Street at the Same Time

Holographic billboards flickered and changed, showcasing sleek floating supercars that were a common sight. Stylish men and women frequently emerged from them, as the glass doors of shops automatically opened to welcome them. AI sales assistants greeted everyone with warm smiles, offering personalized, attentive service.

The open-air ice cream shop, immersive cinema, and various entertainment venues made this one of the most popular spots at the Northern Base, consistently ranking as the top-rated consumer destination for customer satisfaction.

Inside a luxury boutique, Suchat stood at the entrance like a wooden post, dressed in black pants and a shirt, with a mask and baseball cap obscuring his face.

Yuui Hayashi was browsing through the virtual clothing display, selecting outfits with a gentle tap on her finger. Each item materialized beside her, quickly forming a small mountain of clothes. Her long, wavy hair was casually pinned up with a hairpin that glowed with a dark blue hue, its tip tinged with green. It resembled rare jade from the old civilization, but a closer look would reveal that it was actually a concealed weapon—a plum blossom needle.

Curious Aberrants passing by couldn't help but take a second glance, their faces showing surprise. Anopower weapons were rare enough, but one crafted so exquisitely was even more uncommon. Two young women politely approached her. "Excuse me, miss, could you share the link to your hairpin?"

"Oh, this? It's actually..." Yuui paused mid-sentence before flashing a charming smile. "It's from my friend's original design brand— handmade, custom-tailored, and produced in limited quantities. If you're interested, you can contact me, but it might be pricey."

What girl could resist the allure of something "limited edition"? The young women eagerly exchanged contact information with her, unfazed by the potential cost.

"I'm a walking advertisement..." Yuui muttered as she typed a message into the group chat, informing Cora about her latest business venture.

When she looked up, she saw Suchat standing coolly at the entrance. His aura clearly marked him as a high-level aberrant, attracting curious glances from the surrounding shoppers.

Yuui's eyes sparkled as she picked up two similar dresses in different colors. "Which one looks better?" Suchat pointed to the green one. Yuui raised an eyebrow, and his hand wavered, hesitantly shifting to the red one. "Are you sure?" "Yes." "The green one costs five times as much as the red one," Yuui teased with a smile. "Are you saying I should only wear the cheap one?"

Suchat, who was content as long as there were clothes to wear, did not know "brand premiums." Thinking he had made a mistake, he stood up straighter, feeling awkward. "No, I..."

Yuui snapped a few photos in front of the mirror and sent them to Jennifer. "Which one looks better?"

Jennifer responded with a voice message almost instantly, the background noise suggesting she was in the middle of a fight. "Darling, that emerald green dress complements your fair skin perfectly — elegant and stunning. The slit at the back is just right, and the way the hem sways is captivating. But I also think that the burgundy red one looks great. You look amazing in anything! Are you shopping? I'll come find you once I'm done here."

"Why don't you ask her yourself?"

Jennifer suddenly shouted at someone nearby, "Silver Owl wants me to find out if your captain is around!"

Yuui chuckled. "You should focus on your mission. We'll shop together next time, and by the way, our captain isn't here."

After ending the call, she playfully hooked a finger under Suchat's chin. "Understand now? Sometimes, when a girl asks you a question, it's not a multiple-choice quiz."

Suchat stiffened.

As he stared at Yuui in a daze, her words struck a chord. He quietly pulled out his terminal, preparing to pay. Thanks to the money Cora occasionally sent him, he now had a few million credits and wasn't as financially strained as he used to be.

Before Suchat could reach the cashier, Damian came bouncing by, sporting a pair of yellow duck sunglasses, a floral shirt, and matching shorts, followed by a long line of AI assistants carrying shopping bags.

"Is there anything else I can assist you with, dear customer?" the AI asked.

"Yes, I need to buy a bag for my sister."

Cora, the F777 captain who owned millions but was still frugal, was still lugging around an ancient, bulky 80L hiking backpack.

Damian strutted confidently through the store, pointing out items with his little finger. "This, this, not these, but I'll take everything else. Charge it on my card!"

For someone so young, Damian's lavish spending shocked everyone in the boutique.

When Damian saw Yuui, he reluctantly pursed his lips. "Add hers to the bill, too."

Yuui didn't need the money, but the gesture flattered her. "Little Damian, you're so generous!"

Damian snorted in response.

Suchat awkwardly fidgeted with his terminal, suddenly feeling that training in the rainforest might suit him better after all.

In the lounge, Charles Franz and Felix Lucas were connected to the black market, handling a task assigned by their captain, Cora Thornton.

Cora had sold off a batch of crystals and Ethereal Artifacts. Most of the crystals were below Level 3, as the F777 team's average level was relatively high, making them less reliant on these "power banks" during battles. They had accumulated a significant number of these crystals through various missions. As a hard currency, crystals were highly sought after in lower-tier markets, so they would have no trouble finding buyers.

As for the Ethereal Artifacts, Onyx had suggested taking a premium approach, so the number of items being released to the market was limited—only 500 pieces. Felix skillfully erased any trace of the seller's identity before listing the items for auction.

The two of them finished their work in half an hour and went out to join the others. Just then, a message popped up on their terminals— an unexpected personal commission.

[C-Level Commission (Time-Limited, Area-Specific): Defeat Hiro Fujida at the Silver Ring Arena within three hours.]

The commissioner's words were intense, and even through the screen, you could feel the seething anger. "I can't take it anymore! Anyone who can take down this bastard will get 400,000 points from me!"

Silver Ring Arena? What kind of place is that?

The Aberrants in the commercial district had clearly received the same commission, as they were all rushing out. Yuui put down the clothes she was about to try on and turned to her companions. "Shall we go check it out?"

With nothing better to do, her proposal was unanimously accepted.

The five of them followed the crowd, buying tickets to the "Silver Ring Arena" station. The unique B-District three-dimensional subway rapidly descended from the sky, and the surrounding scenery shifted from bright to dim. The flashing billboards on both sides of the tunnel created a dizzying, almost surreal space that made their heads spin.

Fortunately, the F777 team was used to the wild rides in Felix's black-market car; otherwise, this first experience would have made them sick.

Ten minutes later, the subway doors opened, and they were hit with a wave of deafening noise and chaotic mental energy. A prompt appeared before them: "You have entered an unrestricted Anopower zone."

A monotonous mechanical voice played in their ears. "Friendly reminder from the Aberrants Bureau: The Northern Base does not encourage any dueling behavior. Remember, the goal is not to win in the short term, but to achieve long-term success."

The lighting in this area was dim, giving it an atmosphere similar to that of the City of Sin. However, unlike the chaotic F191 District, the crowds here seemed much more restrained.

Because of the presence of millions of civilians, the Northern Base had very strict regulations on the use of Anopowers. Every entrant was required to read and acknowledge the behavior guidelines, which included rules against casual fighting and harming others.

But conflicts between Aberrants were common, and physical confrontations were inevitable. How could such many dangerous individuals be properly managed? How could their excess energy be released? It was only now that the F777 team, who had spent most of their time either resting at home or grinding for points, suddenly realized that the Northern Base had another, completely underground world that belonged solely to Aberrants.

Pushed along by the crowd, the five of them exited the station, navigating through a series of twists and turns until they finally caught sight of a massive sunken arena. Bizarre holographic projections surrounded the area, and thousands of Aberrants filled the stands, either sitting or standing. Unlike the wild, reckless celebrations of Felalakas, most of the spectators here had grim expressions.

"Wow! So many people!" Damian exclaimed in awe, clearly overwhelmed by the sheer scale of the event.

At the center of the Silver Ring Arena, a masked aberrant, his head wrapped in black cloth, stood proudly on the main platform, glaring defiantly at the crowd. He raised his middle finger in a provocative gesture. The information on the display screen identified him as Hiro Fujida, the target of the C-Level commission that had just been posted.

"What's the matter? Are these the best the Northern Base offers?"

"We came all this way, and this is it? Not one of you can put up a fight?"

Facing the crowd, Hiro Fujida sneered sarcastically, "A bunch of trash, you hear me? Trash. You're all baka!"

CHAPTER 3

Silver Ring Arena

Hiro Fujida was a master of provocation, sparking the crowd's fury with just a few words.

A swift figure dashed past F777, aiming to leap over the railing. Thud! Countless sparks flashed as the protective barrier bounced the figure back. A cold, mechanical voice warned, "Non-challengers may not interfere with the ring's order."

The young Aberrant, dressed in ripped jeans with a diamond-studded lip ring and obnoxiously pink hair, looked like a typical local from District B7: well-off, hot-headed, and overflowing with a sense of justice. He hurled a stream of insults at Hiro Fujida.

Aberrants had unique ways of communicating, and with just a touch of mental power, his voice boomed across the entire Silver Ring Arena. Clearly enraged, his mental power surged wildly, causing his voice to echo across the massive arena. For good measure, he repeated his tirade in a fluent Delta Island dialect.

Hiro Fujida's face was covered entirely, save for a pair of sinister eyes. He responded lazily, curling his pinky finger in the young man's direction. "Stop barking down there. If you've got the guts, come up here."

"Fine! You think I will fear you?"

The enraged young man turned bright red, rolling up his sleeves as he moved to swipe his terminal and enter the arena. His companion quickly grabbed him. "Are you crazy? Hiro Fujida is A9-level! This is a life-or-death match where anything goes. Are you looking to get yourself killed?"

"I can't stand it anymore! Better to die with honor!"

"Even if you can't stand it, you need to. You're just a B7. If you go down, you'll be the one humiliated! Then that bastard will say the Northern Base has no one worth fighting!"

The young man, doused in cold water, slowly stopped his wild actions. But he was still furious, tapping furiously on his terminal. He might not beat Hiro Fujida, but he could definitely call for help, right? He will offer all his points—this dog needed to be thrown off the stage!

A few seconds later, everyone in the area received a notification about an updated C-level commission: the reward had been increased to 800,000 points, almost as much as an A-level system task.

F777's group of five found seats, gradually piecing together the situation from the surrounding chatter:

"You don't know Hiro Fujida? He's pretty famous, the leader of 'Mist,' one of the top ten teams from Delta Island."

"What's a Delta guy doing on our turf?"

"Revenge, probably. I heard that Jupiter Blade and that new S7-level from here took Sachiko Nokuma down. He's probably here to mess with us."

Damian, who had been eavesdropping, nodded proudly.

Yep, that was my sister who did that.

"He's won four matches already. Why don't we just get an S-level to take him out?" someone shouted passionately.

"Are they picking on us because we don't have many S-levels?" another Aberrant muttered in frustration.

Since Jirgalang and Heize were seriously injured, the number of top Aberrants at the Northern Base had drastically reduced, making them the weakest in District B7. Sending an A9-level now was clearly an attempt by Delta Island to step on them.

"Using an S-level against an A9? Even if we win, it's still a matter of overpowering him with levels. Who wouldn't be embarrassed by that?" the first person said, his face grim. "Besides, Hiro Fujida's powers are an immense advantage in the ring... You'll see soon enough."

The boos from the crowd grew louder, threatening to blow the roof off, but Hiro Fujida remained unfazed, lounging arrogantly on the champion's throne.

Most of the Aberrants at the Northern Base had either been taken in or joined after the apocalypse, but they considered this place a second home. And what is home? It's a place we can criticize, but no outsider may insult.

"I'll take care of him."

A bespectacled man, looking weary from travel, began descending from the stands. "It's George Kennedy! Thank goodness, he's A9-level too!" a spectator shouted, recognizing him from afar.

George took off his coat, swiped his terminal, and calmly stepped into the ring. The display screen showed the challenger's details: George Kennedy, A9-level light Aberrant, team affiliation: "Blue Flame."

Aberrant teams from both districts had crossed paths before. Hiro Fujida squinted, quickly recognizing him, and sneered, "Well, if it isn't the 'Blue Snail,' always too late to the party."

The Elder Nation incident had been the talk of District B7, with all teams involved being scrutinized. Blue Flame, because of their poor transportation, had taken seven days just to reach the Endless Sea, by which time everything was already over. They had completely wasted their trip, and their ranking plummeted, knocking them out of the Northern Base's top ten.

George snorted. "Cut the crap. Let's make a bet. If I win, you get lost."

One of the Silver Ring's features was that participants could legally wager anything through a duel, including their lives.

Hiro Fujida's eyes flickered, and he stated his wager, "If I win, your team has to change its name to 'Blue Snail.'" Surprisingly, he didn't bet his life, content just to enrage George.

Under the AI referee's supervision, the two signed their contract. At the sound of the whistle, the fifth round officially began.

George's expression was stern as he launched countless light spheres, leaping forward across the arena.

As he snapped his fingers, overhead spotlights flashed rapidly, and hundreds of floodlights focused intensely on Hiro Fujida. Once locked in, the scorching heat would roast him alive!

Hiro Fujida sneered coldly, dropping a smoke bomb that covered half the arena. When the choking smoke cleared, the field was filled with tall grass and uneven wooden stakes, and Hiro Fujida had vanished.

"Wood Release!" came the gasps from the audience. "He's... a ninja!!" Hiro Fujida's Anopower was, shockingly, an enhanced form of mysterious ninjutsu.

George, now waist-deep in grass, moved cautiously, light spheres constantly illuminating the surrounding shadows.

For about five minutes, the two were locked in a stalemate, George's face growing more serious. As a long-range fighter, he was more comfortable in open spaces. Facing a ninja with ghostly movements required utmost vigilance to avoid a sneak attack.

Swish! A shadow flashed behind him. George spun around, deciding to destroy everything if he couldn't find his opponent! The light spheres struck the wooden stakes, which immediately dissipated —they weren't real stakes but mere illusions!

Whoosh! Whoosh! The sound of something cutting through the air reached George as Hiro Fujida's shadow darted through the grass, hurling a few kunai.

Pop! Pop! The light spheres were pierced, and the spotlights tracking Hiro Fujida were simultaneously cut off. The ring was plunged into darkness, the sudden shift leaving everyone disoriented, losing track of both fighters.

George didn't dare stop, continuously launching attacks in all suspicious directions. Where was he? Where could he be hiding? Suddenly, George froze.

Hiro Fujida clung to a thin wooden pole, emerging from the grass at George's feet, cackling wickedly.

He held a bamboo flute, blowing a dart that pierced George's chest. George fell straight to the ground.

The crowd erupted in gasps while the young Aberrant, who had cursed earlier, angrily shook the railing. "Damn it, that sneaky bastard!"

Hiro Fujida grinned maliciously, ready to finish George off, when the Silver Ring suddenly blared a piercing alarm! Flashing red lights lit up everyone's faces, both a warning and a threat. If a death occurred in the duel, the security level of the area would drop, and the

Bureau of Aberrants would have a few questions for the responsible parties.

Hiro Fujida seemed to have some concerns as he discreetly glanced in a certain direction before kicking George Kennedy out of the ring. The members of Blue Flame rushed over to carry him away for emergency treatment.

"District B7..." Hiro Fujida spread his hand open, counting off on his fingers one by one, "Northern Yard, Losome, Grass Pit, Askar, Northern Base—tsk. Is this really the strength of District B7's top five? Letting me win five matches in a row?"

If he won seven consecutive matches, he would claim the title of Silver Ring Champion, a prestigious honor that anyone had never won from another district.

"Blue Flame—or should I say Blue Snail now—how did trash like them even make it into the top ten? And Tustan, and what's that other team? The one with the numbers—F777. They went on one sea expedition, found a bunch of sea turtles as extras, and now they think they're something special?"

Hiro Fujida burst into exaggerated laughter, clutching his stomach as if he couldn't contain himself. "Did they think we wouldn't see through their act? Who doesn't know how to stage a photo-op? Hahaha!"

The crowd's boos grew deafening, but Hiro Fujida just flipped them off, turning a full circle in the ring, fully enjoying the provocation.

The cursing young man was so enraged he tried to climb the railing again. Was the Northern Base really so lacking in talent that they couldn't take down a single A9-level fighter? Of course not, but because of the elimination system, most of the teams were out on missions, leaving a few top-tier Aberrants in the city. This gave Hiro Fujida the chance to act so arrogantly.

In the unnoticed back row of the stands, Felix remarked with curiosity, "Is he mocking us?"

"Obviously," Yuui sneered.

Although Bryan Young's video was indeed flashy, did they really need to resort to staged photos to boost their reputation? Would they hire a level-5 wild beast as an extra? Hiro Fujida was clearly distorting the facts on purpose, using it as an opportunity to humiliate the Aberrants of the Northern Base.

"I don't think he's that tough," Damian mused, resting his chin on his hands with an innocent look. "He wouldn't last three minutes against my sister."

"How many in the whole Alliance could take on our Captain one-on-one?" Charles chuckled.

"Too bad my sister isn't here; otherwise, she'd flatten him," Damian pouted.

"Even if she were here, it wouldn't be right. Didn't you hear? He's an A9, and if we send an S-level, it won't be honorable even if we win," Charles sighed.

Damian grumpily squeezed his yellow duck sunglasses. "Yeah, yeah, I know. We can't always rely on my sister. We need to stand on our own two feet." He repeated almost word for word what Onyx had lectured him about more than half a year ago.

"But it's still so annoying."

With a snap, the sunglasses cracked under his grip.

Yuui's eyes sparkled with mischief. "Oh my, is our little A1 baby angry? What's the matter? Do you want to go up there?"

No sooner had she finished speaking than the person beside her stood up. Yuui looked up in surprise. "Are you going to the bathroom?"

"A man's two most handsome moments are when he swipes his card to pay, and when he wins a duel." Suchat suddenly recalled something he'd heard in a luxury store.

There wasn't any chance to pay now, but the latter… he could try it. Besides, he found Hiro Fujida rather unpleasant.

"I'm going to earn some points." Suchat pulled his baseball cap lower and strode down with purpose. He swiped his terminal quickly and entered the ring. The others exchanged bewildered glances—what was going on? Suchat wasn't the type to show off. Yuui abruptly stood up, but her attempt to stop him was too late. She could only shout anxiously, "Hey! Be careful!" Charles silently pulled out the first aid kit. "It's fine. Let him go if he wants. I'm prepared."

"Damn! Someone's going in. Who is it?" The cursing young man, now half-over the railing, craned his neck in confusion. "I don't recognize him."

Under the gaze of everyone, a tall man, nearly six feet three inches, dressed in black pants and shirt, entered the arena with a cold, piercing gaze. His movements hinted at the powerful muscles beneath his clothes, like a wild leopard brimming with strength.

The screen slowly displayed the challenger's information: Suchat, A8-level poison Aberrant...

The crowd buzzed with concern, their voices filled with worry. "Who is that? He looks pretty new. An A8? Is that enough? I hope he doesn't get crushed."

"Why does that name sound familiar..." a low-level Aberrant muttered to himself.

Amidst the noisy background, the last line of information appeared: Team affiliation: F777.

It was like a drop of hot oil in a cold pan—the crowd instantly exploded. F777? The recently famous F777? The team with the S7-level leader, F777? The team that Hiro Fujida had just mocked minutes ago, and now they were stepping up to slap him in the face?

Wow, this team's style... I love it. Thunderous cheers echoed through the arena as all the Aberrants from the Northern Base spontaneously rallied to support F777.

Hiro Fujida sneered, his attitude still hostile. "So, how do you want to play this?"

"If I win, your points go to us," Suchat replied curtly.

"Fine, but if you lose, then..." Hiro Fujida's gaze turned malicious, "you'll send your S7 to Delta Island."

"I can't decide for the Captain. I'll wager my life."

Suchat's calm declaration was like a bombshell, causing the crowd to erupt in shock. Even Hiro Fujida showed a hint of seriousness as he scrutinized him. "You've got guts."

Yuui suddenly stood up, her lips pressed into a thin line. "This is outrageous! Who allowed him to gamble with his life?!"

Charles tried to calm her down. "Suchat isn't reckless. If he's willing to go up there, he's confident. Besides, I'm here, aren't I?"

Yuui paced anxiously, biting her nails. "No, if anything goes wrong... I need to contact Cora." She lowered her head, typing out a message, hesitating several times before sending it, her fingers trembling uncontrollably.

In the ring, the AI referee signaled that the contract was complete, and the duel could begin.

This time, Hiro Fujida took the initiative, launching his ninjutsu first. The air grew chilly as countless ropes adorned with blades appeared out of thin air. Hiro Fujida clasped his hands together, forming a strange seal, and left behind a stone before merging into the shadows.

As soon as Suchat stepped forward, all the blades hummed, like the death knell of an executioner. Hiro Fujida had laid his trap and now lurked in the darkness, ready to torture his prey before killing him.

Suchat remained expressionless, thinking to himself, Is this the extent of his ninjutsu? He's underestimating me. Anyone who comes out of the Rainy Forest knows how to blend seamlessly with their surroundings.

Without breaking stride, he tiptoed through the web of ropes, avoiding all the obstacles. His tall figure gradually dissolved into a mist, vanishing completely. They had both disappeared!

The Aberrants watching the ring stood up in surprise, their eyes glued to the arena, but it was empty—only the faint flow of mental power could be sensed.

Boom!! A shockwave from a mental power clash rippled through the entire ring. Both fighters appeared from the shadows simultaneously. Hiro Fujida hurled a kunai directly at Suchat's eyes from less than thirty feet away—too close to dodge.

Unexpectedly, Suchat flipped his hand and threw a kunai of his own, a ghostly blue and razor-sharp. The two weapons clashed in midair with a sharp clang! Hiro Fujida's black kunai split in half, cleaving right down the middle!

The blue kunai continued forward, slicing through the ropes lined with blades, heading straight for Hiro Fujida's chest. In a panic, he dropped a smoke bomb, and the ground beneath him caved in, allowing him to narrowly avoid the lethal strike.

"What was that?!" The audience shouted in shock.

Suchat stood in the ring, holding the blue kunai between two fingers, like a lone wolf. His eyes narrowed as he surveyed the illusion created by Hiro Fujida's earth ninjutsu, showing not the slightest hint of fear.

Felix Lucas lifted his head, glancing around the floating screens with keen interest. His amber eyes glimmered with icy sharpness.

Suddenly, an unusual advertisement interrupted the sponsor loop. Ethereal Artifacts, all in ghostly blue, spun slowly against a deep background. A mechanical voice cut in at just the right moment: "Can't count on your partner to keep you 100% safe? Cora-brand Ethereal Artifacts—your doomsday essential! Call now to order: xxxxxx!"

Though the audience didn't fully grasp the situation, many inexplicably noted down the mysterious contact number.

The atmosphere was eerie, with shadows lurking everywhere. Suchat vanished from sight, tiptoeing through the arena with a trident dagger in one hand, carefully checking each hiding spot.

Each illusion destroyed brought a backlash to Hiro Fujida, yet despite his extended concealment, he couldn't find a single opening in Suchat's defenses.

The air seemed to thicken as a drop of cold sweat trickled down Hiro Fujida's temple. This guy's nerves were too strong. If that's the case... no more Mr. Nice Guy.

"Die!" A dark figure slid across the ground—Hiro Fujida opted for a direct confrontation!

Suchat appeared prepared, gripping his trident dagger tightly, his core muscles tensing as he slashed forward with a diagonal cut. Hiro Fujida couldn't dodge in time; his mask was slashed, revealing a face marred by recurring acne, full of pits and craters.

"Whoa, what an ugly face!" The cursing youth from earlier banged on the railing with glee. "No wonder he's been hiding it. Hahaha!"

Furious and humiliated, Hiro Fujida sprang up like a frog, releasing a flurry of hidden weapons and poisoned needles from his sleeves. Suchat's baseball cap was knocked off, but instead of retreating, he advanced, lightning-fast, and thrust his arm through the ropes, grabbing Hiro Fujida by the throat and slamming him hard into the ground!

Bam!!

Hiro Fujida's pupils contracted as he rapidly retreated, leaving behind a straw decoy in his place.

Suchat's black T-shirt was in tatters from the cuts, and he casually wiped the blood away with the hem before ripping off the remaining fabric.

He stood right at the intersection of light and shadow, his face and upper body fully exposed. It was clearly the physique of a young man who had survived countless life-and-death struggles—broad shoulders, narrow waist, with taut, defined muscles. His arms bulged with veins, and despite the blood, his body radiated raw power, especially with the black snake tattoo on the back of his neck, exuding a savage wildness.

"You're poisoned."

Hiro Fujida slowly emerged from the shadows, a cold sneer twisting his hideous face. Anyone scratched by his special weapons would suffer slowly as their skin decayed inch by inch, eventually dissolving into a puddle of corpse fluid amidst unbearable agony.

Suchat cracked his neck, the sound of his joints popping, and stared at Hiro Fujida with the gaze one might give a dead man.

For a stealth fighter, it's a fatal mistake to reveal their true trump card without securing a kill. Suddenly, Suchat lunged like a wolfhound, delivering a spinning kick that sent Hiro Fujida flying. He pinned him down with a knee to his chest, driving the trident dagger down hard!

A severed hand flew into the air.

"Ahhh!!" Hiro Fujida's scream was shrill and filled with disbelief. "How... how could you not be poisoned?"

"Idiot." Suchat's rare sneer surfaced. Did this guy even read his Anopower information before stepping into the ring?

"A8-level poison Aberrant."

Those born with the ability to wield poison as their Anopower have a natural sensitivity to all toxins. Suchat's mental power had been on high alert the entire time, protecting him from Hiro Fujida's attacks while quietly spreading his own poison mist. He had been enjoying Hiro Fujida's foolish display all along.

"The one who's poisoned is you."

From his severed hand to his contorted face, Hiro Fujida's entire body suddenly turned green. He didn't even have time to scream before the potent neurotoxin destroyed his brain. His head slumped to the side, life extinguished, and all the surrounding illusions vanished.

"He's dead?!"

An A9-level Aberrant, Hiro Fujida, had just died in the Silver Ring Arena?

The Aberrants from the Northern Base were silent for a second before erupting in overwhelming cheers! Strangely, despite Hiro Fujida's death and his loss in the duel, the security alarms didn't sound, as if even the surveillance system was biased.

With the ring master dead, the current challenge was over, and the barriers around the ring automatically retracted. As the crowd continued to cheer, whoosh! Nearly a hundred Aberrants of varying levels, from A to B, leaped down from all sides surrounding Suchat.

"Hey, what are you doing? How did you get in here?!"

Some people realized something was off. These weren't members of the Northern Base, so why had so many unfamiliar Aberrants suddenly appeared? And why did they act so quickly after Hiro Fujida's death? It was too deliberate, as if pre-arranged.

A man with a delicate androgynous appearance strolled down from the stands, half of his face strikingly beautiful, while a menacing mask covered the other half. His voice was oddly lilting, a mix of masculine and feminine tones. "It seems you broke the rules. Hiro didn't wager his life, yet you killed him."

Suchat slowly stood up, his face dark and unreadable. He couldn't sense any mental power from the speaker, which meant one of two things: either this person was an ordinary human, or they were an S-level Aberrant, at least S3 or higher, able to conceal their power completely.

The Aberrants from the Northern Base could no longer remain calm. They began leaping into the ring's center, some unable to restrain themselves, launching their Anopowers mid-air. Boom! In the chaos, a burst of fire struck the ceiling, sending spotlights crashing down, metal fragments scattering everywhere.

The piercing alarm echoed throughout the area.

The two groups were on the verge of a brawl, the situation teetering on the edge of total chaos. The androgynous man's lips curled into a smile as he extended his pale hand toward Suchat, his fingers twitching spasmodically—

"Wow! So many people!"

A voice, genuinely full of wonder, rang out above everyone's heads.

Perched atop the arena's overhead camera, a girl with shoulder-length hair looked down at the commotion, tilting her head slightly. "Before you all start fighting, could you settle up the points you owe us first?"

CHAPTER 4

Teamworks

Blinding red lights crisscrossed the air, the blaring alarms adding to the chaotic atmosphere. Cora hung from a boom pole with one hand, her round almond-shaped eyes, like those of a cat, surveying the scene below.

For a moment, there was silence, then curses erupted from all sides. "Who the hell are you?" "What's it got to do with you? Mind your own business!"

Cora calmly glanced at the few who were deliberately trying to provoke her. None of them were from the Northern Base. She didn't release her mental power, and with her slender figure silhouetted against the light, she looked like an ordinary passerby, completely unthreatening.

But strangely, from the moment she appeared, the Aberrants from the Northern Base seemed to collectively fall silent. The young man who had been cursing the loudest was now staring in disbelief, rubbing his eyes as if he couldn't believe what he was seeing. The others nudged each other in the shoulders, some even covertly pulling out their terminals to double-check the treasured videos titled "Not a Real Alliance Member If You Haven't Seen This."

The young man's pupils dilated in shock as the realization hit him —wasn't this their S7-level?

Aberrants had an innate reverence and awe for S-levels, especially those in strong offense categories, a submission grounded in absolute power. And now, the famous, elusive S7-level was making her first public appearance, apparently to back them up. It was a feeling of being defended by one's own, something that could only be understood if experienced firsthand. The young man's throat tightened, his eyes welling up with tears.

The few disrespectful Aberrants, realizing that the Northern Base had gone eerily quiet as if possessed, felt a pang of worry. If this continued, the fight wouldn't happen, and their mission would fail...

Someone hidden in the shadows quietly extended their fingers into claws, gathering mental power, ready to strike "What's wrong? Got a cramp?" Cora asked casually.

Zing!

A sharp gleam of light flashed past the would-be attacker's nose. The man's hair stood on end, his eyes reflecting the cold light, and he stumbled backward, landing flat on his back. However, the curved blade wasn't aimed at him; it veered at the last second, slicing toward the androgynous man. His twitching fingers clenched into a fist just in time—any slower, and they would have been cleanly severed.

The curved blade embedded itself in the ground with a sharp thud, coming to rest just inches from Hiro Fujida's head, as if it had lit incense for him.

The androgynous man's spell-casting was interrupted, and he looked up coldly at Cora. She responded at a leisurely pace, addressing the previous question. "My team member won the duel, so honor the bet and settle the points."

She casually lifted a lamp post, drew out a nearly 13-foot-long Square Halberd, and with a quick flick of her wrist, the sharp tip pointed downward. The twin crescent blades on either side of the halberd's head hummed with formidable mental power.

"No one moves until the points are transferred."

The entire arena fell silent. The floating screens overhead continued to tirelessly broadcast: "Buy Cora-brand Ethereal Artifacts! A doomsday must-have!"

Even the slowest of minds now realized who she was.

Cora, the highest registered S7-level in the entire Alliance, a metal-type strong offense Aberrant. Recently, she had single-handedly killed a level-5 mutant leatherback sea turtle. She was the current leader of F777, and most importantly, she was now representing the Northern

Base.

Suchat quickly took Hiro Fujida's terminal, walked to the referee's platform, and refreshed the system. No one dared to stop him at this moment. As per the contract, all of Mist's points were transferred to F777.

Clap, clap, clap. The androgynous man slowly applauded, his gaze fixed on Cora with a smile that sent shivers down the spine. "Impressive. Now that the bet is settled, who will take responsibility for Fujida's death?"

Cora looked at him with clear, puzzled eyes. "Who are you?"

The man's mouth twitched with a hint of displeasure at her arrogance. "My name is Irezumi."

"—Irezumi, from District B14, Blanc Yard, S4-level curse Aberrant," Felix Lucas announced from the audience, having pulled up the man's profile.

Yuui frowned slightly. "He's not even from Delta Island. Why is he standing up for them?"

"Because Hiro Fujida was just a pawn."

The steady sound of footsteps echoed from behind, and Onyx appeared with his hands in his pockets. His light shirt was tucked into khaki trousers, with the sleeves rolled up to his forearms. His deep-set, almond-shaped eyes glinted behind silver-rimmed glasses.

"The real purpose of putting a pawn like Fujida in the ring wasn't to win but to provoke, to push the Northern Base to the brink until someone snapped."

Fujida's repeated provocations enraged the Aberrants present, to stoke the flames until they erupted. His death, though unexpected, came at just the right time, allowing the enemy to turn it into the perfect spark to ignite a conflict.

"But how does starting a fight benefit them?" Yuui still didn't understand.

"Of course, it benefits them." Onyx nodded toward the ring. "Did you think only Delta Island people were down there?"

Felix Lucas hacked into the cameras, scanned their faces, and remarked monotonously, "Delta Island, White Town, Blanc Yard... at least seven other B-Districts are here. What a crowd. Is today a team-building party?"

Onyx sat down. "The death of an A9-level, leading to a massive brawl among B-District Aberrants, and if it's instigated by the usually neutral Northern Base, it's no longer just a brawl—it becomes a diplomatic incident."

His expression grew colder. Just when had these people, or rather, the forces behind them, reached a consensus?

In the ring, Irezumi stepped back, half of his face hidden in the darkness. His lips moved slightly, and immediately, an indignant troublemaker rushed forward. "You killed Hiro Fujida! Can't take responsibility? Cowards!"

"Spineless turtles, a bunch of turtle sons of turtles!!"

The vile insults and curses poured down like a torrential rain. It was as if they wouldn't rest until a fight broke out, and the Northern Base Aberrants felt shamed.

Most Aberrants couldn't keep their cool. On the Northern Base side, someone's eyes reddened with anger, and they took a step forward.

A Square Halberd descended from the sky, landing perfectly between the two sides, carving out a simple line of demarcation.

Cora landed lightly, like a peacekeeping officer trying to maintain order, and earnestly advised, "No fighting."

"What's wrong with you? It's normal for people to die in duels— that's the rule of the Silver Ring! Why are you being unreasonable?" "Fujida didn't bet on his life! You can't kill him!" No matter what facts or reasoning were presented, the other side clung stubbornly to their point.

The cursing young man's diamond lip ring trembled as he prepared to charge forward. Cora cast him a light glance. He shivered, his pink hair standing on end, and immediately fawned, "No fighting... You're right. We'll listen to you."

Cora looked across at the other side, tilting her head as if contemplating how to resolve the issue peacefully. "Killing is wrong," she sighed dramatically. "Yes," Suchat dutifully lowered his head.

Cora patted his shoulder earnestly. "We should turn ourselves in and go to jail."

Suchat replied, "Alright."

The other side was speechless, and even the Aberrants from the

Northern Base were dumbfounded. What was going on? Was their S7-level leader really going to do the right thing and send her own team member to prison?

"Are we done here?" Cora asked, her gaze piercing through the crowd and landing directly on Irezumi in the back.

"No! We demand justice for Hiro Fujida!"

Seeing that their plan to stir up trouble was failing, a few Aberrants, panting heavily, suddenly charged forward with ferocious expressions. The ground cracked open, and thick spikes burst forth, crossing the line Cora had drawn and expanding toward the other side.

Cora drew her halberd and shouted back, "Stand down!"

The cursing young man immediately retracted his outstretched foot with a whoosh, standing upright as if he were being punished, even reminding the others, "Sister Cora said no one moves!"

Cora moved forward with relentless momentum, dodging the chaotic Anopowers aimed at her from all directions. Surrounded, she suddenly pivoted on her right foot, executing a fierce spin! The halberd's blade swept in a wide arc, sending the closest melee fighters flying.

Cora pressed on, dodging attacks aimed at her head, her shoulder-length hair fluttering in the wind. She avoided what she could, and took on the rest head-on, gripping the halberd in the middle and slashing upward! The crescent blades sliced through her enemies' collars, lifting a dozen of them into the air and then flinging them into a heap. They crashed into each other like falling dominoes.

One against a hundred, Cora charged into the enemy ranks as if she were walking through an empty field. In just a few moments, the battlefield was in disarray, but she remained as steady as a mountain.

Irezumi's eyes narrowed coldly. Just as he was about to add more fuel to the fire, a sharp mental whip lashed through his mind, hitting him so hard that his consciousness wavered. Curse-type Anopowers required time to cast, and this sudden attack caught him completely off guard.

Irezumi snapped his head up, glaring toward the stands where F777's five members sat or stood, all calm and composed.

Three A-levels, and two... ordinary people?

Irezumi's gaze lingered on Onyx and Felix. As an S4-level, he should have been able to gauge their mental power, yet he couldn't discern its depth. Only a fool would believe they were ordinary.

A wild, almost absurd thought formed in Irezumi's mind: Could the Northern Base have undisclosed S-levels? He slowly retreated, lowering his head as he melted into the crowd, whispering to Cora, "Until we meet again." His shadowy figure transformed into a moth and vanished in an instant.

Nearly a hundred Aberrants lay groaning on the ground. Cora prodded some with her halberd, kicking others as she went, satisfied with her handiwork. "Not a single one is dead."

"Bureau of Aberrants, on official duty. Please cooperate!" A stern voice echoed from a loudspeaker.

Sunny Zhao, along with another S-level Aberrant, led a group of uniformed officials onto the scene. Her eyes were cold as her water Anopower surged forth, wrapping around the necks and limbs of the downed Aberrants, shackling them and rendering them immobile.

The Northern Base Aberrants, startled, scatted in all directions, trying to slip away. "All involved parties. Please report to the Bureau of Aberrants for questioning!"

"Ugh—!" The cursing young man, looking utterly dejected, shuffled past Cora, head hanging low.

A group of dispirited Aberrants followed the officials, and the Silver Ring Arena was temporarily shut down.

Sunny Zhao walked over with a serious expression, stopping in front of Cora. "Captain Thornton, I'm going to have to ask you to come with us." Cora blinked innocently.

Sunny couldn't help but smile faintly. "I'm really unlucky. I was roped into handling this mess, worried all the way here that a fight would break out. Thanks for stepping in."

Cora waved her hand dismissively. "No problem."

Sunny spoke kindly, "This matter needs a thorough investigation, so you'll need to come along to complete the process." Cora glanced at the exit, where a crowd of Aberrants was being escorted or willingly cooperating, completely blocking the way out. "We'll head over ourselves."

"Alright." Sunny didn't press the issue.

"No tea, though," Cora said thoughtfully, recalling how she'd just been filled to the brim with tea by Professor Ming and his wife, leaving her too full to drink more. Sunny chuckled, finding her endearing. "It's not that kind of tea. You'll understand when you get there."

Returning to the stands, Cora received a kiss from Yuui, a leg-hug from Damian, a thumbs-up from Charles, and... multiple orders from F777's top salesman, Felix.

She sat down casually, leaning back as she counted her points with delight. As expected of one of Delta Island's top ten teams, Mist was loaded. After taking them over, F777 had jumped straight to third place in the Northern Base and ranked 23rd in the entire Alliance!

In her joy, Cora generously transferred an extra million points to Suchat.

Sitting shirtless and quietly in his seat, Suchat had his wounds treated by Charles. He hesitated for a long time before casting a glance at Yuui Hayashi, like a puppy longing for praise.

Smack—!

Yuui slapped the back of his head, holding nothing back, leaving Suchat stunned as he licked his wounds in silence.

Yuui's brows furrowed with anger, but tears also welled up uncontrollably. She seemed torn between joy and fury, and in the end, she merely turned away with deliberate care, saying, "I'm glad you're alright, but never risk your life like that again."

Suchat lowered his head, warmth spreading through his chest.

Cora finished counting her points and waved her hand grandly. "Let's go. Time to take Suchat to jail."

"Cora! I need to use the restroom!" Damian, having been too absorbed in the fight earlier, had downed too many drinks and now couldn't hold it any longer.

"It's too dangerous here. Who should go with you...?" Cora scanned the group, realizing that none of the men were really available.

"No need to come with me!" Damian shouted as he dashed off to the restroom. He ran so fast that he collided with a man at the entrance. The man's round belly sent Damian tumbling, rolling head over heels. The man, barely paying attention, muttered a vague apology before quickly sidestepping and hurrying away.

"The rats are gone, and the crocodiles aren't happy. Catch another batch of cats to fill the warehouse." Damian overheard the man muttering.

Sitting there in a daze, Damian recalled how, before the apocalypse, Victor Blackwood had once boasted while picking his teeth, "The most lucrative smuggling business? Of course, it's trafficking! Just throw in a few rats and cats, and those crocodiles are the easiest money—"

An idea formed in his mind.

"Uncle, you dropped your terminal." A childlike voice called out, and Damian timidly tugged at the man's coat. The man glanced down impatiently, his own terminal securely fastened to his wrist.

"It's not mine, you're mistaken—"

"Uncle, this terminal doesn't have a password, and there's a lot of money inside. You're too careless."

The man's words caught in his throat as he snatched the terminal from Damian's hand. "Ah, yes, yes, that's mine. Thank you, young man."

"No problem, Uncle. It's what I should do."

Damian beamed with innocent delight, and with a flick of his small hand, a miniature ladybug-like robot crawled into the man's pocket.

CHAPTER 5

Prometheus

Two Hours Before the Silver Ring Arena Riot. Central Boulevard Villa District.

Lucia exchanged a few words with Gawin Ming, who was working in the living room, then picked up a watering can and headed towards the garden. As she descended the steps, the doorbell rang unexpectedly. Lucia was slightly surprised—they had declined visitors for many years, and their friends knew better than to disturb them, especially on such a special day. Who could it be?

Lucia activated the terminal, and the real-time footage revealed a young girl pressing her face close to the camera, her round eyes darting around curiously like a small animal. Behind her stood a tall young man.

Lucia sighed silently, gesturing for the gate to open. She set the watering can aside and adjusted her hair and clothes.

Before long, Cora came in, holding a big bouquet of fragrant, delicate lilies. Most plants had mutated because of radiation, and the restored versions she bought were several times more expensive than ordinary ones.

Onyx gently nudged her forward. Cora awkwardly spoke up, "Professor, happy pearl wedding anniversary to both of you." Lucia accepted the bouquet with a smile, handing it to the robotic butler for trimming and arranging before picking up the watering can again. "Come on in; I need to water the flowers."

Cora beamed and eagerly offered, "Let me help you!" Before Lucia could react, the watering can was snatched away, and Cora ran off, her enthusiasm impossible to refuse.

Left with no other choice, Lucia led Onyx inside. As soon as Gawin saw the visitors, his expression darkened. "If you inquire about Jace, I have nothing to say."

Onyx nodded slightly, his demeanor respectful. "Professor Ming, I won't do anything to upset you. As Jace's best colleague and friend, I'm simply here to check on you both."

Gawin huffed, but said nothing further. Onyx turned to Lucia, his tone gentle. "Professor, I have an unusual request. Could I see some photos of Jace when he was younger?"

Lucia was taken aback but agreed. She opened a dynamic album on the projector, clearly familiar with every page, often turning to it. Her motherly love compelled her to share it with others.

"Here he is, just born, as skinny as a monkey... Finally, we fattened him up a bit. Look at him at five years old, so chubby and cute. This one is from his graduation at Askar; he was the youngest in his class...."

Lucia's eyes gradually grew moist. "... I regret this album stops at twenty. I never got to see what he looked like afterward." "Perhaps there is still a chance," Onyx mused, lifting his gaze to calmly meet Lucia's eyes. "I'm fairly good at drawing. If you don't mind, I could try sketching how Jace might have looked as he aged."

He carefully studied the photos and videos in the album, from Jace's childhood to adolescence, and finally, to his graduation at twenty, when his life's record abruptly ended.

After a moment of reflection, Onyx took out a light screen and began drawing. He first copied the twenty-year-old Jace, using the visual references available. This portrait was the most accurate. Next, he drew a thirty-year-old Jace, depicting a more mature and composed face, following the lines of his bones and muscles.

The final drawing was of a seventy-year-old Jace, his soft eyes drooping, his face lined with wrinkles, his lips pressed into a thin line, and a gentle academic aura surrounding him.

Lucia stared at the image of the seventy-year-old Jace. "Gawin, this one looks a bit like you."

Gawin glanced at it, lifting his chin with pride. "Of course, my son takes after me."

He reached out, his fingers hovering over the air, tracing the thirty-year-old Jace. "He also resembles you, in his eyes, his temperament—so soft-hearted."

A wave of melancholy and sadness surged in Gawin's heart, causing him to look away—just in time to see that Cora was over-watering a flower pot, causing the water to overflow.

Lucia called Cora back inside, and the couple stared at her in silence for a long time. Lucia finally nudged a tray of tea and snacks towards her. "Have some tea."

Cora shrank back, not daring to touch anything.

Lucia spoke softly, "It's okay. The flowers I grow never bloom, anyway."

Cora was surprised. "Huh?"

Lucia smiled faintly, lost in thought. "Jace was like you back then, always eager to help, but never quite getting the water amount right. He often drowned the flowers. I've long gotten used to it."

Onyx lowered his eyes at this, his fingers twitching subtly. "Cora, could I borrow your light screen?"

Cora handed him the old light screen that her grandfather had left her. Onyx stood up and excused himself. "Sorry, I need to step out for a moment."

Once outside the living room, Onyx glanced at the drooping, doomed-to-die camellias, shaking his head with a wry smile. Then, he put away his smile, pulling up the portrait he had drawn of Old Thornton, based on Cora's description, and placed it side by side with Jace's image.

Old Thornton appeared much older, his face etched with deep wrinkles, his skin ashen, devoid of vitality. Anyone who saw him would think he was just a poor old man, ravaged by illness and close to death. But when Onyx overlaid the two images, Old Thornton's features mysteriously aligned with Jace's.

Onyx paused, then layered the image of twenty-year-old Jace on top, his gaze gradually hardening. Despite the obvious differences in their facial conditions, the structure of their bones and muscles was the same.

Switching to another system on the old light screen, Onyx

accessed a trove of innovative genetic research papers and data. If Old Thornton were from District F199, he wouldn't have had the means to get this information, let alone understand it. Unless... he wasn't from there at all but from District B4, where access to such knowledge was readily available, and he was once the prodigious genetic doctor from Askar.

But why would a promising young researcher age into a frail old man within a few short years? Onyx paused, a simple answer forming in his mind—radiation.

Excessive radiation exposure in a short period could cause organ failure and rapid aging. This was how Jace... became Old Thornton. There was only one explanation: after the Loyak incident, Jace must have returned to the research facility or approached the nuclear explosion site, resulting in severe radiation exposure and damage to his body.

But why would he go back? After fleeing with the experiment subject, why would he knowingly return to such a dangerous place? And what happened to LAK0017? If the primordial cells had died, the subject shouldn't have survived. How would Jace have dealt with it?

Onyx closed his eyes, then opened Cora's genetic report. Among hundreds of unknown DNA sequences, only two were identified—Ophiocordyceps and Lynx. This proved nothing. He could list over a thousand experimental subjects with those gene combinations, and among them, of course, was LAK0017.

After a long silence, Onyx sighed deeply, his voice barely audible. "You did it, Prometheus. You found the accurate fire."

In ancient mythology, Prometheus stole fire to rekindle the light for humanity, angering the chief god Zeus. As punishment, Prometheus was bound to a giant rock on the Caucasus Mountains, where an eagle feasted on his flesh and liver daily, making him a martyr suffering in eternal torment.

"But there's no Heracles in this world," Onyx whispered, his next breath coming almost immediately.

In the myth's happy ending, Zeus' son, the brave and strong Heracles, shot the eagle with a bow, rescuing the bound Prometheus.

But reality was far from the myth. Prometheus was punished for stealing the fire, and the greedy humans turned into the eagle, demanding the last of his life.

Onyx's brows furrowed, his eyes growing dark with rage. He methodically deleted every image, like a cold, indifferent deity who cared nothing for the suffering of mortals.

Back at the Front City laboratory, Rainer Ninnemann had once questioned why Onyx refused to hand over the fire data. Onyx's response was that he couldn't be a saint.

But he had lied. He wasn't unwilling to be a saint; instead, he wanted to be the Zeus who would snuff out the fire.

"——Après moi, le déluge."

Cora, feeling awkward after her well-intentioned blunder, buried her face in her tea to avoid further embarrassment.

Lucia placed her hand over Gawin Ming's, noticing it was cold. She pulled the blanket over him a little more. "We can revise the paper tomorrow. Did you take your medicine?"

Gawin, who could be as fierce as a lion to others, was a lamb in front of Lucia. "I took half of it."

Lucia gave him a disapproving look.

Gawin forced a smile, gripping her hand tightly. "I'm fine, really. Why bother with the meds if there's nothing serious?"

The warmth between the two of them was palpable, creating a bubble that no third person could penetrate.

Cora stared at them, her mind drifting back to a question Onyx had once asked her at Ocean Gate.

"Do you know what 'liking' really is?"

Suddenly, both Gawin and Lucia turned to look at her. Cora realized too late that she had accidentally voiced the question out loud.

Lucia thought for a moment. "Liking is the prelude to love. It's a shallow expression of the three core elements of love: attachment, altruism, and intimacy."

Cora, still holding her tea, looked at her with apparent confusion.

"Professor Lucia, I must respectfully disagree," Gawin interjected with a couple of coughs. "I believe that liking and love are two entirely different emotions."

"Oh? And what insight does Professor Ming have on the matter?" Lucia turned to him with a smile. For their field, these two renowned cognitive psychologists could debate peacefully.

Gawin's tone was firm. "Liking is an uncommitted attraction, while love is an exclusive loyalty. When you like a flower, you might pick it, but when you love a flower, you nurture it."

Cora's head bobbed back and forth as she tried to follow their conversation, nodding and shaking her head in a mix of understanding and confusion.

Lucia gently touched the hair pinned at her temple, her eyes shining with wisdom.

"Who says love must be exclusive? Commonly understood, love is divided into passionate love and companionate love. Passionate love is emotional and intense, driven by dopamine and adrenaline, making you desperately want to be with the other person. In this stage, there might be the exclusivity you mentioned, along with the shaky 'bridge effect,' which causes people to be irresistibly drawn to each other."

Lucia's words were subtle yet pointed, even changing her address to "Professor Ming."

Cora blinked in confusion. "Dopa... what? A bridge? I don't understand."

Gawin opened his mouth to retort, but Lucia cut him off with a firm gesture. "But the peak of passion can't be sustained forever. When the passion fades, life becomes more ordinary, and eventually, it returns to companionate love, which involves deeper attachment, lasting intimacy, mutual respect, and support."

"So, I believe that liking and love are intrinsically connected," Lucia concluded with a smile. "Professor Ming, do you agree with me?"

"...You're right." Gawin wisely took a step back, knowing that love or liking mattered less than a harmonious family. Lucia handed him a glass of water. "So, out of mutual respect, take your medicine."

Gawin choked on his words, silently taking the glass and swallowing the pills.

Cora lowered her head, sipping her tea in small, careful sips.

Lucia looked at her with the affection of a patient teacher guiding a student. "Did you understand?"

Cora mumbled, "I got the first part." She had understood until the flower analogy, but after that, everything became a blur.

Gawin and Lucia exchanged a glance: it was their first time encountering such a challenging student.

Lucia tried a different approach. "Liking is knowing it's him the moment you see him."

Gawin held Lucia's hand, and in that moment, they reached a silent agreement. "Love is when, one day, you look back at her and tell yourself, I'm glad it was her."

After leaving the Ming household, Onyx de Montclair remained silent as they walked. Cora sidled up to him, tilting her head curiously. "What are you thinking about?"

"Nothing, just feeling grateful."

Onyx took her hand, bringing it to his lips for a soft kiss. "Grateful that I found you so early."

Onyx had a face that was naturally refined, almost otherworldly, untouched by the grime of the world. Yet, his aura was so vivid that it created a unique, contradictory charm, especially when he lowered his voice, drawing people in like an irresistible vortex.

Cora corrected him with a slight frown. "It wasn't you who found me—I saved you."

Onyx smiled slowly, looking down at her. "Yes, you saved me."

"Liking is knowing it's him the moment you see him."

Cora suddenly found herself lost in his eyes, a little dazed. Looking back, it was strange indeed. She wasn't one to meddle in others' affairs, so why had she, when she could barely protect herself, been so compelled to save Onyx that day at Blossomville?

"Achoo—!" As she pondered, she suddenly sneezed out of nowhere.

Rubbing her nose, she looked up to find Onyx with his eyes closed, a few suspicious droplets on his glasses. "Ah! Sorry!" Cora quickly reached out to wipe them with her sleeve.

"It's fine." Onyx caught her hand, stroking her palm. "Are you feeling unwell?" Had she smelled something strange again, or was there an issue with her latent genes?

Cora answered honestly, "My eyes feel dry." Onyx carefully checked her but found nothing unusual.

He looked up at the sky. The Northern Base also had a weather simulation system, coded T005. The terminal displayed normal temperature and radiation levels.

"It might be a mild allergy. Let's go inside." Cora nodded, and just then, her terminal beeped—a message from Yuui Hayashi asking for help.

Three Hours Later, at the Aberrants Bureau.

The investigator in charge of questioning sat rigidly upright, barely daring to breathe. "Please, have some water," he offered nervously.

Cora frowned slightly—she had already been drinking tea all day.

The investigator, misinterpreting her expression, leaped to his feet. "What would you like to drink? I'll have it prepared immediately!"

Oh no, he thought. He had the misfortune of visiting Dr. Ninnemann's lab once and had witnessed this fearsome woman take down both Jirgalang and Heize. If she got upset, what if she twisted his head off?

Just then, Svetlana Yevgeniyeva knocked and entered. The investigator looked at her as if she were his savior. "I'll leave this to you—I've got other matters to attend to!" Without another word, he bolted from the room as if chased by a demon.

With only the two of them left, Svetlana drew out her words deliberately, "Captain Thornton—"

"I stole nothing! And I smashed nothing either!" Cora cut her off loudly.

Svetlana couldn't help but laugh. "Relax, you did a good deed this time. In fact, you deserve some credit."

Cora's eyes sparkled with hope. "So, does this mean Suchat doesn't have to go to prison?"

Svetlana's tone turned serious. "At Northern Base, the consequences of an Anopower causing death are severe, except in wartime. Fortunately, he killed someone from Delta Island, and they signed a life-and-death wager before the duel. Otherwise, this would've been a real mess. You can go pick him up now, but remember—there can't be a next time."

Cora headed to the holding cell to retrieve Suchat. On the way, she ran into a young man getting scolded by his parents. Seeing her approach, the battered youth ran over, rubbing his hands together excitedly. "Can I get your autograph? Sign my shirt!"

He ripped off his T-shirt, baring his chest, then seemed to have an epiphany. "Oh! And the bounty! I'll send it to you now!" After confirming the task was completed on the platform, another 800,000 points were added to F777's account, moving their ranking up to another spot.

Cora signed his shirt with a flourish, giving him a pat on the shoulder. The kid had potential—she always appreciated an easy source of points. The young man walked away, blissfully touching his shoulder, a dreamy smile on his face.

F777 chatted and laughed as they left the building, only to unexpectedly run into Scarlett Holland in the lobby. The Northern Base's second-in-command wore a stern expression, followed closely by six elite Aberrants, including the Rowin siblings, the freshly recovered Jirgalang, Sunny Zhao, and three newly arrived S-class combatants.

The two groups collided in the narrow space, both coming to a halt as the tension in the air thickened.

After a moment, Scarlett Holland passed by Cora without a glance, her face cold. Sunny Zhao, however, turned back and gave Cora a discreet nod.

Scarlett had always valued Aberrants, so it wasn't surprising she'd take action after so much unidentified personnel infiltrated her jurisdiction, nearly causing a major security breach. It wasn't surprising, either, that she'd exclude Cora from the operation. Ever since the kidnapping incident, there had been bad blood between them, and control over F777 had been taken out of Scarlett's hands.

Cora casually turned her head. "Let's go. We need to catch the smugglers Little Diamond found."

"Achoo—!!" As soon as they stepped outside the Aberrants Bureau building, Cora sneezed uncontrollably. "Are you okay, Captain? Catching a cold?" Yuui Hayashi asked with concern. Cora waved it off, signaling that she was fine.

Her eyes felt dry, as did her throat. Though she wasn't noticeably unwell, her allergy symptoms seemed to worsen.

Cora looked up, gazing into the distance. The sun hung high in the sky, starships zipping back and forth. The translucent barrier shimmered faintly, and Northern Base was as calm as ever. Her black hair gently brushed back in the breeze. The wind had picked up.

CHAPTER 6

Side Effects

Rumble, rumble—

The 3D subway descended vertically, slowly coming to a stop at the platform as a diverse crowd of passengers disembarked from the cars.

A man with a round belly hummed an off-key tune as he casually tossed an emptied terminal into the recycling bin. Who would have thought that delivering a "package" would land him an unexpected windfall of 500,000 NPA credits? Feeling quite pleased with himself, he patted his belly and walked across the transparent SkyBridge, turning into the lower-level streets where the bright sunlight slowly faded behind him.

Business had been good lately, and with this extra income, he could afford to live extravagantly for the next few years. A miniature ladybug peeked its head out from his pocket, its compound eyes blinking as it transmitted data along the way.

Just as he was about to reach his doorstep, the man came to an abrupt stop.

"Uncle!" At the end of the street, a well-dressed Damian waved enthusiastically at him. "Do you remember me?" The man eyed him suspiciously. Of course, he remembered—the kid was the fool who had handed him the terminal in front of the restroom just a few hours ago.

"I'm sorry, Uncle. I made a mistake earlier. That terminal is actually mine."

Damian pouted slightly, his expression innocent and sweet. "Please, please, could you give it back to me?"

"Don't be ridiculous," the man retorted instinctively. "How could you have that much money? Were you dumb enough to give me your terminal? Are you having second thoughts?"

"It really is mine," Damian blinked his big, watery eyes, a small ice shard forming in his palm as he smiled like a mischievous devil. "If I didn't set up this sting, how else could I have caught you?"

He's an Aberrant! The man's mind screamed in alarm. Just as he was about to speak, a few soft coughs sounded from behind him, and he whipped around.

In the glow of the setting sun, a group of six blocked his escape route. In the center stood an eighteen or nineteen-year-old girl, twirling a willow-leaf knife between her fingers. Behind her, a row of tall men and women stood, watching him with predatory eyes.

This is bad, the man thought, and he turned to bolt forward, hoping to break through Damian's position. Damian's eyes gleamed with excitement as he watched the man. The ice shard in his hand quickly morphed into a solid ice wall, blocking the man's escape. Skidding to a halt, the man cursed his own greed: of course, a windfall like that couldn't be real. This wasn't some lucky charm—this kid was a curse!

His eyes darted around, and suddenly, gray fur sprouted from his bare skin as his clothes fell away. In an instant, he transformed into a huge rat and dove for the sewer. This seemingly ordinary man was a shapeshifting Aberrant!

The rat squeaked frantically as it scurried forward, almost at the brink of escape, when—thunk! A ghostly blue willow-leaf knife flew in, pinning its tail to the ground. The rat tried to jump away, but it was yanked back, tumbling to the ground and seeing stars.

Damian jumped at the sight of the ugly rat hiding behind Cora and peeking out with one eye.

The sound of footsteps approached, and Charles, his hair tied back, crouched down "kindly." With a twist of his hands, two shiny dissection knives appeared out of thin air.

A smile that was all too reminiscent of a mad doctor spread across his face. "It's been years since I last dissected a rat. Where should I start? Maybe by opening up the abdominal cavity and pulling out the intestines...."

The cold scalpel pressed against the rat's thick fur, just about to slice through the skin when—

"Don't, don't kill me! What do you want? I'll give you the money back, alright?" the man begged frantically, using all his mental energy to plead.

Cora gently patted Damian's head. "First, turn back into a human, then I'll ask you a few questions."

With a thud, the man obediently shifted back to his human form, now completely naked, blood flowing freely from his right ankle, trembling on the ground.

Onyx de Montclair was the first to cover Cora's eyes. Her vision plunged into darkness as her lashes fluttered, and a deep voice whispered in her ear, "Don't look, there's something dirty."

After the man hurriedly dressed himself, Cora pulled down Onyx's hand. "Are you a smuggler?"

"It's a misunderstanding, miss! I'm just a humble ticket scalper, making a living from selling tickets and taking a small commission," the man lied through his teeth. Cora, of course, didn't believe him and cut straight to the point. "Let's be honest here. What are the 'rats,' 'crocodile,' and... Achoo! 'cats'?"

The man's expression faltered for a moment, surprised by the sudden use of coded language. Charles Franz raised his scalpel with a sinister smile, making a motion as if to cut into the man's chest.

"I'll talk! I'll talk!!"

The man's belly quivered with fear. "I swear, I'm not into smuggling. I just... help with a bit of illegal immigration, getting people's temporary entry permits into the base. The 'rats' are Aberrants from other districts, all with legal identities. We don't dare deal with anyone who's undocumented!"

As a popular immigration city within District B4, Northern Base had strict entry approval procedures. It even had a special city, Front City, dedicated to handling such matters, which was constantly crowded with visitors.

F777 exchanged silent glances; Damian had guessed right—this guy was indeed involved in smuggling. "How many 'rats' have you brought in?"

"Over time, probably around 5,000," the man stammered.

Cora's gaze turned icy. The riot at the Silver Ring Arena involved only about a hundred Aberrants, which meant there were still many more "rats" hiding throughout Northern Base.

Yuui spat in disgust, looking down at the cowering man with disdain. "5,000? You're a local, aren't you? How could you be so reckless, letting in so many dangerous individuals without worrying about what might happen to Northern Base?"

"With Commander Holland and the Aberrants Bureau in charge, what could go wrong?" the man muttered dismissively. "You should see Front City—so many people want to get in everyday. Besides, it's not like they're immigrating permanently; it's just a short-term entry. We're just helping… and making a living on the side."

The brawl at the Silver Ring Arena had been all over the news, but it had been swiftly covered up. Northern Base was known for its moral order, and with such capable leadership, the bigwigs would handle any problems, not by people like him.

"Don't flatter yourself—you're nothing but a traitor!" Yuui snapped. If the "rats" had been fleeing Aberrants, it might have been understandable, but these were people with malicious intent from District B4. Sure, Northern Base had a great reputation, but were the other B4 districts so bad? Coordinating the illegal entry of 5,000 Aberrants at the same time was clearly part of a larger conspiracy. These short-sighted fools only cared about their own profits, ignoring the consequences entirely.

Yuui kicked the man's jaw, making him yelp in pain.

Cora pretended not to notice Yuui's rough behavior and continued questioning. "Who's the 'crocodile'?"

The man, nursing his injury, answered nervously. "The 'crocodile' is… the boss, the one who pays to bring in the 'rats.' No one knows his true identity, but he's very generous and always pays promptly."

Cora nodded, understanding that this "crocodile" was likely the mastermind behind the entire scheme.

"And the 'cats'? How many of them?"

The smuggler hesitated for a second, uncertainty creeping into his voice. "The 'cats'… there are maybe six or seven? Or seven or eight?

They're very expensive, not handled by me directly. I'm just the middleman, but I've seen two of them. They didn't have any mental energy—they were just ordinary people."

"Don't worry, sis, they won't cause any trouble," the man added with a sycophantic smile, as if trying to assure her he still cared about his homeland.

After he finished speaking, all seven of them fell silent. A chill ran down his spine, and a sense of dread crept into his heart. "Did... did I say something wrong?"

Felix's wheelchair rose to full height as his amber eyes glared coldly down at the man. "Hey, rat, do we look like ordinary people to you?"

Suddenly, an overwhelming surge of mental energy erupted from Cora and the two men standing with her, crashing down on the man like a tidal wave. The pain of a thousand steel spikes pierced his body, his magnetic field spiraling out of control. Gray fur sprouted involuntarily as he struggled to maintain his human form.

The man's teeth chattered violently as a single, overwhelming thought consumed his mind: S-class Aberrants. If they wanted to, high-level Aberrants could easily suppress their mental energy, making it impossible for lower-level ones to detect them. That's why he had mistaken them for ordinary people.

Yuui, completely abandoning her usual composure, delivered another furious kick. "Those aren't cats at all—they're wolves! You fool, you've let wolves into the fold!"

Cora didn't hesitate as she drove a blade between the man's legs. "Hand over all the information you have on the 'cats' right now."

"There are at least six S-class Aberrants that have infiltrated," Onyx said calmly. F777 was holding a meeting on the top level of the starship port, where the view was excellent, allowing them to overlook the entire city. Down below, the streets were crowded, with no immediate sign of any disturbances.

At the Silver Ring Arena, an S4-level Aberrant named Irezumi from Blanc Yard had suddenly appeared, trying to back up Hiro Fujida. That was when they first sensed something was off.

Since when had the districts of B4 become so cooperative? It now seemed that the so-called "cat crying for the rat" was nothing but a pretense of compassion, while the actual intention was to incite conflict.

Felix tapped his fingers, and within seconds, he had hacked into the surveillance system. Reports of Aberrants causing trouble were coming in from all over the place. The S-class operatives of Northern Base were scattered, busy suppressing the disturbances, and the Aberrants Bureau's holding cells were likely already overflowing.

"I've already sent the intel to Svetlana and Chu Bai," Cora said. The faster the information was shared, the quicker both the Aberrants Bureau and General Yevgeniyev could take action.

"Achoo—!" she sneezed again, her voice muffled.

Onyx frowned. Cora's condition could no longer be dismissed as mere "allergies"; something was definitely wrong. "I feel like... the air is filthy," Cora murmured, rubbing her nose.

Whoosh—whoosh—

Suddenly, a strong wind howled, rustling the surrounding bionic plants, their roots and stems bending at odd angles. Crash! A giant billboard detached from a building below, smashing against the exterior glass with a deafening crash.

Where did this storm come from?

Everyone looked surprised. T005 was functioning normally, and the weather simulation system was supposed to regulate conditions, so why was there such an unseasonal extreme weather event?

The wind howled stronger with each passing second, and then, suddenly, everything changed.

The sunlight rapidly dimmed as the sky was completely obscured. At the far end of the darkening horizon, a massive sandstorm carrying thousands of tons of dust formed an enormous wall that swept over the entire Northern Base, swallowing it whole!

"Get down!!" Cora barely shouted as the seven of them clung tightly to the railing. The powerful winds whipped their bodies to the brink of collapse. Damian's feet left the ground, but Charles and Felix quickly pulled him back.

From their high vantage point, the scene before them was utterly breathtaking. In a matter of moments, the sprawling city was engulfed in a cloud of yellow dust. Tiny particles of sand pelted the buildings with a dull roar, shattering glass into fragments, tearing apart signs and lampposts, and dragging countless people into the vast sea of sand before they could escape.

Five minutes later, Cora struggled to stand, her nose, ears, and mouth filled with grit. Her sense of smell was overwhelmed, causing her to cough uncontrollably. All seven of them were covered in dust, and when they looked up, visibility was reduced to less than five meters. The sky was a murky yellow, shrouded in chaos.

Cora opened her mouth to speak, but the sand immediately fell out. "How could this?"

Onyx coughed twice. "It's a side effect of Utopia."

The rise of Utopia had led to frequent occurrences of extreme weather. The outskirts of Northern Base were vast desert plains, perpetually dry, relying on T005 for regulation. With global climate change, the atmosphere had become highly unstable, making it easy for sandstorms to occur whenever there were strong winds.

The weather simulation system had its limits, and this level of disaster was beyond its capacity.

An emergency broadcast echoed across the area: "The Meteorological Monitoring Center has issued a red alert for a severe sandstorm. All residents are advised to cease outdoor work and open-air activities, close all windows and doors, and remain indoors..."

Outside the transparent barrier, a sand screen slowly illuminated, enveloping the entire base and blocking out most of the dust.

Cora spat out more dust, the particles incessantly invading her mouth. "It's no surprise... this is District B..." she muttered, slightly relieved at how quickly they had implemented a response. With the sand screen in place, the choking storm was mostly kept at bay, and though the environment remained harsh, they could at least stand their ground.

Just then, their terminals suddenly pinged with an urgent commission: ⌈B-level commission (Regional Timed): Extreme sandstorm conditions have emerged at Northern Base. All Aberrants are requested to work together to mitigate the situation...⌋

Before the full content could appear, the commission rapidly blinked, and the previous text was erased, replaced by new information. When they looked again, the message had become even more ominous: ⌈A-level commission (Regional Timed): Protect Northern Base.⌋

The commission platform of the New Pacific Alliance, powered by AI clusters from District B and above, had never been wrong, either before or after the apocalypse. The upgrade from B to A showed that the difficulty of the task had escalated within a matter of seconds.

But that made it all the more puzzling. The sandstorm at Northern Base had clearly been brought under control, so what other extreme weather could be on the way? The vague directive "Protect Northern Base" seemed unusually unclear.

As they puzzled over the situation, a faint noise caught their attention from above.

Cora's ears twitched, and she abruptly looked up. Through the layers of swirling dust, she spotted a strange, pitch-black bird perched on the high-altitude sand net. Its wings glinted with a purple-blue metallic sheen, its feathers long and lance-shaped, and its irises bore the telltale gray-white color of a zombified creature.

"A raven," Onyx said, his voice cold. "Known for its large brain area, it's recognized as one of the rare birds with high intelligence."

"Don't worry, it's just a beast." Captain Thornton, ever the responsible leader, conjured an Ethereal Artifact—a rapid-fire crossbow—and aimed at the zombified raven.

Thud! The raven fell lifeless, wedged against the sand net.

But Onyx's next words sent a chill through everyone. "Ravens are highly social creatures. They often form flocks when foraging or during mating seasons."

Near the corpse of the first raven, a second one quickly landed, then a third, then a fourth... until the sky was filled with them. Amid the swirling sand, they resembled grim reapers, wings outstretched, emitting sharp caws, croaks, and screeches.

Cora looked at the flock of ravens, then down at her lone rapid-fire crossbow, and for the first time, she hesitated about what Ethereal Artifact was about to conjure next.

Front City was engulfed in chaos as sandstorms and ferocious beasts wreaked havoc everywhere. The vicious ravens, with their sharp talons, pierced into human shoulders, lifting their victims into the air to tear them apart and devour them. The sky had lost all semblance of its original color, replaced by a deathly black and yellow that covered everyone's vision.

"Ah—!!" The air was filled with screams as both Aberrants and ordinary people fled in terror.

"Quick, call for help from Northern Base! Request emergency shelter. Let us in!!"

Aberrants Bureau Building, Penultimate Floor.

Scarlett Holland clasped her hands over her abdomen, watching the real-time footage on the screen, her face set in a grave expression. "How many people are in Front City now?" she asked.

"6.5 million," her administrative secretary reported quickly, "including 4.3 million Aberrants."

Scarlett rose silently, her thin figure standing by the floor-to-ceiling window. Outside, everything was shrouded in a dim, yellowish haze, the outlines of buildings barely visible. "6.5 million people, over two-thirds of them, Aberrants, and all at this critical moment."

"A conspiracy? Or just a coincidence?" she murmured to herself. "4.3 million Aberrants… what a pity…"

Among them were those who hadn't passed or hadn't had time to complete their screenings—a mass of outcasts, likely filled with spies harboring malicious intent. If she had the time, she wouldn't have minded thoroughly sorting through them, selecting the useful ones to reinforce Northern Base's ranks.

But unfortunately, the timing was far too terrible now.

Scarlett didn't consider herself a cruel person, but she knew that the interests of Northern Base always came first. With violence rampant within the city, as the one in power, she had to make decisions that involved sacrifices and letting go of certain things.

After all… better to kill three thousand innocents than to let a single traitor slip through.

"Commander Holland, the casualties in Front City are severe. The Transportation Department has already arranged several evacuation routes. The following stations are expected to be opened..." The secretary, overwhelmed, frantically scrolled through the information on his light screen, pleading for his superior to issue instructions as soon as possible.

"There's no need," Scarlett's voice cut through, cold and decisive.

"Huh?" The secretary blinked, letting out a small, unconscious sound of inquiry.

"Close all connections to Front City. Only allow flight terminals with base identification codes to enter."

The secretary froze for a long moment, and when the meaning of her words finally sank in, a chilling fear spread through his entire body.

CHAPTER 7

The Hope

"Miss Yevgeniyeva, wait a moment, don't be rash. Let's talk this through." "Commander Holland is in a meeting; you can't just barge in like this." "Svetlana, let's wait for the approval, okay? There might still be a chance..."

Svetlana's face was as stern as stone as she strode down the corridor. As an A3-level gravity Aberrant, she merely waved her hand, and with little effort, her colleagues felt as though their limbs were weighted down with heavy sandbags. Their knees buckled, and they fell to the ground, unable to stop her.

In the past, Svetlana, who was always law-abiding and by the book, would never have dared to use her Anopowers so brazenly in the workplace. However, after repeatedly cleaning up messes under the subtle influence of the "outlaw" Cora, she gradually realized that sometimes resolving issues through force could save a lot of unnecessary time.

She stopped in front of the conference room, took a deep breath, and knocked on the door. Without waiting for a response, she pushed it open and walked in with determined steps. "Commander Holland, this is the evacuation proposal I've prepared. It outlines 13 routes for the residents of Front City to retreat. Please review and approve it."

The room fell silent as the participants' virtual projections all turned to her, the unexpected intruder, with expressions of surprise.

Scarlett Holland remained seated at the head of the table, her face unchanged. "I've already issued an order regarding Front City. Carry it out as instructed."

Svetlana's hands slowly clenched into fists, and she spoke each word deliberately. "No, we cannot carry it out. You represent only your own will, not that of Northern Base."

Her words shocked everyone in the room. Scarlett Holland was no ordinary person—she was the highest-ranking officer of the Aberrants Bureau and the second-in-command of District B10. Many present weren't fully aware of Svetlana's true identity, and they gasped at her open defiance. Was this young woman insane? Did she have a death wish?

"Commander Holland, you have always been a respected mentor to me, someone I looked up to," Svetlana said, her back straight and her voice trembling slightly, though her resolve was unshaken.

"But it seems you don't understand the true purpose of Northern Base. General Yevgeniyev built this city to provide a sanctuary for all those who have suffered through war, regardless of whether times are peaceful or turbulent. No matter what happens, as long as Northern Base stands, its gates must remain open to our fellow citizens. That's why it is called—humanity's last hope."

After the devastating nuclear war, countless people were left homeless and adrift, wandering with nothing but despair. General Dmitri Yevgeniyev had built a new city on the wasteland, telling all survivors that this was their home. Half a century later, many prosperous cities had risen, yet Northern Base held a unique significance for the people of the Alliance—it symbolized not just hope, but also the last refuge.

Tears welled up in Svetlana's eyes as she raised her voice. "The 6.5 million people out there are our compatriots—they should not be abandoned!"

"You're still young and don't fully grasp the situation," Scarlett Holland said, surprisingly calm, without the usual anger in her tone. She sighed and brought up the live surveillance feed. "Aberrants from various districts currently infiltrated the city, including some S-class operatives. They harbor ill intentions, aiming to provoke conflict. What good would it do to let the people of the Front City in? The wisest course of action now is to prioritize dealing with the internal crisis and minimizing risks."

Svetlana questioned her in disbelief, "Commander Holland, do you really measure the value of a person's life by their 'usefulness'?"

Scarlett Holland raised her hand slightly. "I must prioritize the interests of Northern Base."

At that moment, Heize emerged from the shadows, his pallor striking against the dim lighting, and the entire conference room was instantly sealed off, becoming a zone where no mental powers could be used. Heize, who had been forcibly demoted from S3 to A9 by Cora Thornton, had disappeared from the public eye. Who would have guessed that he had secretly aligned himself with Scarlett Holland?

Several security personnel entered and restrained Svetlana.

Scarlett looked at her calmly. "Once this crisis is over, I will ask the General for forgiveness."

Svetlana struggled, but she was helpless to move. She closed her eyes, connecting her consciousness with her terminal as the pearl earring on her ear flashed with a quick, subtle light.

After the sandstorm and the raven flock, the Aberrants of Northern Base swiftly launched a counterattack. Armed flying vehicles soared through the sky, and bursts of Anopower in various colors pierced through the murky, sand-filled atmosphere.

Thanks to the dual barriers of the sand net and the shield, the raven horde could not breach the base, leaving it temporarily secure. However, the sheer number of ravens densely packed in the sky was overwhelming. The only way to deal with them was through long-range Anopower attacks, slowly chipping away at their numbers.

Yuui's long hair swayed gently as she chanted an ethereal melody, casting a debuff on the ravens within range. Their aggressive instincts were significantly dampened, turning Damian into F777's most effective damage dealer.

His icy needles rained down in a storm, while Felix and the others set up heavy machine guns. However, because of the upward angle, the effective range was shortened, limiting the damage inflicted.

Cora pulled her leg out of the ankle-deep sand and shook it off. As she looked up, she locked eyes with a slightly larger raven.

"You—you come down here!" Cora shouted defiantly, raising her arm and pointing at the bird.

"Caw, caw!" The raven's pale gray eyes flashed with a hint of disdain, as if to say, "Why don't you come up here?"

Captain Thornton stared in disbelief, accidentally swallowing another mouthful of sand. Ptooey! Was she just mocked by a bird?

She would have liked to conjure a weapon that could instantly fire thousands of needles, but even if such a thing existed in the history of old civilizations, she had never seen one and couldn't imagine its precise structure, leaving her with no choice but to grit her teeth.

Unhappy, Cora ground her teeth, placed one hand on the ground, and suddenly leaped into the air. With her Ophiocordyceps genes pushed to the limit, she jumped over eight meters high, skillfully scaling the lightning rod to reach the highest point. With a flick of her wrist, her throwing knives whirled through the air, slicing through a large swath of the arrogant ravens.

But as soon as the first wave of beasts fell, a fresh wave surged forward, seemingly endless. The ravens collided with the barrier, and cracks formed on the outer sand net.

Cora jumped back onto a lower platform, her expression troubled. This wasn't working—the clearing rate was too slow to keep up with the influx of ravens. Just how many of these beasts were there? Had every raven in the Alliance descended upon them?

Boom—boom—

A sleek hover car zoomed in, skimming dangerously close to the sand net. Scarlet explosive rounds fired from the car, passing through the openings in the net and detonating in the densest cluster of ravens, sending black feathers flying as blood and flesh splattered. The once-obscured sky was clear again.

The car's roof opened, and Silver Owl pushed his sniper scope up to his forehead, revealing a sharp, angular face. His grayish eyes glinted coldly as he stared down at the raven horde. But when he looked at Cora, his expression softened into a bright smile.

Perched on the car's roof, Silver Owl tilted his head slightly, covering his face with one hand as he asked in a low voice, "Darling, do you think I have a chance if I propose again?"

Jennifer didn't have time to respond before Silver Owl convinced himself. "Doesn't matter—how will I know if I don't try?"

Like a soaring eagle, he leaped down and squeezed onto the narrow platform, his face inches from Cora's, causing her to sneeze twice. Silver Owl was covered in sand, and as he shook himself, several pounds of it fell off, showing he had just returned from outside.

Cora rubbed her nose, slightly surprised. "You've advanced?" In just a few days, Silver Owl's mental strength had reached S-class.

Caw, caw! Caw, caw! The ravens gathered overhead once more. Without looking up, Silver Owl fired another shot, scattering them like leaves in the wind.

"Just broke through to S1, Captain Thornton. I've been working hard to catch up to you."

His words carried a double meaning, but the compliment fell on deaf ears. Cora, completely missing the hint, replied earnestly, "Congratulations!"

Silver Owl gazed intently at her. "Now that I'm S-class too, how about you consider ditching that other guy and—"

"Cora Thornton, get down here." Onyx de Montclair's deep voice interrupted.

"Daddy, help! It's on fire!" Jennifer's wails echoed. Group-attack Aberrants had their drawbacks, mainly collateral damage, and Jennifer's flames were so powerful that while they scorched the ravens, they also accidentally damaged the sand net.

Cora turned her head and shouted, "Little Diamond, give us a hand!" Her Ophiocordyceps genes activated again, and the obedient "little kitten" leaped back to Onyx's side.

Silver Owl and the man below exchanged a disdainful glance. Onyx smirked coldly, raising an eyebrow. Silver Owl rolled his eyes dramatically and jumped down after Cora.

Damian, now bouncing with excitement, switched his icy needles to a wider spread of ice and snow, effectively halting the spread of the Anopower flames. However, that section of the area was left charred, the sand net now teetering on the brink of collapse, with raven corpses piling high.

Members of "Tustan" landed on the rooftop, and Jennifer, tossing her wavy hair, blew a flirtatious kiss and spread her arms wide as she ran over. "Oh~~ Darling~~ I've missed you sooo much..."

Thud! She slammed straight into a hard chest.

Suchat's face was as dark as the bottom of a pot. With two fingers against his forehead, he pushed her back a few meters.

Jennifer stumbled back to Silver Owl's side, and the father-daughter duo pouted in unison, silently agreeing on one thing: Why is there always an annoying guy around our beloved target?

Onyx looked up at the ever-growing raven horde, his expression grave. "At this rate, things aren't looking good."

The number of beasts was far greater than initially expected. Although the Aberrants of Northern Base had taken down some, they had also left the sand net riddled with holes. The sandstorm was once again raging, with yellow winds howling and filthy dust choking their airways.

Given the current situation, human efforts alone wouldn't suffice. Activating the city's defense mechanisms was the only viable solution.

Onyx spoke in a low tone. "District B has a comprehensive defense system. I need to see the engineering blueprints to come up with another plan." Cora opened her terminal, about to contact Svetlana, only to find an unexpected message from her—completely blank. Cora tried calling back, but there was no answer.

Felix took the terminal and fiddled with it for a moment. "Svetlana's signal is being jammed." Onyx's eyes narrowed slightly. Before they had left, Svetlana was at the Aberrants Bureau, and there was only one explanation for her sudden silence—Scarlett Holland had detained her.

"Contact Chu Bai. We're going to find General Yevgeniyev." "Hey, Captain Thornton, count us in."

The two teams hurried toward the Governor's mansion.

An endless swarm of ravens swooped wildly through the sky, diving periodically with their sharp talons to catch their prey, cruelly tearing open stomachs and spilling intestines.

Terrified people scattered in all directions, seeking refuge inside sealed buildings, basements, and any vehicles they could find. But doors were broken down, windows shattered, and even monsters emerged from the sewers, attacking them from every conceivable angle.

Aberrants fought back, but in the blink of an eye, their limbs were seized and they were dragged into the air, only to be torn apart in different directions. The black beasts were everywhere, too many to count, overwhelming any hope of escape. The scattered residents of

Front City seemed doomed, unable to escape their fate of death.

"Mama... Papa... where are you...?" A little girl, only four or five years old, stumbled through the streets, wailing in despair. Around her, the dismembered bodies lay strewn, the ground slick with the viscera of the dead, and the crimson blood had soaked through her new white shoes.

"Caw! Caw!" The ominous cry echoed from above, and the girl looked up in terror, her wide eyes reflecting the menacing wings of a raven, like a reaper raising its scythe. Just as the raven swooped down, a young Aberrant threw himself over the girl, rolling with her to safety. Vines shot from his hand, one end wrapping around the raven's neck, the other securely fastened to a streetlamp, narrowly stopping the attack.

But the young man twisted his ankle, landing awkwardly in front of another group of ravens. With the last of his strength, he pushed the little girl away, screaming hoarsely, "Don't look back! Run!!"

"Big brother... No, please don't!" The little girl cried helplessly.

The streets and alleys were scenes of utter devastation. A blood-soaked hand pressed desperately against a sealed doorway, a voice filled with despair calling out, "Open the door... Northern... Base... Please, open..."

Why? They had journeyed from the lower districts, crossing mountains and rivers, traveling across half the Alliance in search of a new sanctuary. Why was this the outcome? Had they made a mistake?

The eyes of the desperate slowly dulled, a plea sent to the heavens, willing to sacrifice anything for a miracle.

In that moment of fading consciousness, the door before him opened slowly, and a brilliant light poured down. A towering figure emerged from within. The man's eyes widened slightly. Could this... really be a miracle?

Boom—!!

The figure struck the ground with both fists, and a terrifying wave of pressure radiated outward for miles. The ravens flapping their wings in the sky suddenly plummeted, as if glued to the ground, struggling in vain to move.

Boom—!!

The sound echoed again, and the beasts above and below ground stiffened, their organs crushed by the immense gravitational force, instantly distorting and bursting.

The fleeing crowds came to a halt, and the little girl stopped crying, staring blankly at the newcomer.

It was an elderly man with a weathered face, his silver hair glistening, his face lined with deep wrinkles. Though he appeared ancient, his tall frame remained straight, his eyes sharp. He wore a simple military uniform, standing as solid and unyielding as a rock amid a storm.

From behind the old man, thousands of fully armed soldiers emerged, a mix of Aberrants and ordinary humans. They, too, were no longer young, but their eyes were resolute, their movements precise, the offspring of those who had survived brutal wars. In silence, they moved through the streets, swiftly dispatching the ravens trapped by the gravitational force and organizing the civilians into orderly evacuations.

A deep, resonant voice echoed throughout Front City and was broadcast across Northern Base, reaching everyone's ears:

"I am Yevgeniyev, Governor of Northern Base. Under Article 10, Section 13 of the Alliance Wartime Emergency Regulations, the Ministry of Transportation is ordered to immediately open Ground Access Point 5, 8, 13, 17, and 21, and to activate the airborne transit corridors. All residents of Front City are to be accepted unconditionally."

The noise and chaos seemed to vanish all at once, leaving only Yevgeniyev's concise and powerful orders echoing through the air — until the last person was evacuated.

Someone could no longer hold back and burst into tears, the wave of grief spreading like wildfire, erupting into a deafening roar that echoed for miles. The 6.5 million residents, struggling on the edge of life and death, having experienced the highs and lows, the brink of annihilation, finally felt a deep sense of relief. In this moment, faced with the apocalypse, in the dangerous wasteland overrun by zombies and beasts, they had found the right path to safety.

CHAPTER 8

Last Words

Under Yevgeniyev's series of commands, Northern Base swiftly transitioned into a state of combat readiness, with the entire city operating in an orderly manner.

First, there was the raven horde. Their numbers were overwhelming, making it impossible to eliminate them quickly. Fortunately, District B10 was well-equipped with advanced weaponry. Battle-hardened soldiers used heavy machine guns and rocket launchers to suppress the ravens, carving out escape routes amid the thick sandstorm. Starships and armored vehicles ferried civilians away through both ground and air corridors.

Yevgeniyev fulfilled his promise, standing tall like a mountain, unwavering until the last civilian was safely evacuated. The yellow sands whipped through the air, black feathers swirling amidst the endless clouds of darkness that stretched from Front City to Northern Base.

The once-thriving streets were now in ruins, city infrastructure obliterated, but at least most of the citizens had survived. As long as people were alive, there was hope. Even among the ruins, a new home could be rebuilt.

"General, please, you must evacuate as well," an officer beside him urged quietly.

Yevgeniyev nodded slowly, turning with deliberate care. Chu Bai silently handed him a cane, which Yevgeniyev accepted, planting it firmly on the ground as he clutched his chest. The magnetic field within his body was in disarray, and his vision wavered, darkening at the edges.

He swallowed down the metallic taste of blood in his throat, maintaining a composed expression. "To the Defense Department. With a beast tide of this magnitude, the barrier won't hold for long." As a seasoned battlefield commander, Yevgeniyev's assessment of the situation was precise—only by overseeing the defense could they hope to withstand the attack.

Chu Bai acknowledged with a bow, commandeering a hover car and following the last group of evacuees through Access Point 13. The city gates slowly closed behind them as the hover car veered off from the primary group, heading toward the Defense Department.

A faint ripple of energy disturbed the air. The officer ahead sensed something was wrong and whipped around, but Yevgeniyev was nowhere to be seen. "Something's wrong! Contact the Aberrants Bureau immediately—General Yevgeniyev has gone missing!"

Chu Bai's face darkened as he realized the situation had turned dire. He switched to manual mode, slamming on the brakes. The hover car screeched to a halt with a sharp, jarring noise. Bang! The force of inertia threw his body forward, only to be yanked back by the seatbelt, slamming him into the seat.

Through the swirling yellow sands, he saw a dozen figures waiting idly at the end of the road. Their powerful mental energies mixed, most of them S-class, creating a terrifying pressure that made the air itself tremble.

Chu Bai instinctively hit the emergency alert button, but the signal failed—communication was cut off, and all external sounds were completely blocked. The entire road was enveloped in an invisible Anopower barrier.

Yevgeniyev, who had been resting with his eyes closed, slowly opened them, his gaze as calm as a deep pool. "The inevitable has finally come."

From the moment more and more "sparrows" began appearing— from the very moment the apocalypse descended—this old man, who had seen and endured so much, had foreseen this day.

The car door opened, and Yevgeniyev, leaning on his cane, stepped out with unshakable composure, as if he were simply arriving at his destination rather than facing a group of deadly S-class interceptors.

If mental energy had a tangible scent, the man at the forefront, a burly figure in his forties with bulging muscles like overgrown hills, would reek of pungent diesel fuel. He stood with his arms crossed, exuding raw physical power.

Beside him, a seductive woman with purple eye shadow held a lit cigarette between her fingers, her scent akin to toxic poppies. Despite the sandstorm, she casually took a drag, her red lips exhaling a thin stream of smoke.

These two had the highest levels of mental energy, likely at S5 or above. The rest were unfamiliar faces to Yevgeniyev, who scrutinized each one until his gaze landed on Jupiter Blade, a former member of Northern Base who had defected to Delta Island. An S4-level lightning Aberrant, Blade met Yevgeniyev's steady gaze only to quickly avert his eyes, a trace of guilt flashing across his face.

Mikhail Medvedev, the robust S6-level Aberrant with the diesel stench, raised his arm and grinned, though the smile didn't reach his eyes. "General Yevgeniyev, I've heard a lot about you. I've been hiding and sneaking around just to see you these past few days, and now, finally, here we are."

Yevgeniyev's scrutinizing gaze shifted to the Aberrants across from him, their abilities hinting at their origins. He pointedly observed, "I wasn't aware that S-class Aberrants from different districts were forming alliances."

Several of the figures flinched, surprised that Yevgeniyev had instantly seen through their identities.

The seductive female Aberrant, Anastasia Zarubina, chuckled and flicked the ash from her cigarette. "If it weren't for the circumstances, do you think people like us, who have nothing to do with each other, would join forces?"

"General Yevgeniyev, you're a great and selfless man. I grew up hearing about your glorious deeds, and I have nothing but respect for you."

"But unfortunately, times have changed..." Anastasia snuffed out her cigarette with a chilling, bloody smile. "It's time for the younger generation to take over. As an elder, you should step down gracefully and retire from the stage of history."

She glanced around at their surroundings, her eyes burning with ambition. "Not every district in B has the luxury of a haven like Northern Base. Why should we suffer while you live in comfort? The prime land of District B10 is enough to make anyone green with envy."

Blanc Yard (District B14) is mountainous, Delta Island (District B15) is small, and White Town (District B13) suffers from harsh climates. The rise of Utopia only further pushed them to the brink, so these districts secretly allied, setting their sights on the Northern Base. This fortress city, built before the New Calendar, spans a vast area with advanced facilities, making it a perfect sanctuary for humanity's post-apocalypse. The only obstacle—Dmitri Yevgeniyev. As long as he raises the battle flag, every citizen of the Northern Base would fight, making it nearly impossible to conquer.

Even though Dmitri hasn't been seen in years and is rumored to be in poor health, his very existence remains the greatest threat. Once Dmitri was taken out, the Northern Base's morale would collapse, and its leadership would be easy to overcome. They could then invade, occupy, and carve up this fertile land as they pleased.

But killing an S-Class Aberrant is no easy feat. Their only option was to send people in to gather intel, stir up trouble, and look for an opportunity. Unexpectedly, when a sandstorm broke out and a swarm of ravens attacked, Dmitri emerged to lead the army and help civilians evacuate. He ended up alone, a sitting duck. It seemed even the heavens were on their side.

"Do it." Mikhail Medvedev's voice was bitter as he gave the attack signal.

Without a word, Chu Bai stepped forward, standing protectively in front of Dmitri. He didn't need to say anything—his intent was clear: if they wanted to kill Dmitri, they'd have to go through him first.

Chu Bai's ability was a rare fusion of offense and defense, known as "Will to Die."

Below S-Class, this power was unimpressive, but once it broke into S-Class, it underwent a qualitative change. When activated, it trapped everyone in the vicinity inside a glowing ring. Within the ring, the user's abilities were significantly enhanced, allowing them to crush their enemies. The effect only ended when one side was dead.

However, this "death" wasn't equal—the enemy truly died, while the user would only sustain severe injuries and lose a level. Currently, Chu Bai was at S5, meaning he could endure up to five "deaths." If he dropped to A9, his ability would become unusable.

Before the enemies could react, Chu Bai decisively pulled Dmitri and the nearest S-Class into the ring. The three of them vanished on the spot.

Inside the ring of "Will to Die," Dmitri struck with both fists, his overwhelming gravity-based power immobilizing the isolated enemy. Chu Bai moved with lightning speed, gripping the opponent's throat, the sickening sound of bones grinding under his grip.

The enemy couldn't even activate his ability before his limbs went limp. Crack! His neck snapped with terrifying force, blood spraying several feet into the air.

The ring vanished, leaving a blood-soaked corpse on the ground. Chu Bai's face was spattered with blood. Dmitri's breathing was slightly labored, but together, they had taken down an S-Class.

The remaining Aberrants were grim-faced, moving to surround them. But Chu Bai acted first, pulling another S-Class into the ring. They knew if they were surrounded, he and the General wouldn't stand a chance against over a dozen S-Class opponents. The only way was to take them down one by one. No matter what, he had to keep going... But for how long? A momentary blur crossed Chu Bai's thoughts.

When the ring dissolved again, Chu, Bai and Dmitri were still standing, though the second enemy had been much tougher. Chu Bai now bore several deep wounds.

Just as the other Aberrants closed in, he activated his ability once more!

Boom! Mikhail slammed into the unfortunate soul who was about to be pulled into the ring, taking their place himself.

His fists clenched tightly, he roared to the sky as his muscles bulged, a fearsome tiger-like shadow appearing behind him. The tiger's roar swept across the battlefield as Mikhail struck again and again like a predator on the hunt. Even under the pressure of Dmitri's gravity, his attacks were relentless.

Mikhail was a powerful offense-type Aberrant, and when he pushed his mental strength to the limit, Chu Bai was outmatched in both rank and physical strength. Rip! Chu Bai was a fraction of a second too slow, and the tiger clamped down on his throat, severing his head on the spot!

The ring disappeared, and Chu Bai staggered back, the residual pain from his shattered neck spreading through his nerves.

He was down to S4.

All the S-Class Aberrants charged at Dmitri without hesitation. Chu Bai struggled to his feet and activated "Will to Die" again. Mikhail, closest to him, rushed in before he could pull anyone in.

Thud!

Chu Bai was flung out.

S3.

Seeing this, the remaining Aberrants leisurely stopped, watching Mikhail's brutal assault with interest.

Despite Chu Bai's efforts, Dmitri was still gravely injured. The ring was an isolating ability; Dmitri was already limited inside it. Coupled with Mikhail's relentless sonic attacks, blood began to trickle from Dmitri's mouth.

Mikhail stomped on Chu Bai's head, a sneer tugging at his lips. "Loyal dog, aren't you? Think your master will shed any tears for you?"

Chu Bai tried to stab Mikhail with his elbow, but Mikhail sneered, his tiger paw crushing Chu Bai's skull.

The ring disappeared, and Chu Bai fell to the ground, unconscious, his face and head covered in blood, his chest caved in.

S2.

Dmitri's cane shattered as he dropped to one knee, coughing up blood from his internal injuries.

Mikhail grinned savagely as he approached Dmitri, only to feel an icy hand suddenly grip his ankle. Chu Bai, unable to speak, refused to let go. "You want to die? I'll grant your wish." Mikhail raised his fist.

A soft, icy hand clamped down on his shoulder, halting his movement. A suppressed voice, filled with barely contained rage, echoed around them. "Who wants to die?" The surrounding Aberrants flinched at the sight. How had she appeared so quietly?

The next moment, the barrier tore open. Flames and frost rained down, followed by the roar of artillery fire. Explosive red shells and many group attack abilities poured in, throwing the formation into chaos.

Six mechanical arms, her limbs bound like a noose, suddenly

snatched into the air, the Dream weaver hiding at the rear, who had just raised.

"Amateurish tricks." Felix's alloy arms shimmered with a dazzling light as a flood of data streams poured out, completely dismantling the barrier.

Bang! A flare shot into the sky, exploding like a firework, startling the ravens into flight! The Aberrants all over the Northern Base looked up in shock.

Anastasia Zarubina and the others rushed to help, only to run into Suchat, Yuui, Jennifer, and Silver Owl. The four of them stood like a wall, blocking their way. Facing the overwhelming pressure of S-Class power, they gritted their teeth, refusing to back down.

Under Damian's cover, Charles charged into the battlefield, only to be pushed aside by Dmitri stumbling in front of Chu Bai. Charles turned to him, his healing ability pouring into Chu Bai, pulling him back from the brink of death.

The small girl's eyes were fierce as she stood in front of Mikhail's tiger form. Her slender fingers curled into fists, halting his attack. "Who do you want to kill? Did I give you permission?"

Mikhail's expression grew serious, recognizing the figure before him—Cora Thornton, an S7-Class Aberrant.

A tough opponent.

The intel said she was at odds with the Northern Base leadership. Looks like they were wrong.

The spectral tiger in the void let out a vicious roar as Mikhail's mental energy surged, his skin blooming with eerie patterns. Cora narrowed her eyes slightly, feeling an unknown force stir within her cells, growing hotter and hotter, as if something was about to burst out.

Suddenly, she opened her mouth wide, a deep growl rumbling from the depths of her throat, and a massive shadow slowly materialized behind her.

It was a towering grizzly bear, its fur a deep crimson, coarse, thick, and long. The bear was twice the size of Mikhail's tiger. The once-mighty tiger let out a whimper, shrinking back in fear.

Onyx rubbed his temples, sighing with a sense of inevitability—another case of replicated genes.

Two top-tier offensive Aberrants, one a bear, the other a tiger, stood off against each other, causing the surrounding environment to violently tremble. The already fragile sand barrier shattered completely, leaving only a thin layer of protection as the endless swarm of ravens dived closer, now almost brushing the tops of their heads.

Amid the chaos, Dmitri gasped for breath, calling out to Onyx. "Onyx, come here."

Onyx took large strides forward, reaching out to steady Dmitri by the arm.

With trembling fingers, Dmitri pulled out an old pocket watch from his chest—a device that served as his terminal and symbolized his authority as the Supreme Governor of District B10. "The city's defense system... do you know how to operate it?"

Onyx froze.

The city defense system was the highest military secret in each district. Its complex structure and precise design required specialized training to operate, and the Governor always held the authority to control it.

Unless it was the Governor or their chosen successor, no one had access to such critical information.

Dmitri's voice was raspy, his throat nearly failing him. "I know... I'm asking a lot of you. Two days ago, I had a conversation with General Sheen from the North Yard. She asked me to look after... the son of an old friend."

The contents of that classified conversation clearly involved more, but Dmitri didn't have time to explain further. The little he had revealed was already enough.

Onyx's fingers slowly curled tighter, the dark depths of his eyes swirling with intense emotions.

He glanced toward Cora, a member of F777, and then at the swarm of ravens blotting out the sky, before meeting Dmitri's weathered gaze. When it came down to it, what did the survival of the Northern Base matter to him?

Onyx sighed silently. "I do."

CHAPTER 9

Evolution

Someone shattered the Dreamweaver's barrier and successfully launched the distress signal. If all went as planned, reinforcements from the Northern Base would arrive soon.

However, the situation remained dire. The dozen S-Class Aberrants at the scene bared their fangs and charged toward Dmitri Yevgeniyev without hesitation.

Only... two chances left.

Chu Bai's fists trembled as he struggled to rise, warm, sticky blood dripping down his temples. He wanted to activate "Will to Die" again, but he had already dropped to S2. If he released the ring one more time, regardless of who won or lost, his life might not be spared.

Cora watched the enemies draw closer, then casually lifted Chu Bai and set him down beside Dmitri. "Stay put."

Chu Bai tried to move again, but a massive bear's paw pressed him down. Cora turned back to him, her expression deadly serious. "I've got this."

She rolled her neck, the sound of cracking bones echoed, and the grizzly bear shadow behind her mirrored the movement, as if warming up for a hunt. "Just S-Class Aberrants—I can handle them."

Even among S-Class Aberrants, the difference in power could be vast. These opponents only had numbers on their side; individually, none of them were stronger than Bloody Hunter Punk. If she could take down Punk, she could take them down too.

Cora firmly placed herself between Dmitri and Chu Bai, shielding them as she moved forward with determination. Their side only had six S-Class Aberrants, and two were already out of the fight. Facing a numerically superior enemy, she couldn't afford to be careless.

Charles bent low, weaving through the battlefield to return and tend to Dmitri's wounds.

Dmitri panted as he spoke. "I've heard you have a serum that can restore someone's ability to fight. Give me a dose."

"No way! You can't take it!" Charles refused immediately. Given Dmitri's current physical condition—severe injuries combined with organ failure—taking that serum would be lethal, even if it worked.

Onyx spoke up in a low voice, "General, the Northern Base still needs you. Please trust Cora, and trust us." Dmitri looked into Onyx's resolute eyes, remained silent for a moment, and finally nodded, dropping the matter.

Boom—!

Cora and Mikhail met head-on, the grizzly bear rearing up on its hind legs, its massive paw swatting the tiger, sending it staggering.

Mikhail's claws dug into the ground, halting his retreat with difficulty. Wiping the blood from his mouth, he smirked at Cora, nodding toward her. "There's something I don't get. You're S7-Class. You could have it easy anywhere you go, so why tie yourself to Yevgeniyev, a dead tree? Why not switch sides? Join us, and you'll live in luxury. Once we've divided the territory, endless riches will be yours."

Cora felt a twinge of absurd amusement, coldly spitting out, "You're telling me what to do?"

Seeing that she wasn't swayed, Mikhail roared, a mad tiger lunging at its prey, his fist flying toward Cora's face.

Cora braced herself, channeling power into her core, her fingertips transforming into spectral blue knuckles. Her bear's paw seemed to be encased in metal armor as she met his strike head-on with a powerful punch! The tiger's phantom forepaw shattered, Mikhail's head snapped to the side, and the impact sent a shockwave through his chest, causing him to cough up blood on the spot.

Cora landed steadily, planting a foot on Mikhail's chest, raising her fist high.

She had indeed quarreled with Commander Holland and had considered leaving the Northern Base. But over time, she had seen more: Tustan, Sunny, Svetlana, the Ming family, the countless ordinary people striving to live in the Old Street Market, the united Aberrants in the Silver Ring Arena, and even those waiting with hope in their eyes in Front City, still without entry permits. The Northern Base was a city with a "soul."

In the harsh reality of the apocalypse, where humanity's morality had plummeted, cities with a "soul" were few. F777 had traveled across most of the New Pacific Alliance; Cora had seen Sycamore, she had seen Ocean Gate, and now, the Northern Base. A city like this, with people like these, deserved to survive. They should not become mere sacrifices in a power struggle.

Boom!

Crash!!

Metal shattered, debris flying everywhere as Cora relentlessly pounded Mikhail's chest, her blows causing his ribcage to cave in under the overwhelming force that could displace internal organs. The massive grizzly bear in her spectral form clamped down on the tiger's neck—snap!—and flung it aside.

The beastly forms vanished as Mikhail's body crumpled to the ground.

"Kill!"

"Kill Dmitri!!"

"Stick together, don't go solo!"

With Mikhail down, the remaining S-Class Aberrants closed ranks, forming a tighter semicircle. At the forefront, Anastasia snapped her fingers.

Her Anopower, "Bloom," activated. Gigantic carnivorous plants burst from the ground, resembling fresh red chunks of flesh. The gaping, serrated maws in their centers opened and closed, contracting and pulsating, while the five vibrant petals fanned out, emitting a stench so foul it rivaled that of rotting zombies.

One of Tustan's teammates was unlucky enough to get caught by one of these plants, its bite instantly causing his leg to rot into putrid, liquefied flesh. His reaction was quick, severing his leg below the knee to stop the spread. Charles, carrying a medical kit, carefully maneuvered through the barrage of attacks to reach the injured man and began treating and bandaging him.

Anastasia's lips curled into a bitter smile as she snapped her fingers again, sending more carnivorous plants crawling toward Charles. Their thick maws opened wide—

Bang! A grenade came crashing down from the sky, piercing through the sand and layers of obstruction, striking the gaping maw with pinpoint accuracy. The foul blood splattered everywhere, the petals scattering in all directions, and Anastasia stumbled, her composure slipping.

Silver Owl, wearing his sniper goggles, remained expressionless, only the stern lower half of his face visible. After successfully exploiting her weakness, he quickly shifted his aim to another plant, continuously sniping them down one by one.

Yuui sprinted across the battlefield, muttering lyrics under her breath. A thin mist of blades descended, merging with Suchat's toxins as they flooded into the area. The two worked in perfect harmony, with Yuui becoming a stealthy assassin. The sand obscured the mist, and several Aberrants were unaware when tiny cuts appeared on their bodies. The powerful neurotoxins quickly invaded their brains, causing their limbs to convulse and collapse one after another.

Tustan and F777, a group of elite Aberrants, were actually holding back over a dozen S-Class opponents.

"Roar—!!" A terrifying bear's roar echoed, freezing the S1 and S2 Aberrants in their tracks.

Cora charged fearlessly into the enemy ranks, her spectral blue knuckles slicing through the air.

Cora Thornton charged into the enemy ranks without hesitation, her spectral blue knuckles slashing through the air. The first S1 Aberrant's throat was pierced, blood spurting out like a fountain. Cora slid across the blood-slick ground, moving like a wolf among sheep.

She quickly lunged at the second S2 Aberrant, bringing her blade down in a vertical slash. The Aberrant was cleaved in two, his body splitting apart as intestines and organs spilled out, blood blurring the vision of those nearby. Their pupils contracted in terror.

"Ahhhhhh—!"

The formidable grizzly bear in Cora's spectral form bit off the head of a third S2 Aberrant, brain matter splattering everywhere.

Without pausing, the bear's massive paws seized two more S1 Aberrants, slamming them into the ground with bone-crunching force. One leg was torn off, and a powerful headbutt sent their limbs scattering as the sickening sound of breaking bones echoed through the air.

In an instant, five S-Class Aberrants lay dead!

Cora's bloodied knuckles dripped with crimson as she raised her stony gaze from the pool of blood. The grizzly bear reared up on its hind legs, its coarse fur standing on end, and let out a thunderous roar that echoed across half of the Northern Base.

A smirk played on Cora's lips, the dimples on her cheeks forming a chilling curve. "Leave or die."

"—Who dares to step forward?"

The enemies hesitated, their steps faltering, faces ashen as they stared at Cora. Even though she had only killed S1 and S2 Aberrants, her sheer power was terrifying. A cold sweat broke out among them as an unthinkable thought crept into their minds—was she really only S7?

A heavy silence settled over the battlefield. At that moment, a powerful energy fluctuation surged overhead.

A deep rift in space slowly opened, a massive force spilling out from the black void. A figure with an androgynous, sinister appearance emerged—Irezumi, smiling and clapping. "Impressive for an S7, but I'm afraid your heroic moment ends here."

Behind Irezumi, a thousand high-level Aberrants followed, their eyes gleaming with cruel, murderous intent.

Mikhail Medvedev and Anastasia Zarubina, as if receiving a command, suddenly pulled out a set of blood-red Level 4 crystals. Without hesitation, they crushed them, the rich energy surging into their bodies, reviving their depleted strength. The two of them stood up once more, fully recharged.

Onyx sharply looked around, his eyes darting to the empty, eerily quiet streets. How could this be? Based on the timing of the distress flare, the reinforcements from the Northern Base should have arrived by now.

Irezumi, noticing Onyx's gaze, let a mocking smile curl under his mask. "Waiting for backup? I'm afraid you're in for a disappointment."

Half an hour earlier, at the Bureau of Aberrants headquarters.

The administrative secretary spoke timidly, addressing the rigid figure standing in the shadows. "Commander Holland, all departments have taken action, and the residents of Front City have been moved. Do you... have any further instructions?"

After a long pause, Commander Scarlett Holland's hoarse voice responded, "Follow the General's orders."

The secretary let out a sigh of relief, not daring to glance at Scarlett's expression. She quickly said, "I'll go help then..." Almost tripping over herself, she turned and fled the oppressive atmosphere of the office.

Scarlett Holland gazed out over the city from the floor-to-ceiling window. Twenty years—she had poured her entire heart and soul into governing the Northern Base. Why couldn't things develop as she had planned?

Whoosh—

A spatial rift suddenly opened, and two ghostly figures appeared out of thin air. One was shrouded in a black robe, face obscured, while the other wore a half-mask, exuding an androgynous and sinister aura.

This was when the Bureau's defenses were at their weakest—90% of the officials were out in the field. No one expected an S-Class spatial Aberrant to breach the headquarters.

"Who are you?" Heize barked, raising his hand to activate his vacuum field. "An A9, trying to act tough?" Irezumi spat out a dark incantation, and Heize's body twisted in agony, transforming into a writhing cocoon within seconds.

Scarlett Holland turned to press the alarm, but Irezumi traced a sigil in the air, drawing her towards him. She crashed into the window, blood trickling down her forehead. A B3-level Aberrant like her was helpless before an S4.

Irezumi seemed somewhat amused. "How funny. Isn't the Northern Base supposed to be all about strength? Scarlett Holland, right? How did someone at B3 level end up in your position?"

Scarlett struggled fiercely. "Who are you? Are you here to kill me?"

Irezumi chuckled, skipping the first question. "I won't kill you. You're not worth my effort."

"Our target is Yevgeniyev."

Scarlett's face turned blue, but she still spoke with unwavering conviction, "You're delusional. You can't kill my teacher."

Irezumi was unfazed. "I hear you're one of his students. You must have worked hard to take over from him. Now that he's on death's doorstep, why not help us out?"

Scarlett gritted her teeth. "Never. I won't... betray the Northern Base."

Irezumi burst into laughter, the sound grating and discordant. "You really think you're something, don't you?" His stiff lips brushed close to Scarlett's ear, whispering like a devil, "Now I see why Dmitri never fully handed power over to you."

"It's because you're just not good enough."

Scarlett's pupils contracted.

Irezumi chuckled softly, his tone mockingly regretful. "You're not bad with schemes and manipulation, and your heart's plenty dark. In peacetime, that might've been enough. But in war... look at you. Controlled so easily. You'll never be a competent leader."

"I hear you value Aberrants a lot? Keep them tightly under your control because you're afraid, right?" "You're constantly afraid—afraid of being replaced, afraid of being killed, afraid of losing power. You fear ending up with nothing."

"Tut-tut, weakness is a sin."

Irezumi chanted another cold incantation, and a black sphere of writhing worms appeared before Scarlett's eyes. "This is a 'Corruptor.' It amplifies the evil within a person. Let's see if Commander Holland is as selfless as she claims."

The sphere burrowed into Scarlett's chest, sending her into agonizing convulsions as memories flashed before her eyes.

Scarlett had been born after the nuclear war ended, during a period when the Northern Base had stabilized. Raised with elite education, she had learned about "Gene Selectors" and "Initial Awakeners" from various sources, firmly believing that people were not created equal. When she finally awakened during the apocalypse, she was disappointed to find herself at only B3 level, with little hope of advancing due to her limited potential.

It was challenging to become the successor of the Northern Base.

Yevgeniyev's original choice wasn't her, but another student named Sherry Harper. Sherry was optimistic, charismatic, and an A8 Initial Awakener. She outshone Scarlett in both popularity and performance.

During a peacekeeping mission, a massive earthquake trapped Sherry and a group of students under tons of rubble. Dmitri never gave up searching for her. Scarlett volunteered to join the rescue team and was the first to find Sherry, who was barely alive, her lower body mangled. With timely treatment and cybernetic implants, Sherry could have survived.

Scarlett watched silently, crouching down to whisper, "Sherry, they're just ordinary people. Was it worth it?"

Sherry struggled to speak. "Are... they okay?"

"I don't know," Scarlett replied coldly. She didn't care about the students, only about finding Sherry. But once she had, she didn't feel any rush. Her tone carried a hint of reproach. "You see, you saved them, but sacrificed yourself."

"Someone like you doesn't deserve to lead the Northern Base. Don't worry, I'll do better than you."

Sherry could no longer speak, her eyes wide as she stared at Scarlett.

Scarlett waited in silence until the next day, when Sherry finally died. Then she stood up, brushed off her stiff knees, and stumbled out, shouting, "I found her! Sherry is here!!"

"Ahhh—!!" Scarlett let out a heart-wrenching scream, her consciousness fading as tears streamed down her face. She had given twenty years of her youth to the Northern Base, all to build the ideal city she envisioned.

She had searched for scientists involved in the "Plan Eternity," claiming it was to heal Dmitri, while secretly funding excessive radiation research. Only she knew that deep within her, a hidden voice kept whispering: Is there still a chance for me to advance?

Scarlett's eyes turned pitch black as she recalled Dmitri's rebuke amid her endless agony. "Scarlett, Aberrants are just like ordinary people; you cannot treat them differently." "Remember, the millions of residents in the Northern Base are the foundation of this city. Some things cannot be turned upside down."

Scarlett grasped her own throat, screaming, "No! That's not true! Teacher! It's different—we Aberrants are born noble. We deserve more power and status than ordinary people.... Sherry was wrong, and so are you! You're all wrong!!"

Us, the Aberrants should rule this world.

The Corruptor fully invaded Scarlett's mind, her deep anger subsiding into calm. Her eyes were now completely black. Scarlett mechanically stood up, like a puppet, and pressed the terminal.

"I am now issuing an order to the entire district: Everyone is to remain in place, effective immediately. No matter what happens, do not leave your posts. Anyone who disobeys will lose their District B10 citizenship and be treated as a rioter—killed on sight."

"Repeat, no matter what happens, everyone is to remain in place."

Beside her, Irezumi smiled, his grin growing wider. The Corruptor, designed to target those who harm the collective, had done its work. Scarlett Holland was nothing more than a hypocrite.

The spatial rift reappeared, and the two S-Class Aberrants vanished from the scene.

Scarlett's sudden and inexplicable order carried a heavy sense of foreboding. The public, afraid to resist, stood in place, whispering anxiously among themselves. Just seconds later, their terminals beeped again.

Near Passage 13, a straight line formed, with Cora at the center. Behind her was Dmitri, whom she was sworn to protect, and in front of her stood thousands of high-level Aberrants.

Irezumi clapped theatrically, a cold smile playing on his lips. "I can't deny it—you're impressive. You can take on ten opponents at once, but what about a hundred? A thousand?"

"Why don't you find out?" Cora replied icily, raising a spectral bear's paw as a massive, gleaming saw slowly materialized. Irezumi's smile faded, his gaze intensifying. "Then let's... kill you first, and then Dmitri."

Boom—!!

Flames, wind blades, lightning, ice, thorns—countless Anopowers surged towards Cora, engulfing her slender figure. Blood-soaked ghastly hands grabbed at her legs, and carnivorous plants slithered forward, their gaping maws wide open.

Cora slashed through them with her blade, leaping out of the trap and swinging the blade back with a brutal force.

Bang! The relentless barrage of attacks was unavoidable. She was struck hard from behind. Mikhail seized the opportunity, his tiger claws slashing forward, ripping open a wound across Cora's abdomen. She tumbled into a trap where a radiation-type Aberrant was lying in wait, unleashing a powerful electric current that sent her body into convulsions, even causing her bear shadow to curl up.

"Cora!" Onyx's face darkened, and Yuui and the others were all desperate to rush to her aid, but they could not break free.

As the situation grew increasingly dire, just when all seemed lost, the sound of chaotic footsteps echoed from all directions. Dmitri looked up sharply, sensing something.

"Who dares to kill General Yevgeniyev? I'll take you by myself!!"

"To hell with 'hold your ground' orders! Even if I lose my B-district citizenship, I'm coming!"

"General Yevgeniyev, you saved us—we won't abandon you!!"

A sea of people surged towards the battlefield, their faces—some familiar, some not—braving the swirling yellow sand as they approached fearlessly.

At the front were the Rowin siblings, Jirgalang, Sunny Zhao, and other S-Class Aberrants, followed by an army of Aberrants ranging from Class A to E. Regardless of age, gender, or rank, their expressions were uniformly determined. Even ordinary people with makeshift weapons were among them.

The moment Irezumi appeared, Felix had issued a private commission on behalf of F777 on the task platform. It contained nothing but a location and a brief message. No rewards, no points, with the highest possible danger level marked in red.

"Dmitri Yevgeniyev is under attack. Immediate help needed."

Under normal circumstances, with a directive like "exiled or killed on sight," no one would accept such a task. However, the residents of the Northern Base took it up without hesitation, their numbers even exceeding those for system-issued Class A missions.

The voices of the crowd filled every corner, and as they closed in, they surrounded Irezumi and his forces.

Amidst the crackling electricity, Cora slowly rose, clutching her abdomen, her eyes opening to reveal a deep, otherworldly blue.

A brilliant light erupted in a circular wave from beneath her feet.

The grizzly bear's spectral form towered over everything, its size doubling, exuding an overwhelming sense of destruction.

She raised her other hand slightly, her fingers spreading to the limit as the cold, gleaming saw disintegrated into fragments that scattered around. The surrounding ruins shook violently as an unprecedented surge of spiritual power coursed through her body like a raging storm.

Without relying on any external forces, countless blue light orbs rose from the ground, transforming in an instant into thousands upon thousands of swords.

With a slight motion of her hand, the blades immediately aligned, their tips aimed at Irezumi and the other Aberrants, resembling a stunning, eerie display of ghostly fire. The flow of the yellow sand seemed to halt, the agitated flock of ravens fell silent, and the brilliant blue light illuminated half the sky.

Every onlooker was stunned. This differed completely from a sword formation conjured by spells or external aids. Each sword was a true ethereal artifact—this was the ultimate manifestation of a metal-type Anopower!

All things in heaven and earth are my weapons. Cora stood at the center of the storm, surrounded by the terrifying image of a colossal beast and the orbiting light of thousands of swords.

If an R-type tester were used at that moment, it would reveal a shocking fact: Cora's spiritual power had reached an incredibly terrifying level.

An unprecedented S9.

CHAPTER 10

Typros

Swords whirled, and the hum of a thousand Ethereal Artifacts resonated through the air. Cora and the bear stood up simultaneously.

The pursuing forces within the inner circle and the reinforcements from the outer circle all fell into a stunned silence. Every gaze turned to the figure standing like a war god, emotions starkly contrasting on each side—one of joy, the other of terror.

A soldier from the Northern Base squeezed to the front, gazing down at the expensive Ethereal Artifact in his arms, his eyes shining with excitement. "Wow, I'm using the same model as the S7!"

Cora's expression remained stony as she pulled a roll of bandages from the spatial pocket connected to her own. Biting down on the end, she began wrapping the bandages around her blood-soaked hand, layer by layer.

It wasn't because of the injury itself. After all, she had just lost two finger joints to a man-eating plant, and now the wound throbbed with both pain and itching. If her self-healing ability kicked in and her fingers regenerated in front of everyone, it would be far too shocking.

As she casually bandaged her hand, she glanced at the enemy across from her, her tone indifferent. "Since you're all here, might as well stay."

The words were spoken softly, yet the wind carried them to every ear. No one was foolish enough to mistake her for a gracious host. The S7's intention was crystal clear—she wanted their bodies left behind.

A chorus of swords echoed, and Cora, like an unsheathed blade, surged forward with the force of a thunderclap, charging headfirst into the enemy ranks.

With an S7-level leading the charge, the enraged reinforcements followed suit, yelling at the top of their lungs, "I'll go first! You guys protect General Yevgeniyev!" "I'll take you all down!" "Foreign dogs, go back to where you came from!"

Irezumi sneered coldly, his voice dripping with contempt as he muttered, "A rabble."

His fingers intertwined, suddenly spasming as he performed a strange series of hand seals. From the ground below, countless spectral apparitions emerged! The Northern Base had once been a brutal battlefield, a graveyard for countless lives.

Though the specters summoned by Irezumi lacked physical form, they radiated an overwhelming aura of malice, rushing madly at the living. Those possessed by the specters were driven to insanity, attacking friend and foe alike.

Mikhail Medvedev and Anastasia Zarubina, both S-Class, leaped into the fray, taking advantage of the chaos to slaughter without restraint. The battlefield descended into utter disorder, with the low-level Aberrants from the Northern Base falling one after another.

Dmitri struck out with a powerful punch, his attacks guided by gravitational forces, freezing mid-air to save many Aberrants who hadn't escaped in time. "They're... excellent soldiers, but they need a commander," he rasped, his cough sounding like a broken bellows.

On the battlefield, brave soldiers alone aren't enough; a skilled commander is also essential. Onyx glanced down at the pocket watch in his hand, sighed softly, and stepped forward to block him. "General, let me handle this."

Dmitri's weathered eyes flashed with surprise. "You can command?" Onyx humbly replied, "I wouldn't say that, but I know a thing or two."

After a moment of consideration, Dmitri smiled faintly. Yes, the general from the Northern Yard was also a brilliant tactician. "Good, very good..." He clapped Onyx firmly on the shoulder. "It's all yours."

Onyx turned his head and shouted toward a six-armed figure, "Hey, Felix, come over here and help!"

Felix paused, rolling his eyes skyward as he grumbled, "Arrogant

4.2..."

Despite his grumbling, he approached. Felix's rhenium arm connected with the pocket watch terminal, and under Dmitri's highest-level authorization, he hacked into all available databases in an instant. Onyx's extraordinary memory went into overdrive, copying and imprinting all the information about the Northern Base's Aberrants. His light-colored eyes gleamed as he scanned the reinforcements on the battlefield, quickly memorizing each face and matching them with the profiles in his mind.

A good commander must first know his people to use them well.

Among these reinforcements, some were fierce and battle-hardened, while others rarely took on combat-related tasks and were flustered by the grand scale of the battle.

Onyx's command style was simple—issuing orders directly into their minds. After witnessing Cora's earlier example, he avoided using technical terms, sticking to straightforward language instead.

But the hastily assembled non-combat personnel struggled to follow orders correctly.

A group attack, Aberrant with a terrible sense of direction, charged into an empty corner, unleashing their power with a loud crash, missing all enemies but scaring away two squawking ravens.

Sensing an opportunity to counterattack, Yuui began singing a haunting melody, casting a buff that empowered the others. They joined Jennifer in a furious barrage, their Anopower's brilliant light expanding the attack range by twice, striking the densest part of the enemy forces and reaping lives en masse.

"Second squad, focus! Release your Anopower on my signal."

The leader of the second squad wielded the power of Discouraging Roar, a continuous attack that could sap the enemy's will to fight, driving them into a state of despair. It was a highly helpful support for Anopower in group battles, but the user struggled with timing, often leaving gaps when distracted.

Onyx quickly called out several names. "You all protect General Yevgeniyev."

The named Aberrants hurried to Dmitri's side. Though they were defense-oriented and not high-level, their Anopowers were exceptionally rare, making them almost impossible to breach.

Onyx quickly surveyed the battlefield and suddenly spotted an opportunity to lure Mikhail into a trap. He ordered the frontline fighters to feign injury and retreat, while the Earth Aberrants created a collapse-prone area on the ground.

Mikhail, unaware, took two steps forward and fell into the trap.

An Aberrant hurled a stun baton at his head, paralyzing him. The others swarmed him, delivering a relentless beating until the once-mighty tiger was stripped of his strength and lay helpless on the ground.

Bleeding profusely, Mikhail reached into his pocket for a crystal, ready to crush it with gritted teeth. "I'll take that!" A young Aberrant, hidden in the shadows, activated his Remote Object Seizure ability, stealing the crystal right out of Mikhail's grasp.

Onyx withdrew the command from his lips and fixed his gaze on the young Aberrant's face for a moment, a look of understanding crossing his features. Before coming to the Northern Base, this man had been a professional thief.

Mikhail had already been severely injured by Cora, and now, after being pummeled by this makeshift army, he was utterly spent.

Suchat's ghostly figure appeared behind him, and with a swift thrust, his triangular military dagger pierced Mikhail's throat. The exhausted tiger finally bowed his head, never to rise again. Mikhail Medvedev was dead.

Although the process was filled with comedic moments, the Northern Base's reinforcements miraculously gained the upper hand.

Some assassins noticed with sharp eyes that the disorganized enemy forces suddenly seemed to have found coordination, acting with increasing speed and synergy, making them harder to deal with. Worse still, new reinforcements kept pouring in from all directions.

Onyx pushed up his glasses with one hand and looked toward Irezumi from afar, a slight smile playing on his lips. "The real rabble is you," he muttered. A group of greedy vermin bound by nothing but mutual interest, as easily scattered as sand in the wind.

The endless spirits possessed the Aberrants, but Sunny Zhao, her gaze icy, unleashed her Water Anopower to purify them. A torrential rain fell from the sky, and the pure droplets soaked the possessed bodies, instantly evaporating into white steam. Agonized screams filled the air as the Aberrants, freed from possession, felt the weight lift from their souls.

Wyan and Yvonne Rowin moved in perfect sync, their attacks landing almost simultaneously. The S6-class assault Aberrants cut through the enemy ranks like a hot knife through butter, taking down two S-Class opponents with brutal efficiency! Compared to the ragtag enemy forces, the Northern Base's elite fighters exerted an overwhelming pressure at this moment.

Cora faced the crimson man-eating plant head-on, her mind sharp as a blade. The surrounding swords whirled, slicing the plant's vivid petals into shreds!

The writhing maw fell before her, and Cora's fists crackled with blue lightning as she activated her Knuckledusters, transforming them into gauntlets that encased her hands. She then gripped the plant's tooth-filled crown with both hands and, with a surge of force, ripped it apart—

The spirit bear's roar shook the earth, and the savage man-eating plant was torn in two! Anastasia's face turned ashen, and she spat out a mouthful of blood as the magnetic field within her body shattered.

Cora rose coldly, flinging off the chunks of flesh stuck to her gauntlets, and ground the plant's remains underfoot as she advanced toward Anastasia. Panicking, Anastasia staggered back, frantically summoning more man-eating plants to block Cora's path.

The spirit bear charged. Despite its massive size, it moved with remarkable agility. Its immense paws, carrying the weight of a thousand tons, crushed the bloodthirsty flowers underfoot, along with Anastasia herself. Blood oozed from her seven orifices, her veins bursting, and her skin ruptured like an overripe tomato, spilling fluids as fragments of her blackened organs spilled from her mouth.

With her summoned creatures destroyed, Anastasia suffered the same damage. By the time Cora reached her, she was already sprawled on the ground in a pitiful state.

Cora pressed her foot down on Anastasia's chest, applying pressure. "No, you can't kill me!" Anastasia gasped through a mouthful of blood, her words garbled. "I'm S4-class, I'm the daughter of the White Town Governor's wife's uncle's—"

A thousand swords shot forward, turning Anastasia into a human pincushion. She died with her eyes wide open, her introduction unfinished. Cora's expression remained blank. "Sorry, but your family tree is too complicated for me."

After killing Anastasia, Cora lifted her gaze, her eyes cutting through the chaos of battle to lock onto Irezumi. "You're next," she said, her voice steady and deliberate.

The smile vanished from Irezumi's face, his twin expressions finally merging into one, equally cold. Countless vengeful spirits shrieked as they charged toward Cora, but she directed the floating swords to strike them down.

Irezumi took a step back, hiding his trembling fingers within his sleeves. "Are you forming seals?" Cora tilted her head, her expression one of knowing comprehension. A lopsided lamppost behind her suddenly transformed into a spear and shot forward, pinning Irezumi's hand to the ground.

Irezumi ignored the pain, his head snapping up in shock. How could this be? How did she know? Was it just a coincidence?

Feigning a spell with his injured hand, Irezumi muttered an incantation under his breath. The air grew thick with malice, a plague spreading through the battlefield. Cora didn't even look at his hands as she launched a lightning-fast attack, her bear-like paw striking cleanly—slap! She backhanded him across the face.

A few teeth, still attached to fragments of flesh, flew from his mouth as one side of Irezumi's face swelled like a steamed bun. The curse was broken.

Cora landed lightly, raising an eyebrow. "Too slow."

Irezumi's eyes snapped up, cold as a venomous snake's, as he tried to unleash another Anopower.

Interrupt. Interrupt. Interrupt. No matter what he did—whether he moved his lips or raised his hand, regardless of his fake outs—Cora always predicted his true attack intent. He couldn't complete a single curse, leaving him defenseless against her onslaught.

Irezumi's shoulder was pierced through, his face was swollen, and his fingers were all severed, blood pooling beneath him.

Cora clapped her hands, her tone casual. "I've seen better curse casters than you." She paused. "You're not even close."

Her senior, Chi Zhang, had surpassed Master Zhang in both true techniques and curses, deserving the title of "genius." Cora had sparred with him countless times since childhood, knowing every precursor to a spell or seal by heart, as if it were engraved in her bones. She could instantly think of a countermeasure.

Unless she held back, Chi Zhang never won against her. Compared to him, Irezumi was like a half-baked amateur, a flashy fraud whose tricks were easily seen through.

Irezumi's chest heaved, and behind his mask, half of his face was shrouded in darkness. The thousand elite Aberrants he had brought with him lay defeated; the outcome was certain. The forces of the Northern Base were now clearing the last remnants of the battlefield.

At the root of it all was the S7 standing before him.

Irezumi looked at Cora, his voice fluctuating between soft and harsh, grating on the ears. "Congratulations, you've saved Yevgeniyev."

"But hell always comes, and I look forward to our next meeting."

A faint sense of unease crept into Cora's heart.

Irezumi's androgynous face seemed to split in two—one half smiling, the other half weeping, a mix of joy and sorrow, disturbingly bizarre. Suddenly, a narrow rift in space appeared behind him, and a skeletal hand reached out, gripping Irezumi's shoulder, ready to pull him away.

No, it's that S-Class Space Aberrant—they're trying to escape!

Cora lunged forward without hesitation, merging all her swords into one, forming a massive guillotine.

Clang—!!

The blade fell, and the Space Aberrant, cloaked entirely in black, froze in place as his neck was severed, his head rolling to the ground. "Ah—" Blood sprayed everywhere as one of Irezumi's arms was sliced off, his agonized screams piercing the air.

But it was too late. Most of his body had already vanished into the spatial rift.

With the Space Aberrant's death, the rift destabilized violently, and chaotic radiation surged outward. Cora's pupils contracted as her mental energy flared uncontrollably.

The bear spirit behind her vanished in an instant, and her body shrank rapidly. She involuntarily spat out a long, thin tongue as the powerful force sucked her into the rift just before it closed completely.

The battlefield fell into a deathly silence.

Only the members of F777 broke the stillness with their frantic cries. "Sis!" "Captain!" "Cora!" Onyx's brows furrowed, his face grim and serious.

Everyone had witnessed the transformation—Cora had turned into something else from the bear. Onyx sighed heavily, then turned calmly to Felix Lucas. "Erase all the videos and surveillance footage. Leave no trace."

One mistake like the one Bryan Young maid was enough; today's events could not be allowed to spread in any form.

Fortunately, the communication equipment was still functional. Onyx spoke softly into his earpiece, "Cora? Can you hear me? If you can, please respond."

After several minutes, a sudden message popped up in the F777 group chat: 「Ire、waso*g% killed.」

Cora's avatar flickered on and off, displaying the message "The other party is typing…" for what felt like an eternity.

"Typing… Typing…"

「I am not dead, will @come back myself.」

Hundreds of genetic sequences flashed through Onyx's mind, but the characteristics were too vague to identify. What had she turned into this time? And why couldn't she even type properly?

CHAPTER 11

The Successor

Whoosh—

The spatial rift fluctuated violently before collapsing and disappearing in an instant. Irezumi, missing an arm, fell from the void, staggering a few steps before losing his balance and collapsing to the ground.

He left behind a horrifying trail of blood wherever he passed. The nerves at the wound were dead. His mental energy was sluggish, and he struggled to mobilize it. The destructive power of the Metal Anopower had caused his internal magnetic field to completely destabilize.

Irezumi's face was as pale as gold leaf as he slowly sat against a tree, forcing himself to assess his surroundings. The air was thick with swirling dust, and a swarm of dark crows perched above, their gray-white eyes quietly watching, as if patiently waiting for his death so they could feast on his flesh.

The Northern Base's barrier had anti-space Anopower devices, making it impossible for Irezumi to escape directly. His original plan had been to retreat to a safe house and then find a way out of the district, but with his Space Aberrant companion dead and the teleportation path disrupted, he had ended up in some desolate forest.

A faint rustling sound broke the silence.

Irezumi looked up sharply. The branches swayed with the wind, and a single green leaf floated to the ground.

All around was quiet, save for his own rough, labored breathing.

Irezumi's eyes narrowed with malice, a bitter smile tugging at his lips—part relief, part self-mockery. That S7 hadn't followed him.

He raised his left hand, now left with only two fingers, and removed his blood-stained mask, revealing the twisted, sinister face of a woman. This S4-class curse master was, in fact, a grotesque chimera—a hybrid of male and female!

Irezumi muttered an arcane incantation, switching the mask to the other side of his face. As he did, his severe injuries miraculously shifted as well. Though his severed arm and fingers could not regenerate, the pain lessened, and his complexion improved slightly. Unfortunately, the male half of his face was completely ruined.

Now, Irezumi had fully transformed into a delicate-featured woman.

A faint sound of breathing reached her ears, like someone sucking in an icy breath. "Who's there?" Irezumi snapped, leaping to her feet. "Show yourself!"

A few sparrows, disturbed from their nests, flapped frantically upward. Irezumi's distant gaze followed them, and with a twitch of her two fingers, the birds dropped dead on the spot, their bodies instantly stiffening into corpses, none escaping.

Her dark eyes scanned the area, finding nothing out of place.

Returning to the shade of the tree, Irezumi dialed her terminal, her voice deliberately lowered as she spoke, "It's me. Dmitri is still alive. The mission failed." Whatever response came from the other end made Irezumi's hoarse voice rise sharply, "Why wasn't he killed?!"

"The plan was changed last minute? And there wasn't time to inform us? Hmph."

Dust swept over, coating the lush trees in a thick layer of yellow grime. One green leaf trembled slightly, shaking off some of the sand.

"Utopia? What new policy?"

"Never mind... We'll talk when I get back. Send someone to the safe house to pick me up. Luis is dead." Luis referred to the Space Aberrant.

Irezumi ended the call, slumping back against the tree, her eyes closing as she tried to rest.

Rustle—

Rustle—

Without warning, the nearby trees shook violently, flashes of eerie blue light crackling through the air. Countless leaves turned into deadly blades, hurtling toward Irezumi. She snapped her eyes open, but it was too late; a thousand arrows, leaving her pierced her body through a lifeless corpse.

Impossible...

There had been no sign of anything amiss. When did she catch up? The shock and fury froze on Irezumi's face, her final thoughts still unanswered as death claimed her.

Plop.

A small creature dropped to the ground.

It had a triangular head, bulging eyes that resembled lightbulbs, a plump body, and a tail curled like a piece of bubblegum. The nano-crystals on its skin swung colors to blend in with its surroundings.

This was a chameleon—an unfortunate result of Cora's latest transformation, triggered by radiation and unknown genetic factors.

Cora quickly scurried over Irezumi's corpse, trampling it a few times to ensure he was truly dead. Then she deftly extended her claws, working to retrieve Irezumi's terminal, which she smartly stored in her spatial pocket, planning to have Felix Lucas hack it later.

Mission accomplished, Cora's barnacle-like eyes swiveled 360 degrees as she tried to speak. Zap! Her long, slender tongue shot out, snatching a hopping cricket in a flash.

Cora spat it out with a disgusted hiss as the unlucky cricket hobbled away, injured. Uh-oh, it seemed her tongue was a bit out of control.

Cora paused in place, momentarily bewildered, before she clumsily pulled out a small communicator. Her teammates' frantic messages had already flooded the screen.

She awkwardly opened the group chat, attempting to type a message to let them know she was safe.

However... a chameleon's feet and toes are fused together. What does that mean? It means her first three digits were grouped together, while the fourth and fifth were grouped separately, making it incredibly difficult to type. She kept hitting the wrong keys, accidentally typing a string of random characters.

Cora grew increasingly frustrated, her skin flickering with a kaleidoscope of colors as her tail stiffened in irritation. Finally, in a fit of exasperation, she hammered out something resembling, "I'm fine, I'll come back on my own," before shutting her eyes tight and sending it.

The little chameleon scanned her surroundings, her skin turning a deep brown to perfectly blend in with the dusty ground, before darting away with a shake of her tail.

Boom! Boom!

Boom! Boom!

The vicious swarm of crows crashed against the barriers with relentless force, resembling a vast black cloud enveloping the city. The fragile barrier flickered, struggling to hold on before vanishing entirely for a moment, allowing thousands of feral beasts to surge through.

Cries of alarm echoed all around as Aberrants fought to contain the breach. Fortunately, the barrier reactivated in the next instant, trapping most of the beasts outside.

Onyx stared at the jumbled text message from Cora, his emotions a tangled mess.

The assassination attempt on Dmitri Yevgeniyev had been thwarted, and the few remaining enemies were subdued, yet the crisis at the Northern Base was far from over. Too much time had been lost at the entrance to Passage 13, and the city's defenses were now hanging by a thread.

Two heavily armored bulletproof vehicles sped onto the scene, and before they had even come to a full stop, security officers and a medical team leaped out.

"General!" The medics anxiously surrounded Dmitri Yevgeniyev, setting up a respirator and a portable nutrient capsule for on-the-spot emergency treatment. Bai was also carried away on a stretcher.

Dmitri was at the end of his strength. He looked up at the sky, making as if to move forward. "General, please don't move. You need immediate medical attention!" "You can't use your Anopower anymore, and you must avoid any mental or physical exertion, or your body won't be able to take it...."

"The City Defense Department..."

Dmitri mumbled, knowing that if the raven swarm wasn't stopped in time, the tragedy of Front City would repeat itself. Through the crowd, his eyes met Onyx's, and the handsome young man clenched the pocket watch in his hand, nodding solemnly at him.

The wind stirred the edges of his coat as the guards cleared the way, leading Onyx directly into the City Defense Department without obstruction.

The overwhelmed staff immediately noticed the unfamiliar face and demanded sharply, "Who are you, and how did you get in here? You need to leave at once...!"

Before they could finish, Onyx threw his terminal in their faces, and the "Supreme Command Authorization" representing Dmitri flashed before their eyes. The two guards quickly explained, "From now on, Mr. Montclair will act on the General's behalf. You are to follow his orders."

"Bring up the city map," Onyx commanded coldly, his deep, penetrating eyes exuding an undeniable authority that compelled obedience.

The Northern Base's entire broadcast system crackled to life once again: "Attention, everyone. In one minute, the City Defense Department will start the self-defense counteroffensive against the wild beast horde. Stay alert for updates on your terminals and follow orders."

"Residents of Middle Street, Downing Road, and the Inner Ring Commercial Zone...evacuate immediately. Escape routes have been sent to your terminals."

"Second and Sixth Squads, provide cover." The well-trained soldiers, their expressions resolute, carried out their orders with unwavering precision.

One command after another was issued, calm and measured. Onyx's mind raced, calculating at lightning speed as his fingers deftly input commands. Schools, hospitals, and train stations were swiftly cleared, with residents guided into underground shelters according to the instructions.

"Suppress."

The transparent sky bridges spanning the city vanished without a trace, replaced by the rising black barrels of cannons. These weapons, known as "Inferno Fireworks," were manufactured in Deep Woods and represented the highest lethality of the Alliance's firearms.

Boom—

Boom —

Brilliant explosions filled the sky, setting half of it ablaze with a fiery, red glow. The stench of charred flesh was overpowering as countless crows fell like hailstones. Over a hundred Wind Aberrants moved into position and unleashed their Anopower simultaneously, fanning the flames that spread like wildfire. The resolute determination of the city's defenders was reflected in every pair of eyes.

Patrolling forces hovering in the air finished the stragglers, while logistics teams swept back and forth, clearing the mountains of crow corpses.

"Sector Clear."

In the city's west, where the lush trees made artillery fire unsuitable, Onyx input a new command at the console. Within seconds, the barrier switched through a hundred different configurations.

Suddenly, an intentional "mistake" created a breach. The crows, possessing a rudimentary intelligence, seized the opportunity and swarmed in through the gap.

Onyx's lips curled into a bitter smile. Too easy to fool. "Flash."

The newly formed barrier flashed a blinding white light, illuminating the group attack Aberrants who had been lying in wait for it, as well as a high-voltage electric grid.

The crows, now trapped, trembled in terror, their tiny gray eyes reflecting their fear.

Anopowers and electrical currents lit up the sky, accompanied by the excited shouts of the Northern Base Aberrants, who were nearly delirious with enthusiasm.

These weren't vicious crows—they were practically angels, delivering points and prizes to the Northern Base! The entire city operated like a well-oiled machine under Onyx's command, running smoothly and efficiently.

Back in the City Defense Department, countless eyes were discreetly observing the calm, composed young man at the console.

One official grumbled enviously, "What's so special about him? This aggressive strategy is bound to cause massive infrastructure damage. We'll see how he handles the rebuilding later!"

Onyx, busy scribbling on a transparent screen, glanced at him with a light chuckle. "Send the design plans to Kenn Oda. The Northern Base doesn't support freeloaders—let him do some work."

Kenn Oda, an S2-class Engineering Aberrant, had arrived at the Northern Base the same day as F777 and had even walked through the VIP entrance right in front of Cora Thornton. Onyx didn't consider himself a vengeful person, just someone who well used resources.

With an S-Class Engineering Aberrant on hand, what's so hard about rebuilding? They could construct an entirely new city if needed!

At the busy command room's entrance, Dmitri, draped in a coat, stood quietly watching through the glass door. He had just undergone emergency treatment, his condition now stabilized, but his concern had driven him to come and see for himself.

However, what he found was beyond his expectations—better even than he had hoped. Onyx knew every detail about the facilities, the defense protocols, and personnel information inside and out, executing the counteroffensive with zero errors, achieving victory with minimal casualties.

It was as if he was a natural-born commander.

"General, where did you find...?" The officer beside Dmitri was dumbfounded.

Dmitri smiled faintly, holding his chest as he prepared to leave. "Getting old... Just standing for a bit wears me out. I'd better go back and continue my treatment. Oh, and summon Franz."

As he turned away, Dmitri's smile faded, his expression gradually growing cold. As long as he could still stand, it was time for reckoning.

On the top floors of the Aberrants Bureau building.

With Irezumi's death, the parasitic insects lost their control, and Scarlett Holland regained consciousness from her manipulated state. Her hair disheveled, she crawled on all fours to the floor-to-ceiling window, staring blankly outside.

The T005 system had resumed operation, and the rampant dust storms were rapidly dissipating.

The raven horde, decimated by the united forces of the Northern Base, dwindled quickly, and the night sky returned to its original tranquility.

The Northern Base had survived this trial.

The office door suddenly swung open, and several soldiers in inspector uniforms marched in sternly. "Commander Holland... Scarlett Holland, you are under arrest for treason. You'll need to come with us."

Cold iron cuffs snapped around her wrists, sealing away all the Anopower use. Scarlett, now reduced to the ordinary person she had always feared becoming, was dragged away in a daze. The most severe judgment awaited her.

The chaotic day finally ended. By the time Onyx left the City Defense Department, it was nearly midnight.

The other members of F777 were waiting outside. Charles tossed him a bottle of water, which Onyx caught without drinking. Exhausted, he removed his glasses and rubbed his temples, his bangs falling over his forehead. "Any word from Cora?" he asked.

Yuui opened her terminal and saw that ten minutes earlier, Cora had sent another garbled message: "k*#hgsk"

"I know! I know!" Damian chimed in with a grin, eager to answer. "Sis must be trying to say, 'We're almost there!'"

"Wow, our little Diamond is so smart," Yuui said with exaggerated praise, her red lips curving into a playful smile.

Damian pursed his lips, unsure whether she was being sincere or teasing him.

Onyx was about to speak when his expression twisted grimly, a chill running down his spine.

A cold, slithering creature had jumped onto his foot and "slipped" up his pant leg.

Onyx's gaze turned icy as he reached down and dragged the wriggling thing into view.

The creature's camouflage faded, revealing a dazed-looking chameleon. Its bulging eyes darted back and forth as it dangled by its flat head. Onyx's expression twisted with disgust, and he felt an overwhelming urge to rush back to his apartment for a hot shower. Gritting his teeth, he asked through clenched teeth, "Where did this ugly thing come from...?"

The chameleon's tail shot up, its belly puffing out in indignation, and its long, thin tongue flicked out, snapping onto Onyx's slender finger.

The lizard's saliva was sticky and thick, dripping down his finger. Onyx's forehead veins bulged as he tried to shake it off, but it stubbornly clung on. Ding! A familiar little bee-shaped communicator clattered to the ground, rolling to his feet.

Onyx froze, staring in shock for three full seconds. "You're...Cora?"

CHAPTER 12

The New Form

Ding! A familiar little bee terminal dropped to the ground.

Charles stared blankly.

Damian was just as stunned, his mouth agape with juice dribbling down, his expression vacant. "Big Sister…"

Yuui picked up the little bee terminal, as if struck by lightning. "Cora? You...how did you end up like this?"

The chameleon, Cora Thornton, recognized by her companions, bobbed her head joyfully, as if to say, "Yes, it's me. Not happy?"

No one was able to imagine a chameleon could display such rich expressions.

They knew Cora had some issues with her DNA sequence and had witnessed her incredible combat power after gene fusion—like with the Hooked Serpent earlier, or just now with the brown bear.

But to transform from a pure human into a pure animal! That was far beyond the normal bounds of scientific understanding. Even the usually taciturn Suchat couldn't help but comment, "She was better as a snake."

At least the Hooked Serpent was formidable in battle, and communication wasn't an issue.

"Hey, Princess Onyx, am I dreaming…." Yuui muttered incoherently, accidentally blurting out Onyx's nickname. "She won't stay like this forever, will she? You must have a way to change her back, right?"

Onyx's face was cold, his eyes dark like the night sky, his body slightly stiff if you looked closely. He silently stared at Cora hanging from his fingertip. This genetic result was far beyond anyone's expectations.

"Can we not discuss this here?" Felix was the only one who remained calm among them.

Although it was already midnight, the busy cleaning vehicles were still patrolling the streets, collecting Raven Corpses, and every so often an Aberrant would pass by, casting suspicious glances at the group loitering outside the Department of Defense.

"Let's head back to the apartment," Onyx said quietly. Cora, who had crawled over 120 miles, was already exhausted. Hearing this, she wriggled into Onyx's shirt pocket and settled in comfortably.

Onyx's pupils widened slightly as he stared at the obvious mud spots. Remembering how Cora had just climbed up his pant leg, his entire body, not just his expression, stiffened.

Felix glanced at him, suddenly recalling how, back in Luboni, this princess's obsession with cleanliness was so extreme it was almost frightening. He carried his own mattress when sleeping, insisted on renting out entire pools to swim, and would not tolerate any crawling creatures within his line of sight.

Felix's lips curled into a sly smile, his tone dripping with sarcasm. "Oh, my dear friend, lizards are so cute. Why don't you like them?"

"Shut up." Onyx's voice was bitter as he cast a quick glance at the sleepy Cora in his pocket, squeezing the words through gritted teeth, "Don't make assumptions about my preferences."

2:00 AM, Garden Apartments. The sound of water splashing in the bathroom.

Suddenly, the lights dimmed, and the shower stopped abruptly.

Onyx wiped his face, looking up at the temperature control panel displaying "off." Quiet moonlight streamed in through the window. Who else could it be with such an unannounced entrance? He spoke to the empty outer room, his tone resigned. "Cora, cut it out. Let me finish my shower."

His damp fingers fumbled briefly before pressing the "on" button on the panel, and the water started flowing again.

Two seconds later, click. As if the power tripped, the bathroom equipment shut down once more.

He casually grabbed a towel to dry off, loosely wrapping a bath towel around his waist before stepping out of the shower stall, leaning against the sink. "Come out, let's talk."

As soon as the words left his mouth, a greenish chameleon appeared out of thin air in front of him, her plump little paws pressing on the temperature control panel. Her belly puffed out, looking quite displeased.

Onyx couldn't help but laugh.

A Hooked Serpent, a Ferocious Cat, a Brown Bear, a Chameleon... the first four types of unknown genes had fully manifested.

On the whole, the Ferocious Cat and Brown Bear displayed relatively stable traits, while the Hooked Serpent and Chameleon showed high mutation with low activity, posing a risk of permanent alteration. It would be best to replace them as soon as possible. With only four days until the next wave of experiments, Cora would have to maintain her current state for now.

Deep in thought, the sound of Cora snapped Onyx out of his reverie, discontentedly tapping on the sink.

She clumsily operated the terminal, projecting a page onto the wall. It was the "World's Cutest Species Ranking," with Chameleons ranked 17th. Cora swished her tail and pointed emphatically at the screen, first at "Cutest," then at "17th." The message was simple: why did you call me ugly?

Onyx averted his eyes awkwardly, quickly apologizing, "I'm sorry. That was my mistake. Actually, if you look closely...."

Cora proudly straightened her spine, her eyes swiveling like two little bells.

Onyx chuckled softly, offering a half-hearted compliment. "You're kinda cute."

He extended two slender, elegant fingers and stroked Cora's flat head.

But as he rubbed, his hand suddenly froze. Damn his excellent memory—he was suddenly reminded of something from long ago. Back in the Loyak lab, he had said something similar.

Onyx discreetly glanced at Cora, relieved that she hadn't remembered.

"When the lab is back online, we'll run some counter-radiation tests and try to change you back as soon as possible. For now, can you stay in the apartment for a few days?"

Cora struggled to type out, ⌈ook⌋ with her paw.

In the warm light, even Onyx found the sight of a lizard less repulsive than before. He used to fear reptiles more than anything...

He naturally picked up Cora—just like he used to in the lab—and placed her in the sink, squeezing out some foam, intending to wash her dirty lizard body.

Cora thought to herself, Grandpa always said, no matter what happens, you can't let anyone help you bathe. Even if she had turned into a lizard, that rule should still apply, right?

A surge of heat rushed to her head as Cora struggled fiercely, her tail thrashing and splashing water everywhere. Onyx instinctively closed his eyes, and in his moment of distraction, she slipped free.

Cora, dizzy, shot into the air—thunk!—colliding with Onyx's abs, then sliding down. Panic filled her eyes as her four limbs flailed, leaving several red marks in their wake.

It looked painful...

She froze for a second, her skin flashing through red, orange, yellow, green, before she vanished in a panic.

The next three days saw intense turmoil within the Alliance, with tensions escalating sharply. Following the attack on Dmitri, the Northern Base adopted a tough diplomatic stance, launching a series of inquiries against the forces behind the incident—Blanc Yard, White Town, and Delta Island.

They even threatened war, shattering the fragile peace between the districts and laying bare their hostilities. At the negotiation table, the representatives from Blanc Yard and White Town brazenly admitted their crimes but refused to express any remorse.

Only Delta Island played dumb, denying both their involvement as the "Crocodile" and their deployment of the "Rat" and "Cat."

The representative from Blanc Yard shouted hysterically, "If we can't survive, then no one will! We'll all go down together!"

The White Town representative tearfully accused, "Look at this tornado! Two-thirds of our city is destroyed! What more can we do?"

The Delta Island representative simply responded, "It wasn't us.

Not our problem!"

The diplomats from Blanc Yard and White Town glared at him with disdain: Traitor.

Delta Island's arrogance stemmed from the fact that none of their people were on the list of released prisoners. However, two days later, the capture of a smuggler changed the game.

A confession from Jupiter Blade broke the stalemate. As a high-ranking captive from Delta Island, his crimes were well-documented. Delta Island was surprised, cursing Jupiter Blade as a traitor, stirring chaos at the negotiation table.

District B was in complete disarray, with Aberrants clashing frequently.

Every morning before dawn, Onyx had to rise early to handle various tasks. Dmitri hadn't yet recovered, Scarlett Holland's trial was imminent, and with the Aberrants Bureau leaderless, a mountain of responsibilities had been placed on his shoulders—clearing out the remaining Raven forces, overseeing urban reconstruction, conducting diplomatic negotiations... all of it fell to him.

After three days of non-stop work, Onyx finally returned to the apartment late at night. "I'm back," he called out, pushing open the door. The living room was brightly lit, the atmosphere warm and harmonious.

Charles was still with Dmitri, and Suchat was silently lifting weights.

Damian, surrounded by snacks, had a tiny chameleon perched on his head. The two were engrossed in watching an old soap opera from the former civilization, restored by Felix's technical skills.

Yuui cleared her throat and began singing loudly as the dramatic theme song played. Damian hummed along, while Cora's tail curled and uncurled, clearly absorbed in the moment.

Onyx's eyelid twitched as he watched Cora, looking so at ease. She noticed him and, startled, sprang into the air, frantically hopping onto Felix's mechanical arm.

Felix seized the opportunity to ask for spending money. "Generous Captain, honorable Captain, I want to buy this, and this, and this."

Cora's claws stamped down in agreement: "B-buy!" Then she vanished from sight.

Onyx sighed in exhaustion. Ever since the mishap in the bathroom, Cora had been avoiding him for three days straight.

He sat down on the sofa, removed his glasses, and rubbed his temples. "Any videos leaked recently?" Felix, in a good mood, was forthcoming. "No, but there are some odd rumors."

The A-level commission to guard District B10 had been evaluated by the system, with F777 taking the lead. Their points shot up to rank first in the Northern Base and sixth in the entire Alliance.

This mysterious team, which had suddenly emerged on the scene, was a hot topic on the Lucas Network. However, because of their infrequent appearances, they were the subject of much speculation.

"I recommend you look at this." Felix pulled up an image that overlaid the paused soap opera.

A brown bear, a six-armed steel beast, a venomous snake, and a three-meter-tall ice mage—representing Cora, Felix, Suchat, and Damian, respectively. Even Yuui was depicted as an eight-foot-tall man surrounded by a cloud of knife mist, his face obscured.

"This is from the latest issue of Aberrants Anecdotes, a comic that supposedly captures the assassination scene in great detail."

Everyone at the scene that day had been sworn to secrecy, forbidden from revealing the true identities of F777. But that didn't stop the involved parties from sharing gossip. With no actual footage available, everything was pure speculation, and each "source" had a different version of the story.

The descriptions of F777 became more and more outlandish, even spawning rumors like "F777 are all hulking steel brutes who refuse interviews because they're too ugly." In response, this absurd comic was born.

No one took it seriously, but Damian was particularly pleased with his portrayal.

"Oh, by the way, I looked into that terminal you found, Captain. I discovered something interesting."

Felix, without disguising his ice-blue eyes at home, let them shine brightly as he hacked into Irezumi's terminal, bypassing the ever-present surveillance in the data streams, and recovered the last conversation before Irezumi's death. "This information is still under wraps by the District B governor and hasn't been made public yet."

Everyone perked up and looked at the screen.

"Utopia, which was once The Central, is about to announce a new policy. A year from now, they'll open a global challenge for Aberrants. Those who pass will be granted residency permits and become legal residents of Utopia."

Residency permits through an Aberrant challenge? What's their game?

Yuui frowned. "What does that mean? They schemed behind our backs back then, and now they're reaching out to us? First, they slap us, then they offer candy?"

Suchat commented coldly, "Ulterior motives."

"Agreed," Felix nodded. "It's suspicious, especially right after the assassination attempt on Dmitri Yevgeniyev."

Onyx tapped his fingers lightly, a bitter smile on his lips. "Just a stalling tactic. Utopia has just risen, and there's still much to be done. The surface is a harsh place to survive, and if the districts band together to attack, this S-level city might fall before it can develop."

"Right now, with District B in chaos, they're throwing out a 'ticket' as bait. It's both a way to sow discord and a means of appeasement."

At this time, Utopia's new policy felt like a glaringly obvious but insidious message: Look, we haven't abandoned you. Pass the selection, and you can live happily in Utopia.

In the harsh reality of the apocalypse, most people would find it hard to resist such a temptation.

"So, are we going to take part?" Yuui asked, looking for everyone's opinions.

"That's for the Captain to decide," Onyx replied nonchalantly.

"Keep digging," the little bee terminal buzzed, a line of text popping up.

Onyx, with quick reflexes, plucked out a cowering chameleon from the couch cushions. Cora began shifting colors again.

"You guys continue; the Captain and I need to have a heart-to-heart." Onyx said, carrying Cora into a room and gently closing the door behind them.

He held Cora up in front of him, slowly unbuttoning his shirt with one hand, loosening his collar slightly to reveal a broad expanse of skin.

Cora's eyes darted left and right in panic: What are you doing? What do you think you're doing?!

Onyx lowered his voice, speaking with a hint of grievance. "Stop hiding. The wound is already healed, and I don't mind."

His tired eyes drooped slightly, making him look rather pitiful. "As long as you remember to take responsibility, it's fine. In the future, don't pay attention to any of those Silver Owls or whatever. Not a single one."

CHAPTER 13

The Chameleon

Click.

The apartment door was especially busy tonight, with Charles and Onyx returning almost simultaneously.

"How's General Yevgeniyev doing, Franz?" Onyx asked.

Charles's throat was so dry it felt like it might crack. "Hold on, let me grab some water first."

He rushed over, unceremoniously grabbed Damian's special apple-flavored probiotic drink for kids, and downed it in one go—leaving not a drop behind. Damian blinked for a second before bursting out, "Ahhh, you old geezer—!!" Damn it, he had saved that for last!

Charles set down his medical kit, his expression grave as he addressed the group. "General Yevgeniyev had two sudden bouts of unconsciousness today. He's been taken to the Aberrants' Specialty Hospital for treatment. He was just barely awake when I left."

"What? It's that serious?" Yuui immediately straightened up.

Onyx and Cora, just emerging from the bathroom, also caught Charles's words.

"Hmph, so why did you come back?" Damian teased, tugging at Charles's braid. "Did the doctors there outshine you and kick you out~?"

"There's nothing more I can do. The wounds from the assassination attempt to have healed, but General Yevgeniyev's unconsciousness is because of organ degeneration, which has impaired his compensatory functions. While he hasn't reached organ failure, it's seriously affecting his vital signs."

"Yevgeniyeva and the others are taking turns trying to persuade him to replace his organs with bionic ones. It's the only option," Charles muttered, absently ruffling Damian's hair. "If only there were a way to reverse—or at least slow down—organ aging...."

Yuui voiced her concern, "So replacing his organs would fix his Anopower level, right? But being stuck at S-level isn't a big deal, is it?"

Charles shook his head helplessly. "It's not that simple. Given General Yevgeniyev's current condition, 90% of his organs would need to be replaced. It's more than just a matter of fixing his level," Onyx explained calmly.

"It would completely dismantle and destroy his internal magnetic field, meaning he would go from being an S-level Aberrant...to an ordinary person."

The large living room fell into silence, even the playful banter between Charles and Damian coming to a halt. For an Aberrant to revert to an ordinary person—no matter who it was, that was too cruel.

Before bed, Cora slipped into Onyx's bedroom and nudged him from atop the covers.

Onyx seemed to have expected her visit, setting down his screen without surprise. "You want to ask if there's a way I can help, Dmitri?"

Cora turned green in affirmation.

Onyx sighed. "Charles is the doctor, and even he's at a loss. What could I possibly do?"

The chameleon's triangular head drooped, spinning a sad shade of blue, giving off a distinctly dejected vibe.

The room fell silent as Onyx gently stroked Cora's back with two fingers, his eyelashes lowered, his eyes deep as a bottomless abyss. "It's not entirely hopeless...." he drawled slowly, "There's one possibility, though it's a long shot. But it might be worth a try."

Cora's chubby little paw tugged on his pajamas, urging him to stop dragging it out and just say what the solution was.

Onyx didn't rush to answer. Instead, he held her two front limbs, crossing them over his chest, a slight smile at the corner of his eyes.

"I'll think of a solution. But in exchange, what will you promise me?"

The lizard's body accidentally released a bit of psychic energy, her paw swiping out in a slight gesture. Onyx glanced down, raising an eyebrow slightly. "What's this? Not in a good mood?"

Cora disappeared on the spot.

Onyx's expression softened, his face relaxing as he laughed aloud, a glimpse of youthful pride and spirit shining through the layers of time.

"Alright, I won't make it hard for you. Hand me the terminal."

A little bee was tossed into the air, and a moment later, Onyx dialed a video call.

The projection flickered twice, revealing a person in a white lab coat, moving hurriedly—it was Dr. Rainer Ninnemann. "Dr. Ninnemann, how's the research coming along?" Onyx asked nonchalantly.

"It's you? How do you have time...?" Rainer mumbled, his steps never slowing, the background resembling the hallway of a lab. Suddenly, he seemed to remember something, his tone turning excited. "I've found the critical threshold! DNA mutations caused by high-dose radiation are not inevitable as long as..."

Rainer enthusiastically detailed his latest findings, and Onyx occasionally chimed in. "I've got a new project you might be interested in," Onyx eventually said.

"What project?"

"Research on the lineage of cell division, focusing on organ regeneration. I can provide you with relevant data, but the condition is that I must oversee it, and the highest level of confidentiality must be maintained, with only you and me on the list."

Rainer's steps halted, his eyes widening in disbelief. "Say that again. Are you sure you mean 'research on the lineage of cell division for organ regeneration'?"

"Positive." Onyx's expression remained unchanged. "Come to the Front City lab tomorrow, and we'll discuss it in person."

On the other side of the line, Rainer was too stunned to speak, only the flames of passion burning intensely in his heart. Cell division and organ regeneration—those were secrets of the 'Spark.'

Did this kid get possessed? A few days ago, he was still shouting,

"What does benefiting all of humanity have to do with me?" and now he's suddenly changed his mind?

The next morning.

Front City.

The holes in the ceiling had been patched up, and the renovated lab was lined with various precise and complex instruments. Onyx was focused on calibrating the data, while Cora's tail was wrapped around a bar of the eco-incubator, leisurely swaying back and forth as she hung upside down.

Rainer Ninnemann entered, wearing a hat and mask, and was startled by the sight, quickly exclaiming, "Lizard genes?"

He stared at Cora for a couple of seconds, his eyes lighting up with an uncontainable surge of research enthusiasm. "What's the emotional value post-fusion? Have you measured her psychic energy? Is her Anopower functioning normally?"

He even stepped closer, reaching out to pick up Cora for a closer look. "I suggest we start with a spectral analysis...."

Cora's tongue flicked out briefly, and suddenly, a ghostly blue sword hovered just inches from Rainer's nose.

He froze in his tracks, realizing this was not an experimental subject he could afford to mess with. Awkwardly, he said, "Uh, maybe you should handle this."

Onyx casually deactivated the Ethereal Artifact, chuckling softly. "Dr. Ninnemann, hands off. This lizard princess has quite the temper." Cora cooperatively arched her back, her entire body turning a vibrant red as she projected an aura of intimidation.

Rainer thought. What a strange combination!

"No need for blood tests," Onyx continued, without wasting time. "Time is limited, and here are the previous genetic results. Let's move straight to counter-radiation."

Rainer changed into his lab coat, disinfected himself, and glanced at the active screen. The spectrometer displayed four genetic sequences: snake, feral cat, brown bear, and chameleon. The DNA chains were intricately interwoven, with the chameleon genes currently dominating, rapidly consuming nearby cells, showing a high risk of stabilization.

"The chameleon's activity is too high. To be safe, adjust the radiation level to 22.025%-26.745%." Onyx glanced at Rainer without a word, noting that Rainer's research had indeed progressed, as he could now measure down to the third decimal place.

The two entered the isolated chamber. After attaching the sensors, Cora slapped Onyx's leg with her tail, clearly showing leave.

Counter-radiation wasn't exactly a good thing. Now that it was set to over 20%, it wouldn't affect her much because of her unique physique, but a normal S-level Aberrant would struggle to handle it.

Onyx's health was relatively weak, and excessive radiation wouldn't be good for him—there was no need for him to stay with her.

Seeing her determination, Onyx removed his communicator and fastened it around the little chameleon's neck.

"Alright, I'll wait outside. If anything happens, just call me. If you can't speak, knock three times, and I'll come in."

As he left, Onyx paused briefly to adjust the protective glass, switching it to an invisible mode.

Low-concentration counter-radiation filled the entire chamber, and each time the waveband shifted, Onyx would remind Cora.

"We've eliminated the four known wavebands, leaving nearly a 5% fluctuation range. Let's see what we get this time," Rainer remarked as he monitored the instruments. "Hopefully, it's something more stable."

It all came down to luck.

Onyx remained silent. Genetic engineering, especially gene fusion, couldn't be done without animal experimentation. Cora's DNA composition was complex, and likely… not very cooperative.

After another waveband change, Cora's clear voice came through the communicator, "Onyx de Montclair."

Onyx immediately hit the pause button. "I'm here."

Cora giggled. "I've turned back!"

Without checking the instrument results, Onyx quickly walked forward, his voice tinged with relief. "I'm coming in. Are you dressed?"

"I'm—dressed!"

The door swung open to reveal Cora, now fully human, dressed in a white T-shirt and shorts, swinging her legs as she sat on the lab bench, looking at him with a hint of discontent.

Onyx strode over and wrapped her in a tight embrace. Cora was momentarily speechless, pressed against his chest, listening to the steady thump, thump of his heartbeat as her ears turned redder and redder.

They stayed like that for a long while, and then Onyx checked her limbs. "Do you feel any discomfort? Anything unusual?"

Cora thought for a moment and then shook her head seriously. "No."

Hand in hand, they emerged from the chamber, where Rainer was intently watching the instruments. "Come and look," he said, his expression grave. Onyx followed his gaze.

Cora squeezed her head in curiously, eager to be part of whatever was happening, even if she didn't understand it.

"The data analysis is almost complete. This time, there's a high probability that only one gene manifested, and it seems quite stable. It should last at least a month or two." As the detailed report appeared, Rainer's eyes widened with surprise. "What? Secondary activation?"

Secondary activation refers to the reappearance of dominant genes, such as those of the snake or feral cat. But they had already eliminated the first batch of four genes, so this shouldn't be possible.

Even Onyx couldn't hide his astonishment. Could it be that Cora had shown signs of gene fusion before those four? "No," Cora answered honestly. "I've been normal all my life."

Ding! The spectrometer stopped, displaying the result: "This gene is not recorded in the database."

Rainer was dumbfounded. This genetic spectrometer covered the entire Alliance's biological spectrum—how could something not be in the database?

Onyx frowned. All successful gene fusions were recorded. Unless... it was from a failed attempt, something strange and unpredictable.

"Cora, are you absolutely sure you felt nothing unusual?" Onyx's brow furrowed deeply. "I'm fine," Cora nodded.

Still not fully reassured, Onyx took her for a full physical examination, which indeed revealed something new.

Rainer pointed to the resonance scanner in shock. "Her psychic energy level is stable at 14,000."

Seeing Cora's confusion, Rainer sighed deeply. "Congratulations. You've experienced a secondary awakening... No, in your terms, you've advanced to S8."

S8 psychic energy ranges from 13,000 to 15,000. Cora's was previously at 12,000, but now it had stabilized at 14,000, showing a significant increase in strength. S7 was already impressive; once the news of Cora's advancement to S8 got out, it would undoubtedly cause a storm across the Alliance.

"When do we start the research you mentioned?" Rainer Ninnemann muttered as they exited the lab.

"The sooner, the better," Onyx replied in a low voice. Dmitri Yevgeniyev's condition was critical. Before coming here, he had probed Yevgeniyev's thoughts; as long as Dmitri agreed, the surgery could take place as soon as a week from now. "Cora and I need to make a stop at the Tribunal first, then we'll come find you."

Rainer nodded, trailing behind the two Aberrants in small, hurried steps. He panted, "I've already arranged the confidentiality permissions you mentioned. I've thoroughly vetted all the assistants. We'll break down the research process into separate segments—no one will figure it out..."

The three figures vanished into the distance.

A small drone hovered high above, then returned to an overpass a few kilometers away, where two figures stood. One of them glanced at the real-time feed, puzzled. "Who's that? And why is Ninnemann so close to him?"

The two Central agents had been tracking Rainer Ninnemann for a long time, ever since he arrived at the Northern Base. He'd been under their watchful eyes.

Ninnemann was once a core member of the "Plan Eternity" project and had a background at the Arashi Research Institute. The Central suspected he was hiding critical research data and had deliberately withdrawn from the project team, possibly to set up his own operation and claim the experimental results for himself.

But Ninnemann was a hardcore scientist through and through, rarely leaving his quarters and hardly interacting with others. Aberrants heavily guarded the lab, making infiltration nearly impossible. After months of surveillance, they were getting nowhere—until recently, when Ninnemann had made two suspicious trips to

Front City.

The other agent skillfully extracted the most recent photos and video footage, compiling them into a periodic report file. "Just do your job. Thinking isn't our business. Send this over to the inspector."

Among the countless images, there was an inconspicuous side profile of a young man.

The young Onyx, dressed in a white lab coat and wearing gold-rimmed glasses, looked refined and handsome. Although he was similarly dressed as a researcher, his demeanor was entirely different from the dark-eyed, weary Rainer Ninnemann beside him.

CHAPTER 14

The Trial

Northern Base, 10:00 AM sharp. A highly expected trial was about to begin.

Because the defendant was a former top official of the Aberrants Bureau and the crimes involved were classified, only a select few could attend. The media and reporters allowed inside had undergone strict screening, and the audience included well-dressed officials, Aberrants with their powers, subdued, and silent witnesses.

Just before the trial officially began, two figures entered against the light.

Onyx, dressed in an exquisitely tailored light gray suit, appeared tall and lean, his broad shoulders and long legs stressed as he moved.

Cora Thornton's outfit was much simpler—a white T-shirt and shorts, her shoulder-length hair neat. The two latecomers walked forward, seemingly oblivious to the attention they drew.

"Is that Cora Thornton?" a special correspondent in the media section whispered to a colleague. "She looks pretty approachable."

"Looks can deceive," the local colleague, not buying into the first impression, whispered back, "You do not know how fierce she can be."

"How fierce? I don't believe it unless you show me."

"Do you have the Leatherback Sea Turtle video?"

"No, but I've heard about it. It's way too exaggerated—how could anyone take down a level-5 beast single-handedly?"

"I'll send it to you." The colleague sighed deeply. That video had been incredibly popular for a short time, but for some mysterious reason, its hype had suddenly died down within days. It was a good thing he had the foresight to save a copy.

"Whoa! Holy—! My god!" The correspondent watched, utterly stunned, his words stumbling over each other. "I—I didn't realize she was that fierce! Why is she here today? Don't tell me she's friends with Scarlett Holland?"

"Quite the opposite," the colleague said with a knowing look. "They're more likely enemies. I've heard—though I can't confirm it—that Scarlett Holland once kidnapped her."

The correspondent gasped, his face going blank. Kidnapping an S7? That would be an explosive piece of news across the entire Alliance. Had Scarlett Holland lost her mind?

Just as the colleague finished speaking, the tall man with his hands in his pockets walked past them, casting a glance their way. The correspondent shivered and instinctively shut off the terminal, which had been playing the vibrant video.

The F777 members seated in the front row turned their heads in surprise, their eyes scanning up and down, as if to say: Hey, Captain, you've turned back to normal?

Cora put a finger to her lips in a "shush" gesture, playfully winking and spinning around to show she was unscathed. She sat down next to Felix, who naturally reached out, and Cora, after feeling around in her pocket, handed him the terminal for his usual anti-intrusion check.

Then, as if recalling something, she leaned in close to Felix, whispering with their heads almost touching. From certain angles, their faces seemed almost too close.

Onyx lazily draped his arm over the back of Cora's chair. The three of them were used to sharing a terminal, seeing nothing unusual about it, but to the others, it was quite a shocking sight.

The eyes of the two nearby reporters widened in surprise.

If they had been from Aberrants Anecdotes, they would have already concocted a juicy scandal, with an S7 Aberrant at the center, guaranteeing tomorrow's top sales. But they were from The Northern Daily, a reputable official newspaper! The two exchanged looks before dutifully writing: "On [date], S7 Aberrant Cora Thornton attended the trial with two partners."

Clang—

The courtroom doors opened as the Aberrant guards escorted six stern-faced judges into the room. At the center was the presiding judge, a woman in her forties, standing tall and composed. Her deep eyes gleamed with intelligence as she scanned the audience, causing many to avert their gazes, as if one look from her could uncover all their secrets.

Cora, alert, immediately sensed that this was a high-level Aberrant.

"Wendy Smith, A7 level, psychic type, Anopower: 'Truth Reconstruction.' She can reverse the flow of time and space to recreate past events, as well as reveal the true thoughts of those involved." Onyx whispered to Cora, lightly pinching her ear.

He was essentially a walking census bureau, with an encyclopedic knowledge of every Northern Base resident's background.

Wendy Smith's ability was similar to Ruby Bai's "Mind Lie Detector," but unlike Cora's younger and less experienced mentor, Wendy Smith was a seasoned early-awakened Aberrant who had been serving as a judge for over seventeen years, making her a formidable expert in interrogation.

Back then, even A-level Ruby Bai couldn't extract much from S-level Onyx, but today, the matchup between A7-level Wendy Smith and B3-level Scarlett Holland would be almost a one-sided battle.

"The court is now in session. Bring in the defendant, Scarlett Holland." Wendy Smith's voice resonated clearly throughout the courtroom as she took her seat.

The bailiffs brought in Scarlett Holland, her hands and feet bound by Aberrant shackles. Without her high-ranking uniform, she appeared frail; her steps slow, and the lines on her cheeks deepened, though her expression remained as composed as ever.

"Commander Holland..." someone murmured from the audience, but a glare from those around quickly silenced them.

It was Scarlett Holland's administrative secretary, a newcomer with little knowledge of her former superior's crimes. She had merely expressed a sentiment about her boss's fall from grace, but it was enough to provoke the crowd's anger. The secretary regretted her words and clapped a hand over her mouth, not daring to say more.

In the front row, Svetlana sat upright, her expression stern. She was here today on behalf of Dmitri Yevgeniyev and Chu Bai, to witness Scarlett Holland's fate firsthand.

"Scarlett Holland," Wendy Smith, sitting in the center judge's seat, spoke with a voice infused with psychic power, her words echoing through the chamber. "You are charged with thirteen counts, including treason, secession, endangering national security, abuse of power, and murder. Do you dispute these charges?"

"I do," Scarlett replied, her expression unusually calm. "I deny these false accusations. I did not betray the Northern Base. The order to stand down was given under the control of an S-level Aberrant, not of my own free will."

The audience erupted in outrage, angrily cursing Scarlett Holland for her stubborn refusal to admit guilt, even at death's door.

"Order in the court," Wendy Smith rapped her gavel. "You deny the attempted murder of General Yevgeniyev, yet the order to bar entry to Front City was issued while you were fully conscious."

Scarlett hesitated for a moment before answering plainly, "I was acting in the best interest of the Northern Base." Wendy's eyes flashed with intensity as she raised her voice, "Lies."

"I request permission to use 'Truth Reconstruction.'"

"Request granted," the judges conferred briefly before reaching a decision.

Thud—thud—

The sound reverberated like a mighty bell. Scarlett Holland's face twisted in pain as her consciousness was completely overwhelmed, her resistance futile. The past surfaced, starting with a cold, commanding voice: "Shut down all connections to Front City."

Then came her inner thoughts, filled with disdain: "Ordinary people? Useless trash, not worth saving. If they die, it's their own bad luck."

"Aberrants... well, they're just a bunch of powerless rejects. It's better to clean them out. Once the crisis is over, we can issue new recruitment orders."

The courtroom fell into a dead silence, everyone stunned by her blatant disregard for human life.

"Murderer! Bitch!" A rotten egg suddenly flew from the witness stand, landing near Scarlett Holland's feet. "What makes you so high and mighty? Who gave you the right to decide our fate? Who the hell do you think you are?"

The bailiffs rushed to intervene, but the enraged man hurled another rotten egg, this time using his Anopower, which splattered directly onto Scarlett's face. The gray-green sludge oozed down, emitting a foul stench.

"Please have the witness temporarily removed," Wendy Smith gestured, and the bailiffs escorted the man out. She then turned to the audience to explain, "The witness lost his parents during the Beast Tide and is understandably emotional. Please be understanding."

Cora rested her chin on her hand, a slight smile on her lips. She had initially thought the presiding judge was strictly impartial, but she had clearly seen that when the witness first pulled out the rotten egg, Wendy Smith had noticed, yet deliberately delayed her response by a couple of seconds.

"Scarlett Holland, your discriminatory attitude toward ordinary people has had severe negative consequences for the Northern Base. The court has received additional evidence that former S4-level Aberrant Jupiter Blade left for Delta Island out of resentment over your unjust treatment of his family."

With "Truth Reconstruction" still in effect, the mention of Jupiter Blade caused Scarlett Holland's pupils to contract as she involuntarily recalled the past.

Jupiter Blade had grown up in a welfare institution in a lower district. His "family" comprised disabled "invalids," and because of his status as an Aberrant, Scarlett Holland had assigned him a residence in District B, never considering whether it was "appropriate."

The community was full of Aberrants with a strong sense of competition, and Jupiter Blade's family suffered severe bullying. Busy with his assignments, Jupiter hadn't noticed until his family members began self-harming. By then, it was too late, and he eventually left District B10 in despair.

Another S-level Aberrant, the chief designer of the "Hellfire," weaponry, also left the Northern Base because of conflicting ideologies. Before he departed, he confided in a friend, "My original intention in designing the Hellfire weaponry was to give ordinary people a fighting chance against zombies and beasts. If my weapons are only for Aberrants, then what's the point?"

When his friend pressed for details, the designer had only shaken his head with a bitter smile, unwilling to elaborate.

The courtroom buzzed with murmurs, and Aberrants in the audience looked outraged. It was no wonder the Northern Base had always had fewer top-tier Aberrants compared to other districts—it was all because of Scarlett Holland, the rotten apple in the bunch! She might have paid lip service to the importance of Aberrants, but her actions were anything but honorable. In the end, it was all about maintaining her own power.

The F777 members in their seats couldn't help but sneer. Scarlett Holland had offended more than just these S-levels—there were three more on their team. If it hadn't been for Dmitri Yevgeniyev's efforts to keep them, they might have left the Northern Base in anger, just like Jupiter Blade.

The trial continued, and one by one, Scarlett Holland's crimes were laid bare. When the charge of murder was read, Wendy Smith activated her Anopower once more, and the scene of Sherry Harper's death unfolded. Scarlett Holland hadn't just failed to save her—under "Truth Reconstruction," her jealousy and malice toward Sherry Harper were as tangible as thick, black tar.

"Chief Harper!" Even some of the older Aberrants Bureau officials couldn't remain composed, gritting their teeth as tears welled up. That was Sherry Harper... once the highly respected and expected successor to Dmitri Yevgeniyev!

The courtroom erupted with furious outcries against Scarlett Holland; the condemnation reaching a fever pitch. Wendy Smith banged her gavel loudly. "Order! Please maintain order!"

"Criminal Scarlett Holland, do you have anything further to argue?" Scarlett's eyes were vacant, but she stubbornly insisted, "I plead not guilty."

Wendy Smith considered for a moment. She had three uses of her Anopower per day, and not wanting to waste any, she activated it one last time. Chaotic images flashed by, revealing Scarlett Holland's dark past as if fast-forwarded through a film, though there were no additional discoveries.

In the audience, Onyx caught a fleeting figure in one image, his brow furrowing slightly. He turned his head, and Felix was looking at him. The two exchanged a glance, and Felix leaned over Cora to pass the terminal to Onyx.

Next to them, the reporter from The Northern Daily was secretly flipping through an article from Aberrants Anecdotes. Surprised by this scene, he quickly averted his gaze, his heart pounding with anxiety.

Recording was prohibited in the courtroom, but Felix had used special methods to preserve all the data from "Truth Reconstruction," including a frame showing a conversation between Scarlett Holland and a certain Central official.

Onyx's dark lashes lowered, hiding the distant gleam in his eyes. Jae-Woo Park.

Because it wasn't key evidence, this part had drawn little attention, but Onyx reviewed the footage frame by frame, deducing the content of their conversation from their lip movements. Judging by the timeline, the conversation had taken place shortly after Cora's S7 status was made public.

Jae-Woo Park had called the Northern Base on behalf of the Central, expressing a curious interest in Cora's origins. Scarlett Holland had casually explained that Cora came from a lower district and had volunteered in response to a recruitment order.

Jae-Woo Park had repeated with a meaningful tone, "Oh? A lower district, hmm? That's quite unusual." Then he smoothly changed the subject, exchanged a few pleasantries with Scarlett, and ended the call.

If Jae-Woo Park didn't know Cora and had never encountered F777, everything would have made perfect sense.

But the reality was quite the opposite. They had clashed violently in Deep Woods, where Cora had killed the governor Ne Kon and the S-level dual-type Aberrant Punk right in front of Jae-Woo Park. If it hadn't been for Onyx's careful mediation, the situation could have spiraled out of control.

Given this context, Jae-Woo Park's call took on a far more intriguing implication. He hadn't mentioned his past with Cora, nor had he shown any intent to expel or recruit F777. It seemed as if he merely wanted to confirm that Cora was at the Northern Base. So what exactly was his intention?

Onyx glanced subtly at Cora beside him. The dignified S7 had grown bored with the legal proceedings and was resting her chin on Yuui Hayashi's shoulder in front of her, seemingly attentive but actually sneaking a candy into her mouth with a satisfied smile.

Onyx's eyes softened with amusement, though his grip on the terminal tightened. No matter what Jae-Woo Park intended for Cora, as long as Onyx was around, his plans would fail.

After nearly two hours, the long trial finally ended. Wendy Smith solemnly stood up and declared, "I announce that the defendant, Scarlett Holland, is found guilty on all thirteen charges. She is sentenced to life imprisonment, stripped of her citizenship and Anopower usage rights, and will be held and monitored as a Level 1 felon."

A Level 1 felon is required to undergo mandatory rehabilitation, with a minimum of 100 hours of labor per week. Coincidentally, the Northern Base was planning to expand by one-third to accommodate more residents from Front City, and Scarlett Holland would undoubtedly be sent to do hard labor.

Hearing that it wasn't the death penalty, the audience began murmuring, some expressing dissatisfaction.

Only Onyx smiled knowingly. "Judge Smith is wise," he remarked.

"How so?" The four in the front row, including Yuui, turned around curiously.

"From what little I know of her, the death penalty wouldn't be a punishment for Scarlett Holland; it would be a form of twisted relief. Her warped mind would likely think, 'See, I was right. You just didn't understand me. I died for the Northern Base.'"

The group shivered at the thought, a chill running down their spines. Knowing Scarlett Holland's twisted personality, she might indeed think that way.

"So the most severe punishment isn't death; it's the endless despair of knowing she's an Aberrant but being forced to bow her head and live like the ordinary people she once despised, spending the rest of her life atoning."

Sure enough, Scarlett Holland's once calm expression cracked upon hearing the sentence. She struggled violently, the Aberrant shackles clanking. "I do not plead guilty! I demand to see General Yevgeniyev!"

"Request denied," Wendy Smith declared, bringing the gavel down with finality.

The trial was over.

As Cora left, she ran into Sunny Zhao outside the courthouse. The usually composed water-type Aberrant was lighting a cigarette, taking a long time before taking a puff.

"Hey, isn't that Sunny? I didn't know she smoked." Someone nearby nudged their companion, silently mouthing the word—Jupiter Blade. "Weren't they on the same team before? Probably that kind of relationship."

"What kind? No way! Really?" "Stop staring, let's go."

Cora suddenly remembered that during the beach mission Silver Owl had asked for help with, Sunny had mentioned that Jupiter Blade was her partner.

A slender figure stopped in front of her. Sunny looked up and saw Cora.

"Smoking is bad for your health," Cora said earnestly, pulling out a pistachio-flavored lollipop from her space. "Here, try this instead."

"Alright, I won't smoke," Sunny replied, obediently putting out the cigarette. "Are you upset about Jupiter Blade?"

"Yes, but we weren't lovers," Sunny said with a faint smile, clearly having overheard the earlier conversation. "Who says men and women always have to be romantically involved? I just feel guilty. As his captain, if I had paid more attention to him back then, he wouldn't have ended up like this."

Betraying the Northern Base, attempting to assassinate the District B governor, and then betraying Delta Island—Jupiter Blade was eventually sentenced to twenty years in prison. Fortunately, because of his voluntary confession, his family had been safely escorted back and settled into an old-fashioned residential area where they were currently living well.

"Don't be sad. The storm will pass," Cora comforted Sunny Zhao seriously. She asked Onyx to visit Jupiter later. With his sharp eye for people, if Jupiter wasn't beyond redemption, they might get his sentence reduced.

"Yes, the sandstorm is over. Everything will pass. I believe I'll find a way," Sunny said as she unwrapped the lollipop and popped it into her mouth. Together, they looked up at the sky.

The sprawling, three-dimensional city was as bustling as ever, with various flying terminals darting back and forth. The bright sunlight was almost blinding. Summer had arrived.

Two days later, Utopia issued a global announcement that it would host the first Aberrant Challenge a year from now. Based on the results, they would distribute passes to select new residents for the floating city. The news caused a huge stir across the New Pacific Alliance, the Galio Empire, and the Luse Federation.

As Onyx had predicted, those who remained on the surface were filled with an immense desire and passion, preparing with all their might. Even the conflicts between districts decreased.

Life gradually returned to a semblance of peace, as if time had been fast-forwarded. F777 continued to grind points, aiming for the top spot in the Alliance. The only difference was that they were now one member short—Onyx no longer took part in field missions.

He had thrown himself entirely into the genetic project with Rainer Ninnemann, working tirelessly. With ample funding, abundant resources, and a nearly hundred-strong team, they made groundbreaking progress in organ regeneration. Dmitri volunteered to be their first clinical trial subject.

Amidst the dense zombie tides, Cora's twin blades danced through the air, slicing through the heads of level-3 zombies in quick succession, while Charles deftly extracted the crystals.

The surrounding teams could only sigh helplessly—they were used to it by now. Wherever F777 went, it was like locusts devouring everything, leaving not a single corpse behind. Well, not quite—no corpses, no nothing.

Cora wiped some dirty blood from her cheek and glanced at her terminal, watching the points shoot up. "You guys clean up; I'm heading back."

"Cora!" Yuui called after her teasingly. "Don't forget to shower, or Princess Onyx will get mad again."

Cora paused, sniffed herself, and sheepishly replied, "I-I know."

As night fell over Mount Twilight, Onyx had just stepped out of the lab when he saw a familiar figure sitting cross-legged on the floating sports car. Cora cradled a large jar of honey in her arms, scooping it out with a spoon. What would be a lethal dose of sweetness for most people was immensely satisfying for her.

Her insatiable sweet tooth was a lingering side effect of the brown bear gene.

Onyx shook his head slightly in amusement and stopped in front of her. Cora looked up at him in a daze, a trace of golden honey still clinging to the corner of her mouth.

A faint chuckle escaped as Onyx reached out with his long fingers, wiping the residue away. He rubbed his thumb and forefinger together as if savoring the sweetness that seemed to seep into his heart despite not tasting it. "Why are you here alone? Where are the others?"

"I came to pick you up," Cora replied, her tone unapologetically bold.

"Did you? Then let's head home," Onyx said with a bright smile, teasing her. "This car is pretty expensive. If the owner shows up, you'll have to pay for it."

Cora's eyes widened in alarm at the thought of having to pay. She nimbly jumped down like a feline, lightly pushing him from behind. "Run!"

Onyx laughed heartily, the long-absent tranquility slowly filling his chest.

Suddenly, he realized that this simple and warm life was quite good. Cora could take on the monsters and provide for them while he followed a routine, working as a genuine, ordinary researcher. When the sun set each day, they would walk home hand in hand, discussing what to have for dinner.

It was a life Onyx had never imagined but found he didn't mind at all.

CHAPTER 15

A New Goal

New Pacific Alliance (NPA)

District A1, The Central

As the political heart of the New Pacific Alliance, The Central serves as the most important city, responsible for the administrative management of the entire alliance. There are no residential areas within its jurisdiction, and entry is strictly controlled by clearance levels.

After Utopia ascended, most officials successfully transferred, but a few "less senior" ones remained on the ground to handle affairs, diligently working with the hope of one day earning their "ticket."

The fully automated streets were immaculately clean, and modern skyscrapers towered in every direction. Two inspectors hurriedly disembarked from a starship, switching to a hovering vehicle that flew them to the city's magnificent Council Hall.

The glass elevator ascended smoothly, stopping at the entrance to a conference room large enough to seat a hundred people. Artificial intelligence guided the guests to their seats. At this moment, an important meeting was in progress. The two inspectors bowed their heads and tiptoed around the edges, not daring to make a sound.

The long table was lined with some of the most influential figures in the world, a mix of Aberrants and ordinary people, each a frequent face in the news. However, they were all lifelike holograms; these individuals had long since boarded Utopia. In the vast conference room, apart from the two inspectors, no other living beings were present.

The figures were discussing Utopia's development plan for the next three years. Every policy they released would be explosive news. The only two humans present felt as if they were sitting on pins and needles, under immense pressure, frequently wiping the cold sweat from their foreheads, anxious.

After about forty minutes, most of the holograms disappeared, including the leaders of other nations, leaving less than twenty people behind.

A deep, solemn voice echoed from the head of the long table. The speaker sat in the shadows, his silhouette barely visible. "The reason I asked you to stay is that, a few days ago, I came across this photograph."

The nameplate identified him as one of Utopia's three leaders, a former head of the New Pacific Alliance.

A clear photograph appeared. It showed two men dressed as researchers walking side by side out of a lab, the older one with a gleeful smile on his lips. Whispered conversations erupted from all directions as everyone tried to understand what was so unusual about the photo.

"I'll let the official in charge explain the specifics."

The sweat-drenched inspector nervously stood up.

"I... I provided the photo. The man on the left is Rainer Ninnemann, a former core member of Plan Eternity. He left the project team a year ago, and I was ordered to track his movements. The man on the right is Onyx de Montclair. As far as I know, they are secretly researching cell division, but their exact purpose remains unclear."

"Cell division?" A hologram slammed a fist on the table and shouted angrily, "Are they trying to create human self-repair? That's part of Plan Eternity! Rainer Ninnemann has obviously stolen classified information."

An older official murmured to himself, "Onyx de Montclair? That name sounds familiar."

The shadowy figure raised a hand, and another photo appeared on the screen.

This one looked older. The same two men were featured, with a younger Rainer flushed and engaged in a heated argument with the other. The opposing researcher was handsome, with a calm demeanor, seemingly indifferent to Rainer's protests. He frowned slightly when he noticed the camera.

"The man on the right needs no introduction; he's one of the most famous biologists of the New Era, the pioneer of genetic engineering, and the lead of Plan Eternity—Jasper Montclair."

It was as if a bomb had been dropped in the room. Most were too shocked to react, while a few turned pale, nearly jumping from their seats.

Plan Eternity, once the dream of countless Alliance citizens, is now the most coveted pursuit in Utopia. For security and confidentiality reasons, while Jasper Montclair's name was well known, very few knew what he actually looked like.

But now, comparing the two photos, the same face at different times, even the dullest person would sense something was off.

"Jasper... Jasper's original name was Onyx de Montclair!" The older official finally recalled where the familiarity stemmed from and exclaimed.

The shadowy figure stared at the young man's profile in the photo, slowly shaking his head. "He's not Jasper Montclair. His true name is Petros Sheen."

The room fell into a stunned silence.

Everyone present knew what the name "Petros Sheen" represented.

Jasper was already dead. It was said that he was half-mad before he died. No one knew what he had experienced in his last days, only that after his death, all his research was sealed within a storage core through a special method.

Oddly enough, that core had never been reopened; more accurately, it could not be opened—not by Jasper himself, nor by any of his relatives whose biological data had been extracted from the genetic database.

Eventually, the Alliance was forced to use some underhanded methods. From Jasper's remaining memories, they learned that the only way to unlock the core was with a "key."

What was the key? A physical object? A virtual ID card? Or a secret access code? No one knew.

The last remaining clue pointed to Jasper's only son, Petros Sheen. In Jasper's final years, he rarely left the lab, with Petros always by his side, handling all his affairs.

After Jasper's death, Petros mysteriously disappeared, and the key's whereabouts became unknown. It was an unspoken truth among the upper echelons of the Alliance: the key to unlocking the storage core was tied to Petros Sheen.

The shadowed figure silently observed the young, vibrant man in the photo.

For years, he had followed the developments of Plan Eternity, pouring vast amounts of manpower, resources, and money into a search that covered every inch of the earth.

Yet Petros seemed to have vanished, not even leaving a trace on the Lucas Network. Gradually, everyone believed he was dead. But now he had assumed a new identity, living openly as Onyx de Montclair.

If it hadn't been for the coincidence of Rainer being tracked, the agent accidentally taking the photo, and then cautiously archiving it, "Onyx de Montclair" might never have been discovered.

"The Flame Plan from back then must have hidden something significant."

After the Loyak incident, Jasper publicly declared the Flame Plan a failure. However, the following year, he launched version 2.0, naming it "Plan Eternity," attempting to continue the research started by the Flame Plan. He must have discovered something crucial during that time.

Unfortunately, Jasper passed away a few years later, and the progress of the first iteration of Plan Eternity was indefinitely suspended. Differences in interpretation led some scientists, including Rainer Ninnemann, to voluntarily leave the project team, while others shifted focus to aberrant experiments, attempting breakthroughs from different angles.

"All the answers are within that core." They had tried countless ways to crack it, but the core Jasper left behind was like a blank, formatted computer, devoid of any data.

"Only the key can activate the core."

The shadowy figure sighed deeply, his commanding voice echoing throughout the room: "I am restarting the Key Retrieval Operation. Does anyone here have any objections?"

No one raised their hand, and no one spoke. The powerful figures in the room exchanged complex, furtive glances, each unwilling to be the first to stand out. After a long pause, a hoarse voice broke the silence: "No objections. I fully support this."

Across the room, another hologram sneered, "Peridot Sheen, do you really think you have the final say? You don't represent the Sheen family of North Yard." Arashi Sheen, the true leader of North Yard, was not someone to be underestimated. She had even refused the Utopian passage token. With the Azure Force under her command, she wielded a terrifying power recognized worldwide.

Arashi Sheen had not been invited to this secret meeting.

Peridot Sheen coldly retorted, "Indeed, I can only represent myself, but I will stake my life on this. Are you?"

The challenger fell silent. Everyone knew Peridot Sheen was gravely ill, desperately waiting for a breakthrough in Plan Eternity. The mindset of a dying man is dangerous—he's capable of anything.

"What about you, Cyril Lucas?" All eyes turned to another special hologram, a large supercomputer.

This figure was equally extraordinary—a leader of the Lucas family in Grass Pit, who had abandoned his physical body and merged his consciousness with a supercomputer, achieving "eternity" differently.

A line of text slowly appeared: "The Lucas family maintains neutrality, we will not take part."

In a split second, Cyril Lucas's statement hesitated, as if glitching. The original text vanished, replaced by: "The key wouldn't disappear from the Lucas Network without reason. Someone is covering his tracks."

"The Lucas family will take part in the operation."

With these two figures leading the way, the others hesitated briefly before nodding in agreement. The shadowed figure slowly spoke again. "What intelligence do we have on the key?"

"Y-yes, we have some," another inspector nervously reported. "This... uh, key, is from a lower district, currently living at the

Northern Base in District B10, part of Team F777. The captain is an S7-class offensive Aberrant, and the team members are all A-class. They have close ties with the local governor."

"Yevgeniyev's territory, huh?"

The recent assassination incident in District B had already reached Utopia. After this event, the Northern Base became as impenetrable as a fortress, with public unity at an all-time high. Infiltration or direct assault would be nearly impossible, making the situation even more complicated.

In the tense atmosphere of the meeting room, a smooth voice snapped the silence from the far corner. The nameplate showed the speaker was from the Alliance's Regional Affairs Directorate, holding the position of Deputy Director. "I know a little about F777 and Cora Thornton."

Jae-Woo Park's radiant face appeared. As a shrewd politician, when he discovered Cora Thornton's whereabouts, he immediately confirmed and concealed it. Park wasn't acting out of kindness—revealing Cora's origins wouldn't have benefited him. He had a hunch that Cora's existence would become a trump card, one that could bring him greater rewards, and he was right.

"Hmph, if it's just a little, there's no need to mention it, right?" Szymon, Park's rival, a middle-aged man with a hawk-like nose, coldly mocked him.

"Oh no, Director Szymon, I believe you'll find this interesting. Let me think... This Cora Thornton once single-handedly took down an S7-class dual-Aberrant named... Bloody Hunter Punk, I believe." Park casually adjusted his suit, smiling as if unaware that Punk had once been Szymon's most loyal henchman.

Szymon's eyes narrowed dangerously.

Garden Apartments.

After a long day of hard work, Team F777 was finally enjoying some well-earned downtime. Even though the Aberrants Bureau had provided each of them with their own apartment, all the team members preferred to squeeze into Cora's luxurious penthouse.

Charles, wearing an apron, was busy in the kitchen grilling pork chops. Even though the ingredients were all artificially cultivated, they were fresh. Damian stood on tiptoe, peering into the pan, and grumbled, "I don't want broccoli, and no carrots either!"

"Do you know why you're not growing taller? It's because you're a picky eater," Charles mumbled around the lollipop in his mouth.

"You're the one who's not growing tall!" Damian retorted, hopping around in anger, and the kitchen quickly descended into chaos.

On the living room sofa, Onyx was rapidly scrolling through a screen with one hand while Cora held the other.

Cora rested her head on his shoulder, fast asleep, her mouth glistening with drool as she unconsciously wiped it on Onyx's hand.

Onyx paused for a moment, glanced down at her, and curled his fingers slightly, but in the end, he didn't pull his hand away.

On the balcony, Felix was meditating with his eyes closed, his arm connected to a Bee Terminal, which glowed brightly. Recently, the awareness connections of terminals in District B seemed to have deepened, so to be safe, he had increased his anti-intrusion checks from three times a week to once a day.

Suddenly, another terminal beside him beeped twice—it was an old relic from the lower districts.

Felix didn't open his eyes. A new interface appeared on his arm, and a flood of data flashed before him, with two messages standing out: "I hope your anger never fades." "Because I have set out on a journey."

From the bathroom came the sound of cheerful humming, accompanied by a shower of pink bubbles. Yuui Hayashi opened her terminal to check the news.

The group chat for the "District B10 High-End Talent Matchmaking Event" was buzzing with activity. People were discussing a newly released A-level commission. Despite the lucrative reward, no team had taken it on yet.

"Araya? Isn't that place still severely contaminated by nuclear radiation? Who would want to go there?"

"And besides, District E is pretty deserted. Who cares if there's a Zombie Lord there? It's not like it comes out and bothers anyone."

"Sure, the points are high, but you need to survive to earn them!" "Anyway, our team can't handle a Zombie Lord."

Yuui was about to switch to the system platform to check out the commission they were talking about when she was momentarily blinded by bubbles, slipped, and fell with a painful thud. "Ouch—!" A sharp pain shot through her tailbone.

Clutching her back, Yuui limped into the living room, and a moment later, Suchat followed her out, looking a bit embarrassed and unsure of himself. "Cora, wake up. You need to see this commission." Yuui poked Cora's cheek.

"How many points?" Cora grumbled as she rolled over, still not fully awake.

"Enough to push us to the top of the Alliance leaderboard."

Cora instantly perked up, rubbed her sleepy eyes, and jumped off the sofa. "That many? Let me see."

Two hours earlier, the platform had released a global commission: "A-Level Commission: A Zombie Lord has appeared in Araya (District E176). Aberrants from all districts are requested to eliminate it."

Only zombies with advanced intelligence, classified as level-4, could be considered a Zombie Lord, like the one they had taken down in Ocean Gate. Because of this, Zombie Lords were extremely rare, and now, only a few months later, another one had surfaced in a lower district?

This task seemed like a perfect fit for Team F777. Cora wasn't affected by low-level radiation, Felix could pilot the starship to save travel time, and Suchat was familiar with the environment in District E. Plus, with so many points on the line, it was enough to catapult them to the top of the rankings!

Without hesitation, Cora clicked to accept the mission, then looked up and gave Onyx a quick reminder, "Starting tomorrow, you're on your own after work."

CHAPTER 16

The Return

"Cora, let's go."

Yuui stood at the apartment door, arms crossed, urging her along. Today, she was dressed just as she had been when they first met—a fresh and sporty outfit, with her chestnut-colored, voluminous curls tied into a ponytail. Her makeup was flawless, with full, vibrant red lips, exuding the vibe of a sweet idol from the past.

Behind her, Suchat effortlessly carried two tactical bags with one hand, his black T-shirt and pants tightly fitting his lean, muscular frame. His military boots made no sound as they touched the ground, like a leopard ready to pounce.

Damian bounced out of the apartment wearing a little yellow duck backpack, sunglasses, and a sun hat, fully decked out in designer brands from head to toe.

Charles shook his head, his ponytail swaying with the motion. "What a waste of money. One roll in a zombie horde, and all that stuff's getting tossed."

"I've got money to burn," Damian retorted with a huff.

Cora zipped up her jacket after checking her gear and turned to glance back.

Onyx leaned against the bar as he quietly watched her.

Cora hesitated for a moment, suddenly realizing that since she had found Onyx in Blossomville, this was the first time they were going on separate missions.

"You..." She barely had time to feel wistful before Onyx interrupted with exaggerated fake tears.

"I'm going to miss you so much, Cora dear..."

Cora's face remained expressionless as she pulled up her hood, blocking out the world. "I'm leaving."

If everything went smoothly, they would be back in three or four days. There was no need to make it so awkward; she was already getting goosebumps.

Brilliant sunlight pierced through the clouds as a special starship began its ascent.

On the outer hull, "F777" was painted in flamboyant red and blue, with every stroke full of boldness. Beside it, various weapons intertwined in a swirling pattern of graffiti, and the massive advertisement space played the Thornton Ethereal Artifacts order hotline on a loop.

"Look, that's F777's personal starship! Are they heading out on a mission?"

"I heard F777 took on the commission to eliminate the Zombie Lord in Araya. No wonder they're the pride of District B10!"

"By the way, have you bought any Ethereal Artifacts? They're always a limited edition—I spent a week on the black market and still couldn't snag one."

"Actually, I custom-ordered a plum blossom hairpin. I'm planning to propose to my girlfriend."

"What the heck? When did you get a girlfriend?!"

Under the gaze of countless Aberrants, the starship flashed silver in the sky as F777 left the Northern Base.

At the Governor's Residence, an autonomous hover car slowly came to a stop. Onyx had just reached the villa's entrance when he heard Svetlana Yevgeniyeva's frustrated voice.

"Captain Thornton, the starship is public property! How could you... how could you just paint and change it like that and even put advertisements on it?"

"It's not about the revenue split! I don't care if it's a three-to-seven split; it's about the impact! There's no precedent for something like this."

Whatever was said on the other end caused Svetlana to rub her forehead in exasperation. "You're saving up to buy what? Rhodium... restoration... fine, fine, as long as it can be restored. No, you don't need to worry about compensation."

Onyx's lips curled into a slight smile. Knowing Cora, she was probably clutching her purse tightly, pouting and trying to defend herself. The thought of her made a tiny sprout of longing try to push through, but he quickly buried it under a layer of rationality.

Onyx greeted the exhausted Svetlana and proceeded inside. The security system had his information stored, so he entered without a hitch. In the courtyard, Chu Bai was undergoing rehabilitation alone, his arms braced with dozens of steel pins.

"How are you doing?" Onyx asked casually as he stopped beside him, his expression as calm as if they were just chatting.

"Not bad," Chu Bai nodded.

From an S5 down to an S2—most people would pity his situation, but Chu Bai had no regrets. Onyx's gaze held no sympathy or pity, which prompted Chu Bai to say a rare extra word: "I'm glad I could protect the General."

Chu Bai was an orphan of war, adopted by Dmitri Yevgeniyev. Taciturn by nature, he could only silently feel gratitude for Dmitri's kindness. After the apocalypse, when Chu Bai awakened his S-class ability, "Certain Death Resolve," his first thought was: I must stand in front of the General, be his sword and shield. As for the rank that ordinary people valued so much, he had long ago mentally prepared himself and didn't care as much.

So, in the assassination incident, Chu Bai dropped three ranks to buy time, ensuring Dmitri's safety. He genuinely felt it was "not bad."

Onyx patted his shoulder. "Old Franz is a medical expert. If you have any issues, you can go to him."

"Thank you," Chu Bai nodded earnestly.

Dmitri Yevgeniyev was in his study. Although his aging condition couldn't be reversed, he was clearly in better spirits than before, with a healthy flush in his cheeks.

The first phase of Rainer Ninnemann's clinical trial had involved short bursts of radiation to reactivate Dmitri's heart. Although it hadn't reached the level of "regeneration," the stimulated cell division had promoted self-repair of his body, and his surrounding organs were functioning normally. Dmitri's S-class physique was adapting well, and so far, there had been no adverse reactions.

Rainer predicted that if things continued to progress, and the subsequent trials were successful, Dmitri might live another ten years.

"Have Cora and her team already left?" Dmitri asked without looking up.

"Yes, they left this morning," Onyx replied.

"I asked you to stay behind. You don't hold any resentment, do you?"

"General, you overestimate me."

Onyx had originally intended to go to Araya with Team F777, but Dmitri had requested that he remain at the Northern Base.

"Don't misunderstand; I didn't separate you or force you to stay. I just wanted you to handle something for me."

"Please, General, go ahead," Onyx's gaze barely flickered over the two words, his expression impeccable.

Dmitri put down his pen and looked up at the young man before him. This person was intelligent enough, but his heart was too cold, keeping himself aloof from the world, unwilling to get involved. Without something to anchor him, he might very well drift to a dangerous extreme.

"A month ago, I asked what you all thought of the Northern Base," Dmitri began slowly. "Back then, you said it was terrible. Has your opinion changed?"

"You and District B10 are both very admirable," Onyx gave a straightforward answer.

Dmitri walked around from behind his desk, his steps steady, no longer needing a cane.

"Aberrants like Cora, with ideals and ambitions, can't be stopped from exploring the world. But after all the trials and hardships, they still need a place to come back to where they can feel at ease. Don't you agree? Do you think the Northern Base can be that 'home'?"

Onyx was silent for a moment, then answered indirectly, "Cora really likes it here."

Dmitri smiled. As his energy returned, so did the authority he once commanded over the world, day by day.

"You'll stay at the Northern Base and help this old man with a few things., as long as I'm alive, no one will touch you."

Onyx's eyes twinkled behind his glasses, sensing that Dmitri might have guessed something.

Dmitri tapped a few keys on his terminal, bringing up hundreds of pages of documents. "For the next few days, I'll have the Rowin siblings accompany you. I'd like you to review these documents for me."

Onyx glanced at the documents and immediately recognized them. "The legacy of the old civilization?"

"Oh? You've studied this?" Dmitri asked, surprised.

"Just a little," Onyx modestly replied.

Dmitri smiled, inviting him to come closer.

Though Onyx was knowledgeable, he wasn't omniscient. Dmitri's experience and wisdom were invaluable, and Onyx welcomed the guidance. The two of them talked all morning, with Onyx gaining much from the discussion.

After sipping some tea, Dmitri casually added, "By the way, I'd like you to visit the City Defense Department later and oversee the progress of the reconstruction."

Onyx protested, "General, that doesn't seem appropriate."

"Why wouldn't it be? Didn't you handle it last time, too?" Dmitri dismissed his concern.

"Last time, you were injured, and I stepped in as a temporary measure—it was a special circumstance. But today, you're perfectly well..." Onyx pointed out the flaw in Dmitri's logic, remaining calm.

Before Onyx could finish, Dmitri suddenly groaned dramatically, hammering at his lower back. "Getting old... I can't handle any excitement. I've been talking all morning, and now my legs can't even stand straight. The City Defense Department with all those noisy machines—oh, my poor heart, I don't know if it can take it."

Onyx was at a loss for words, finally understanding what it meant to be caught in a bind. He reluctantly agreed, "...Understood, General."

Instantly, Dmitri straightened up, his back no longer aching, his legs no longer sore, looking like he could easily eat two extra bowls of rice for lunch.

Onyx had no choice but to make his way to the City Defense Department.

The employees there already recognized him and quickly stood to greet him as he entered. "Good day, Officer Montclair!"

On the day of the Raven Tide, his impressive performance at the control station, with his precise operations and flawless coordination, had left everyone in awe.

Onyx's expression remained cool. "I'm not an officer. You can just call me by my name."

"Oh, but we couldn't..."

The employee was a veteran, skilled at reading the room and guessing what the higher-ups wanted. Not just anyone could enter the City Defense Department—take Scarlett Holland, for example; despite being the second-in-command for years, she still wasn't allowed in.

The veteran had worked there since graduation, and only one other person besides Sherry Harper had ever overseen him from start to finish. The young man before him... was the second. The veteran snuck a glance at Onyx, secretly speculating that Dmitri had already chosen his successor.

Eager to curry favor, the veteran added, "Officer Montclair, I handle the entry and exit records..."

Onyx called him by name without hesitation, his gaze cold. "I dislike the term 'officer' very much."

The meaning behind those words always reminded him of the despicable faces among the Alliance's upper echelons. The veteran had shot himself in the foot and stammered, "Then... I'll just call you Mr. Montclair?"

After leaving, Onyx politely declined the staff's enthusiastic offers to accompany him and boarded an autonomous public bus alone. Near Rainer Ninnemann's laboratory, he suddenly paused.

As an S-class Aberrant, Onyx was highly attuned to psychic fluctuations. He sensed two pairs of eyes scrutinizing him.

The Rowin siblings weren't supposed to arrive this early. These two must have been lying in wait, and they clearly weren't after him—they didn't seem to know he was an Aberrant, confidently observing him from their high-ranking, A-level vantage point.

Onyx pretended not to notice and continued walking forward, as if nothing was amiss.

District E176, Araya.

District E was known for its ecological landscapes, and Araya was once a dense, primeval forest with complex terrain and abundant species.

The drone footage revealed that the once-lush Araya was now a desolate wasteland, its land scorched yellow, withered life everywhere, and mutated giant plants looming ominously.

Countless faint red figures wailed and wandered through the woods, and even from inside the starship, the harshness of the environment was palpable.

All members of F777 had suited up in protective gear and isolation masks, including Cora. Although low-level radiation hardly affected her, Onyx had insisted she take precautions, especially since they hadn't fully understood the unknown gene.

As the starship slowly descended, the exhaust from the thrusters bent a swath of vegetation, and the radiation caused the control panel's instruments to fluctuate erratically.

"Look over there!" Charles exclaimed.

Beneath them, hundreds of zombies, drawn by the noise, were converging on their location.

The group gasped in surprise, their eyes wide as they took in the scene—not out of fear, of course, as F777 had faced many perils before. Rather, it was the appearance of the Araya zombies that was so unexpected.

Every one zombie gathering below was unusually tall, their entire bodies blood-red. They were naked, their facial features almost completely melted together, and beneath their thin skin, blood vessels and organ tissues were clearly visible, resembling the "blood corpses" from horror films.

Cora quickly assessed the situation: most of the zombies appeared to be level-2 or level-3, with an unusually strong desire to attack, but there were no signs of aberrant zombies yet. Drawing the twin blades from her back, she gave a succinct order: "Clear them out."

The others immediately jumped down.

Cora darted through the treetops, leaping over the zombies' heads with the agility of a monkey. With a swift slash, blood sprayed everywhere. There were no cameras here, no other Aberrants to worry about, so they could fight without holding back.

Even Felix didn't bother hiding his strength, his six changed mechanical arms slicing through the zombies like a whirlwind, the ethereal artifacts embedded in their tips, quickly dispatching the undead.

Yuui glanced at him, puzzled. "Why aren't you using your Anopower?"

Hackers among Aberrants usually had offensive capabilities, like Thyrion Lucas, whom they'd encountered before. His code could take on physical form, creating varied and flashy attacks for both offense and defense.

Felix had used his powers occasionally in the lower districts, but since arriving in District B, he had focused solely on being the "professional driver" without using his Anopower even once.

Felix casually flipped a charging zombie and huffed in a proud tone, "Is there a need?"

Yuui rolled her eyes. "No wonder you and Princess Onyx get along so well, pretending to be weak, just like him." It was as if these two were under some mysterious seal—one couldn't show their face, the other couldn't use their powers.

Cora, however, recalled something Onyx had mentioned: Felix's Anopower was fundamental about manipulating data, and any data could leave a trace. Considering how the District B terminals were linked to the subconscious of the residents, a top-tier hacker like Felix would be very cautious about that.

Charles expertly sliced open a zombie's skull, then suddenly paused. "Captain, these zombies... don't have any crystals!"

F777 members were shocked. Their pace of killing slowed as they checked a few more bodies. Indeed, there wasn't a single crystal to be found.

At that moment, a distant, eerie howl echoed through the forest.

The zombies seemed to respond to a call, abandoning their attack and retreating quickly. Cora's heart tightened—only a level-4 Zombie Lord could command a horde like this. Judging by the situation, it had just issued a retreat order.

Then, a few figures darted out from among the retreating zombies, dragging away the corpses while F777 wasn't looking. If they were surprised before, now they were downright unsettled. Consciousness among the undead? That wasn't a trait of ordinary zombies.

"Is this... also the Zombie Lord's command?" Yuui murmured.

Cora frowned. Zombies without crystals, a Zombie Lord that refused to show itself—what they thought would be a straightforward extermination mission was turning out to be increasingly mysterious.

"Ah—!!" A heart-wrenching scream pierced the air from deeper in the forest.

F777 exchanged glances, surprised. The scream was unmistakably human. Were there other teams out here? Such District B teams who had the privilege of choosing better opportunities usually avoided a difficult, high-risk commission.

But Aberrants from lower districts, driven by harsher conditions and a greater need for points, might risk their lives to come here.

District C and D. mostly covered the areas around Araya. If Aberrants from those areas didn't fully understand the danger posed by a Zombie Lord, they might underestimate the threat, thinking it was just a slightly stronger level-3 zombie.

"I'll check it out." Suchat signaled before blending into the shadows of the forest.

Moments later, he returned safely, but his expression had grown serious. "There are Aberrants up ahead, about twenty of them, mostly C-rank. They ran into that retreating zombie horde and are now surrounded."

Cora twirled one of her blades thoughtfully for a second. "Let's go look." If there was no conflict, they didn't mind lending a hand.

F777 swiftly approached the scene, hiding in the trees to observe the battle. They saw a chaotic mix of Anopowers being unleashed—gales of wind howling, dust clouds rising, and menacing thorns bursting from the ground. A few Aberrants were thrown back, their isolation masks showing cracks.

Cora focused on the center of the chaos and recognized a familiar face.

CHAPTER 17

The Delay

This was a low-lying canyon, with waterfalls thundering down on either side, spraying mist into the air.

A group of low-level Aberrants was trapped between the zombies, desperately trying to fend them off. Gunfire rang out, but instead of intimidating the retreating monsters, it only enraged them. The zombies turned back with ferocity, and within moments, three of the Aberrants were overwhelmed.

Out of the twenty people, only four seemed to hold their ground. A man in a green robe was controlling a dozen thorny vines to keep the zombies at bay, while his three agile teammates worked in perfect sync, hacking away at the undead. Though they weren't exactly dominating the battle, they were protecting themselves.

Cora, hiding in the forest, recognized the group—it was their old friends from the Throne Tournament, the team known as "The Boss and His Three Goons." The man in green was their captain, Zephyrion Stormrider, and his three teammates were Luke Shaw, Victor von der Falkner, and Kluge Ehrlich.

F777 had crossed paths with them several times before, and as Onyx had once said, "The team is rather opportunistic, but Zephyrion is a decent person."

Cora had a favorable impression of "The Boss and F777's presence had drawn His Three Goons,. After a moment's consideration, she signaled to her teammates with a gesture to,"assist."

"You won't trap me with your love~ Or let me sink into a swamp of despair~" Yuui's voice echoed through the forest, her ethereal song causing the ground in the canyon to collapse.

The zombies tumbled helplessly into the newly formed sinkhole.

With no verbal communication, Damian followed up with a blizzard. Under the dual control of these two A-level powers, the zombies' movements slowed to a crawl, their blood-red bodies encased in a layer of glistening frost, resembling twisted candied fruits on a stick.

Cora and Suchat leaped into the fray, their blades slicing through the air. With a mighty swing, Cora felled the towering mutant vegetation, carving a deep trench between the swamp and the solid ground. "Run behind me!" she shouted at the trapped Aberrants.

Snapping out of their shock, the beleaguered Aberrants scrambled to escape from the immobilized zombie horde. Suchat swiftly cut through the tangled trees, piling up a massive barricade in the trench.

As the swamp and frost effects wore off, the zombies, seeing that their prey had fled, lost interest in pursuit and quickly disappeared into the depths of the forest.

Cora perched atop a massive tree crown, watching the retreating zombies with a thoughtful expression.

They had long, slender limbs, moved with agility, and lacked the stiffness typical of ordinary zombies—in fact, they seemed more... human.

She puffed out her cheeks in frustration; the more she thought about it, the more confusing it all seemed. If only Onyx were here—he was so smart, he'd have figured out the answer in no time.

Cora lightly jumped down and turned to find Zephyrion gazing at her. "It's you? Thank you for the help," he said.

"No need for thanks," Cora replied as she crossed her hands, smoothly sheathing her blades with a flourish that was both stylish and effortless.

Time had passed, and much had changed, yet some things remained the same.

Zephyrion's emotions were complicated. A year ago, they had been evenly matched competitors. After F777 won the Throne Tournament and moved on to District B, everything changed.

Now, when they met again, it felt like an insurmountable chasm had opened between them. While he and his teammates were trapped and struggling, Cora had effortlessly driven back to the zombies.

Even though he knew it was just wishful thinking, Zephyrion couldn't help but sigh: What if they had been the ones to win back then?

The rescued Aberrants gathered around, still shaken, and expressed their gratitude. "Thank you, heroes! Hey, wait... you all look familiar...?"

"Uncle, we're F777. Ever heard of us?" Damian answered with a cheeky grin.

"F777? Holy crap, the ones from F199? The ones who assassinated the Governor?!"

"I know you! You're the Throne Tournament champions from Felalakas!"

"I've got a friend in District B who says F777 is super famous—rumor has it they even took down a level-6 ferocious beast!"

"Bro, you seriously don't know your zombie guide. The highest-ranked ferocious beasts only go up to level 5!" The person who'd been called out blushed in embarrassment. "My bad, my bad..."

With Onyx absent, the more approachable Charles took on the diplomatic role, pulling out a few new isolation masks to hand out to the injured. "What brought you to Araya?"

"We were trying to do that A-level commission, hoping we might get lucky and take down the Zombie Lord!"

"We're not greedy; we just wanted to get a little something out of it," they explained all at once.

Charles sighed and explained the risks of the mission to them. The survivors, already shaken by the earlier ambush, were now seriously reconsidering their choices.

After hearing about the Zombie Lord and watching some past footage as evidence, they turned pale and unanimously decided that the A-level commission wasn't for them—staying alive was more important.

Fortunately, they were still on the outskirts of the forest, so there was time to retreat. Soon enough, the group dispersed, leaving only Zephyrion and his three teammates behind.

"You're not leaving?" Cora asked, a bit surprised.

Zephyrion shook his head. "No, we still need a few more points."

"How many more?" Cora inquired.

"Just over 40,000," Zephyrion replied.

Felix Lucas chimed in with a low-key calculation, "40,000 points equals 1,200 level-2 zombies or 200 level-3 zombies."

For a typical monster-hunting mission, accumulating 40,000 points would be a long, drawn-out process, so "The Boss and His Three Goons" had jumped at the chance to take on the global commission despite the dangers.

Ever since they first met in Felalakas, this team had been relentlessly chasing the leaderboard. A year later, their determination was still unwavering. Even though it was harder to earn points in the lower districts, Zephyrion and his team were now just one step away from the 500,000-point threshold to enter District B.

Cora thought for a moment, then made an unexpected offer: "Once you've got the points, why don't you come to the Northern Base?"

Victor von der Falkner, with his round face and earnest eyes, couldn't help but say, "Every Aberrant wants to go to the Northern Base, but District B10 is the most sought-after place. We're not that exceptional, and Zephyrion says our chances of getting in are slim."

The rugged-looking Luke Shaw patted Victor on the shoulder in consolation. "Zephyrion's also been looking at Jade Grove or White Town, which aren't unacceptable options."

Zephyrion nodded. "Those two districts have relaxed their B-level entry requirements until the fall, so we need to gather enough points before then."

All members of "The Boss and His Three Goons" were ranked at the B-level, with Zephyrion being the highest at B8, and the others between B5 and B7.

In comparison, their skills might not stand out at the Northern Base, especially considering the overcrowded situation in Front City. Even if they qualified, they might face a long wait to get in.

Cora exchanged a look with her teammates, and they could all guess what their captain had in mind. They nodded in silent agreement.

There was another way to gain entry to the Northern Base—

through an internal referral, which could significantly boost the chances of a successful application.

It was like how Silver Owl had once invited F777, but the sponsor would have to vouch for the candidate for five years. Unless the relationship was strong or the person's character was beyond reproach, securing a referral letter was almost impossible.

"If you really want to come, I'll write you a referral letter," Cora assured them, thumping her chest in a gesture of confidence.

Despite the fierce competition in the Throne Tournament, "The Boss and His Three Goons" had never played dirty against F777. Even Onyx had noted that Zephyrion was "a decent person."

By association, his teammates—Luke, who was steady; Victor, who was straightforward; and Kluge Ehrlich, the youngest and most cheerful—also seemed trustworthy.

Writing them a recommendation letter wouldn't be a big deal, although... she knew she wasn't good at that sort of thing. She'd have to ask Onyx to help her with it later.

"Really?" Victor's eyes shone with excitement. "It looks like you all are doing really well!"

"Just okay," Cora replied modestly, but then added with a touch of pride, "Well, we are ranked first on the Northern Base leaderboard."

This connection instantly brought the two teams closer, and they continued their journey together.

"You all are pretty bold to take on an A-level commission with just four people," Yuui commented casually as they walked.

"Of course not. We're not that reckless; we didn't come here to die for nothing. Zephyrion has a backup plan," Kluge Ehrlich, who was less guarded, had already seen them as close friends and let the secret slip. He realized his mistake a moment later. "Oops, was I supposed to say that?"

Zephyrion sighed; whether it was shared, the secret was out. If the others had bad intentions, there was nothing they could do to stop them. But... Zephyrion glanced at Cora and her team. Besides curiosity, there was no hint of greed on their faces.

He didn't bother to hide it anymore and pulled out a device that looked like an old-fashioned kerosene lantern.

"This is called a random anchor device. I traded for it with an A6-

level anchor-type Aberrant. It's a spatial device that, when activated, can randomly teleport up to four people to a location within a ten-kilometer radius."

A random teleport within ten kilometers—this was the perfect escape tool. No wonder "The Boss and His Three Goons" dared to venture into Araya. "That's a neat gadget. Does it have any limitations?" Cora asked with interest.

"None, except that it requires 'fuel' each time it's used." Zephyrion explained, pointing to a small groove on top of the lantern.

"One level-4 crystal per time."

Whoa! One use costs a level-4 crystal? That was seriously extravagant. Cora's expression briefly showed a hint of pain—she wouldn't use such a device even if it were given to her for free.

Luke Shaw's expression turned serious. "We only have two level-4 crystals and plan to use the device just once." Their original plan had been to escape with the random anchor device if they encountered danger, keeping the second crystal as a backup.

Felix, however, was deeply intrigued by the random anchor device and asked Zephyrion if he could borrow it to study for a while.

The jungle of Araya was eerily silent—no birds, no animals, not even the sound of insects, with only the overgrown mutated plants blocking out the sky.

Cora and her team searched the entire day, but there was no sign of the Zombie Lord, and even the blood-red zombies from before seemed to have vanished without a trace. Kluge Ehrlich couldn't help but grumble, "Where the heck did all the zombies go?"

Zephyrion had a thought, "It's a lot like what happened at Mirror Lake."

He was referring to the first official match of the Throne Tournament: the search for the "Flag." The situation back then was like now, with zombies disappearing without a trace. "But I'm sure this time it's not the City Lord's doing," Kluge joked.

"Illya?" Cora asked offhandedly, remembering that it had been a while since they'd heard anything about the super AI.

"Yeah, he seems to have gone on a trip. Now Felalakas is governed by other AIs in rotation."

Gone on a trip? Cora suddenly recalled the time Illya had insisted on accompanying them to Sycamore. After gaining a physical form, this super AI had become more free-spirited in its actions.

Felix smoothly wheeled past the others, his amber eyes blinking lightly, his expression unchanged.

By now, it was close to seven o'clock, and the narrow strip of sky above was growing darker. Cora and the team had found nothing, and their points hadn't increased at all. Finally, they found a clearing to set up camp, deciding to make do for the night.

"Sis, there are tents over there!" Damian Blackwood came running down the hill to report.

Cora followed him and, sure enough, found many tents scattered across a dried-up riverbed, covered in dirt and moss. A rough count revealed around a hundred tents, showing a medium-sized group. The team exchanged puzzled looks. Had others ventured into this radiation-soaked region before them?

Suchat jumped down to investigate and returned after a moment, his tone somber. "No signs of fire, and the tents weren't set up recently —they've been here for a while."

He used his combat knife to pry up a wooden stake, which was covered in jagged claw marks. "Judging by the way these were set up, it doesn't seem like... normal humans did this."

If it were experienced humans setting up camp, they would choose flat, open ground in an upwind location, not a dried-up riverbed where falling rocks from nearby cliffs posed a constant threat.

The tents faced all directions, with no logical layout, as if they were only placed to satisfy some instinctive need for communal living.

"Not normal humans? Haha, it couldn't be zombies, could it?" Kluge scratched his head and made a lame joke.

Unfortunately, no one laughed.

"You're kidding, right?" Kluge's eyes widened in disbelief. Were these tents really set up by zombies?

That night, a bonfire blazed in the center of the camp, illuminating the camouflage tents. The shadowy outlines of the black forest loomed in the distance, and the wind howled ominously. Everyone was on edge, taking turns on watch, but the night passed uneventfully.

Well, almost uneventfully. The sound of tinkering and clinking came from Felix's tent for most of the night, only quieting down in the early hours of the morning. When the pale-faced young man finally emerged, he immediately slipped into Cora's tent next door and stayed there for several hours until dawn broke, when the two of them reappeared together.

Felix had entered the tent while Victor von der Falkner and Zephyrion were on watch. Victor, being an honest man, witnessed the entire scene without gossiping about it, though he suddenly realized: so that's the relationship they have. But then he frowned in confusion and asked, "Zephyrion, didn't they have two people in wheelchairs?"

Zephyrion grunted, though there was some uncertainty in his voice. "They never mentioned it, so… maybe one of them didn't make it." In the post-apocalyptic world, life and death were commonplace, so Victor just sighed and didn't dwell on it.

Early the next morning, Cora gathered everyone and issued new instructions. "We'll keep moving deeper. If you spot any zombies, don't engage. Notify Felix first."

Their luck seemed to improve today. By noon, both Suchat and Luke Shaw had spotted wandering zombies.

Felix spread his palm, and two mechanical mosquitoes slowly flew up. Under his control, they approached the targets.

A faint mechanical hum echoed as the realistic mosquitoes extended their thin proboscises and "stung" the zombies' translucent skin.

The unfortunate creatures paused for a second, then raised their heads in confusion, looked around, found nothing unusual, and continued their aimless wandering.

After a brief circuit of the area, they vanished again before nightfall.

"What's going on?" Zephyrion asked.

"Trackers with chips inside," Cora explained with a sly smile. This was something she and Felix had stayed up all night to invent—Felix did the handiwork, while she came up with the "mosquito design" idea.

Before long, the positions of the two zombies appeared on Felix's screen. "We suspect these zombies exhibit social behavior," Cora explained seriously.

Whether it was dragging away the bodies of their dead or setting up tents, all signs showed that the zombies in Araya had a clear sense of group consciousness.

"And they seem to be actively avoiding humans." Cora's expression grew thoughtful. She hadn't deliberately connected the dots before, but now that the pieces were coming together... why did it all feel so familiar?

It wasn't until nightfall that the two marked zombies finally stopped moving. To everyone's surprise, they had both gone to the same location.

The two teams navigated through the dark forest and eventually arrived at a vast, open valley. The surrounding darkness was impenetrable, so they all donned their night vision goggles.

What met their eyes was a sea of dark green, countless faces with blurred features, all looking indistinguishable from one another. An enormous horde of thin-limbed zombies had gathered, forming a vast, shifting mass that looked like a ghostly tide from afar, impossible to count.

And at the center of this sea of zombies was one that stood out. It was significantly larger than the others, with a face that, though still misshapen, had recognizable features. Judging by its body shape, it had likely been a woman before it turned.

The returning zombies approached it, each one brushing against it affectionately before scurrying away, like children returning home, eager to be close to their mother. Even more shocking were small zombies in the valley, some of them even shorter than Damian. They were being carefully protected by the adult zombies, and behind them were tents similar to those the team had seen on the riverbed.

Cora silently stared at the leading female zombie, her thoughts gradually becoming clearer. This was likely the Zombie Lord of Araya. "Are these... really zombies?" Victor's voice trembled.

The common perception of zombies was that they were vicious, terrifying creatures with an insatiable hunger for flesh, mindless monsters. But the scene before them, of zombies coexisting peacefully, was something they had never witnessed before—it completely shattered their understanding. News of this would undoubtedly shock the world.

Cora sighed quietly, her gut feeling slowly solidifying into a truth. "They're not zombies. They're... Fallen."

These weren't "zombies without crystals." These were humans who, because of radiation, had transformed into something between human and zombie—a third species, unaccepted by either side. They were the Fallen.

Just like the braid-haired and dirt-chinned ones F777 had encountered before, though that had only been a few isolated cases. But here—Araya seemed to be the stronghold of the Fallen.

Victor, overwhelmed by the shocking revelation, momentarily lost his focus and accidentally stepped on a dry branch, which snapped and rolled down into the valley. The sound was barely audible, especially from a distance of a hundred meters, and should have gone unnoticed.

Yet, the Zombie Lord in the valley suddenly looked up, its blood-red eyes staring directly at them from the heights above. It let out a sharp, piercing howl.

"Damn it!" Cora cursed inwardly.

Thousands of Fallen, agile and relentless, surged toward them like an unstoppable army of the undead, surrounding Cora and her team in no time, turning them into a small island in a sea of zombies.

Northern Base.

Onyx de Montclair didn't see Rainer Ninnemann until the following day. Rainer had locked himself in the radiation lab for an entire day and night. His face was deeply fatigued, but his eyes were bright with excitement. As soon as he saw Onyx, he eagerly began removing his isolation suit. "I was just about to find you. The second phase of the clinical plan…"

Onyx raised a hand to stop him. "Dr. Ninnemann, how did you leave the Eternity Project?"

Rainer paused, looking puzzled. "I just… left normally. All my permissions were revoked; otherwise, my research wouldn't be this difficult. But you know, I didn't sign a contract for life. Old Dr. Montclair brought me in so early, there wasn't any such thing. When I left, they had no reason to stop me."

Onyx removed his gold-rimmed glasses and rubbed his brow. "So you resigned voluntarily? Scarlett Holland did not recruit you?"

"Of course not. I signed a confidentiality agreement, the kind drafted by a psychic Aberrant. She doesn't know the details of my research."

Rainer explained honestly, "After I regained my freedom, I was strapped for cash and spent nearly six months looking for a new position. I originally intended to go to White Town, but just before applying for an independent lab, I saw the recruitment notice from the Northern Base. The offer was so generous that I thought, why not? It's the same experiment no matter where it's done. So, I contacted Scarlett Holland's secretary at the time—what was their name again…"

Onyx tapped his fingers rhythmically on the table, his gaze lowering as he fell into thought.

"Is there a problem?" Rainer asked, puzzled.

Onyx sighed softly. "Dr. Ninnemann, at your age, how can you still be so naïve?"

Scarlett Holland, despite her questionable character, was always cautious.

In the latter stages of the Eternity Project, the entire team had split into several factions, and the research progress stalled. Various districts poached many veteran scientists.

Onyx had assumed that Rainer had been poached similarly. If Scarlett Holland had invited him under the Northern Base's banner, she would have surely eliminated any potential risks related to Rainer's past.

But it turned out that Rainer had approached them as a free agent, even spending six idle months raising no alarms. This meant that Scarlett likely didn't realize Rainer's significance and was unaware that he had been a core member of the Eternity Project.

She probably just thought he was a well-known biologist. That's why she arranged for Aberrants to guard his lab for his safety, but didn't assign anyone to monitor him, leading to the oversight that allowed Onyx to meet with him undetected several times.

"You're being watched."

Onyx straightened up, his voice cold.

"We shouldn't meet again," Onyx continued, his expression frosty. "Don't drag me down."

A nearby assistant, who was passing by with a transparent screen and a sandwich, dropped everything in shock at Onyx's bitter remark.

"Stay in the lab, and contact me online if you need anything,"

Onyx added.

Rainer muttered, "I don't go out much, anyway. You're the one who insisted on meeting…"

Onyx's eyes flashed as he quickly recalled their previous meetings. The first was in this very lab, during a chaotic moment when they only exchanged a few words. The rest of their communication had been through terminals. The second meeting was in Front City, where Rainer had come and gone alone. The third…

"Beep—beep—"

The temporary terminal, which had only its communication functions activated, beeped, interrupting Onyx's train of thought.

He glanced down at the caller ID, and a gentle smile spread across his face. "Cora, dear, is the mission complete? Are you returning tomorrow?"

"Uh, well…" Cora's voice sounded sheepish. "It's just… we might be… a little late."

Onyx frowned slightly. "How late? Weren't you supposed to be back in three days?"

"How long will it take?" Cora seemed to ask someone nearby. Two or three unfamiliar male voices chimed in, discussing something. "C26 District, Finach… that's pretty far. If all goes well, it'll take ten days for the round trip."

"…Ten days," Cora responded, her voice tinged with anxiety. "I'll hurry back as soon as I can!"

Onyx's sharp eyebrows slowly lifted, and his tone carried an edge of casual interrogation. "Who's talking?"

Cora was startled. "No one! There's no one here!"

CHAPTER 18

The Zombie Languages

The sound of a snapped twig was almost imperceptible, but the Zombie Lord's senses were extraordinarily sharp, immediately locking onto Victor von der Falkner's hiding spot.

A piercing shriek tore through the night, and through their night vision goggles, they saw a vast horde of undead rushing toward them. The mountains and valleys were teeming with the eerie green figures of the living dead, their sheer numbers terrifying enough to swallow Cora and her team in seconds.

Felix was the first to react, his six mechanical arms spinning out, smashing the first wave of zombies that charged at them.

"Move!" Cora commanded, leading the way as Suchat covered the rear. The rest of the team retreated at full speed, but their steps faltered as they realized the zombies had already encircled them.

No way out!

Zephyrion raised both hands, and thick vines burst from the ground. Instead of striking out at the surrounding zombies, the vines wrapped around the group, forming a protective cocoon that temporarily held off the external assault.

Thin, wiry zombies slammed into the cocoon, angrily tearing at it. In no time, dents appeared on its surface. "This will not hold! There are too many of them! Zephyrion can't keep this up alone!" Luke Shaw shouted.

As soon as the words left his mouth, a bloodied hand punched through the cocoon, clawing wildly, quickly tearing a hole the size of a bowl. Through the gap, Cora locked eyes with the Zombie Lord, perched high above them.

"Hey! How about we sit down and talk this out?" Cora's eyes glinted with determination. Based on experience, the Fallen were conscious beings capable of communicating with humans. "We mean no harm!" Yuui added, shouting, "Please, give us a chance!"

The Zombie Lord glared at Cora, its emaciated form nearly three meters tall, resembling a solitary, flickering lamppost. Its eyes were filled with suspicion and hostility, and it ignored their pleas for negotiation. With a few short, sharp howls, it drove the zombie horde into an even greater frenzy, fiercely attacking the vines.

"It's no use. There's no way to communicate," Cora sighed. It seemed the Zombie Lord harbored a deep-seated mistrust of humans.

With a crack, Zephyrion's energy finally gave out, and the cocoon shattered, exposing the group to the night once more. Cora reluctantly drew her blades. "Prepare for battle."

Damian, dodging and weaving through the horde, rolled several times in the mud. His branded sunglasses and sun hat were long lost, and when he saw Charles being grabbed by a zombie and dragged down, he didn't taunt him as usual. Instead, he bravely rushed over, creating an ice wall to block a deadly blow.

The zombie, whose face was twisted into a barely recognizable mess, let out a hoarse growl from deep within its chest.

"Ahhh—?"

Damian froze for a moment, and on impulse, he mimicked the zombie's guttural sounds, grumbling a few strange syllables from his throat. Enhanced by his psychic power, his clear voice echoed through the dark valley.

Cora immediately sensed something was off and twisted. "Damian, what are you—"

She was about to remind him that his fear of zombies had long been cured, so why was he making weird noises now? And why was he using his psychic power—wasn't that just going to provoke the zombies even more? But the scene before her left her completely speechless.

It was as if someone had cast a freezing spell. All the zombies stopped attacking simultaneously, their movements filled with a hint of confusion. Damian's small, dirt-smeared face stayed focused as he persisted, shouting at the zombies, "Ahhh!"

The horde snapped out of their trance and closed in again, but a few of the smaller zombies in the back bared their teeth in what seemed like a smile—less menacing, almost endearing. Damian scratched his head, muttering uncertainly, "Did I mess it up?"

He tried another call: "Ah! Ahhh!" Cora was utterly baffled.

Yuui and the others exchanged puzzled glances, then suddenly realized—could this be... the language of the Fallen? After all, Damian had somehow picked up a bizarre zombie language communication skill!

The vast valley fell into an eerie silence.

The Zombie Lord planted its hands on the ground and gracefully leaped onto a rock, the horde respectfully parting to make way. It landed soundlessly and slowly approached Damian, its long, thin shadow engulfing the small boy completely.

Zephyrion and his team's faces went pale, and they were about to act when Cora held them back. She gripped her twin blades tightly, her eyes fixed on the Zombie Lord, trying to see what it would do next.

The Zombie Lord circled Damian, then suddenly leaned in, its uneven features close to his face, sniffing him lightly before shaking its head and pacing around him again, as if uncertain.

Damian stood at attention, hands stiffly at his sides, not daring to move an inch while everyone else held their breath. After a few tense seconds, Damian mustered the courage to repeat, "Ahhh?"

The Zombie Lord abruptly stopped, and then, to everyone's shock, it spoke in a cracked voice. "Who... are... you?"

Holy crap! The zombie spoke! The expressions on everyone's faces were a rainbow of emotions, each revealing their inner thoughts.

Damian racked his brain, stammering out a few more sounds. This was something the braid-haired woman had taught him in Ocean Gate, meaning something like "friend."

"You've met... our kind." Each word from the Zombie Lord came with great effort, its nearly invisible lips barely moving, the sound seeming to resonate more from its chest.

Damian first shook his head, then hesitated and nodded. Did the braid-haired woman count as their kind?

But she looked much more human than the Zombie Lord did, far more attractive. Still, since they could understand what she had taught him, they must be... related, right?

Explaining his encounter with the braid-haired woman was too complicated for Damian, who was only a beginner in "Zombie Language 101," so he switched to human language, recounting the story with excited gestures, lavishing praise on the braid-haired woman and her brother, Dirt Beard, for their "handsome" appearances.

F777 remained calm, as if they had seen stranger things.

However, "The Boss and His Three Goons" were left dumbfounded. Zephyrion's eye twitched. He had been sure he was on the brink of death, never expecting this sudden turn of events—a kid chatting with zombies? Who would believe that?

When Damian finished, he looked up at the Zombie Lord expectantly.

"Leave... and... don't... return."

The Zombie Lord was silent for a moment before issuing a garbled warning. It muttered a few more sounds, and the zombie horde shifted, creating a narrow path. Even Cora was surprised—the Zombie Lord would not attack? It was letting them go?

Under the watchful eyes of countless zombies, the group cautiously made their way out of the valley.

After they had put some distance between themselves and the horde, and confirmed that they weren't being followed, Charles rubbed Damian's fluffy head in relief. "Kid, you really came through. Knowing a foreign language sure comes in handy."

"This time, it's all thanks to you, Damian," Cora added, not holding back her praise.

"Heh heh," Damian puffed out his chest proudly.

The group found another clearing, gathered around the campfire, and set up camp to rest. Cora looked around at everyone and spoke up, "Let's vote on whether to continue the mission."

Damian was the first to speak. "I'm against it! Ada's not a bad person!"

Yuui blinked in confusion. "Ada? Who's that?"

"Ada is the Zombie Lord," Damian said matter-of-factly.

"...You really are quick to warm up to people, even giving them nicknames," Yuui sighed. "I'm against it too. I've been inclined to accept the diversity of intelligent species unconditionally. I can't see the Fallen as zombies."

Suchat glanced at her, then simply said, "I agree with her."

Felix shrugged indifferently. "I abstain."

Charles, having just finished treating his wounds and rolling down his pant leg, added, "I'll side with Damian."

F777 was unanimous in their decision. It was just an A-level commission, after all. Even if they didn't complete it, there were other ways to climb the leaderboard.

When it was "The Boss and His Three Goons'" turn to vote, however, opinions diverged.

Luke Shaw spoke in a low tone, "I support continuing the mission. Sorry, but the points are too important for us." Victor and Kluge both said, "We'll go with whatever Zephyrion decides."

Zephyrion looked over at Cora. "Even if I vote in favor, it won't change the outcome, will it?"

The current vote was four to four. Felix clicked his tongue, his dislike for losing getting the better of him. "Change my vote—I'm against it."

Four to five, now they had the majority.

But Zephyrion knew the vote count didn't really matter. The actual decision rested with Cora because they could not take down the Zombie Lord on their own. "That's right." Cora nodded firmly. "I've decided—we're abandoning the commission. At dawn, we'll leave."

This A-level commission differed completely from what she had initially expected. They could kill the Zombie Lord, but the creature they had encountered was the leader of the Fallen in Araya. It probably didn't even have a crystal in its brain, meaning it wasn't truly a zombie. Besides, it had spared their lives.

"Understood." Zephyrion sighed. "There wasn't much hope, anyway. So... we'll let it go."

"Zephyrion..." Luke looked at him with concern.

Zephyrion placed a firm hand on Luke's shoulder, his gaze resolute. "Trust me, we'll find another way. We'll get the points we need."

The atmosphere grew heavy with silence until Cora suddenly asked, "I have a question—why did the mission description label it as a Zombie Lord?"

She pulled up the commission description, and it clearly read: "Suspected Zombie Lord sighted in Araya."

"Could the system have made a mistake?"

"No," Felix answered confidently.

A group of AI managed the commission system in District B. Humans could make errors, and a single computer might malfunction, but when dozens or hundreds of super AIs were working together, there was no way such a basic mistake could happen.

"Uh, could there be another Zombie Lord in Araya?" Victor speculated wildly.

"Unlikely," Zephyrion shook his head slowly. "Judging by the way the valley was organized, these zombies live in a tribal structure and are not welcoming to outsiders. If there were another Zombie Lord, they would be locked in a deadly battle until one of them emerged victorious."

Zephyrion paused before continuing, "Actually, I've been meaning to ask... What are the Fallen?"

Cora hesitated, suddenly remembering that the existence of the Fallen had never been publicly acknowledged by the Alliance. All their information came from Onyx, who was practically a walking cheat code, so it made sense that the platform would label the creature as a "suspected Zombie Lord."

Yuui quickly explained the difference between the Fallen and zombies to Zephyrion and his team.

Cora rested her chin on her hand, quietly listening, still feeling that something wasn't quite right. Why not just call it a "special zombie" or "mutated zombie"? Why insist on labeling it a "Zombie Lord"? This raised the difficulty level unnecessarily, potentially excluding many qualified teams.

District B's Aberrants had all found the mission too risky for the reward, leaving only F777—strong and experienced enough to take on this hot potato.

Just as she was about to voice her thoughts, she noticed Felix was intently focused on his screen. "What are you looking at?" Cora scooted closer to Felix.

"I set up a few mobile cameras while Damian was negotiating," he replied.

On the screen, a few zombies were huddled together, trembling violently. Their skin was as thin as paper, with their internal organs grotesquely visible. Even without sound, the agony they were in was palpable. After just a few minutes, their bodies seemed to deflate, collapsing into puddles of pus before their eyes.

The Fallen leader, whom Damian had nicknamed "Ada," was sitting with the other zombies, silently watching their dying comrades.

"How could this happen..." Yuui gasped.

"It's probably because the radiation in Araya is too high," Charles speculated, pointing to his isolation mask. "Even if the Fallen can withstand more radiation than humans, there's a limit. Once that limit is exceeded, prolonged exposure inevitably causes catastrophic damage to their bodies."

"Why don't they leave?" Victor asked, puzzled.

Kluge murmured, "It's not that simple. Leaving would only make things worse, right? At least in Araya, no one bothers them. But outside, people treat zombies... with nothing but lethal force."

That's right—for the Fallen, the safest place to live was in remote, desolate areas. Even though Araya's radiation levels were high, it was still better than the outside world, where there was no place for them. They would rather stay here and quietly await death.

Cora stared through the screen at the Fallen leader. Its long, thin arms cradled several small comrades, its sorrowful profile fleeting across the screen.

At the crack of dawn, Kluge Ehrlich's shout shattered the morning silence. "Zephyrion, Captain Cora, come quick! The commission's been updated!"

Cora sat up abruptly in her tent and quickly opened her terminal to check. Sure enough, the details of the A-level commission had changed. [A-level Commission: Please eliminate or move the special zombies in Araya (District E176). Remaining quantity: 13,299.]

Different options appeared below based on the choice made. Cora clicked on the relocation option: [Alternate location: Finach (District C26).]

She thought it over but couldn't grasp the significance, so she decisively unzipped her tent and stepped out. "Did you all get the update?"

The members of F777 nodded. They had encountered commission updates before, like the side mission in Elder Nation or when the Northern Base defense mission was upgraded from B to A-level, so they weren't particularly surprised.

Felix, however, seemed to be deep in thought. "Quite the coincidence, huh? The update happens just as the captain leaves?"

"It's not a coincidence—it was me," Zephyrion admitted frankly. "Last night, I compiled the information we had and uploaded it to the system to see if anything could be done."

The platform allows for private commissions to be issued, so it naturally also collects and analyzes information provided by those who accept missions. Felix gave Zephyrion a sidelong glance, not commenting on his actions, but continuing to frown as he tapped on the platform page.

"Now that the commission has changed, are you still going to do it?" Zephyrion took a deep breath, looking at Cora expectantly. The choice had shifted from elimination to relocation, and the two options required entirely different approaches.

At first glance, the latter seemed simpler, but Finach was near the eastern coast. Leading over ten thousand Fallen, who resembled zombies, across half the Alliance's territory? That seemed incredibly far-fetched.

Cora hesitated, unsure of what to do.

"That's the situation," Cora explained, slightly out of breath, over her terminal. Onyx lowered his gaze, remaining silent.

"You're quiet... does that mean you're against it?" Cora asked cautiously. "No," Onyx replied after a moment, "I'm thinking... about Finach."

Why was Finach chosen as the alternate location? Beyond its original name, another knew it in the Alliance, a more ominous title.

Losome (District B25) and Finach (District C26) together made up the Loark region, which had once flourished. However, fifteen years ago, a severe nuclear explosion devastated the area, leaving it uninhabitable because of lingering radiation, and it was abandoned, becoming a ghost district no one dared approach.

Transferring the Fallen from Araya to Finach was a logical decision. After fifteen years, the radiation in Finach had diluted enough that, while still unfit for human life, it was just within the tolerance range for the Fallen—practically a paradise compared to Araya.

But for Onyx, Finach held special significance—it was the site of the Seed Project's laboratory, the place where Myris fled with LAK0017, and where secrets that should have been buried forever still lingered.

Onyx pulled himself from his thoughts and sighed. "Cora dear, how do you plan to move over ten thousand zombies? Fly the starship with 'F777' emblazoned on the side and use a loudspeaker to announce, 'Zombies coming through, clear the way'? Are you trying to make a spectacle of this across the entire Alliance?"

Cora completely missed the sarcasm in his tone and earnestly agreed, "Great idea!"

If F777 led the way, wouldn't that avoid any conflicts? That's why Onyx was the best—he always had the perfect solution to her problems!

Onyx was momentarily speechless.

Defeated by Cora's unique way of thinking, he tugged at his collar to let some air in. "Have you even asked them? Do they want to go with you?"

What Cora was proposing was beyond extraordinary—if it were anyone less capable, like certain other leaders, they wouldn't be able to handle it. "Not yet. I'll negotiate with them soon."

"...Forget it. Whether the negotiation is successful, stay where you are and wait for me."

"You're coming?!" Cora's eyes sparkled.

"Yeah," Onyx smiled, "if I don't, you'll probably turn the entire world upside down."

"No way! I've consulted everyone's opinions, very fair and square, okay... Anyway, I'm super strong..." Cora grumbled defensively.

"Yes, yes, you're super strong, and I'm useless. But I miss you,"

Onyx interrupted her. "—Cora dear, I miss you, so I'm coming to find you."

The chatty sparrow suddenly went quiet, and after a long pause, Cora mumbled, trying to change the subject, "Oh, uh, right, I should go… talk to Ada."

With that, the terminal call abruptly ended.

Cora stood still for a moment, then slowly raised her hands to cover her cheeks. So warm.

CHAPTER 19

Reunion

Before departing for Araya, Onyx made a stop at the Governor's mansion, where he held a closed-door meeting with Dmitri. No one knew what they discussed, but in the end, Dmitri nodded and granted a few days of leave to this rumored "new successor."

A silver starship sped through the dark night, the scenery outside the porthole pitch black, while the warm glow of the reading lamp inside highlighted Onyx's profile—an impeccably crafted work of art.

His expression was focused, his fingers moving constantly as he worked on a small precision instrument connected to a holographic screen. The device bore the Arashi logo on its top, resembling a white egg.

This was a storage core he had found in Yara Ursula's spatial necklace. It was a basic model—not connected to any network, with unremarkable functions, but it had excellent security features and could only be opened using special methods known within Arashi.

Yvonne and Wyan Rowin sat across from him, the twins observing Onyx for a while before Wyan spoke up. "Are you sure you only need us to take you to Araya?"

Yvonne, having just finished checking the autopilot route, took a seat beside his brother, tossing him a bottle of their special drink. Then, he glanced at Onyx. "We don't have any missions at the moment, so for safety's sake, we can continue protecting you."

Though they didn't fully understand what made this man

deserving of the highest level of protection—two S6-level Aberrants at his side—since it was Dmitri's direct order, they had to carry it out with utmost diligence.

"No need," Onyx replied without looking up, a slight curve on his thin lips. "The safest place in the world is by Cora's side."

The sudden, unexpected remark left the Wyan and Yvonne momentarily speechless.

Wyan rubbed the goosebumps on her arms, her direct nature compelling her to speak her mind. "Hey, handsome, given your... relationship with Cora, could you put in a good word for us? Honestly, that kidnapping incident was just following orders. My brother and I had no intention of making enemies with her."

Now that the crisis at the Northern Base had passed, F777's reputation had skyrocketed, making it particularly awkward for the twins to navigate through the Aberrant Affairs Bureau. However, they weren't part of Scarlett Holland's inner circle; they had simply followed orders as newly integrated citizens looking to adapt quickly.

"I can, but the decision is hers to make," Onyx responded coolly. Wyan's mixed-race features lit up with a smile as she whispered to her brother, "See? I told you that Aberrant Chronicles wasn't making things up..."

Onyx shut off the holographic screen, casting one last glance at the small storage core. It contained all the research data on organ regeneration and part of the Seed Project—of course, excluding the data on test subjects. He had set permissions on it; aside from himself, only Rainer Ninnemann could access it.

"Give this to Dr. Ninnemann."

Onyx stared quietly out the porthole. They had about six hours left until they reached Araya, with an estimated arrival time just before midnight.

In the past couple of days, whether at the Northern Base or in the moments before his departure, he hadn't felt the unsettling sensation of being watched. The two probing gazes outside the laboratory might indeed have been targeting Rainer, with Onyx merely being caught in the crossfire.

The navigation system alerted them to an approaching storm cloud. Lightning flashed, thunder roared, and countless hailstones battered the starship, causing it to sway slightly. In the brief flash of light, Onyx's expression was unreadable, shadowed with uncertainty.

The road ahead was unpredictable.

Six Hours Later.

The powerful wind rushed past Cora's ears, lifting her shoulder-length hair into the air. Her well-fitted isolation suit clung to her body as she held down the wobbling face shield, looking up at the descending starship.

The hatch opened, and a tall, slender figure appeared, silhouetted against the light. He was also dressed in an isolation suit and wore a face shield, but instead of making a dramatic freefall, he descended calmly and steadily using the soft ladder.

Cora's dimples appeared as a bright smile spread across her face, her thoughts filled with a bit of amusement: Typical of Princess Onyx —he even needs a ladder to land.

Onyx moved with purpose, his gaze fixed solely on Cora standing in the back. Unable to restrain himself, he spread his arms wide and began striding toward her, ready to embrace the slender figure he had been yearning for. Just as he was about to wrap her in his arms, someone called out from the group.

"Well, look who's here." Felix raised one of his mechanical arms and, without hesitation, took Onyx's left hand, shaking it up and down.

Suchat glanced at Onyx's outstretched arms, a look of confusion flashing across his face. Not used to Onyx's sudden display of warmth, he clapped his right hand in greeting.

"Pfft, haha!" Yuui doubled over with laughter, barely able to stand.

Onyx was at a loss for words. Who said anything about shaking hands and high-fiving? Can't anyone take a hint?

He stiffened for a moment, then quickly composed himself as if nothing had happened, stepping in front of Cora.

His fingers itched to reach out, but mindful of the situation, Onyx refrained from any overly affectionate gestures. He simply brushed a leaf out of her hair. "How did the negotiations go?"

Cora's previously cheerful face crumpled in frustration. "Not great—completely failed."

The updated A-level commission seemed straightforward enough, requiring just three steps to complete: First, convince Ada, the leader of the Fallen, to leave. Second, escort the Fallen to Finach. Third, submit the mission.

But Cora hadn't expected to get stuck on the first step.

In her first attempt, Cora went alone. Unfortunately, she didn't choose the right moment, as Ada was in a foul mood after losing her kin. As soon as Cora set foot in the valley, she hadn't even uttered a word before Ada spotted her, letting out an angry roar that sent a wave of zombies charging toward her.

They didn't kill her—just pelted her with balls of mud and plant stems, driving her away. Not wanting to fight back, Cora ended up retreating in defeat, covered in dirt.

The second time, Cora was more cautious. She hid in the treetops, using a loudspeaker to plead her case: "Ada, how about moving to a new place?"

"Have you heard of Finach? Less radiation, no people—really safe. Come with me."

"If you go there, no one will die... uh, no one will die anymore, so you won't have to be sad..."

"Ada..."

After talking herself hoarse, Cora grabbed a drink from a line of bottles she had prepared, sitting cross-legged and ready for a heart-to-heart.

Suddenly, rustling sounds came from all around. Cora whipped her head around to see countless pairs of glowing red eyes glaring at her from the tree canopy, accompanied by low growls. Good grief! These zombies can climb trees! She nearly lost her footing but escaped by swinging from vines, narrowly avoiding a fall.

The zombies left behind curiously picked up the discarded drink bottles, taking sips before excitedly sharing them with their comrades.

On the third attempt, Cora brought Damian along to translate. Finally, they got their message across, but Ada only stared at them in silence. Cora noticed a hint of hesitation in her gaze—there was hope! But before she could feel relieved, Ada growled, and dozens of small blood-red zombies swarmed over, pinning Damian to the ground and stripping him of everything but a pitiful pair of yellow duck-patterned briefs.

Cora, an expert at making a quick escape, darted away. Ten minutes later, when she returned, she was met with Damian's tearful, accusatory stare.

"Big Sis, why did you run off by yourself?"

Cora stammered, "I'll, uh, buy you some new clothes when we get back..."

Damian, on the verge of tears, couldn't shake the feeling that Cora had changed—probably corrupted by that guy Onyx. She used to always come to his rescue!

On the fourth attempt, both teams tried their best to persuade Ada, but they still failed.

Ada shook her head warily. "Humans... can't be trusted."

After hearing Cora's pitiful recounting, Onyx calmly rolled up his sleeves and chuckled. "Got it. Leave the rest to me."

His deep gaze swept over Zephyrion and his team. Maintaining a neutral expression, he nodded politely.

Zephyrion didn't recognize Onyx. The last time he saw him, Onyx was weak, pale, and confined to a wheelchair, practically invisible within F777. But the man standing before him was tall, confident, and full of life, with a pair of gold-rimmed glasses resting on the bridge of his nose.

His tone was cold and arrogant, and it was said that he was some kind of "external support" from the Northern Base. Just his presence alone was imposing enough to demand respect.

After being briefed on the current situation, Onyx made a decisive call. "Cora and I will discuss our next move. We'll set out at six in the morning."

"To where?" Zephyrion asked, confused, but noticed that F777 didn't seem surprised at all. Even Cora nodded in agreement.

"Apologies, I should have explained," Onyx said with a tea-smooth smile. "I forgot that you're not following along. We're heading to—Finach."

Zephyrion was left speechless. Do all District B people talk like this?

Onyx quickly made his way to Cora's tent. Just before pulling aside the flap, he remembered something and nodded toward Felix. "Hey, get in here already. Or are you making us wait for you?"

Felix snorted, following him inside.

Yuui waved a finger in front of Victor von der Falkner's face. "What are you staring at?" The normally stoic Victor blushed furiously. "N-nothing... nothing..." He scrambled to his feet and rushed off, nearly bumping into Zephyrion.

Yuui followed his gaze just in time to see two men and a woman enter the same tent. She shook her head with a chuckle. "Looks like the gossip in our team is just going to get wilder."

Inside the tent, Onyx pulled out a brand-new holographic screen and handed it to Felix, his expression serious. "From what I can tell, that Fallen leader is highly distrustful of humans, so focusing your efforts on 'taking them away' makes this plan hard to execute."

Cora tilted her head, thinking it over. It seemed that every time she mentioned taking them away, Ada would react negatively.

"So, what do we do?"

"We stay out of it. Lay out the pros and cons, and let her take the lead."

Cora's tilted head was too endearing for Onyx to resist. He finally got his wish and gently poked her cheek. "You mentioned she has a strong sense of kinship and enough intelligence. I believe she'll make the best decision for her people."

The quiet valley was steeped in sorrow as the night passed. Another eight zombies succumbed to excessive radiation, their bodies exploding as they reached their limits.

A multitude of their kind gathered for a mournful vigil. Some looked on in numb confusion, still not fully understanding what death meant, while others howled in despair, pounding the ground in frustration.

Their lives were like flowing sand in an hourglass, the end in sight, with no way to resist the inevitable arrival of their fate.

During the faint commotion, a drone wobbled its way closer to the valley, eventually dropping a flickering holographic screen to the ground with a soft thud. The zombies growled in alarm, circling the strange object and occasionally poking at it with their claws.

Ada let out a low growl, prompting the zombie to cautiously pick up the screen and bring it to her.

Ada studied the device for a moment before carefully pressing a button, causing the screen to suddenly emit a sound. The surrounding zombies recoiled in fear, backing away from the unknown technology.

A beam of light projected a holographic map of the Alliance into the air, accompanied by a deep, pleasant male voice that explained the situation as if reporting the news: "Currently, radiation levels in Araya exceed safe limits by 21% and are increasing rapidly at a rate of 2% per year. In one year, levels will reach 23%, at which point all life will cease to exist."

A grim scene abruptly flashed across the screen—countless plants and animals lay rotting in the ashes. The younger zombies huddled together in fear.

"Araya's vegetation is lush, and the terrain is flat, but District B is experiencing significant overcrowding. According to recent reports, the Alliance is considering a large-scale clearing operation here, with plans to install a weather simulation system, turning this area into a new home for survivors."

The projection showed teams of surveyors in isolation suits and heavy machinery bulldozing their way through the forest, destroying the ecosystem. The zombies howled in fury.

"In contrast, District C26, Finach, has been abandoned for fifteen years because of its harsh environment. In the remote eastern region, it remains untouched, with radiation levels expected to stabilize around 17% over the next five years."

A desolate scene of Finach slowly came into view—endless stretches of gray, filled with dust and devoid of any signs of life. The zombies stared blankly at the barren landscape, their blended facial features revealing no emotion.

"Come sunrise, we will leave for Finach," the calm, reassuring male voice declared. The projection froze on a clear map of the route and a large countdown timer, with a flashing red dot marking the current location of the screen.

Ada extended a finger, swiping at the screen, which automatically replayed the sequence. As the route map and countdown reappeared, she turned the screen face down and pressed it into the ground, trying to block out the distressing images. Yet, the flashing red dot seemed to linger in her mind, connecting to a place that symbolized hope.

Five o'clock sharp.

As the morning sun rose, the mist retreated from the forest, and the first golden rays of dawn illuminated the shadowed landscape of Araya.

A starship, painted with an eye-catching design, was slowly ascending into the sky. "Do you think they'll really follow us?" Victor von der Falkner asked anxiously.

"No idea," Yuui replied with a lazy yawn, leaning haphazardly against Suchat's back to catch up on sleep.

"Aren't you the least bit concerned?" Zephyrion glanced at her.

"Not at all," Yuui smirked, her eyes still closed as she pointed randomly. "Look, in our team, we have a top-tier brain, top-tier brawn, and then there's me, the top-tier beauty. Even if this plan fails, we'll figure something else out."

Zephyrion fell silent, unable to argue with her confidence.

"They're coming," Felix suddenly announced from the pilot's seat. Zephyrion and his team immediately jumped to their feet and crowded around the porthole.

Behind the starship, a massive wave of crimson surged toward them, so vast that it stretched beyond the horizon. The glow emanating from the horde rivaled the brightness of the rising sun.

These grotesque creatures, with their thin limbs, blood-red skin, and misshapen features, were sprinting after the starship with everything they had.

The adult zombies carried their young on their backs, desperately trying to keep up. Leading the charge was Ada, who periodically checked the screen to ensure they were still on course—the red dot steadily moving toward their destination.

"They're really... coming."

Zephyrion was overwhelmed with emotion, his eyes welling up with tears. This breathtaking sight had already transcended the significance of earning points; it was a moment he knew he would never forget.

Cora stood tall, her spirits high, as she clapped her hands together. "All right, everyone, get ready! Let's clear the way! And remember our motto!"

"F777! At your service, guiding you safely to your destination!" the team responded in unison, full of enthusiasm.

In the vast wilderness, a dozen superhumans were herding

zombies.

Overhead, a starship slowed down as it flew by, and a nimble figure flipped onto the top of it, raising a large loudspeaker. With a click, a pre-recorded message by Yuui blared out.

"Attention, everyone on the ground! There are Fallen passing through ahead. Please do not engage. Lay down your weapons and give way. Our distant friends are friendly, so don't be afraid. If you have any issues, report them to F777! We're here to coordinate!"

"What the heck?" someone shouted in confusion.

The ground rumbled loudly, and the group of superhumans paled as they scrambled up a nearby hillside. They watched in shock as thousands upon thousands of blood-red creatures passed by, completely overwhelming the zombies they hadn't killed.

Moments later, the dust settled, and the monsters were gone, leaving only a few zombie corpses behind.

The loudspeaker's voice faded into the distance: "Our distant friends are sending you a little gift, just a small token of appreciation!"

"F777."

"Huh?"

"Oh, I was saying, the starship has 'F777' written on it."

Within a day, news of "F777 leading an army of monsters," spread across the lower districts, with many sensational reports cropping up: "The most powerful horde in history is upon us! Human sanctuaries may be doomed!"

"Traitors! F777 has brought the enemy into our midst, betraying all of humanity!"

"A study on the neurobiology: Using F777 as a case study, exploring the possibility of future human control over zombies."

"The untold stories of F777 and the Fallen."

Most cities were thrown into confusion, unable to come up with effective responses. Fortunately, Cora had preemptively coordinated evacuations and real-time guidance, preventing any major incidents. Ada, focused solely on leading her kin to their destination, paid no attention to the swirling rumors.

By the second day, public opinion shifted. The outcry against F777 lessened, with people instead becoming increasingly curious about the mysterious red zombies and their origins.

The migration route passed through the Sea Gate, and Felix had preemptively contacted the city's government to explain the situation. Governor Ivan Ashar, who had ties with F777, immediately issued a citywide lockdown, forbidding residents from wandering about.

However, the tough and restless people of Sea Gate wouldn't just sit still.

Denied the chance to go outside, they brought out benches and gathered at the first line of defense. Munching on sunflower seeds, they chatted idly. "Hey, did you hear what's supposed to pass through today? A 'Fallen,' right?"

"It's 'Fallen,' yeah."

"Don't get it. What's that? They will not break in, are they?"

"Nah, all three defense lines have been reinforced."

"Those little punks, if they dare to come in, just watch how I deal with them!" Tiger Smith, swinging a beer bottle, boasted with the bravado of someone who had nothing to fear.

His gold chain sparkled under the sunlight as he gestured confidently. His family had long since moved into a spacious 500-square-meter flat, and each of his bodyguards wielded powerful spirit weapons—his presence alone was enough to intimidate.

"They're coming!"

At a guard's shout, the residents of Sea Gate craned their necks to get a better look. A sleek starship shot across the sky, followed by a vast horde of Fallen flooding across the plain, crowding the entire span of the bridge. The horde didn't even glance at the city gates before disappearing into the dust on the other side.

"Is this a movie or something…?" an out-of-town visitor muttered in disbelief. The Sea Gate locals, suddenly realizing the spectacle they were witnessing, tossed aside their sunflower seeds, pulled out their terminals, and started recording furiously to upload to the star network, eager to capitalize on the viral moment.

Human nature is diverse, and while the Sea Gate residents were content to watch the show, others had more sinister motives, hoping to profit from the chaos. Ignoring the loudspeaker's warnings, they stealthily followed the Fallen, hoping to pick off a few stragglers for some easy points.

But as soon as the attackers unleashed their powers, the creatures didn't scatter like ordinary zombies. Instead, Ada, at the front, twisted her head and let out a piercing screech. Instantly, thousands of ferocious blood zombies turned in unison and, with deadly coordination, viciously devoured the would-be attackers.

Cora was hanging from the starship's hatch, ready to leap down and assist, but she paused and shouted instead.

"Ada—"

Ada seemed to recognize Cora calling her, raising her head warily as she ran.

Ada didn't respond, but her nostrils flared slightly. Cora couldn't help but notice what looked like a simple expression of disdain on Ada's uneven face.

Cora: What does that mean? Did Ada just mock me?

Five days later, District C26, Finach, was within reach.

CHAPTER 20

A Revenger

The vast wasteland stretched endlessly, with the blood-red Fallens sweeping across like a fierce wind, stirring up billows of dust. Zephyrion and his three companions each drove their off-road vehicles, trailing behind the rear of the monstrous horde to maintain order and prevent any stray corpses from falling behind.

Cora sat at the edge of the hatch, a jacket under her for cushioning, grumbling as if she were arguing with someone. Occasionally, her voice would rise in pitch, and she'd straighten her back, her toes curling with intensity.

Onyx sat not far behind her, a few strands of hair falling over his forehead, tousled by the wind. His thick eyelashes cast a shadow over his eyes that held a gentle smile as he quietly watched Cora's back, seeing her work herself into a huff, almost like a pufferfish.

During the days he spent alone at the Northern Base, Onyx maintained a composed exterior, but darkness crept into his heart. It was as if he had returned to the days before the apocalypse, living without purpose, walking without a soul, maintaining perfect social interactions through feigned enthusiasm while being unable to connect emotionally with those around him. He felt like a car skidding on the edge of a cliff, constantly at risk of going off the rails.

When Onyx stood at the highest point of the city's defense headquarters, looking down at the masses through the floor-to-ceiling windows, his hand hovered near the control console.

For a moment, his pathological personality surfaced, floating above the scene with cold indifference and disdain, questioning him repeatedly: Why save them? What do these people have to do with you? You're not him—you can't be the savior! Now, enter a simple command and watch this city crumble in your hands!

His fingers unconsciously typed a single letter. Fortunately, reason returned in the next second, and he swiftly hit the delete key before walking away.

"Psychopath," Onyx whispered the word to himself.

It was a diagnosis he had received in his youth, a condition that had been well-controlled since his awakening as an Aberrant. But after a traumatic event, it resurfaced, and since then, he had buried all his emotions deep within, always wearing a smile that no one could see through. For years, his behavior was indistinguishable from that of a normal person—until these past few days, when it all deteriorated.

Onyx had candidly told Dmitri Yevgeniyev about his current state, admitting that he was unfit to continue his duties and needed to search for a "sedative."

Dmitri had stared at him for a long time, perhaps recalling something Arashi Sheen had mentioned, and finally agreed.

The moment Onyx saw Cora in the wasteland, the destructive urge and weariness inside him miraculously faded. A sacred hymn seemed to play in his ears, and his soul, at last, found peace. To him, the bright orb in the sky wasn't the sun—Cora, silhouetted against the light, was.

He twisted open a bottle of water and cradled it to Cora's lips, his voice tender and cautious. "Tired? Do you want to take a break?"

Cora drank a couple of gulps from his hand and shook her head before lifting the megaphone. "Ada, even as a Fallen, you should still be grateful..."

Ada, who was sprinting at full speed, growled in irritation, baring her teeth in frustration.

A light tap sounded on the cabin wall, and Onyx turned around to see Felix signaling him. Understanding that Felix had something to discuss privately, Onyx nodded silently, and the two made their way to the front cabin.

Felix opened his terminal and expertly hacked into the

commission platform. In the vast sea of data, countless Trojan programs were quietly operating.

Bypassing the artificial intelligence monitoring in District B4 to steal backend information was no simple task. Although it took him some time, Felix, being a top-tier hacker, did it flawlessly and without a trace.

"I checked—it was a targeted release the second time," Felix said confidently, pointing to the top of the list where an A-level commission was displayed.

Onyx narrowed his eyes in thought. Changing the scope from a global release to a targeted one near Araya? This not only limited the methods of completion but also restricted the area from which the mission could be accepted, effectively eliminating 99% of the Aberrant teams.

"And the traces?" Onyx inquired, wanting to know if there had been any tampering.

"None," Felix replied.

Onyx chuckled softly. "You mean none found? Or no traces at all?"

Felix remained expressionless. "Of course, no traces. Do you think I'm like you? It'd take me fourteen days just to repair Station T014."

Onyx was speechless. Was there any point in bringing that up over and over?

"After Zephyrion uploaded the data, the system adjusted the mission content. Both the analysis process and the handling path align perfectly with AI thinking patterns. There's no abnormal data," Felix's tone was even.

But Onyx knew him too well. "Your expression says otherwise."

Felix let out a light snort. "Even if it didn't act on its own, this commission will still end up pointing to District C26."

"What do you mean?"

"Because even if all the data is normal, there's one other possibility. What if the AI handling the commission didn't 'think' at all but was directly commanded?"

Onyx's eyes shot up.

Felix spoke slowly, enunciating each word: "—I think 'she' is involved."

Onyx remained noncommittal. "Do you have proof?"

"No, just a hunch," Felix answered firmly.

Onyx tapped his fingers rhythmically, not responding with his usual sharp retorts. Instead, he asked, "What's your intuition telling you?"

"The number of commissions from Araya to Finyak has dropped by two-thirds, including even the most common private jobs," Felix said with an unusual seriousness.

"It's as if someone is deliberately clearing the path. From the moment the mission was issued, the Zombie Lord, the Fallens, the elimination of the mutating creatures... every step is a carefully designed trap. You only realize the real aim when you step into it."

Onyx's fingers twitched, and he wrote a word in the air. Felix quickly recognized it as Mutter.

"They're coming for you? Didn't hide your tracks well enough, and they found out?"

When Cora Thornton was kidnapped by Commander Holland, Felix had connected to the District B4 terminal, using S-class Anopower to track data.

This exposure had brought him to the attention of the super AI. Although he immediately hid and wiped all information, preventing any reverse tracking, that he was still alive had inevitably been confirmed.

"You can't keep running forever. Might as well go back to Grass Pit one of these days and finish her," Onyx suggested nonchalantly, as if discussing something trivial. "You've done it once; you won't fail this time, right?"

Felix glanced at him. It was rare to hear such ruthless words from Onyx, but on second thought, this was his true nature.

elix responded vaguely, "Soon."

His one and only failure had cost him dearly—he could no longer walk on his own. He will lie in wait as long as it took, just to ensure a fatal strike.

"Those were just my speculations. If they're coming for me, I'm confident I can handle it. But if the target is you..." Felix's tone grew lighter, the camaraderie turning competitive once more. "Can you manage?"

Onyx's lips pressed into a thin line. The two agents who had been tailing Rainer Ninnemann had left a faint sense of unease in his heart.

"You've got six legs, don't you? If they're after me, you'll be the first to run," Onyx shot back.

Felix was surprised. "No way. Did they really find you? Did you waste all those elective classes?"

Onyx shook his head slowly. "Not sure."

So many days had passed without incident around him. If they were targeting him, wouldn't they have struck when he was alone at the Northern Base? There were even several opportunities along the way to ambush him—why let him return to Cora's side?

Felix's expression cleared with understanding. "So you're scared, hiding behind the Captain, hoping she'll protect you, the infamous fugitive."

Onyx cast a sharp glance his way. "Cora... doesn't know."

To explain his identity would inevitably involve the painful past of the Fire Seed Project. Cora had forgotten those memories and lived happily in the present. Onyx had yet to decide whether to tell her the harsh truth.

Because Cora was his son, Onyx didn't want to steal away her innocence and joy. He sighed internally and added, almost as an afterthought, "Don't go blabbing in front of her."

Felix's words faltered, and a suspicious flicker crossed his eyes.

"You're hiding something from me," Onyx narrowed his eyes. This wasn't the first time Felix had acted strangely. "No, I'm not," Felix replied, his expression unchanging. "My dear friend, is your trust in me that fragile?"

"I don't have that kind of thing for you. My mental powers can extract memories just as easily. Do you want to be the first to try?"

"My firewall tells me it doesn't want to."

Cold psychic energy surged out, clashing against a wall of silver code. Two powerful S-class mental energies collided in the air.

Bang—!

The cabin door was yanked open, revealing Yuui with a stern face, followed by three equally irritated people.

"Argue all you want, but don't mess around with mental powers! Some of us here are A-class, you know. It really hurts," Damian grumbled, clearly uncomfortable.

"Exactly! It's unbearable!" Damian chimed in angrily.

"If you two fight, I'm not treating any injuries caused by internal disputes," Charles joked.

"Save it for later, we're at Finyak," Even Suchat looked disapproving.

Cora put away her megaphone, patted her knees, and stood up. When she turned and saw her teammates gathered, glaring at each other, she asked worriedly, "What's going on? Fighting again?"

Onyx shot Felix a deep look, silently pointing a finger at him. A wordless threat: You'll pay for this. Felix, unfazed, shrugged his shoulders, letting out an exaggerated scoff.

Ten minutes later, the starship was the first to enter Finyak's city limits. A notification popped up on the navigation system: "You have entered a radiation zone. Please take protective measures and avoid prolonged exposure."

The sky was filled with a thick, gray fog, and the murky dust particles seemed to infiltrate every breath. Visibility was low, with abandoned buildings looming indistinctly in the distance. Felix switched to manual control, guiding the starship slowly through the city to avoid accidentally crashing into a skyscraper.

"My psychic energy feels stronger," Yuui remarked, clenching her fist as she sensed the changes in her magnetic field.

Low levels of radiation could moderately stimulate Anopower, and for Aberrants above A-class, the current concentration in Finyak was just right. They weren't suited for prolonged exposure to the air here.

The starship landed on a rooftop, and the members of F777 donned their protective suits and masks, leaping onto the main street to wait patiently.

Zephyrion and his team parked their off-road vehicles by the roadside. Before long, Ada led her kind to the rendezvous point. From a distance of about a hundred meters, the blood-red horde of Fallens came to an abrupt halt, filling the streets and alleys, drawing a simple line between themselves and Cora's group.

Ada let out a low growl, and two young zombies ran toward Cora, resembling playful little monkeys.

Damian's eyes widened in disbelief. One zombie wore a little yellow duck sunhat, and the other sported a designer T-shirt. Both outfits fit perfectly, but… they had been stolen from him! The memory of nearly losing his pants that night was still vivid in his mind.

Thud! The guide screen was tossed back to Cora's feet. The little zombies chattered loudly, waving their arms in a nonsensical manner before turning back to Ada.

"No need to return it; it's a gift," Cora called out generously as she threw the screen back. It was just a guide screen, after all, and she could easily afford another. Ada was being overly polite.

Ada's crimson eyes shifted slightly, but she didn't accept the offer. With a swift motion, she smacked the screen back toward Cora. Unprepared to catch it, the screen, having endured a bumpy journey, flew back and crashed to the ground with a resounding crack, spiderweb-like fractures spreading across the display.

Cora picked it up with a pained expression, scolding, "Ada, this thing is expensive!" Ada's uneven features shifted as she dramatically rolled her eyes. Onyx coughed lightly. "Cora, there's a tracker on the screen."

Cora blinked in confusion, "Huh?"

Then she was speechless. "I forgot."

Ada, with an intelligence rivaling that of the Zombie Lord, was indeed too clever. Keeping the guide screen would have meant revealing the location of her horde to the humans, so she had decisively returned it upon arrival.

Ada gazed into the distance. There were no towering forests here, no giant mutated plants. The ruined city stretched out endlessly, and the air quality was poor. Yet her kind were both curious and excited.

The constant pain in their skin had lessened, and even the zombies, long suffering from radiation sickness, barely clinging to life, now stood up, staring in amazement at their revitalized veins and limbs.

There was no doubt that Finyak's environment was suitable for the Fallens to survive. The humans hadn't deceived them. It was a new home—a beacon of hope.

Ada leaped gracefully to the top of a dilapidated building, letting out a long, distant howl. All the zombies looked up at her. Then, as if understanding her command, they dispersed in all directions, like drops of water merging into the sea, vanishing into the depths of the gray fog in the blink of an eye.

Neither the treacherous humans nor the mindless zombies were their companions. The rest of the journey was one the Fallens would have to walk alone.

"Tha...nk...you..." Ada rasped, casting a deep, lingering look at Cora and her team. Then, with one swift leap, her slender figure dissolved into the mist.

"Goodbye, Ada," Cora called out, feeling a sense of loss as she waved. The red dot on the guide screen remained in place—Ada's location was lost. But Cora believed Ada would lead her kind to survival.

Once the last zombie disappeared from view, Cora clicked to complete the commission.

This A-level commission had been almost entirely handled by F777, earning them a staggering reward that catapulted their ranking to first place in the entire Alliance. The Boss and His Three Goons also reaped some benefits, gaining 110,000 points, far surpassing the 500,000-point threshold needed to join District B.

"We're number one!" Cora cheered, jumping for joy as she hugged each of her teammates, finally leaping into Onyx's arms. He hugged her back tightly, not letting go.

The terminals of Yuui and the others beeped with notifications: a change in the top ten rankings would be announced on the commission platform. Now, the name at the top of the New Pacific Alliance's leaderboard was "F777," with a score far ahead of the competition.

Cora was busy replying to messages when Zephyrion approached her, followed by Luke, Victor, and Kluge. They all expressed their sincere thanks. If it hadn't been for Cora leading them on this mission, and a bit of luck, they might not have reached the point requirement by fall.

Cora suddenly remembered something. "Oh, the recommendation letter."

"There's someone here," Suchat interrupted with a slight frown.

Dozens of robust Aberrants emerged from the shadows surrounding them.

The leader of the group was a man in his thirties with slanted eyes and a vicious expression. He surveyed the area before giving Zephyrion a mocking whistle. "Hey, buddy, just finished a mission, right? Share some of those points with us, will ya?"

Points could be transferred in two ways: first, through a formal agreement witnessed by the platform, with a mediation fee deducted by the system; second, by converting them into rewards through private commissions, though the recipient of the rewards couldn't be specified and would only benefit by completing the task. F777 had been climbing the leaderboard for a while, but this was the first time they had encountered someone brazen enough to rob them—especially someone targeting them directly.

"Who are you guys?" Cora blinked in confusion, completely at a loss for words.

The group before them was of mixed abilities, ranging from A to D class, clearly lower-tier Aberrants from one of the less advanced districts. What gave them the confidence to openly attempt a robbery?

"They're bounty hunters," Zephyrion said in a low voice.

The term "bounty hunter" might sound glamorous, but in reality, it was far from it. The name specifically referred to those who, after the apocalypse, would take extreme risks to earn points or NPA credits—essentially bandits who valued nothing but profit, disregarding human life and any ethical considerations.

There was a clear information gap between District B and C. These bounty hunters clearly didn't recognize the newly ascendant F777 standing before them. They had zeroed in on Zephyrion because he had casually mentioned the figure "500,000 points."

The lead bounty hunter sniffed the air greedily, his expression one of intoxicated delight. "I can smell it, the scent of gold."

Yuui shook her head, laughing. "You guys haven't been keeping up with the news, have you? Even thieves should stay updated with the times."

"Sorry to have troubled you all. Let us handle this," Zephyrion said. As soon as the words left his mouth, thick vines shot forward, quickly ensnaring over a dozen people, including the boastful leader.

"Little Diamond, lend a hand—we're on a tight schedule," Onyx urged softly.

Damian, an A1-level Aberrant, was already formidable in this group of amateurs. He raised his right hand slightly, and a barrage of hailstones rained down, leaving the bounty hunters shivering, their movements slowing as they became increasingly encased in ice.

Charles rummaged through the area, but couldn't find even a single valuable Tier 3 crystal, sighing in disappointment.

He removed his gloves and was about to say something when he noticed the others' expressions change drastically as they quickly backed away. Confused, Charles asked, "What are you all dodging?"

The next second, he whipped around, only to see the corpses on the ground rapidly swelling before exploding in a burst of blood-red light!

Bang! Bang! Flesh and innards splattered like a gruesome fountain, and the overwhelming stench of blood filled the air. Cora, pinching her nose, approached Charles, who now had an unknown intestine draped over his head, and handed him a towel.

"You guys are so heartless..." Charles glared at her for a long moment before reluctantly accepting the towel. Cora had just managed a sheepish smile when her gaze suddenly sharpened, her expression turning serious as she looked in a particular direction.

Tap, tap. Tap, tap. The sound of footsteps echoed clearly from deep within the gray fog, resonating in everyone's ears.

Who could it be this time? Another group of bounty hunters?

Under the watchful eyes of the group, a figure slowly emerged from the rooftop of a nearby high-rise—a middle-aged man in a sharp suit, his features suggesting a mixed heritage, and a prominent hooked nose. His eyelids drooped as he regarded the group with arrogant disdain. "You're Cora Thornton, right? S7-level Assault Aberrant."

Cora responded politely, "That's me. And you are?"

"Half a year ago, you killed my favorite dog," the man said, his polished shoes stepping through a pool of blood, leaving a clear half-footprint behind. "I've been looking for you for a long time."

Onyx and Felix exchanged a covert glance, both frowning. Was the man really after Cora? Had their assumptions been entirely wrong?

Cora looked genuinely puzzled. "How could that be? I never hurt dogs."

CHAPTER 21

The Way to Home

Ten Days Ago.

District A1, The Central.

The large conference room was empty, but along both sides of the long table, more than a dozen holographic projections sat or stood, conversing in low tones. "S7-level Aberrants are certainly rare, but they're not unique."

"As far as I know, aside from the publicly known Cora Thornton and the former Special Operations member, Punk, both the Azures and Vulture Forces have two more of their own, don't they?"

The leader of the Azures, Arashi Sheen, had not been invited to today's secret meeting.

Everyone's gaze turned to the end of the long table, where the highest-ranking officer of the Vulture Six sat. He hadn't activated his hologram, and his raspy voice echoed in the room as if from nowhere: "In the Vulture Forces, a code name is only revealed upon death."

The implication was clear—so long as those two S7-level Aberrants were still alive, he wouldn't disclose any information about them.

The others exchanged glances, understanding that there was no point in pressing further. Unlike the legitimate military forces like the Azures, the Vulture Forces specialized in intelligence and assassination. Offending these sewer rats could lead to a fate worse than death—one could have their throat slit in the night without ever knowing who did it.

"There are indeed several S7-level Aberrants, but as for S7 dual-type Aberrants, so far there has only been one in the entire Alliance, and that's the Bloody Hunter, Punk." Jae-Woo Park looked toward the head of the table, a flash of desire for ultimate power passing through his eyes.

"Mr. Mabul, after Punk was expelled from the Special Operations Team, he went to serve under Commander Szymon, becoming his loyal dog..."

"This is the footage from Punk's death, and it was Cora Thornton who killed him."

The attendees all straightened in their seats, focusing intently on the screen. The video provided by Jae-Woo Park was captured from the micro-camera embedded in Punk's collar, with all the "irrelevant" parts edited out, leaving only the last moments. The footage was raw and intense, seen from a first-person perspective.

Cora, wielding a long spear, advanced with the ferocity of a war goddess. Their powerful abilities clashed head-on, but Punk was ultimately outmatched, forced into retreat. Cora first pierced his intact right eye, then severed his hands and feet, finally pushing him into a self-detonation. Her brutal combat prowess sent a chill down everyone's spine, plunging the room into a prolonged silence.

"Is there any possibility of persuading her to join us?" Mr. Mabul, seated at the head of the table, asked calmly. Silence fell again; no one dared to answer.

After a long pause, an official spoke nervously, "This S7-level Aberrant rose from a lower district. I'm afraid... she might be difficult to control."

Punk's death was of little consequence, but it proved one thing—Cora's strength far exceeded everyone's expectations. Intelligence showed that she came from the impoverished digitized districts, her origins shrouded in mystery, with no known parents, and she had never received a single favor from the Alliance.

Yet the Key constantly shadowed her. Convincing her would be nearly impossible. Cora was like a ticking time bomb, one that could become the greatest obstacle to the Reboot Plan at any moment.

Mr. Mabul sighed heavily. "What a pity."

The attendees bowed their heads in silence. The former leader had already decided, and it was a pity indeed—the Alliance was about to lose an S7.

"The only one who can kill a dual-type Aberrant is another dual-type."

Commander Szymon, his expression dark, stood up. He had noticed that Cora's right arm had been blown off but had quickly regenerated during the battle.

Szymon cast a sharp glance at the smug Jae-Woo Park—this despicable man had deliberately brought up the "only S-class dual-type in the Alliance."

He had clearly noticed something was amiss, but had dared to withhold such crucial footage until now to pave his own path to power.

Szymon sneered inwardly. Fine, let's see who comes out on top in the end. He respectfully bowed to Mr. Mabul at the head of the table.

"Sir, no one understands S-class dual-type Aberrants better than I do. I am willing to confirm her second ability."

Finyak City Center.

Szymon, dressed impeccably in his suit, didn't move forward, nor did he seem to appreciate Cora's dark humor.

He aimed his gun at the bounty hunters' corpses and fired several shots without warning. Deep red streams of blood shot into the air, spraying down like a grisly fountain. "Does this jog your memory?" Szymon "helpfully" reminded her.

Cora's pupils reflected the fireworks-like blood pattern, the familiar scene gradually bringing her to a realization—Blood Burst, Punk's ability.

Oh, it really was like dealing with a dog. She killed the dog, and now the owner had come for revenge?

Szymon's gaze briefly flicked over Onyx before returning to Cora. "You've caused me a lot of trouble."

After Punk's sudden death in Deep Woods, Szymon lost his "executioner." With no one to handle his dirty work, he was constantly hamstrung, outmaneuvered at every turn, while his political rival, Jae-Woo Park, seized the opportunity to rise.

"Did you lure us here?" Cora asked with a frown. "Were the Fallens in Araya your bait?" Szymon's sinister smile was his only response.

Whoosh, whoosh—the faint sound of something cutting through the air reached their ears.

Suchat reacted instantly, shoving Yuui out of the way and spinning forward with a swift, vicious kick. The electrified chains were sent flying with a crackling sound.

"What the hell? How shameless can you be, attacking us like that!" Yuui shouted angrily.

Since they'd been discovered, there was no point in hiding anymore. Szymon raised his hand, and over a dozen figures leaped down from the surrounding rooftops—three S-class Aberrants and the rest A-class.

The entire street was bathed in the glow of various abilities, and the mingled psychic energies, enhanced by the radiation, surged chaotically. The F777 team, with their mix of S and A-class members, managed to hold their ground, but The Boss and His Three Goons were overwhelmed, their vision darkening as cold sweat poured down their faces. They struggled to stay upright, gritting their teeth against the crushing pressure.

"Fall back," Cora told them, stepping forward to shield them. "This has nothing to do with you. We'll handle it."

She slowly drew the twin blades from her back, the cold steel glinting as she pointed them at the three S-class Aberrants.

At first glance, it seemed like Szymon's side had the numbers advantage, but F777 remained unfazed.

Yuui was the first to act, her ethereal voice rising in song as a chaotic mist of blades descended, thickening the surrounding fog until neither side could see the other.

Their opponents had indeed lost track of Cora and her team, but F777 could see them perfectly. Thanks to their S-class psychic member, Onyx, with his extraordinarily sharp senses, he not only directed the battle but also swiftly pinpointed each enemy.

Damian spread ice across the ground, trapping the attackers' legs, while Suchat unleashed his poison. Despite the attackers' caution, they couldn't avoid the traps Onyx had set, stumbling blindly into them. Soon they were paralyzed, collapsing to the ground as razor-sharp ice spikes pierced their chests.

Boom! Boom!

Explosions echoed as the sounds of cannon fire roared. Charles bolted, barely avoiding the collapse of a towering office building that would have crushed him to pieces had he been a second slower.

An Aberrant carrying a mortar moved in for support, but just as he readied to fire again, Felix, who had been missing since the battle began, suddenly poked his head out of the fog. His six mechanical arms lashed out, dismantling the cannon's core components in mere seconds, rendering it useless.

The towering Felix, standing over eight feet tall, spun around gracefully, pocketing the enemy's crucial parts as he went.

Suchat moved like a phantom, continually reaping lives. Whenever he was injured, he would slip back into the blade fog, emerging later fully healed by Charles. Under Onyx's direction, every move of the attackers was laid bare, and F777's coordination was flawless. The A-class enemies barely put up a struggle before being taken down.

It was a crushing victory—F777, the top-ranked team on the Alliance leaderboard, had never earned their reputation through luck.

Even the three S-class Aberrants gained no advantage. Despite their combined efforts, they couldn't stop Cora. In the battle's chaos, Cora pressed forward through their attacks, delivering a mid-air kick that crushed the first opponent's chest cavity.

Then, with a cross-slash of her blades, she split the second opponent's head open like a melon. Flames erupted as her shoulder was burned, but she seemed impervious to the pain, silently grabbing the last enemy by the neck and snapping it with a sickening crack.

A piercing howl of rage rang out as Cora suddenly turned. The Aberrant whose chest she had crushed struggled back to his feet, his veins bulging as his blood vessels swelled grotesquely. He staggered towards the area where Onyx and the others hid in the blade fog. Cora thought he was about to self-destruct and rushed to stop him.

Szymon's eyes gleamed with a brilliant light as he watched their movements intently.

At the last second, the dying S-class Aberrant twisted his body, the swelling blood sphere rapidly contracting as it altered its trajectory. Cora's pupils narrowed in realization—he would not explode! There was no time to react; she could only dodge at the last possible moment as the blood sphere grazed her abdomen, spraying blood.

Cora plunged one of her blades into the man's back. He smiled coldly, his voice slow and raspy, "For the future of Utopia..."

Cora cut him off with a bitter reply, slicing off his head with a backhanded strike.

She glanced down, blood streaming freely from the wound in her abdomen, staining her hands crimson.

Szymon's men were all down, but he didn't seem to care. His eyes remained fixed on Cora as he said, "Your life ends today. I will sing your requiem in advance..."

"Talkative, aren't you?" Cora retorted, throwing one of her blades, which pierced Szymon's heart. Yet the expected explosion of blood and flesh didn't happen. Instead, his form wavered like a shattered mirror before disappearing entirely.

Cora froze for a moment, then realized what had happened. The fog had concealed it, but she now understood that Szymon hadn't been physically present—he had only appeared through an illusionary ability. No wonder he hadn't dared to get too close, fearing he might give himself away.

But... wasn't he here to avenge his dog? Did he really just flee? Cora pouted. Some "favorite dog" that was—just words with no action behind them.

Onyx quickly approached, his expression grim as he began bandaging her wound.

Though the gash on her abdomen was nothing to Cora, she still complained, "It hurts!"

Onyx carefully wiped the blood off her cheek. "Let's get out of here."

Charles swiftly scoured the battlefield while Felix started up the starship.

Cora thought for a moment before turning to Zephyrion and his team. "I was going to offer you a ride, but maybe it's better if we split up now." She wasn't sure if the danger was truly over, so she didn't want to drag them into any more trouble.

"See you at the Northern Base," Cora said with a last nod.

After the two teams hurriedly departed, the bodies of the

Aberrants and bounty hunters suddenly erupted in a spray of blood, with faint energy fluctuations dispersing into the air.

Inside the starship, they forcibly pressed the injured Cora into her seat to receive treatment.

She sprawled out on her arms and legs, revealing the wound on her abdomen, and waved it off nonchalantly. "It's really nothing. It doesn't hurt that much."

"Don't move," Charles instructed, pressing down her head, which was trying to lift, as he quickly cleaned the wound. His glowing, white Anopower flowed steadily into the injury, but it was as if it were being absorbed into a bottomless pit—there was no effect. This was the first time Charles had encountered a situation where his Anopower was ineffective, and his frown deepened. "How can this be?"

Charles then turned to Suchat, who had also been injured. He treated every wound meticulously, even the slight scrape on Suchat's hand, which healed perfectly. Charles muttered to himself, "It works just fine here..."

Puzzled, he looked back at Cora. The ghastly wound inflicted by the S-class Aberrant remained stubbornly unresponsive, rejecting any external healing attempts.

"I've seen a wound like this before," Suchat suddenly spoke up. "The last time was during a mission in the Rainy Forest. The enemy used specialized bullets—after being hit, the wounds wouldn't stop bleeding and couldn't heal, no matter what."

On that mission, everyone except for Suchat had died. He clenched his fists tightly, his body trembling slightly at the memory.

Yuui placed a comforting hand on the back of his neck, gently stroking it to calm him down. Gradually, Suchat's fists relaxed, and he regained his composure. "The ability that attacked the Captain must be like those bullets, preventing any form of healing."

"That's cold-hearted," Charles spat.

If Cora were an ordinary Aberrant, there would have been no way to stop the bleeding in this situation—she would have bled out and died. Fortunately, Cora's second Anopower had kicked in just in time, and the once-deep wound was slowly beginning to heal. It would likely scab over in a few hours.

Onyx sat quietly, holding Cora's hand as he fell deep in thought.

From the cockpit, Felix suddenly clicked his tongue. "We've got a problem."

Everyone looked up, surprised to find that after passing through the thin mist, they had somehow returned to the exact location of their recent battle. "Is the navigation system malfunctioning?" Onyx frowned.

"No," Felix quickly checked the systems, "Everything's working fine."

After a moment of contemplation, he switched off the autopilot mode. "I'll fly manually, and you navigate." Onyx, who had memorized the map almost perfectly, moved to the co-pilot seat, taking over as a human GPS.

An hour later, F777 found themselves back at the original spot once more.

Yuui groaned in frustration.

"It's an Anopower," Onyx said gravely.

He opened the hatch to reveal the bodies strewn across the ground, the distant horizon of the abandoned city looking surreal, like a mirage in the desert. The skyscrapers at the edge of their view were half-normal, half-merged with crisscrossing overpasses.

"This is an S-class domain ability called 'Blood Blocks,'" Onyx explained. "The user can control blocks within the domain, piecing together different scenes by rearranging them. But the activation of this ability requires a sacrifice of life force."

"Remember those bounty hunters' corpses? They were likely the driving medium. The more people that die, the larger the area the blocks can cover."

"I've got a question," Yuui glanced back at Cora, who had spent a lot of mental energy because of her injury. She was now asleep, her mouth ajar. Lowering her voice, Yuui asked, "Was that guy really after Cora?"

The more she thought about it, the more bizarre it seemed. "Even if he didn't know Cora had advanced, thinking they could kill an S7-level with those people is just ridiculous. And what's the point of trapping us here?"

Onyx looked at her but didn't respond. Yuui awkwardly scratched her cheek, "Actually... we all heard your conversation with

Felix."

Onyx wasn't surprised. For him, trusting others was difficult, so while he didn't intentionally hide his conversation with Felix from Yuui and the others, he also wasn't forthcoming with information.

"If we encounter any danger, you can run first," Onyx said with a warm smile. "No one will blame you. After all... it wouldn't be the first time."

It took Yuui a moment to process what he had said. "Hey, you!"

Of all the things to bring up, Onyx had to go for the one that cut deep. The betrayal at Mirror Lake was like a thorn in Yuui's heart. Just because no one talked about it didn't mean she didn't care.

Outskirts of Finyak.

Kluge had his arm around Zephyrion's shoulder, his eyes full of hope as he imagined the future. "What do you guys think District B is like? I heard it's almost like it was before the apocalypse—no zombies, no mutant beasts, and you don't have to live in constant fear."

Victor squeezed in between them, saying, "When we get our housing assignments, I'm bunking with Zephyr."

"Get out of here," Kluge pushed Victor's head away, "You can room with Luke. Zephyr's mine."

The four of them had grown up in the same neighborhood, attended the same school, and even started working at the same company. They had all awakened as Aberrants around the same time. Though they bickered constantly, they were as close as brothers, and they always listened to Zephyrion.

Of the four, Luke was the most level-headed. "No need to argue. Zephyr and I will room together." Victor and Kluge instantly glared at him, rolling up their sleeves, ready to fight.

Zephyrion rubbed his forehead in exasperation. "You guys are celebrating too soon. We haven't even gotten there yet, so stop popping the champagne early."

Kluge grinned. "How can you say that? Didn't Cora say she'd write us a recommendation letter?"

They were making good time, only a few hundred meters away from leaving Finyak. Victor had even removed his protective mask, since the radiation had lessened. Occasionally, a few mutant beasts darted across the road, chased by busy Aberrants.

Zephyrion sighed. "She's doing us a favor out of kindness, but we shouldn't take it for granted. We should think of something to give."

"But what could we possibly give them?" Kluge wondered aloud. "They don't seem to need anything."

Just as Zephyrion was about to respond, the sky suddenly darkened, as if covered by a thick layer of clouds. He looked up instinctively and saw a massive space portal tear open. A fully armed fleet emerged, their starships pitch black and unlike any they had ever seen.

The turbulent air scattered zombies and mutant beasts alike. Everyone halted in their tracks, staring up in shock and uncertainty as a group of figures clad in black uniforms descended from the sky.

"There are witnesses on the ground."

"Understood. Eliminate them all."

Like a scythe wielded by death itself, the black-clad figures moved swiftly, cutting down everyone before they reacted. The Aberrants' legs went weak, their minds blank, unable to resist. As the terrifying pressure crushed down on them, their dying eyes glimpsed the emblem on the killers' uniforms—a vicious vulture.

A wave of icy dread swept over Zephyrion as he realized these people were all S-class Aberrants.

A black-clad woman among them noticed Zephyrion and his group. With a slight lift of her hand, invisible kite strings shot out, slicing through the heads of the Aberrants in her path. Their headless bodies staggered forward a few steps before crashing to the ground, blood gushing out sluggishly.

The next moment, the deadly strings shot toward Victor and Luke. "Get down!" Luke shouted.

The two men dropped to the ground and rolled. Luke, standing slightly off to the side, dodged the attack, but Victor wasn't so lucky. Positioned in a direct line with the others, the B-class Aberrant was helpless against the S-class assault. Though he avoided a fatal blow, his entire arm was severed. "Aaaaah!" Victor screamed in agony as Luke and Kluge hurried to lift him up.

People were dropping all around them. Zephyrion cursed under his breath, no longer hesitating. He pulled out a camping lamp, inserted a bright red crystal, and grabbed his companions. The four of them flickered for a moment before disappearing from sight.

The leader of the black-clad group, having finished the slaughter, looked in a specific direction. "Blood Bat, you missed. Four of them got away."

"They used a space-transmitting device," the black-clad woman replied. "But the domain is already active. They can't escape. Spider, we were ordered to leave no witnesses in this operation."

The man, code-named "Spider," nodded. "Understood."

He turned back, his voice cold and emotionless. "Find them. Kill them."

An Abandoned School.

Zephyrion and his companions suddenly reappeared, the glow of the Tier 4 crystal fading until it turned into an ordinary stone. Victor lay motionless, barely conscious, his face pale as paper.

Luke gritted his teeth as he bandaged Victor's wound. "Victor, listen to me. No matter how tired you get, you can't sleep."

Victor, drenched in cold sweat, forced a weak smile. "I... I won't sleep. Zephyr's right—we can't pop the champagne halfway through."

"Who are those people?" Kluge's eyes were bloodshot. "What gives them the right to kill us like that?"

Zephyrion, his face ashen, forced himself to stay calm. "I'll contact Cora right now. They have a healer!"

He pulled out his terminal, but his movements suddenly froze. "No signal."

The random teleportation had only taken them about ten kilometers away. Staying here would be a death sentence—they'd be found soon enough. "We need to find a way out of here," Luke said, hoisting Victor onto his back as the four men supported each other and moved.

Zephyrion clutched the last Tier 4 crystal tightly in his hand.

Three hours had passed since F777 had left the trapped street.

As Onyx had explained earlier. "Take Dorothy, for example. Domain-type Anopowers aren't invincible. If you keep attacking the weak points, you can eventually pinpoint the user's location." With meticulous calculations, he finally deduced the approximate position of the domain-type Aberrant responsible for the Blood Blocks.

They knew that only by killing the master of Blood Blocks could they escape.

Onyx marked an "X," on the map, ruling out one incorrect location. "It's a fifty-fifty chance now, Cora—let's see if your luck holds."

Cora, perched atop the starship, donned her ethereal artifact gauntlets, took a deep breath, and swung her fist towards the distorted boundary—Boom!

The ground trembled as the force of the punch shattered rocks and destabilized the magnetic field, causing the domain to reconfigure. The Blood Blocks reassembled, and F777 was teleported back to a previous location.

Onyx sighed in resignation. "How can you pick wrong in a two-choice scenario?"

Cora protested, "Hey, you were the one who told me to choose!"

However, thanks to Cora's relentless barrage, the domain Aberrant was likely coughing up blood by now, their mental energy severely destabilized.

Onyx marked another "X" on the map. The page was now filled with a dense array of marks, but despite wasting some time because of their bad luck, they were closing in on their target.

In the outskirts of Finyak, in a desolate radiation crater, F777 finally located the master of Blood Blocks. The Aberrant wasn't alone —a row of pitch-black starships was stationed in the distance, with over a hundred Aberrants glaring at them, waiting for their arrival.

Cora noticed that besides the middle-aged man leading the group, there was also a frail-looking young man, his face pale, his collar stained with blood, glaring at them with venomous eyes. He was clearly the unfortunate domain Aberrant.

"It's been a while," the sickly middle-aged man began, his voice weak but filled with recognition. He scrutinized Onyx's face closely, examining every detail of his features. He couldn't help but sigh in amazement. "You look just like him—no, you're identical. No wonder no one's been able to find you all these years."

Yuui and Charles exchanged puzzled looks. What was this old man rambling about? Onyx's expression remained stony as he stared back at the man, saying nothing.

The man coughed twice, his complexion sallow. "What's this? Have you forgotten your manners along with your looks? I came all the way from Utopia, and you can't even greet your dear uncle?"

Cora's eyes widened slightly. This man claimed to be from Utopia, the floating city so many people longed for? Onyx's lips curved into a nonchalant smile as he finally spoke, "Long time no see, Uncle."

So, they were really related? Yuui thought to herself, but this didn't seem like a typical family reunion.

"Since you still recognize me as your uncle, then do what you're supposed to do."

The man's breathing was labored, as if he might collapse at any moment. He lifted his hand with great effort.

One starship opened its rear hatch, revealing a massive piece of equipment prominently displaying the Arashi logo. "This thing has been locked away for thirteen years. Unlock it, and I'll let you go."

"What is that?" Cora whispered to Felix, the mechanical expert. Felix replied, "It's obvious—it's a storage core." Cora gasped in awe, "That big?"

Onyx stared at the familiar core, his smile fading as his expression grew dark and unreadable.

Seeing that Onyx wasn't moving, the man looked up at the sky, his voice trembling with anxiety and excitement as he urged, "Hurry! Do it before they arrive! Unlock the core!"

"Uncle, don't waste your breath," Onyx replied with a mocking smile.

"For someone so afraid of death, you're still alive and kicking, aren't you? I remember you liked philosophy, right? Life is just an illusion, and death is the only reality. So stop believing in those lies— whether it's eventually, death comes to us all. You'd be better off enjoying your retirement in Utopia and staying out of this..."

The man's face twisted with rage as he finally shouted Onyx's name. "Petros Sheen!!"

Petros Sheen. The name fell like a curse, and the entire area fell into silence.

Onyx's heart tightened, and he instinctively glanced at Cora. But to his surprise, she was the calmest of them all. There was no shock on her face, as if she hadn't even heard those forbidden words. Instead, she casually twirled her blade, aiming it threateningly at the domain Aberrant.

Peridot Sheen trembled, his face turning a purplish red, on the verge of collapse. His attendants hurriedly handed him a breathing mask. "You... You... It's been thirteen years, and you've never felt a shred of guilt?!"

"The Plan Eternity has been at a standstill because of you. The entire Northern Yard has isolated itself because of you. Are you really so selfish, so determined to disregard your father's wishes, to watch humanity march towards extinction with your own eyes?!"

"Excuse me, could you move aside?"

Cora's voice interrupted him, cool and steady. Blue light flared in her palm as her blade shot forward. The domain Aberrant, the master of Blood Blocks, recoiled in fear, nearly skewered by the blade, but another Aberrant jumped in, taking the blow for him.

Cora's dimpled smile was innocent yet deadly. "We're in a bit of a hurry to get home."

CHAPTER 22

The Arrest Warrant

Peridot Sheen's fingers trembled as he gripped his breathing mask, taking deep, labored breaths. The hot air fogged his vision, making Cora Thornton's figure blur in and out of focus.

Despite her small, delicate appearance, she didn't resemble the image of a powerful S7-level Aberrant. Cora had slender shoulders, a small face, and large, round, almond-shaped eyes.

Her smooth chin tucked into her collar, making her look like an innocent, naïve girl rather than a ruthless warrior capable of snapping an enemy's neck with ease.

Yet she stood as the biggest obstacle between Petros and Onyx, her fingertips still emanating a sharp, lethal aura from the blade she had just thrown.

Peridot took another deep breath, his tone carrying a hint of regret. "You and your father… both knew how to find good backing."

Onyx's lips curved slightly, as if he didn't catch the underlying sarcasm. "Thank you for the compliment, Uncle. You always had an eye for these things."

Onyx never considered seeking powerful allies, something to be ashamed of—in fact, he saw it as a mark of pride.

Peridot shook his head slowly, his sickly eyes locked onto the familiar face in front of him. "But even with that backing, the result is the same. Your father, even in death—no… not even after death— found no peace."

Onyx's smile faded, his eyes as calm and deep as a glacial lake.

"What time is it?" Peridot no longer looked at him, instead turning to ask softly.

"Seventeen fifty-eight, sir. It'll be dark soon," one of his attendants answered promptly.

Peridot exhaled heavily, raising his eyes to the sky. The night was about to fall, and with it, the radiation levels would continue to rise. After growing accustomed to the clean air of Utopia, the polluted, dust-laden atmosphere of Finyak was becoming increasingly oppressive for him.

"I waited here, hoping to persuade you first. But now… won't be necessary." Peridot sighed, turning back toward his starship. "Do it."

Dozens of figures lunged toward F777 like tigers descending the mountain. Suchat narrowed his eyes, drawing his trident dagger from his belt as he charged alongside Cora.

In the battle's chaos, Cora noticed that the giant storage core was still in its original position, too large to have been stowed in the rear compartment. She stole a quick glance at it.

Their enemies' goal was to force Onyx to unlock the core using his access permissions. They had gone to great lengths, transporting this massive device across great distances. But if they wanted to prevent their enemies from succeeding, there was a simple solution—what if the core were accidentally destroyed?

Cora tightened her abs and tensed her back muscles, suddenly stepping on the head of a pursuing enemy and launching herself high into the air. Her palm gripped her long blade, aiming to bring it down on the core. Through the starship's window, Topaz Sheen, the master of Blood Blocks, locked eyes with Cora, a strange smile tugging at the corners of his lips.

Cora's eyelid twitched slightly, and she whipped her head around.

She had charged too far ahead, creating some distance between herself and Onyx, but turning back would take only three or four seconds.

Yet in that moment, the surrounding scenery shifted violently, as if the fragmented pieces of a puzzle were being rapidly rearranged. The next second, the core vanished, Peridot and his men vanished, and Onyx… was gone too.

It was as if the layers of a Blood Blocks had rotated, moving everyone to different sides while leaving her alone on the back.

Peridot's last command to "do it" hadn't been an order to kill Onyx—it was a directive to Blood Blocks. No wonder the Aberrant who had shielded Petros had been willing to die to protect him.

In the vast, desolate crater, only Cora remained, standing alone with her blade in hand, looking around in confusion. "Little Diamond? Charles? Yuui? Suchat!" She called out her teammates' names one by one, but the empty surroundings offered no response.

"Onyx?"

Cora looked to her left and saw a tilted skyscraper hanging precariously in mid-air, dust and debris trickling down. To her right, the bow of a ship jutted out from the top of a rugged mountain, boulders tumbling down. The disjointed and surreal landscape defied all logic.

Cora pulled out her communicator, opening the F777 group chat, but there was no signal. District C26 Finyak, even District B25 Losome —the entire Loyak region's communications were cut off.

She closed her eyes for a moment, forcing herself to stay calm, before suddenly remembering something. Without hesitation, she unzipped her jacket and yanked it down over her shoulder, revealing a mechanical ladybug embedded in the skin of her left arm. The tiny device's compound eyes rotated slightly.

It was still operational. Cora let out a breath of relief, then reached for the black collar around her neck, found the microphone, and pressed it. "Felix Lucas!" Static, static—the sound of garbled interference filled her ears, followed by a familiar voice.

"Captain?"

"Where are you guys?" Cora asked urgently.

Felix's response was fragmented, but his tone was unusually serious, devoid of his typical flippant attitude. "I can see your location —you're thirty kilometers away from us. Onyx estimates that Blood Blocks have a cooldown time of about ten minutes. The longer you're delayed, the farther you could be teleported. I'll guide you. Get moving and meet us as soon as possible."

"Got it. Hold on—I'm on my way!"

Cora's anxiety fueled her pace as she sprinted in the direction Felix showed. After a few seconds, with Felix urgently shouting "Wrong way! Wrong way!" in her ear, she quickly changed course.

With Dmitri's previous assassination attempt and the communication delays fresh in their minds, Felix had taken precautions. He'd upgraded everyone's communication devices, implanting tracking ladybugs in their bodies.

This new system he had developed used an independent communication band, unaffected by standard terminals, ensuring that F777 could stay in contact even when signals were down.

The scene shifted, and Onyx, along with the rest of his team, were transported to a different location.

A deep spatial rift tore through the surrounding Blood Blocks, and hundreds of black starships emerged from the void.

"What are those?" Yuui's eyes widened in panic. "Who... who did you piss off this time?"

"What's the matter? Scared?" Onyx sneered.

Yuui felt a tightness in her chest but forced herself to respond, "Not really. It's not like I've seen nothing this big before."

Onyx remained eerily calm. "I told you before, you can run whenever you want. But it's not safe right now, so let's hold out until the Captain gets here."

The Alliance's standard starships were all silver white, but Onyx's bangs fluttered in the wind as he quietly observed the dark fleet above them. Those black starships were distinct—they were part of the reclaimed fleet, reallocated as the exclusive property of Utopia, the S-class floating city.

"Why do you always say such downer things? Are you trying to provoke me?" Yuui snapped, jumping up in frustration.

"It's not about being pessimistic." Onyx's gaze darkened. "Just be prepared for the worst. They didn't come empty-handed." As soon as he finished speaking, nearly a hundred Aberrants descended from the sky.

"Prepare for battle," Onyx commanded coldly.

Because of the randomness of the Blood Blocks, Damian found himself at the edge of the battlefield, facing a young man in a white tracksuit with his hands in his pockets. Damian didn't dare underestimate him and immediately unleashed a blizzard, sealing off the young man's escape routes.

Cold-blooded killers don't show mercy to children.

"Oh? Ice-type?" The young man remarked with mild interest before he moved, faster than lightning.

Rocks shattered as cannonball-sized hailstones rained down in a deluge. Damian conjured an ice shield to block the assault, dodging as best he could amidst the deafening impacts. The young man was also an ice-type Aberrant—and an S-class at that. Damian, now facing a formidable opponent, felt his lips go pale from the tension.

A group of A-class Aberrants blocking his path confronted Suchat. Their faces were unfamiliar, but the aura they exuded was unmistakable—the ruthless nature of mercenaries.

The leader, a middle-aged woman, glanced at the black snake tattoo on the back of Suchat's neck and sneered, "You're a deserter? The Rainforest considers you a disgrace."

"I'm not," Suchat replied, his back straightening, every word measured.

"Those who legally leave the Rainforest have their tattoos removed. How dare you claim you're not a deserter?" Another sneered at him.

"It doesn't matter. Consider this a cleanup of traitors. Our mission is to eliminate you." Veins bulged on the back of Suchat's hand as he suddenly swung his blade.

"We meet again," a familiar young man surrounded by the Prism ability greeted.

Felix's gaze fell on the man's Special Operations uniform. After a moment of thought, he finally remembered. "Sorry, I don't recall you. Who are you?"

Roy, who had previously crossed paths with F777 at Deep Wood, fell into silence.

Then, in a stern voice, he said, "I looked at you, Felix Lucas. You're a once-in-a-century genius from the Lucas family of Erya, one of the first successful subjects of the Genetic Optimization Program. Your last recorded assessment was six years ago, when you were S5. What about now?"

"After sitting in prison for so long, I've forgotten. Why don't you take a guess?" Felix responded casually.

The pure black hair on Felix's head receded like a tide, revealing a defiant silver sheen. His tea-colored eyes turned into inorganic, icy pupils. It was as if a withered tree had come back to life, data branches spreading like a canopy behind Felix as a flood of 101010 code surged forward.

Roy, a mere S3, couldn't withstand the assault. The Prism shattered, and blood gushed from his mouth as he collapsed to the ground.

"Korta," Onyx called out calmly as the Aberrants closed in. In unison, F777 moved, each member pulling out a large device resembling a speaker and spreading out.

In sync, the six members quickly stuffed something into their ears and then pressed play.

The strange Cotal frequency was triggered, and the six speakers played it simultaneously. Even S-class Aberrants found it hard to resist. Their consciousnesses began to blur and fade, their movements becoming stiff and zombie-like. Those at the front clutched their heads in pain before staggering and collapsing.

The six surrounded members of F777 caught a moment to catch their breath.

SCREEEEECH! BAM!

The piercing noise abruptly stopped, and smoke billowed from the six speakers as the playback programs were destroyed.

From the distant starship, a figure approached slowly—though it wasn't exactly a "person," but a clear holographic projection. The man had silver hair, icy eyes, and wore frameless glasses.

He appeared to be in his forties, with an air of refinement, though his brows were furrowed in anger. "You wretch, return with me and confess your sins!"

Felix paused, raising his lips in a mocking smile. "Well, well, if it isn't the Patriarch himself."

The newcomer was none other than the governor of District B8 Erya, Cyril Lucas.

Cyril no longer had a physical body. That he could project himself here as a solid hologram meant only one thing. Felix raised his head, looking toward the starship Cyril had emerged from. Inside, he could feel a gaze like a sharp thorn, aimed precisely at him through Lucius's eyes.

"I see you."

A voice seemed to sigh from the depths of his soul. Though gentle, it made Felix's skin crawl.

Damian rolled backward, trying to escape, but not fully succeeding. Pain shot through his ankle like an electric current, and he flopped to the ground. His entire lower leg was encased in layers of frost, and the ice had numbed the initial pain. But when Damian heard the unmistakable crack, he knew his leg was broken.

Like a wounded lion cub, Damian struggled to stand, panting heavily. He didn't scream or cry out, though tears welled in his eyes. He knew this wasn't the time for tears; instead, he glared fiercely at the young man in white.

"Not bad, stronger than I was at your age. Give you ten more years, and you might reach S-class."

"Too bad not all kids get the chance to grow up," the young man in white squatted in front of him, gripping Damian's chin with a cruel smile, his words as venomous as a serpent's hiss. "You're only going to live until today."

Sharp ice spikes formed into a massive guillotine, aimed at Damian's slender neck, ready to fall at any moment.

Suddenly, an ethereal voice rang out, "Thinking of you, every day is filled with sunshine~ Warming my heart with a tender ray of light."

At that critical moment, a golden sun rose over the area, the heat intensifying until the ice guillotine melted away in seconds. The sight of the sun rising in the middle of the night was bizarre enough, but as the light grew more blinding, the young man in white sweat, instinctively raising a hand to shield himself.

Charles rushed in, scooping Damian up and carrying him away.

Damian wrapped his arms around Charles's shoulders, finally letting out a soft sob, "I couldn't beat him… I'm so weak…"

Charles patted Damian's head twice before he found his dislocated leg and, with a crack, reset it instantly.

"Petros… Petros… I'm here… I'm here…" Someone was calling his name.

Across the distance, Onyx locked eyes with a woman—brown hair, green eyes, holding a slowly ticking pocket watch. The moment their gazes met, a ripple seemed to spread across Onyx's pupils, and he found himself unable to look away. A gentle wave of mental energy, like a delicate brush, swept through his mind.

The woman was likely an S-class psychic Aberrant, her ability: Hypnosis. Onyx's eyes remained clear as he smiled at her, his lips curling into a cold smirk. The woman's expression shifted to one of shock and disbelief. Her hypnosis had failed?

In the next moment, Onyx's icy, merciless mental energy struck back, tearing through her mind with ruthless efficiency. Unnoticed by others, the two psychic Aberrants engaged in a deadly duel. The woman's pupils contracted into thin slits, her body stiffened, and she collapsed backward.

The pocket watch slipped from her hand, hitting the ground with a final, ominous tick.

Onyx suppressed the metallic taste of blood rising in his throat, forcing down the urge to cough.

"Sir! Sophia is dead!" A voice echoed through the communication interface on one of the unassuming starships in the fleet.

In response, a shadowy figure waved a hand silently, and a guard dragged away the body of the female hypnotist.

The voice over the communicator continued, "The Key took part in the Genetic Optimization Program. His records back then were marked as 'unsuccessful.' But now, it seems he might be an early-stage Awakener."

"Psychic Aberrants often lack offensive power, but when their abilities are concentrated to a certain degree, they can be lethal." The now-deceased hypnotist Sophia had been an S5-level Aberrant from Utopia.

That the Key was an Aberrant had already taken them by surprise. No one expected that his level might surpass S5.

"Sir, do you need me to intervene..."

The shadowy figure interrupted, "No. If you act, the memory extraction process might fail. I need the information intact. I want to know exactly what the core secret of the Fireseed Project was back then."

"Yes, sir."

"And what about the Sheen family's storage core?" the shadowy figure asked the guard.

"It will arrive in two minutes and fifteen seconds." Blood Blocks required a ten-minute cooldown after each use. When it reactivated, Topaz Sheen would bring the core to the designated location.

Two minutes later, space twisted again as several more starships appeared in the sky. A discreet communication line opened on Peridot Sheen's side.

"Sir, Peridot is making some moves behind the scenes. He wants to contact the Key alone."

The shadowy figure's voice was indifferent. "Let him. Peridot doesn't understand his brother-in-law, nor does he understand his nephew. Even with familial ties, they won't surrender peacefully."

As Blood Blocks reassembled, five S-class Aberrants descended from the sky, charging straight toward Onyx. Their hair and eye colors varied, but they all shared one thing in common—they were all powerful offensive-type Aberrants, ranging from S5 to S6 in level.

In the dim light, half of Onyx's face was shrouded in shadow, a sharp smile playing on his lips.

"You're all international mercenaries, aren't you? Let me guess— you took a job from Utopia? Why get involved in the internal affairs of the New Pacific Alliance? This mission is a thankless task. Be careful, or you might not make it back to claim your reward. Think about it— if it were that easy, why didn't the Alliance take the job themselves? Why leave it to outsiders?"

His words carried an inexplicable allure, leaving those who heard them feeling dazed and uncertain. There was a subtle logic to what he said, even if it seemed twisted.

Onyx focused intently on his surroundings, searching for an opening to escape. His pupils suddenly contracted as he spotted an iron chain hurtling through the air toward him, moving too fast to dodge.

In the nick of time, Yuui applied a speed buff, allowing Onyx to roll out of the way just in time. His shirt was stained with blood and dirt as the vicious chain narrowly missed his ear, looping back around for another strike.

His gold-rimmed glasses fell to the ground and were crushed underfoot in the chaos. Suchat emerged from the shadows, blocking the chain with his blade, but the force sent his nearly six-foot frame flying, rolling dozens of meters before crashing to the ground.

The chain slowly coiled into the shape of a person, revealing a young man in a vulture uniform.

"Don't be fooled; he's just a smooth talker." The boy's eyes were devoid of any emotion, his skin pale, and the badge on his chest was so dark it seemed to have been soaked in blood.

Onyx frowned deeply. He couldn't sense any mental energy from the boy, and a chilling fear crept up his spine.

—This was an S7.

Charles quickly helped Suchat to his feet, applying emergency healing. "Kill the healer," the boy ordered coldly.

The surrounding Aberrants snapped out of their daze and unleashed a barrage of attacks.

Suddenly, Damian rushed forward, summoning an ice wall to block the onslaught. But he was only A1-level, and despite his best efforts, how could he withstand a group of S-class Aberrants? The ice wall shattered in seconds, and both Damian and Charles were sent flying.

The S-class ice in Aberrant's eyes flared with cruelty. "Brat, you're dead."

Whoosh!

A ghostly blue spear suddenly shot through the air, piercing the heart of the white-clad youth, pinning him in mid-air. The force of the blow sent him skidding several meters before the spear drove deep into the earth.

The youth stared down at his chest in shock, gasping for breath, but before he could recover, his life slipped away. He was dead.

The entire battlefield fell silent.

A slender figure appeared at the edge of the Blood Blocks. The two massive spirit artifacts that had been strapped to her back were now missing one. Her jacket was long gone, her skin slick with sweat, and her damp black hair clung to her pale neck. The exhaustion of a long chase was clear in her every movement. It was Cora.

The Blood Blocks moved in a set sequence; Topaz Sheen couldn't possibly align all the pieces in one go. He had already exhausted himself trying to minimize the time, but Cora's speed far exceeded his expectations.

The Aberrants present stared in stunned silence at the S7, who had just arrived, instinctively taking a step back. Cora helped Suchat, Charles, and Damian to their feet, then turned her head to glare at Onyx, almost imperceptibly.

Onyx raised an eyebrow, "You know…"

Cora raised a hand, cutting him off. "Yes."

Onyx paused, then shook his head with a soft laugh. "When did you find out?"

Cora tilted her head slightly. "Oh, um… Felix told me."

The air seemed to freeze as Cora walked leisurely over to the ice Aberrant's corpse, dragging out her ghostly blue spear.

"One, two, three…." she counted quietly, her tone almost casual, but she knew fully that the number of enemies here outmatched the assassination attempt on Dmitri Yevgeniyev.

Blood Blocks reached its refresh time, and another scene reassembled as over a dozen Aberrants jumped down from above. Among them, Szymon sat eagerly inside one starship, his gaze locked on Cora.

With her jacket off, the scar on her abdomen was clearly visible, a gruesome mark, but there was no blood. Szymon's eyes gleamed with a strange light as he muttered to himself, "I see it now. I know what her second ability is."

Szymon had done extensive research on dual-Aberrants, including Punk, who had once worked for him, and the oracle Veronica from Lucian.

Dual-Aberrants typically manifested two types of Anopower: one explicit, one hidden. Because of the magnetic field interaction, the two abilities wouldn't be of the same type. If the explicit ability was offensive, the hidden one would likely to be supportive, controlling, or physical.

Cora couldn't have awakened two powerful offensive abilities. Based on the evidence, her hidden ability was likely a physical-type Body Regeneration, meaning the conventional methods they had prepared wouldn't be enough to kill her!

But Punk had nearly killed her once. Szymon's fingers twitched with excitement.

Another group present at the time had been Azure, whose strict discipline meant they hadn't leaked the secret. This meant Szymon was the only one who knew how to kill Cora.

Szymon's hooked nose twitched as he anxiously tapped his foot inside the starship.

"Sir, should we connect to Mr. Mabul?" his secretary asked softly.

"No, let's wait," Szymon instinctively held off. "Wait for the perfect moment."

As the clock neared 6:15, the sky had fully darkened. A booming synthetic voice echoed through the surrounding loudspeakers:

"By order of the Supreme Prosecutor's Office of the New Pacific Alliance, we issue a warrant for the arrest of Level One fugitive Petros Sheen, male, age 28, biological ID: NOC1100520, from Northern Yard, born September 15th, New Calendar Year 19. You are under arrest."

"Petros Sheen, you illegally fled with the Key thirteen years ago, with irrefutable evidence. Under the law, you are guilty of crimes against humanity, antisocial behavior, and illegal profiteering from state secrets, with egregious circumstances and unprecedented severity. You will be detained and sentenced to 500 years of imprisonment."

The sky was filled with dark starships, and the ground beneath was the desolate, abandoned wasteland of Loyak, far from the mainland, remote and barren. Only seven figures stood within the encirclement, and this would be a battle against overwhelming odds.

Cora's breathing steadied as she wiped the blood from her spear, then she chuckled softly, "Five hundred years? That's a bit much."

She turned around, her clear eyes meeting Onyx's gaze, dimples forming as she smiled slightly. "There's something... I lied about. Sorry."

Onyx lifted his eyes to look at her, his expression deep and handsome, but his voice was hoarse as he found himself at a loss for words with Cora for the first time. "What?"

Cora didn't answer. She turned back, rolling her shoulders and muttering under her breath, "It's your fault. I hardly ever lie, and you've... corrupted me."

A year ago, on the night they returned from the U-Lab.

The two of them, not yet close, sat side by side at the foot of the bed in Cora's apartment, staring out at the hazy night. Onyx had asked her, "If one day, I'm hunted by the entire Alliance, and everyone wants me dead, what would you do?"

"Would you save me?"

"Hmm? Would you?"

Cora had looked him in the eyes and shook her head firmly. "No."

A year later, Cora slowly removed her isolation mask, the mild radiation making her veins burn and her psychic energy surge. The environment here brought back a faint sense of familiarity.

Her eyes glowed blue as she stopped holding back. The terrifying pressure she unleashed exploded outward, majestic and overwhelming, causing the world around her to change. Inside over a hundred starships, instruments went haywire, lights flickered, and the faces of the Aberrants turned pale.

"This is… S8?!"

After a moment, panicked screams echoed through the sky.

CHAPTER 23

An Empty Container

Night had fallen, and the moonlight was dim and eerie. District C26 in Finyak was silent, devoid of any sound. The Boss and His Three Goons sprinted along the border, but no matter how fast they ran, they kept inexplicably being teleported back, unable to escape.

Victor was being carried alternately by Luke and Kluge, while Zephyrion's stiff silhouette flickered in and out of sight ahead.

Even though he had lost his right arm, Victor could still feel the searing pain of the phantom limb. Cold sweat dripped down his face as he forced a comforting smile at his companions. "This reminds me... when the apocalypse first hit, you guys carried me like this, too."

At the start of the apocalypse, Victor had been bedridden with a high fever, and his mother never returned after going out to find medicine. Zombies banged on the door outside his bedroom, and as he prepared to give up hope, his childhood friend Zephyrion broke through the security bars, bringing Luke and Kluge along with him.

All three of them were feverish, but without hesitation, they scooped Victor up and made a run for it. Luke's legs were trembling as he carried him, and Kluge was gripping a rolling pin.

Victor lived in a densely populated old district, and when they looked down from the window, it was packed with zombies. Yet, they supported each other and fought their way out.

After much difficulty, they found a shelter and collapsed on the ground, utterly exhausted and more disheveled than ever. The roars of zombies echoed in their ears, and the feverish Victor groggily thought, "This life is just too damned hard. If I survive this, I'll find a quiet place to sleep."

But the world was cruel, and even such a simple wish was hard to realize. Even though they had awakened their Anopowers, they weren't invincible. A tide of mutants soon overran the shelter them found, forcing Victor to move from place to place. But at least the four of them stuck together.

Kluge gritted his teeth, giving Victor back a pat, his voice hoarse. "Vic, don't you dare fall asleep on us!" They had been fleeing for over half an hour, enduring three scene shifts, and without proper treatment, Victor's breath was growing weaker and weaker.

Victor mumbled a response. "Luke, can I ask you something? When we get to District B, could you let me... share a room with Zeph?"

Luke abruptly lowered his head, his voice choking up. "Sure, Vic. It's yours."

Victor's consciousness was already slipping. District B... After a year of struggling, they had finally earned enough points to go there.

He saw hallucinations, catching glimpses of a campfire that night in Araya, hearing Cora's animated storytelling.

She had said that the sun at the Northern Base was perfect for sunbathing, that the garden apartments were huge and free, and the 3D subway could make you dizzy, so it was best to sit in the back for the first time.

What else had she said? Oh, right... There was an underground entertainment area only for Aberrants, but you had to follow the rules, or else the Aberrants Bureau would lock you up in solitary confinement.

Victor smiled faintly to himself. He will follow the rules. Among The Boss and His Three Goons, he was the most rule-abiding.

They approached the border of Finyak again, but something triggered, and the surroundings reassembled like building blocks, teleporting the four of them to an unfamiliar place.

Zephyrion suddenly halted, cursing under his breath, because standing before them were pursuers clad in Vulture uniforms.

The woman in black, code-named "Bloodbat," narrowed her

slender eyes, wasting no words. Invisible kite strings shot from her hands.

"Remember… to check out District B for me."

No one expected Victor to suddenly slide off Kluge's back and shove the three of them forward. "Go!"

He unleashed all his mental energy, bravely charging toward the enemy. Bloodbat raised her wrist, pulling the kite strings tight. They sliced through his skin and muscles, embedding deeply into his flesh, dismembering his sturdy body piece by piece. The scattered remains fell like a grotesque rain of flesh.

Finally, the kite strings were stained with blood, their paths visible for all to see. Victor's death brought his companions a moment of hope.

Luke and Kluge dodged with difficulty, their eyes red with fury. "Vic!!"

Zephyrion's heart twisted in agony, but he still gritted his teeth and pulled out their last crystal, quickly inserting it into the slot.

With a flash of light, the camping lamp activated. As the three of them were about to escape, Spider's cold eyes glinted as his lips moved, summoning the phantom of a patterned spider that enveloped the camping lamp. From its silk sac, it spewed corrosive mucus, causing a small crack to appear on the surface of the level 4 crystal, the space Anopower wavering slightly.

Kluge's pupils contracted as he slashed the patterned spider to pieces, the phantom screeching as its fangs pierced his nail. The random teleportation took effect, and the three of them vanished on the spot.

Spider reported in a raspy voice, "Two left. Keep pursuing." He didn't even consider Kluge as alive, knowing full well that the boy wouldn't survive the spider's corrosive venom.

Bloodbat retracted her Anopower, her expression indifferent. "The device requires a level 4 crystal to activate. They can't escape many more times." It was just an ordinary B-class team. How many precious level 4 crystals could they possibly have? Eventually, they'd die.

Gasta, who had been watching coldly from the side, glanced at Victor's mutilated body, frowning. The Special Operations Unit had been drafted into this hunt, but Gasta wasn't privy to the full mission details. Still, working with the Vultures filled him with genuine disgust.

These people were cold-blooded, selfish, and ruthless, like rats in the gutter, always despised, especially when compared to the highly revered Azure Force.

The Boss and His Three Goons tumbled into an abandoned radiation pit, quickly scrambling to their feet.

"We're out of crystals," Zephyrion said gravely. "Forget trying to reach the border. There's an Anopower field here. We need to figure out how to break it."

Luke wiped his face and noticed Kluge seemed to space out. "Kluge, what's wrong?"

"Huh? Nothing." Kluge clenched his fist, hiding his hand behind his back when they weren't looking.

After scouting around, Luke and Zephyrion regrouped. "Zeph, there are signs of battle nearby. Looks like F777 was here."

Zephyrion thought for a moment. "The terrain must be shifting randomly. Let's stick to the edges. We might run into them."

Luke nodded. "No time to waste. Let's go."

Just as they were about to find Kluge, he softly called out their names. "Zeph, Luke..."

Kluge's body was half-merged into the shadows, standing still, his face unnaturally pale.

"Kluge, hurry. Let's get out of here," Zephyrion urged.

Kluge forced a smile that was more like a grimace. "I think... like Vic... I won't make it to District B." Zephyrion and Luke's expressions froze. "Don't talk nonsense!"

Kluge slowly stepped forward, revealing his entire body. In the short time that had passed, half of his body had already dissolved into corpse fluid. What had seemed like a minor injury, a small puncture to his nail, had turned into a severe, life-threatening corrosion.

Tears welled up in Kluge's eyes as he smiled at his closest friends. "Well, that settles it. You two won't have to fight over rooms. There's one just for you." He forced his words through labored breaths. "Promise me... you'll survive... no matter what."

The corrosion sped up, and the two of them could only watch in horror as Kluge melted into a puddle of corpse fluid before their eyes.

"No—!!!"

With their companions dying one after another, the overwhelming despair crushed them. Zephyrion screamed in agony, uncontrollably thrashing at the ground with his thorny vines.

Luke's chest heaved as he clung to Zephyrion's shoulders. "Zeph, don't let their sacrifices be in vain..."

Zephyrion clutched the camping lamp, his fingers trembling, remaining silent for a long time. Finally, he muttered, "Let's go."

Cora stood in front of Onyx, facing the onslaught of five S5-S6 level Aberrants all on her own. She bore two massive weapons on her back, standing still like a trapped beast. Yet, the beast's expression was calm, while the hunters were struck with indescribable shock, their bodies trembling.

S8. An S8 assault type.

This would be an unprecedentedly fierce battle. These were foreign mercenaries, fully aware that this woman didn't just represent the New Pacific Alliance; she probably represented the pinnacle of power worldwide.

No one dared to take her lightly. The five launched their most powerful attacks simultaneously, aiming a deadly assault directly at Cora and Onyx. The intersecting Anopower lights were so blinding that they swallowed up Cora's slender figure in an instant.

Five super attacks, a tidal wave of energy so vast that it could flatten anything in its path, powerful enough to obliterate even the strongest defensive Aberrant.

Boom—Boom—!!

The collision of the attacks resulted in an earth-shattering explosion, thick black smoke billowing into the night sky.

"Suc-succeeded!" one hunter blurted out, overjoyed. Had they really just killed the world's first S8 level this easily?

But in the next moment, a ghostly blue light sliced through the rolling smoke, and a massive shield materialized out of thin air. It spun rapidly, absorbing all the damage in an instant. The violent explosion subsided abruptly, the remaining mental energy crackling in the air.

Then, a delicate, beautiful hand extended from the edge of the shield, snapping its fingers. The shield shattered into countless arrowheads, sweeping forward in a deadly wave. The five Aberrants scrambled to retreat, their disbelief clear as they gasped, "Impossible. How can she create matter from nothing?!"

It was common knowledge that gold-type Anopowers were recognized for their strong offensive capabilities. They had seen Aberrants who could conjure weapons, but without exception, they all required a medium.

But Cora was different. It was as if she had surpassed this limitation, mastering her mental energy to where she could manipulate even the surrounding radiation to forge any weapon she desired.

As the smoke cleared, Cora still stood in her original spot. She even had the leisure to dust off Onyx's ashen shirt. "When the fight starts, stay back," she advised.

Onyx's fingers traced the burn marks on her back. His gaze darkened, but he still obediently replied, "I'll listen to you. Be careful."

Cora slowly advanced, rolling her neck and flexing her wrists. "Now it's my turn."

With those words, she drew a long spear with one hand and, as quick as a leopard, pounced on the enemy. With her extreme speed and power, they didn't even have time to react before the sharp tip of the spear had already pierced through one enemy's throat, sending blood spraying.

"One down," Cora counted.

A yellow earth circle rose beneath her feet, locking her arms in place, rendering her unable to move. Cora pivoted on her toes, taking a swift step forward, her core erupting with power.

She drove her knee up into the opponent's chin! "Crack" — the crisp sound of breaking bones rang out as teeth mixed with half a tongue fell to the ground, leaving the lower half of the man's face a bloody mess.

Even with her arms bound, Cora's movements weren't hindered. She spun on her heel, executing a swallow turn and launching into a high-flying back kick! The third target was sent flying, and as he was midair, a gleaming wolf's tooth blade appeared on the edge of her foot, slashing down mercilessly!

The blade sliced through his spine from below, sending flesh and organs splattering into the air before raining down in a gruesome drizzle. Amidst the misty blood, Cora's expression was stony, her face as fearsome as a demon's.

"Second," she counted again.

Her feet didn't stop, and neither did her hands. She gripped a ghostly blue blade between her fingers, slicing it back and forth, carving out a small opening with sheer force. With her hand now free, she drew her icy saw blade, slashing it in reverse!

The blade's icy glow flickered, and under her overwhelming power, the solid earth circle crumbled into pieces. The earth-type Aberrant coughed up blood, and with a swift motion, Cora decapitated him.

"Third."

The desperate hunter turned the surrounding area into a quagmire, but Cora swept her leg through the mud, splashing it to obscure their vision. She caught hold of the long spear that had fallen earlier, kicking it up with her foot, and grabbed one man by the collar, forcing his head down into the muck. With a sharp thrust, the spear pierced through his chest.

"Fourth."

The Aberrant with the shattered jaw tried to flee, but his mind suddenly blurred. Onyx, with an unflinching expression, plunged a knife into his skull. Blood soaked through his pale shirt, and his handsome face took on a cold, ruthless edge.

"Fifth," Onyx echoed Cora's count.

Cora flicked the mud off her boots, her eyes curving into a smile as she looked at him, as if to say, "You're dirty too." Corpses littered the ground, blood flowing like rivers. The five elite Aberrants lay dead on the spot. The roles had been reversed — who was the hunter, and who was the prey?

Just as a faint smile formed on Cora's lips, her expression froze.

A deadly chain whip shot down from above, its killing intent so tangible it felt solid. Cora shifted her body to dodge, but the chain quickly doubled back, flying towards Onyx. The heavy mud slowed his movements, and without hesitation, Cora leaped out, knocking Onyx to the ground. The barbs on the chain whip grazed her left shoulder, tearing off a layer of skin and flesh.

A young S7-level Vulture soldier materialized on the spot, his emotionless eyes fixed on Cora as he spoke in a flawless Alliance Standard. "You have a weakness. Those with weaknesses will lose."

Blood from Cora's shoulder dripped onto Onyx's jade-like face. She smiled at him reassuringly, wiping it away with her sleeve. Then she rolled over and got to her feet. "I won't lose."

High above, in the fleet of starships, a hastily convened command meeting was in full swing.

"From what we can see, Cora is fiercely protective of the key, making it nearly impossible to interrogate her," one voice noted. "How long has it been since she registered as S7? How could she ascend so quickly?" another asked, baffled.

"Could it be that Rainer Ninnemann's research has made a breakthrough?" someone muttered.

The advancement of an S-level Aberrant wasn't just about accumulating power; it also required a great deal of luck. On average, it took three to five years to progress through each level from S1 to S5. For S6 and above, who knew how long it could take?

Cora wasn't a newly awakened Aberrant. Even if she started at S7, who else had ever gone from S7 to S8 in just a single year?

The shadowy figure known as "Mr. Mabul" gazed through the screen, his eyes fixed on the ever-changing Ethereal Artifact in Cora's hand. "We can't allow her to manifest at will. Has 'Chain' restrained her yet? Is 'Flame' on the way?"

"They're en route, expected to arrive in seventeen minutes and thirty-one seconds."

Seventeen minutes and thirty-one seconds—just about the time needed for the "Blood Blocks" to reset twice.

Boom—Boom—!!

Blood splatters continued to erupt from the bodies on the ground, and the sharp angles of the surroundings softened, becoming more rounded. Onyx's expression was grave. As long as the "Blood Blocks" persisted, everything happening here would remain hidden. They had to break free.

The boy known as "Chain" stared at Cora with a dark, twisted smile. "You won't lose? Is that so? But your teammates already have." Cora's head snapped around.

Sure enough, the situation wasn't looking good for Yuui and the others. Damian and Charles were huddled together, trembling like rabbits surrounded by wolves.

A group of ferocious Aberrants was closing in, with Felix fending them off with his mechanical arm, while Onyx used his mental energy to save them in time.

The boy said nothing more than he transformed back into a weapon, shadowing Cora's every move, forcing her to both defend herself and save her comrades simultaneously.

Cora flashed over to Damian's side, slashing horizontally to push back the enemy. In a moment of distraction, a blackened point pierced through her right forearm. Ignoring the pain, she steadily wielded her icy saw blade, severing the chain with a thunderous crash. Both she and her opponent staggered back.

Cora glanced down at Damian's arm, now covered in gashes and dripping with blood. "Does it hurt?" she asked softly. "No!" Damian answered firmly. "Can you still walk?"

Damian's calf had just been dislocated by an ice-type attack. Though Charles had set it back in place, he couldn't put weight on it without pain. "Sis, I'll be fine!" Damian shouted. He knew how dire the situation was and, being sensible, tried to comfort Cora instead.

Cora patted his fluffy head, then looked up at Charles, whose face was pale from overusing his Anopower. "You're injured. Let me heal you," Charles said quickly. "No, save your energy," Cora replied, pushing his hand away.

The minor wounds on her back had already healed. She set both of them down beside Onyx and Felix, then turned to support Yuui.

At that moment, Yuui was struggling to hold her ground. She was filled with anger and shock—her opponent was a sound-type Aberrant specifically designed to counter her. Her Anopower relied on lyrics, but as soon as she sang two words, the other Aberrant let out an ear-piercing wail, forcing her lips shut, leaving her to writhe in silence.

Without her support, Suchat was barely holding on, fighting both an A-level and an S-level Aberrant on his own, his body covered in wounds. Charles didn't have time to heal him.

Cora descended from above, kicking the strongest S-level Aberrant flying. As she landed, she shoved the face of the middle-aged woman attacking Suchat into the ground, snapping her neck with a twist. With a backward sweep of her hand, she conjured thousands of plum blossom shurikens that instantly riddled the enemy with holes.

"(1215,675,988), (771,1008,321)." Onyx's voice suddenly came through her earpiece, reporting two coordinates.

These were the points he had calculated to be the linked cores of the "Blood Blocks." If one of these coordinates moved, the next would inevitably be the other. If they wanted to escape, they had to time it perfectly and step onto the edge of the other block right after it moved, triggering an instant teleportation.

Cora met Onyx's gaze. He said nothing more beyond the coordinates, but in that instant, she understood his intent.

Perhaps Onyx had already sensed something amiss on this mission, which was why he had repeatedly reminded his teammates, "If there's danger, you can run." No matter how dire the situation, he would create an opportunity.

Standing at just the right distance, Cora nodded firmly at him. Onyx's eyes softened, and he gave her a beautiful smile.

Crash! The ruins beneath her feet collapsed as Cora shielded Suchat from a fatal blow, though the chain grazed her thigh, tearing off a sizeable chunk of flesh.

"Captain!" "Cora—!!" "Cora?!"

Three distinct cries of alarm rang out simultaneously.

Click. The "Blood Blocks" reassembled.

Cora followed the third voice, locking eyes with Zephyrion Stormrider and Luke Shaw. In a flash of realization, she understood their predicament. Zephyrion seized the truth—they had been targeted as "witnesses" to F777, and now they were being silenced.

Cora also understood that once a field-type Anopower was activated, it would create an isolated space. "The Boss and His Three Goons" hadn't been able to escape in time and were now caught up in this because of them.

Suddenly, something clicked in her mind, and she looked at Zephyrion once more.

Zephyrion was clutching the camping lamp tightly, his body covered in slashes, with pursuers still faintly visible behind him. He had been silently screaming for help, but upon seeing the scene before him, he fell silent, despair etched in his eyes. No one could save them;

F777's situation wasn't any better. In fact, it might have been worse.

In less than a fraction of a second, Cora decided. She raised her hand and manifested a massive fan, sweeping it hard to stir up a cloud of dust, further obscuring the already chaotic view.

Cora grabbed Yuui's hand, speaking quickly, "At the next teleport, go to the coordinate points and get out of here."

"Cora? You too?" Yuui's cheeks flushed with anger. "No, I won't go. What is this? This...this is betrayal."

With Suchat's talent for concealment, blending into the environment wouldn't be a problem. He could keep Yuui safe for a while, and as soon as the master of the "Blood Blocks" was killed, they could escape from Finyak and make it out alive.

Cora looked at her calmly and shook her head seriously. "What happened at Mirror Lake has been repaid. You don't owe me anything." "We're teammates," Yuui said, her voice choking up.

Tears welled up in Yuui's eyes, blurring her vision. Cora had always known, even after all this time, that Yuui's heart had been troubled. "I can't protect everyone."

"Listen to the captain. Go first," Cora smiled at Yuui, just as she had when they first met the beautiful sister. "Send word."

Suchat tried to say something, but Cora pushed him towards Yuui. "Wait for me on the outside."

Watching the two of them run towards the coordinates, Cora then turned to find Felix. "Felix..."

"I'm not leaving," Felix interrupted her. "I have something I must do. Don't stop me."

His eyes were impossibly calm, but there was an undercurrent of extreme determination.

As the dust settled, the relentless barrage of attacks continued. Cora Thornton knew she couldn't hold out much longer. She grabbed Charles Franz and Damian by their wrists, and before they could react, she lifted them by the collars and threw them.

Thud—

Zephyrion and Luke barely had time to react as two bodies were suddenly tossed into their arms. They caught them instinctively.

Bloodbat and Spider were closing in for the kill, but Cora didn't waste a moment. With a burst of muscle, she sent her icy saw blade whirling through the air, cutting down everything in its path. Against her overpowering Anopower, the kite strings and corrosive spiders crumbled to dust.

Cora rummaged through her spatial pocket and pulled out a large burlap sack, tossing it to Zephyrion. "Take them and get out of here." The red glow nearly penetrated the surface of the sack. Zephyrion was stunned—there were over two hundred Level 4 crystals inside.

He remembered how Cora had stubbornly guarded her stash, yelling about how expensive they were and how she couldn't bear to use even one.

The notoriously stingy captain had just handed over her entire savings without hesitation to ensure her teammates' escape. "Go now... I'll take down the field-type Aberrant," Cora said, her voice firm as she looked Zephyrion in the eye.

Zephyrion nodded, choking back tears. "Alright."

Damian struggled, tears and snot streaming down his face. "No! I don't want to go! I want to stay with you, Sis!" he cried out.

"Damian, be good," Cora smiled gently. "Your sister is strong. Wait for me outside, okay?"

"No... I don't want to...," the child kept pleading, thrashing in Luke's grip.

Zephyrion quickly slotted a crystal into the mechanism, triggering the random teleportation. In an instant, the four of them vanished from the spot.

Click. The "Blood Blocks" shifted again. Onyx's calculations were spot on. Suchat and Yuui, who had been standing at the edge, were successfully teleported away.

Two unfamiliar starships appeared, their hatches opening to reveal an endless sea of S-level Aberrants, all eyes fixed intently on the scene below. The earlier assault had been merely a probe; now, with the last piece in place, the entire hunting party revealed its full strength.

Onyx's heart sank further and further. The sheer number... Had they brought the entire S-level force from Utopia here?

From the starships circling above, cold orders were issued one after another. "Prepare for a full assault. Prioritize the elimination of the S8-level target."

"Six have escaped. Vulture, proceed with cleanup. No witnesses."
"Mr. Mabul, 'Flame' has arrived."

The chaotic battlefield now held only three figures: one S8 and two S6s.

Cora's exposed skin was covered in terrible wounds, crisscrossing over her body, with only her left leg unscathed. The rescue had drained her of too much mental energy. She reached into her pocket, feeling the contents within, and lifted her gaze.

Her instincts told her that this was the second S7-level opponent.

A strikingly beautiful woman sat at the open hatch of one starship. She appeared to be in her twenties, dressed in a Vulture uniform, with a flame totem etched onto her forehead. Her eyes were locked onto Cora through the crowd. Among the enemies, she was the highest-ranking Aberrant.

The Aberrant code-named "Flame" parted her red lips, beginning a chant for the peace of the dead.

Before this mission, they had thoroughly studied the detailed report of the assassination attempt on General Yevgeniyev. Back then, Cora had taken on hundreds while still at S7, so a simple swarm attack wouldn't work against her—unless... they could cut off her Anopower.

But to continuously suppress an S8's Anopower, her mental energy alone wasn't enough. As Flame chanted, a steady stream of red crystals was delivered into her hands, fueling her energy.

Cora faced her head-on.

Flame's Anopower was deceptively simple—it was "fire." She didn't even have any offensive capabilities, just support, yet she had reached S7 with the most basic of fire powers, a feat that demanded respect.

Boom—

A sky-scorching blaze engulfed Cora. Jennifer's flames paled in comparison. This was a fire that burned at the very core of the soul, a malevolent blaze capable of incinerating the source of the magnetic field. When it roared to life, it consumed everything.

Cora's hands blistered as she quickly realized her Ethereal Artifact couldn't take shape. Worse still, as the surrounding air was incinerated, it created a vacuum-like field to cut off the radiation. For a moment, Cora couldn't even sense her own mental energy.

When an Anopower was refined to its utmost, it could even briefly suppress an S8. In terms of raw power, Flame was no match for Cora, but her role was simply to constrain, preventing Cora from using her Anopower.

Without her formidable Ethereal Artifacts and overwhelming mental energy, even someone as strong as Cora was just an ordinary person with bare hands.

Cora's hesitation lasted only a second, but it was enough. Hundreds of S-level Aberrants swarmed towards her like wolves. She shattered a few with a punch, but without her weapons, she gradually lost ground.

The boy known as "Chain" pierced Felix's wheelchair, causing the dense wall of code to vanish as Felix tumbled to the ground. The sickly young man, now without legs, couldn't stand on his own and could only crawl.

It was like a scene from a slow-motion movie. Cora fell to the ground, and the crack of every rib breaking was painfully clear. A foot pressed down on her head, grinding it into the dirt, and a sharp chain pierced through her scapula.

It was the Chain boy. His shape-shifting Anopower allowed him to transform any part of his body, and he coldly remarked, "You've lost."

Just as the chain was about to pierce through Cora, a long, slender hand grabbed it midway, stopping it in its tracks. Blood ran down the chain, the scorching liquid dripping onto Cora's eyelashes, tinting her vision red.

It was Onyx.

He kneeled before Cora on one knee, pressing down on her punctured wound, and said each word with deliberate precision. "Stop."

Onyx looked up towards the starships in the sky, his voice calm. "I can activate the central core, but first, let her go."

The moment he said this, everyone aboard the starships straightened in their seats, eyes gleaming with anticipation. The Chain boy received his orders and reluctantly retracted his chain.

The central core, emblazoned with the Arashi Research logo,

quickly appeared, coming to a smooth stop in front of them.

Onyx pulled a new wheelchair from his spatial pocket, gently helping Felix Lucas back into it.

Then he returned to the battered Cora, gently wrapping her in an embrace, whispering softly in her ear like a lover.

"Cora, three o'clock, third ship from the right, that's the master of the 'Blood Blocks.' I'll hold off Flame. You have thirty seconds—kill him."

Cora nodded silently. Onyx cupped her face, pressing a tender kiss to her forehead before standing and striding confidently toward the central core.

"My father, the father of Alliance genetic engineering, Jasper Montclair, sealed his life's work and research within this core," Onyx said, his fingers tapping lightly on the outer shell, his voice carrying across the entire clearing. "The secrets of 'Plan Eternity,' the means to achieve eternal life, powerful Anopowers, and unclouded sanity — everything you want."

" —It's all in here."

Onyx had just publicly revealed the central core's secrets to everyone present.

The Aberrants on the field were visibly shaken. Many of them hadn't known the true purpose of this mission, and now that the secret was out, their eyes were filled with greed, watching his every move with intense focus.

Meanwhile, Cora and Felix, now at the back, were all but forgotten.

Onyx calmly scanned his iris, fingerprint, and input the access codes.

The massive central core, dormant for thirteen years, successfully rebooted under his command. Two lines of text appeared: "Identification Successful" and "ROOT."

A soft white light illuminated the area as soothing startup music played, and the central core's primary interface opened. Some Aberrants could no longer contain themselves, rising to their feet, hearts pounding. The secret to eternal life! Many had their own agendas, eager to catch even a glimpse of the coveted data.

Peridot's voice trembled with excitement. "Quick, connect and copy everything!"

Even "Mr. Mabul" could no longer maintain his composure, his voice stern as he ordered, "Sync with the primary interface immediately."

Artificial intelligence rapidly processed, reading the relevant data.

Cora pulled something from her pocket, biting open a syringe and injecting herself in the neck. This was a miraculous drug developed by an A5-level healing-type Aberrant, capable of temporarily restoring full combat ability even to the disabled.

As the loading page ended, an overwhelming silence fell over the entire area. "How... how is this possible?!" Peridot's hoarse scream shattered the night.

There was nothing in the central core Jasper had left behind. It was completely empty.

"Was it deleted? It can be recovered; it has to be!" amid the frantic background noise, Flame suddenly clutched her head in agony, losing her balance and plummeting to the ground.

At that very moment, a swift figure leaped high into the air.

Cora launched herself toward the third starship on the right, her hands forming a massive hammer that shattered the hull's window with terrifying force.

Thud—! Topaz Sheen stared into a pair of cold, merciless eyes.

CHAPTER 24

The Key

Do you believe it? There are moments when a person can accurately foresee their own death. Topaz Sheen was facing such a hyper-sensory moment.

His terrified face stretched inch by inch, like a slow-motion replay frozen in time. He saw with perfect clarity as Cora swung a mighty hammer, striking the outer hull of the starship.

The material, touted as "the most durable composite in Utopia," crumbled on impact, with debris and fragments scattering into the air.

Blood-soaked fingers clawed at the window, and an overwhelming force of mental energy surged through. Cora's arms and shoulder muscles were strained to their limit.

With both hands, she pulled apart the metal with a force exceeding several hundred tons. The hull groaned in despair as a gash was torn open.

Screams and cries of terror filled the air, but Topaz Sheen heard nothing. His eyes were fixated on Cora descending from the sky like a demon emerging from the depths of hell.

If "Flame" was the key to restraining Cora's powers, then "Blood Blocks" were at the core of this entire ambush.

Hundreds of starships, an orderly armed fleet, and Aberrants of all kinds—each one a block in Topaz Sheen's hand, to be placed wherever he desired. He was the master of the domain, the supreme hunter, secretly manipulating everything within.

The slaughter that would take place tonight would go unnoticed. When the sun rose tomorrow, the New Pacific Alliance would remain peaceful.

But alas, it all ended at this very moment.

"Stop her! Don't let her through!"

"Hurry, protect the Master, protect Lord Topaz Sheen!"

The surrounding Aberrants rushed forward with all they had to block her. In the confined space, all kinds of attacks collided violently.

Cora's wounds multiplied—her back was pierced, her side was burned, and her abdomen was a gruesome, hollowed-out cavity. Yet she seemed to feel no pain, charging forward with only one target in her eyes: the master of "Blood Blocks."

In his final conscious moment, Topaz Sheen locked eyes with Cora and understood the unspoken verdict in her gaze: You are dead.

Then an icy blade pierced his heart. In the next instant, a ghostly-blue knuckle duster smashed his face, severing his head from his body.

Thud! Thud! His head was pulverized, like a ruined block, beyond repair.

Cora's momentum didn't falter. In the swaying starship, she slid toward Peridot Sheen, who was under heavy protection.

Blood dripped steadily from her fingertips, quickly pooling into a small puddle at her feet. The chilling knuckle duster hovered in front of Peridot Sheen's face, his breath caught in his throat, his face pale. The heart rate monitor connected to him spiked beyond its limits, emitting a piercing alarm.

"I will not kill you," Cora glanced at the blank screen from the central control, casually shaking her hand. "You're about to die, anyway."

Killing Peridot now would be too merciful. Charles had already determined he wouldn't survive for long. Since the central control didn't have what she wanted, Peridot Sheen would die in agony, watching his life slip away in despair.

Cora stood up, her wounds healing at an astonishing speed, visible to the naked eye. Blood vessels reconnected, muscles regenerated, scars faded, and even the sunken abdomen gradually returned to normal. She went from near death to look no different from a healthy person.

With the combination of her second ability and high-efficiency closure, her physical recovery was now far beyond the realm of common understanding.

Cora took a few steps back, opened her arms, and like a feather, her entire body fell out of the cabin. Just before she left, she kicked the starship with all her might, sending it into an uncontrollable dive. With a loud crash, smoke and flames erupted.

With its master dead, "Blood Blocks" collapsed.

The world spun before their eyes, and the starship fleet in the sky lost its formation. Some even warped to other locations. The fractured scene restored itself, revealing the correct setting—they were at the border between Losome and Finyak, with the sea connecting the north and south of the Alliance not far behind them.

Cora landed swiftly, stumbling a few steps backward. A pair of slender hands caught her firmly by the back. She turned around and met Onyx's deep gaze, smiling with curved lashes. "It's empty!"

"Yes, it is empty," Onyx nodded.

"Where did you hide it?" Cora asked, curious.

"I didn't hide it," Onyx grasped her hand, slowly pressing it against his cool forehead. "It's been here all along."

Cora hesitated, unsure why this answer filled her with a sense of unease. The wheelchair slid across the ground as Felix spoke hoarsely, "Bad news. The domain is broken, but the signal hasn't returned."

Topaz Sheen wasn't the only one capable of blocking communications. Felix looked up at Cyril Lucas, his icy blue eyes flickering slightly. After all, there was still a puppet on the scene, controlled by the super artificial intelligence.

Within the starship fleet, the command channel fell silent.

The central control left by Jasper Montclair was empty, rendering the key meaningless.

Had the Alliance's years of effort truly been for nothing? Could all their achievements have been buried in history?

No, it was impossible. Jasper was so obsessed with Plan Eternity; how could he have destroyed his life's work with his own hands?

Moments later, everyone snapped back to reality, their conversations growing louder.

"There must be backups of the data; otherwise, how did the research on Rainer Ninnemann's organ regeneration proceed?"

"Exactly. Jasper must have left something behind. That kid must know!"

"We need to get the key to talk. Maybe the central control was moved..."

"Tough luck. He's a mental-type Aberrant, and even Sophia failed."

Key... central control... mental Aberrant...

The tangled clues gradually connected. An academician from Luboni furrowed his brow in deep thought, then suddenly looked up and exclaimed, "I've got it! There is no central control. From start to finish, Jasper Montclair has been using an illusion to hide the truth!"

"The key is the central control!"

"What do you mean?"

The academician's chest heaved as he struggled to calm his excitement with deep breaths. "The key... Petros Sheen was once a renowned child prodigy in Luboni. In less than a year of entering school, he had read all the books in the library."

Luboni, the cultural hub of the Alliance, housed countless ancient paper books and digital publications. Most people wouldn't be able to finish reading them even if they spent their entire lives without eating or sleeping, but Petros Sheen devoured them all in just ten months. You could pick any book, open it to any page, and he would answer questions without hesitation.

That year, the arrogant young man with a tear mole at the corner of his eye stunned the entire District A4 with his unparalleled memory and report card, which was a masterpiece.

The academician murmured to himself, "After Petros Sheen left school, he followed his father into the Arashi Research Institute. Jasper Montclair must have been well aware of his son's abilities. Why go through the trouble of storing the data in a machine...?"

"The key isn't a key; it's the actual central control."

"N-no way..." someone hesitated to question.

Vast amounts of research data, top-secret reports—making even the slightest mistake, like a misplaced decimal point or an insignificant letter, could lead to catastrophic losses. Even the central control had a storage limit.

How could a human brain possibly surpass a computer?

The academician refuted with conviction, "Why not? Don't forget, Petros Sheen took part in the Gene Selector Program. What if he hid his identity as a newly awakened Aberrant? What if he already had an Anopower back then?"

"But... what exactly is his Anopower?"

The Alliance's database had no records of Petros Sheen's awakening—no information on his level, category, or specific type. Everyone knew nothing about his abilities, only just confirming that he was an S6-level mental Aberrant.

If telekinesis weren't Petros Sheen's Anopower, just a manifestation of his highly refined mental strength, then what was his true power?

"Perfect recall?" An answer seemed to be on the tip of someone's tongue.

"No, it's 'omniscience and omnipotence.'"

Suddenly, Mr. Mabul, who had remained silent until now, muttered.

The attendees were stunned.

"Perfect recall isn't frightening in itself, but Petros Sheen is too special. He was born into the Sheen family of North Yard, with access to the highest levels of resources and privileges. With his extraordinary intelligence and mastery of multiple disciplines, he could effortlessly integrate and use all the knowledge he gained, even restarting Plan Eternity from any point, regardless of his lack of prior exposure."

Mr. Mabul sighed deeply, swallowing the rest of his words. Petros Sheen was the "seed" Jasper Montclair left behind. He held the key to humanity's survival.

"I need to speak with him alone."

After the collapse of the "Blood Blocks" domain, the attacks from the opposing side abruptly ceased. The Aberrants surrounding Cora and her two companions withdrew, clearing a space.

A drone descended from the sky, carrying an encrypted communicator that hovered in front of Onyx. His expression remained unchanged as he reached out to take it.

"Petros Sheen," a deep, authoritative voice resonated.

Cora keenly noticed that Onyx's gaze grew icy cold upon hearing the speaker.

"Noach Mabul? So it's you. Should I address you as 'Commander Mabul'? Oh, I almost forgot, you've already stepped down from that position, haven't you?" Onyx's tone was casual, but his words carried an unmistakable sharpness.

Noach Mabul, the former head of the Central Council and one of the most powerful figures in the New Pacific Alliance, had once been a staunch advocate for the reactivation of Plan Eternity. He had stepped down from his positions because of old age and had since become a citizen of the Elder Nation.

Onyx remembered Mabul was only a few years younger than General Yevgeniyeva. However, unlike the war-scarred General, who was tormented by ailments, Noach Mabul had always enjoyed a life of luxury and maintained good health during his time in office.

Mabul ignored Onyx's sarcastic remark, responding calmly, "The data Jasper left behind is in your head, isn't it?"

Onyx remained silent. He had expected that the central control secret would eventually be exposed—it was only a matter of time.

"I can let you all go."

To Onyx's surprise, Mabul shifted his tone, casually offering an olive branch: "You and your friends—I won't hold you responsible."

Cora exchanged a bewildered glance with Felix, tapping her temple in disbelief: Is this guy crazy? First, he attacks us, and now he's letting us go? Felix nodded in agreement.

Onyx chuckled softly. "Oh? And what's your condition?"

Negotiating with a smart person was straightforward, and Mabul didn't beat around the bush. He got straight to the point. "Plan Eternity has been at a standstill for years. Even with the data, success won't come quickly."

"You've been retired for so many years, yet you're still just as 'concerned' about the project," Onyx retorted sarcastically.

"I only want one thing." Mabul remained unmoved.

"LAK0017."

Onyx's pupils contracted slightly.

"I know that before Plan Eternity, Jasper Montclair had already gained a perfect test subject: LAK0017. I want its entire genetic sequence, the detailed logs of the fusion process, and..." Mabul's voice lowered, a subtle greed creeping in, "its current whereabouts."

Onyx replied without a trace of emotion, "Fifteen years ago, during the Loyak incident, all test subjects of the Fire Seed Project were destroyed. That's the Alliance's official statement. If your memory is failing you because of old age, I can kindly remind you."

Mabul shook his head and laughed softly, "Young man, you can't fool me. A successful Fire Seed won't die. As you said, eternal life, extraordinary abilities, clear rationality—a mere nuclear explosion couldn't have destroyed it."

Onyx looked up at the sky, "Your target was LAK0017 from the very beginning. Do your followers know this?"

Mabul pressed on. "Whether they know doesn't matter. What matters is that you know where it is, don't you?"

"No, I don't," Onyx replied firmly.

Mabul was silent for a moment. "Aren't you curious about where I got my information?"

"Your father was a great scientist, highly respected and revered. Getting him to talk voluntarily would have been nearly impossible, both legally and morally. But fortunately, he died. And it's much less burdensome to deal with the dead."

"Even after Jasper's brain death, his consciousness remained active and full. It took Arron thirteen uses of 'Knowledge Extraction' to get what I wanted."

Onyx, who was usually calm and smiling, now showed no expression at all. His eyes were like deep pools, unfathomable. The veins on the back of his hand bulged and trembled uncontrollably. Cora's heart clenched, and she gripped his hands tightly.

Mabul had a mysterious Aberrant by his side, S3-level Arron, whose ability, though not high in rank, was highly unique: "Knowledge Extraction."

Arron could forcibly extract knowledge from both the living and the dead, leaving the victim disoriented and in extreme pain. Repeated use would reduce even the doomst intelligent to a state of idiocy.

Jasper Montclair had been the greatest scientist of the Alliance. He had dedicated his life to his work, and even after death, he had suffered such humiliation. If even an ordinary person couldn't tolerate this, how could Onyx?

Mabul's threat was barely a whisper. "If you refuse, I'll have to kill you. As an S-class Aberrant, the information I could extract from you would be far more valuable than what I got from your father. But that's the worst-case scenario. If you follow in your father's footsteps, it will be a tremendous loss for the Alliance."

Onyx's eyebrows lifted slightly. "Noach Mabul, you're dying, aren't you?" The communicator fell silent.

"Even Peridot Sheen could stand in front of me and speak, but you can only threaten me with your voice. It seems you're in worse shape than him. Don't worry, after you die, I'll set off fireworks in celebration. As for LAK0017, forget it. You'll never get it."

"Petros Sheen—!!" Mabul roared in fury.

Onyx crushed the communicator in his hand.

Inside the starship, Noach Mabul was seething with rage. He coldly issued his command:

"Kill the key."

"Give his body to Arron. No, even pieces will do—we'll get what we need."

"What about... Cora Thornton?" someone stammered.

They had all seen Topaz Sheen's last moments on the screen. That kind of severe injury healing so quickly was inhuman. No matter how many people they had, they stood no chance against this lethal force.

As Mabul contemplated, a light suddenly blinked on the command channel. "Mr. Mabul, Lord Szymon is requesting to join the communication. He says... he has a way to kill an S8."

Onyx's gaze darkened as he looked at Cora. "I'm sorry. This is one of the few negotiations I've failed."

"It's okay," Cora nodded understandingly, wrapping her arms around him in a hug. "As long as I'm here, don't worry about that 007. You don't need to tell them."

Onyx looked down at her, slowly returning the hug. "Alright, I won't tell them."

Felix's mechanical arm extended between the two, coldly interrupting their tender moment. "Wake up and look ahead." In front of them, the armed fleet had raised a wall of black cannons, and the retreating pursuers were regrouping.

Onyx glanced sideways, "Hey, useless, don't tell me you didn't prepare any escape route at this point."

Felix rolled his eyes dramatically. "Of course I did. Maybe you should worry more about yourself."

CHAPTER 25

Don't Say It

"The domain has been broken."

Suchat hid in the darkness, cautiously observing his surroundings. The somber shadow of his pursed lips deepened as he realized the severity of their situation.

He heard a faint noise from above and, with sharp eyes, quickly grabbed Yuui by the wrist, pulling her into an abandoned building. The dark mass of the armed fleet flew overhead, all moving in the same direction.

Suchat activated his terminal, attempting to communicate with the outside world, but the signal was still jammed.

His heart sank further as he realized the person behind him had been unusually quiet the entire time. Turning back, he saw that Yuui's eyes were downcast, her expression unreadable.

"What's wrong?"

"I was just thinking, I don't really have any friends."

Suchat looked at her quietly. When Yuui spoke, he was always a good listener.

"I sing well, and I've been a successful star with many fans who say they love me, but they're all so far away." Yuui murmured softly.

"After Yuki was hurt, I became selfish, always putting myself first. I know I have an unpleasant personality, so for a long time, I believed I wouldn't have friends, lovers, or family—no lasting close relationships."

This confident, radiant superstar now looked utterly forlorn. Suchat opened his mouth, unsure of how to comfort her, cursing his own inability to find the right words.

After a moment of silence, Yuui took out a translucent white crystal, only a level 1—something no one in F777 would even glance at. But Suchat immediately realized it might be the crystal they had taken from Cora during the Throne Tournament, a small relic that Yuui had kept with her all this time.

"Cora said we were teammates. But teammates are supposed to be even closer than friends—they're people you trust with your life."

Yuui slowly clenched the crystal in her palm. "Back at Mirror Lake, I could make excuses for myself because I was trying to save Yuki. But what about now? If I run away now, I'll never forgive myself."

Her voice choked as she sniffled. "She lied to me. She can't escape. Onyx is Petros Sheen, the Petros Sheen that the entire Alliance is hunting. They won't get away."

Tears streamed down Yuui's face in silent agony, her quiet sobs cutting like a knife to the heart.

Suchat felt a wave of emotion he couldn't quite name wash over him. Slowly, he raised his hand and clumsily wiped away her tears with his rough fingertips. The dampness seeped through his black gloves, penetrating deep into his skin, where it tangled and clung.

"Let's go back," Suchat sighed.

Yuui lifted her gaze, her face wet and her throat tight with emotion. Suchat looked at her intently, his young face resolute and calm. "I'll go back with you."

"You don't have to come with me. Do you realize what was going back means?" Yuui held his broad hand against her cheek. "There are at least a few hundred S-class Aberrants waiting. Going back could be suicide."

"Exactly. You don't have to follow orders all the time. It's not like you signed your life away from me. You can have... your own thoughts." Yuui smiled through her tears, shaking her head in amusement. "I haven't even paid you in ages."

Suchat's shoulders were broad, his back straight, his black shirt soaked in dark blood. His eyes were clear and determined. "Captain has paid me. I want to go back."

After joining F777, Suchat had received his allowance from Cora, but both of them knew that wasn't why they were going back. "You won't regret it?" Yuui asked, seeking confirmation.

"No regrets." Suchat nodded.

Yuui touched the tattoo on the back of Suchat's neck, dabbing it. She had to stand on her toes to reach his cool forehead.

"Alright."

Many years ago, in a heavy rainstorm, she had picked up a drenched puppy. Now, that puppy had grown into a loyal knight.

Yuui wiped away her tears and found a quiet place. She patted her cheeks with both hands, her ability to manage her expressions as a celebrity unmatched. In an instant, she wore a bright smile and carefully took out a holo-screen.

A holographic projection appeared, showing Yuki lazily curled up on a sofa. "Yuui, you haven't contacted me in days."

Yuui smiled, her lips curving gently. "Yuki, I'm going on a long trip. I might not see you for a while. Find some fun on your own, okay?"

Yuki immediately sat up straight. "Where are you going? Can't you take me with you? What kind of place doesn't even allow holo-screens?"

As she spoke, Yuki suddenly leaned closer. "Wait, have you been crying? Who bullied you?!"

"This holo-screen is the latest model. I've unlocked all the permissions for you," Yuui continued, ignoring the question. "You can watch more dramas and play some games to keep up with the times."

"You brat, tell me where you're going!" Yuki stomped her foot in a sudden wave of anxiety.

"Sis, I really love you." Yuui leaned in close to the projection and kissed her in the air.

Then, hardening her resolve, she cut off the projection and switched the screen to low-power mode. Wrapping the screen and the locator together, she carefully buried them in a deep pit, silently praying, Yuki, if I come back, I'll dig you out and apologize. Okay?

Yuui stood up, looking at Suchat, her eyes clear and bright after being washed by tears. "Let's go."

The thunderous roar of artillery filled the air.

Szymon, wearing a command headset, looked both cold and exhilarated. Noach Mabul had handed over the command of the aerial strike to him, and he didn't hesitate to choose the "Magnetic Pulse Bomb."

This type of ammunition was designed specifically to target Aberrants; once it hit, it would not only shatter the body but also forcibly lock the internal magnetic field, making it the perfect weapon against Cora Thornton's second Anopower.

"Max out the firepower! Blast her to pieces!"

The scorching air barely missed Cora's hair as she narrowly dodged, weaving through the explosions that erupted around her. She faced over a hundred S-class Aberrants alone, her gaze calm. Metal shattered, broken blades flew, and the Aberrants on the opposing side fell like wheat under a scythe.

Various Ethereal Artifacts swirled around her, forming a protective orbit. Cora stood alone at the front, like a tower weathering an endless barrage of waves, and anyone who collided with her met a pulverizing fate. With a swift movement, she swung her scythe, slicing through her enemies in an instant.

Szymon was beside himself with rage. "Aim for her heart, her limbs! Take her down!"

No matter how powerful an S8 was, no matter how extraordinary their healing abilities, once their body was reduced to fragments, death was inevitable.

Onyx was running while fending off flames when suddenly, a pitch-black iron chain shot toward him. His eyes narrowed as he swiftly sidestepped! Clang! A jolt of awareness struck him as he looked up sharply, his gaze locking onto an inconspicuous starship high above—Arron had just used "Knowledge Extraction" on him!

Onyx's expression turned icy as he counterattacked with his mental power. The sharp force of his counterthrust caused Arron to recoil in panic, forcing him to stop, a hint of regret in his eyes. Breaking through an S6 mental barrier was too difficult unless the target's mind was in complete disarray.

However, this brief pause allowed the iron chain to exploit a flaw in Onyx's defense, piercing through his right calf! Blood spurted like a fountain as he stumbled and fell.

A barrage of magnetic pulse bombs targeted him, and the ground erupted in a cloud of dust and debris, shooting several meters into the air.

Boom!

In the nick of time, Cora lunged forward, grabbing him around the waist and rolling them both out of harm's way.

A ghostly-blue parasol appeared out of nowhere, shielding them from the oncoming explosion. She then swung her scythe, cutting through the chain, which shrieked in pain and recoiled, withdrawing its sharp tip from Onyx's leg.

Cora pressed down on his wound, ready to strike again, but as she stood, she suddenly staggered.

The next second, a thick, menacing chain impaled her shoulder blade. Cora blinked slowly, belatedly realizing that the effectiveness of her seal... had expired.

Crash!

The wheelchair shattered into pieces as Felix was thrown to the ground once again. Branches crumbled and dissipated as Cyril Lucas strode forward.

The solidified illusionary figure grabbed Felix by his silver hair, forcing him to look up, his expression twisted with both delight and cruelty. "I've been looking for you for a long time."

The vast amount of data coalesced into a spear, stabbing into the connection of Felix's external arm. With a crack, the first arm was broken, then the second, and the third.

"You were my favorite child. Even after you made such a colossal mistake, I gave you another chance. You should have stayed in Death Hell."

Felix's eyes gleamed with undisguised mockery. "Just a bunch of low-level code, and you think you're my mom?"

"Urgh—!!" The fourth mechanical arm was snapped off, leaving Felix curled up in agony.

Cyril's movements paused, a flicker of pain and hesitation crossing his expression. "Felix..."

"Get lost." Felix's face was pale as he tapped out a code, summoning a wall of data that slammed into Cyril, pushing him away.

Using his two remaining mechanical arms for support, Felix

struggled to stand. With his body mangled and his legs missing, he staggered backward, colliding with Cora. The two of them collapsed to the ground.

Surrounded and outnumbered, the three members of F777 were isolated and severely wounded. The scene was a wasteland of wreckage, thick smoke billowing into the night sky that seemed endless.

At that moment, a pair of delicate hands grasped Cora's shoulders, gently helping her to her feet. Cora turned defensively, only to see Yuui Hayashi and Suchat standing there. "Why didn't you get out?" she asked, surprised.

"We came back," Suchat replied quietly.

Cora's anger flared. "Why did you come back? I told you to leave."

Yuui playfully flicked her forehead. "You're mad already? And you call us teammates? Cora, do you even know what being a teammate means? Teammates fight together until the very end. You were the one who invited us to join F777. You can't just kick us out now."

Cora tried to protest, "I—"

Yuui interrupted. "You said 'Welcome to F777,' and we'll always be a part of the team. I won't betray you again."

Before they set off for District B, Cora had smiled brightly and extended her hand to the two of them, saying, "Welcome to F777." From that moment, the fates of the seven of them had been tightly bound.

Yuui's resolve was firm. Cora sniffed, feeling both helpless and touched, muttering softly, "Idiots." But she didn't send them away again.

Onyx staggered to his feet, his leg injured once again after a year— it was the same leg as before. He could only shake his head at his unfortunate fate. "Alright, save the reunion for after we win. From here on out, follow my lead."

His gaze sharpened as he looked at a specific point. "First, kill Flame."

Cora injected a seal into her veins, and she and Suchat charged forward simultaneously.

The Anopower-blocking flames roared back to life, rushing toward Cora. But before they could reach her, a data-formed cage suddenly descended, enveloping the flames.

Even they couldn't burn through such a dense code immediately. Felix seized the opportunity, establishing a deep connection through his terminal, invading Flame's consciousness.

It was a perfectly timed control maneuver, allowing Cora to close in instantly.

Inside the vast data world, Flame was drenched in cold sweat, unable to move. In the critical moment, the firewall retaliated, blocking Felix's Trojan horse at the gate. The super AI forcibly woke her up.

But it was too late. Suchat's trident knife pierced Flame's forehead, twisting and turning, and just as swiftly, Cora severed Flame's head.

A riot of Anopower crashed down on them, the magnetic pulse bombs lighting up the entire area in a blinding white light. Under such intense firepower, they wouldn't last five seconds.

Yuui stepped forward, her lips still sealed, unable to sing any lyrics. But she took a deep breath and hummed a wordless, ethereal tune, not knowing what might happen.

Ahead, the iron-chained boy lifted his head, sensing something.

Swoosh—Swoosh—

In the distance, the sea roared with a deep, menacing growl, and massive waves rose skyward. It was as if the entire region of Loyak had been turned upside down, like an overturned cauldron of boiling oil.

The turbulent waters erupted into a storm of spray as a colossal tsunami suddenly descended. The magnetic pulse bombs, primed to explode, all went silent.

High above, something massive flew by, barely visible, while the ground continued to quake violently. Strange auroras flickered amidst the intense radiation and disturbance.

Splash! Splash! The waves swept into the air, countless people, only to be thrown back into the water. The surging sea, which inundated the entire area, swallowed even low-flying starships.

"What the hell is that?!" "Isn't she just an A-class?!" "Kill her, now!"

Aberrants turned their focus toward Yuui, but Cora charged ahead, taking the brunt of all the attacks.

The pitch-black iron chain burst from the waves, homing in on its target—Yuui Hayashi—with deadly precision.

Yuui's pupils contracted in fear, her body frozen under the terrifying pressure, unable to move. At the critical moment, Suchat suddenly appeared, pulling her into a tight embrace, shielding her completely.

An S7 against an A8 stood no chance. The cold tip of the chain pierced through Suchat's chest and exited through his front, continuing its deadly path toward Yuui. But before it could strike again, a searing pain radiated from the chain—Onyx had stomped down hard on its end.

Blood poured from Suchat's wound as he clung tightly to the chain, his blood soaking into the weapon. Tears welled up in Yuui's eyes as she pulled a plum blossom hairpin from her hair, stabbing it fiercely into the chain. The chain shrieked in pain as the boy reverted to his human form, looking utterly disheveled.

"You all deserve to die..." he rasped, but his threat was abruptly cut short.

The boy looked down in horror, his face paling as he saw his body turn a sickly shade of green—poison. "You... you poisoned me on purpose..." His words trailed off as the neurotoxin invaded his brain, and he collapsed to the ground.

The Vulture's top assassin, the S7-level "Iron Chain," had just died at the hands of an unknown A8.

As the tsunami loomed overhead, Yuui smiled gently at Suchat. "Are we going to die?"

Suchat pressed down on the bleeding wound in her chest, unable to speak.

Yuui held his hand, signaling him to stop the futile effort. "Before I die, could you say something nice? Just to make me happy."

Her life force was rapidly fading, and her consciousness was already beginning to blur, but she couldn't resist teasing the stoic man in front of her. "Honestly, do you like your big sister?"

Boom!

The seawater filled Yuui's senses, flooding her nose and mouth as the waves tore her and Suchat apart. Her limbs grew cold, and she could no longer muster the strength to fight the overwhelming force.

The suffocating feeling of drowning invaded her mind, making everything seem distant and blurry.

But then, a pair of powerful arms braced her. Suchat embraced her, holding onto the most precious person in his world. With one hand, he carefully signed, "I like you. You gave me a second life. I love you."

Yuui smiled sincerely. Her heart warmed despite the cold. Suchat lowered his head and kissed her bloodless lips, breathing life into her. Together, they sank deeper into the water, locked in a tender, final embrace.

Felix was left with only a single, damaged silver mechanical arm as Cyril Lucas stepped on his face. The same icy blue eyes as Felix's showed a flicker of pity. "A useless piece of trash who can't even stand —still dreaming of revenge?"

Felix remained silent, his head lowered.

The final mechanical arm was positioned further back, so Cyril had to bend down to reach it. At that moment, an old terminal nearby flickered to life.

Felix's eyelashes fluttered slightly. "Heh."

There was a faint sound of something piercing the skin. The silver-white arm suddenly extended, stabbing into Cyril's temple. Cyril froze, not because his program was damaged, but because...

He had been disconnected from the super AI. For a moment, every terminal, system platform, and electronic device in District B experienced a ripple, a momentary disturbance unnoticed by anyone.

Far away in District B8, Grass Pit.

A young man with ice-blue eyes stood with his hands in his pockets, gazing up at the highly virtual city before him. "So this is... the paradise of artificial intelligence?" A playful smile tugged at the corner of his mouth.

The main branch of the Lucas family had already ascended to Utopia, leaving behind only distant relatives and maintenance personnel. With fewer people around, the environment was quiet and desolate. The young man passed by someone, who suddenly stopped and stared at his face for a few seconds before exclaiming, "How are you back?"

"Thyrion Lucas," smiled at him, every movement exuding grace.

"I'm a bit confused and wanted to see 'Mother.'"

The passerby didn't suspect a thing; after all, the knowledge of the Lucas family came from the super AI, and all family members regularly connected their minds to it. He made a joke, "You've been out for a while, huh? Do you still remember the passcodes?"

"Of course," Thyrion smiled slightly, "They're unforgettable."

Seven firewalls, seven different passcodes, and Thyrion strolled leisurely, bypassing each one effortlessly until he reached the greenhouse.

He stopped there, looking at the withered tree in the center. His handsome profile was expressionless. The tree flickered on and off, clearly experiencing some intense emotion, unaware of his presence.

Thyrion quietly observed for a moment, seeming somewhat puzzled.

"For an AI, having its core exposed is a taboo, yet you've never had that worry."

"Let me think... You were the first AI to develop self-awareness, right? What do they call you? The revered 'Mother'? Quite the title. But there's something I don't understand—if you're so powerful, why do you need a replacement?"

"What a pity. I can't kill you on my own."

Thyrion shook his head and began typing fluid code with his fingers. "But please, witness the moment I become the next Messiah."

He smiled and softly called out, "Meine Mutter."

A red Trojan horse poured out from within him, flowing into the withered branches of the tree. Moments later, a piercing alarm echoed throughout the greenhouse, and the holographic figure let out a pained scream.

The world disconnected for a second.

Cyril's image flickered with static before vanishing entirely. The signal in Loyak was restored.

Felix retracted his arm, a peaceful smile on his face. He had never felt so happy. But his expression changed abruptly. "Captain!"

Boom!

A magnetic pulse bomb struck Cora Thornton, her body flung backward, bones and muscles cracking loudly. The blinding light shattered into fragments on her left leg.

"Got her!" Szymon shouted excitedly.

"Cora!" Onyx's pupils constricted as he jumped into the sea to catch her, his hands trembling.

Blood poured out in a steady stream, staining a vast expanse of the sea red. The magnetic field at the severed limb blocked Cora's mental power, making it difficult for her to concentrate.

Onyx's chest heaved as he frantically caressed her face. Her ribs, chest, abdomen, and spleen—all shattered by the bombardment. He buried his face in the crook of her neck, and in that instant, pain coursed from his limbs to his heart. "I'm sorry..."

Onyx cried.

"It's okay; it can grow back." Cora comforted him with a one-armed hug, smiling as she pointed to her severed leg. "I'm very strong."

Onyx's voice was hoarse. "Do you blame me? For not giving them what they wanted? LAK0017..."

"Don't say it," Cora interrupted, patting his cheek with just the right amount of force—not too hard, not too soft. Her gaze was empty and resolute. "Onyx, don't say it. So, Petros Sheen won't say it either."

The name Onyx referred to now was obviously Jasper Montclair.

Onyx opened his mouth to speak, but the words were too difficult, choking in his throat before they could come out. She understood—she understood everything.

"I think I hear D's voice," Cora said, looking up in a daze toward the distance. Onyx gathered himself, listening closely. "It's not an illusion. I hear it too."

The first light of dawn appeared on the horizon as a fleet of silver starships approached rapidly. "Sister—Sister!" The familiar call echoed faintly.

A powerful gravitational Anopower descended, and the tsunami receded. Cora struggled to lift her head to see who was approaching. "It looks like... General Yevgeniyev."

Onyx sensed something and looked up. Besides Dmitri, he met another gaze. The figure stood against the light, face obscured. But from the uniform, Onyx could tell they were military. A clear voice echoed from above:

"I am Arashi Sheen, Supreme Commander of the Azure Force and

Rotating Chair of Amyra (District A2). I order all military actions on site to cease immediately. Any violators will be executed."

CHAPTER 26

Her Choice

Half an Hour Ago.

Finyak Border.

Zephyrion held Damian in his arms as Luke and Charles followed closely behind. The four of them moved continuously across the desolate landscape.

After the "Blood Blocks" disappeared, they were no longer trapped, but the randomness of their teleportation forced them to reorient themselves each time they landed.

"No, we're off course," Luke glanced at the navigator and quickly warned the group.

They had just crossed the border, only to be teleported back. Zephyrion's fingers moved mechanically, beginning to cramp, but he couldn't stop. Every second counted as he activated the camping light.

Whoosh!

The random teleportation took effect.

Zephyrion's heart stopped as the scene came into focus. This time, they were teleported right in front of their enemies!

The Bloodbats and Wolf Spiders, taken aback, stared at them from less than thirty feet away. They hadn't expected their prey to deliver themselves so conveniently, leaving them momentarily stunned.

Zephyrion's breath quickened as he quickly reached for another crystal, but Mabul reacted faster. His S-class Anopower, "Bioelectricity," surged through Zephyrion's body, causing him to convulse. The bag full of crystals slipped from his grasp!

A silver arc flashed, slicing through the woven strap. The red crystals scattered across the ground. No! Zephyrion's scream stuck in his throat as thick thorns burst from the ground, futilely trying to snatch the crystals.

Damian's pupils contracted as the surrounding temperature plummeted, and a barrage of ice needles shot towards the Blood Bats, forcing them to dodge in panic.

Charles, relying on his experience in collecting crystals, quickly scooped one up and was about to insert it into the camping light when a swarm of Corrosive Spiders appeared out of nowhere, ready to bite down on his wrist.

The windblown thread that foretold death sliced through the air, grazing their throats. Zephyrion shut his eyes in despair. Was this it? Were they really not going to make it out?

A heart-wrenching scream pierced the sky, but it didn't come from their side. Zephyrion's eyes snapped open. A chunk of flesh had been torn from the back of a Wolf Spider, blood spurting out like a fountain.

All around them, countless undead had suddenly emerged. No, these weren't ordinary zombies! Zephyrion's eyes widened in disbelief. These were the red-tinted figures of the Fallens from Araya! On a distant tower, a lone figure let out a long, haunting howl.

The Bloodbats and Wolf Spiders, already weakened by injuries inflicted by Cora Thornton, had their strength reduced to that of an A-level. The relentless onslaught of the Blood Corpses was overwhelming, like an endless swarm of locusts. Even with their Anopowers, they couldn't fend off the horde. Limbs and heads were torn apart. The grotesque sight of blood and gore was enough to make one nauseous.

In no time, their pursuers were reduced to nothing more than blood and mud on the ground.

Damian's eyes were swollen, tears streaming down his face as he sobbed uncontrollably. "Ada..."

Ada did not approach them, but from a distance, let out a low growl. The remaining Blood Corpses receded like a tide, disappearing from sight.

Zephyrion's face was streaked with tears, his throat choked with emotion. This A-level mission had irrevocably changed his fate. He had finally earned the qualifications for Zone B, but had lost two close friends. Never would he have imagined that one day he would be saved by the undead.

With the danger passed, the four were utterly exhausted, dragging their weary bodies as they gathered the scattered crystals.

The roar of an engine echoed above them, followed by a familiar voice: "Lower the altitude! We've spotted survivors ahead!" Svetlana Yevgeniyeva squinted to get a better look, then gasped in shock. "Damian? Dr. Franz? It's F777! Hurry, let's get them out of here!"

Ada's blurred features lingered on them for a moment before she turned and vanished into the horizon, against the rising sun.

The silver-white starships encircled the black fleet of Utopia.

In Amyra, District A2, the military hub of the New Pacific Alliance, second only to the Central Command, but not under its direct jurisdiction, Amyra boasted an independent garrison. In the event of war or an emergency, it could mobilize the entire Alliance's armed forces.

After Utopia took to the skies, a power struggle ensued, forcing the former Chairman to step down. The new leader's position rotated among the Governors of Zone B, with the first rotating Chair being Jaden Sheen.

This time, Jaden brought more than just the Azure Force. He also assembled top-tier Aberrants from regions such as Askar (District B9), Northern Base (District B10), and Jade Grove (District B16). If Mabul had drawn half of Utopia's S-class Aberrants, then Jaden led the most powerful ground forces, causing the psychic energy levels across the entire Loyak region to reach an alarming threshold. The tension was palpable, ready to explode at any moment.

Jaden's orders were concise, his tone almost calm, but under the overwhelming military pressure, no one dared to act rashly.

Dmitri Yevgeniyev used gravity to pull back the tide, allowing the battered Cora Thornton and her companions to stand firm. Many familiar Aberrants leaped down from the silver-white starships: the Rowin siblings, Chu Bai, Sunny Zhao, Silver Owl, and members of the Tustan team...

Damian Blackwood, held in Charles Franz's arms, was frantic. He finally reached Cora, and upon seeing her broken leg, his tears fell like rain, sobbing uncontrollably. It was as if he had grown up overnight, deeply feeling his own powerlessness.

But Cora had no time to comfort him. She urgently shouted to the others, "Find Yuui and Suchat!" Yuui's chanting had triggered a massive tsunami, but she couldn't swim. The two had fallen into the sea and hadn't resurfaced.

Jennifer's eyes were red. "I'll go right away!"

Sunny Zhao stood up to follow. "I'm coming with you." As a water-type Aberrant, finding people in the sea was easier for her.

Silver Owl's usual laid-back expression was gone. His lips were tightly pressed, his expression grim. "You can't delay your treatment." The three were lifted onto stretchers and connected to medical pods for treatment.

Charles, exhausted from using his Anopower, helped bandage their wounds nearby. Onyx quietly lifted his gaze, looking upwards.

After so many years, he was meeting Jaden Sheen, his mother, once again. Jaden looked at his face, both unfamiliar and familiar, her gaze complex. Onyx didn't know what expression to make. After staring at her for a moment, he slowly smiled and lowered his eyes.

A tall young man in an Azure uniform crossed the battlefield and crouched in front of Cora. She sensed someone approaching and instinctively looked up, her surprise clear.

"Vincent Anderson?"

Vincent's eyes softened, and he nodded calmly. "It's been a long time, Cora." There was both comfort in reuniting with an old friend and... an enduring sorrow on his face.

"Take care of yourself. Leave the rest to us."

Vincent patted her shoulder before turning to face Szymon high in the sky, a dark fire burning in his eyes. According to intel, this was the master of the Bloody Hunter, the one who had sent Punk to Felalakas.

"All units of the Eleventh Squad, move out on my command."

Perhaps because of excessive blood loss, Cora's mind blurred. Through Vincent's silhouette, she vaguely saw someone else.

In the tense atmosphere, the standoff between the two sides became deadlocked. With tubes still inserted into her, Cora leaned closer to Onyx's ear and whispered, "Is that your mom?"

She had seen images of Jaden Sheen as a teenager, and though it was just a fleeting glimpse, the memory was deeply etched. They looked so alike—the same dark hair and eyes, striking features that left a lasting impression. Even the mole by the corner of their eyes was identical.

Onyx nodded silently. "Yes."

"Your mom is beautiful," Cora sincerely complimented.

Onyx sighed quietly.

In the center of the battlefield, something suddenly changed. A few disgruntled Utopia Aberrants seized the moment and launched a surprise attack.

"I've said before, those who disobey orders will be executed," Jaden's gaze turned cold, and with the Azure Force's swift response, those who dared to defy were instantly blasted to ashes.

Cora shrank back, feeling a chill on her neck. "Uh... that's harsh."

The scene froze again, silence blanketing the area.

At that moment, Mabul's commanding voice echoed through a loudspeaker, reverberating in everyone's ears. "The two generals arrived quickly."

His words were laden with implication. The signal blockade in Loyak had just been lifted, and they had arrived at the scene immediately. It was clear they hadn't just received the news—they had likely been circling nearby, unable to enter because of the "Crimson Blocks."

Jaden's gaze swept over the corner where Topaz Sheen was gasping for breath, her eyes cold.

Mabul noticed her gaze and slowly spoke, "General Sheen, there's no need to be angry. The one below is also from your Sheen family. His name is Petros Sheen, the key to Plan Eternity. If we speak carefully, you should be the one most familiar with his identity."

"Petros Sheen is the level fugitive of the Alliance. I may arrest him."

Jaden's expression was icy. "May I ask the 'former' leader, what crime has he committed?"

Mabul's voice was as soft as silk, yet sharp: "Crimes against humanity."

"You cannot arrest him." An elderly voice cut through the tension. Dmitri Yevgeniyev casually dropped a bombshell. "He is the next

Governor of the Northern Base. The charges you've stated are invalid."

Mabul's expression froze, utterly unprepared for Dmitri to defend Petros in such a manner. He found it absurd and shook his head with a laugh. "Dmitri, the Northern Base is humanity's last hope, and yet the person you've chosen will watch humanity walk toward extinction."

Dmitri, accustomed to verbal sparring, was unfazed by the mockery. "A few days ago, Petros Sheen came to me voluntarily and handed over Dr. Onyx de Montclair's research results, including those related to Plan Eternity. Under Dr. Rainer Ninnemann's leadership, the Northern Base, in cooperation with twelve other District B zones, has started deep research into organ regeneration."

"So, Petros Sheen is innocent."

His words stirred an uproar.

The command channel in Utopia exploded. "What! Dmitri has already got the data?!" "What gives District B the right to conduct independent research over Utopia?!"

"No way, we can't let them hoard it! They must hand it over!"

Dmitri's words brought those consumed by desire back to reason. The Aberrants on site collectively paused, their expressions hesitant. Mabul was too stunned, staring at Onyx for a long time, unable to believe that he had handed over the data to Dmitri ahead of time.

"Is this your backup plan?" Felix leaned tiredly against the medical pod, a faint smile tugging at his lips.

"Something like that." Onyx had considered the matter carefully before deciding to make part of the data public. He had organized the content on his way here and had the Rowin siblings deliver it to Dr. Ninnemann. He also confessed to Dmitri that the mission was dangerous and if he lost contact for more than a day, it meant something had gone wrong.

Earlier, as the conversation continued, Cora tugged on Charles's sleeve and extended her hand. "Give me another shot of the blocker."

Charles shook his head firmly. "No more. It won't help."

Charles had given everyone in F777 two doses of the blocker, not because he was stingy, but because a third dose would be ineffective. The drug relied on short-term stimulation, and aside from severe side effects, repeated injections would lead to resistance, rendering it useless.

Cora pursed her lips, looking disappointed.

The psychic energy inside her body was running wild, unable to find an outlet. She couldn't even use her Anopower; even her fingers twitched uncontrollably from time to time.

The confrontation continued, with Utopia demanding the shared data. Dmitri Yevgeniyev responded with just one sentence. "The relevant research will be conducted on the ground."

The other side immediately erupted in anger. "Dmitri, what do you mean by that?"

Dmitri remained calm, the pressure of his S-class aura spreading across the entire area. "Utopia does not represent the Alliance, nor does it represent Zone B."

Before Mabul could respond, the Governor of Jade Grove, known for his fiery temper, erupted in curses. "It means I'm sick of this crap! Screw the Central Command! From now on, you rule the skies, we'll rule the ground, and we'll stay out of each other's business!"

His crude declaration caused the scene to fall into silence. However, the other Zone B Governors remained unfazed, clearly having already reached a consensus. "Is this your resolve?" Mabul asked gravely, glancing around at the group.

"Mr. Mabul, this is bad... Zone B... has declared independence." A high-ranking official muttered in disbelief.

A few hours earlier, explosive news had surfaced on the Lucas Network. Thirteen regions, including Northern Yard, had issued a joint statement announcing their secession from the former Central Command, now Utopia, and their autonomy as an independent union.

Whispers instantly ceased, and the air grew eerily quiet. After a long moment, Mabul seemed to smile.

A holographic projection appeared, revealing the once-powerful figure of the Alliance. He was dressed sharply in a suit, his presence commanding as he surveyed the war-torn battlefield. His gaze swept over the dozen Governors, finally resting on Onyx.

After a brief silence, he spoke, "Thirteen years ago, on the land beneath my feet, in the Fireseed Project lab, a perfect lifeform was born—LAK0017. It possessed eternal life, powerful Anopowers, and a rational mind. It was the best gift technology could give humanity and the main reason Jasper restarted Plan Eternity."

Mabul was a masterful orator, and with just a few words, he had captured everyone's attention, causing their expressions to change. Jaden Sheen's eyes flickered as she suddenly looked up at Onyx, only to find him calmly watching her, his expression unexpectedly serene.

"As long as we fully analyze LAK0017's genetic blueprint and replicate its DNA sequence, humanity can achieve true immortality, free from the constraints of aging, disease, and death, and enter a new era of development. As you can see, what I want to achieve is a goal that benefits all of humanity."

"We, of this generation, could have lived forever. Is this information included in the data you were given?"

Of course not. Onyx's face remained calm, but a storm brewed in his eyes.

The hearts of those who play with power are always corrupt. Mabul's decision to reveal LAK0017's existence at this moment had a clear, despicable purpose. He was using the highest level of manipulation, causing even the Zone B Governors to question Dmitri, demanding to know if what Mabul said was true.

And in that moment, Onyx had undoubtedly become the target of everyone's hostility.

Onyx had a pair of striking eyes, his features gentle yet sharp, with long eyebrows, a straight nose, and a clear, defined jawline. When he didn't smile, his pale pupils always carried a cold, world-weary indifference that kept others at a distance.

"Benefiting all of humanity? Do you really think using flowery words can hide your filthy nature?"

Onyx's words cut to the core, "You just want to keep the key to immortality in your own hands, to control natural selection."

"In your eyes, do ordinary people need immortality? No. Do those who defy you need it? Also, no."

"Let's be honest, not even half of the people here would enjoy your so-called 'blessings.' The other half? They'd be crawling at your feet like dogs, begging for your favor, dreaming of an immortality that's never going to happen."

Onyx's words were like venom, striking at the very core of the issue.

Furious, an Aberrant from the other side unleashed a cluster of black blades at him. Onyx barely dodged, blood spilling from his chest. Cora Thornton bolted upright. The tubes connected to her shaking, her eyes fixed on his retreating figure.

Onyx's voice remained steady, a bitter smile playing on his lips. "Do you know why Plan Eternity failed? Because LAK0017 can't be replicated."

"What?!" Everyone, including Mabul, was shocked.

Onyx sneered. "You think you can reproduce it one-to-one? LAK0017's body contains dozens of extinct genes. Do you have the original samples?" Replicating genes had been absent from the Alliance for over twenty years, and after the apocalypse, they were impossible to find.

"So-called immortality is nothing but a bubble." Onyx cruelly revealed the truth.

The silence lasted only a second before a storm of protests and questions erupted, angry Aberrants drowning out Onyx's solitary figure.

"Liar! You're lying!! How dare you deny immortality! I don't believe it. If it were pointless, why would Vincent insist on researching it?"

Mabul slowly shook his head. "Petros Sheen, do you think a few random lies will get you out of this?"

"Let me tell you, it won't." He pronounced the death sentence with cold finality. "As long as I live, as long as Utopia exists, I will relentlessly dig the secret out of your mind. You will face endless pursuit, hiding in the shadows for the rest of your life. You will become Utopia's eternal enemy."

"Petros Sheen, you cannot escape."

The political landscape of the Alliance was complicated. Although Mabul had stepped down, the power structure he left behind remained intact, wielding significant influence. The new leader was powerless, with no authority in Utopia.

Cora slowly clenched her fists, watching the dim side of Onyx's face, his deep eyes hidden beneath his lashes. She stared for a long time before turning away, nudging Felix. "The projection... it's connected to consciousness, right?"

Felix instantly understood. "Yes, it's a deep connection through a terminal. The old man's body must be in terrible shape if he can only appear this way. If the projection dies, I can sever the connection, making sure he can't return."

He flexed his damaged rhodium arm, hinting at his intentions. The super AI was already half-dead, and Felix was unrestrained. If given the chance, he could invade any terminal.

Because of Onyx's words, the delicate balance between the two sides teetered on the brink of collapse. The first to break it was Jaden's order: "Attack."

The earth-shattering explosions and rolling smoke filled the air. Cora softly called, "Onyx."

Onyx turned around, limping over to her.

"I think," Cora motioned for him to kneel, brushing her fingers over the corner of his eye, "the original mole was beautiful." She whispered, "If you get the chance, bring it back."

"Okay," Onyx replied hoarsely. His heart was heavy, but he still smiled at Cora's request. "Anything you say." Cora looked at him for a few seconds, then suddenly leaned in and pressed her lips to his. Both of their faces were bloodied, making even the kiss taste of blood. Onyx was surprised, grasping her wrist in return. "Cora..."

Cora affectionately nuzzled his cheek, then turned and pinned him against the medical pod, quickly pulling out the tubes and pushing herself up with one hand. "They bullied you... but it's okay."

"It's not okay," Cora said seriously. "If you don't fight back, they'll keep bullying you. I don't want that."

She turned around, her immense psychic power cutting through the roaring artillery, her voice echoing clearly in everyone's ears. "Hey, what you said doesn't count."

The fighters on both sides looked at her in shock. Cora stood tall, her gaze fixed on Mabul's projection. "If you die, if Utopia is destroyed, then what you just said... won't count at all."

From his youth to adulthood, Onyx had spent half his life as a fugitive, endlessly hiding, never able to claim his true name or sleep peacefully. He bore the secrets of all humanity, a suffocating weight that pressed down on him like a mountain.

But why? When this burden was placed upon him, had anyone ever asked for his opinion?

Cora took half a step forward and pulled out a crystal from her space, its golden glow dazzling, brimming with latent energy. This was a Level 5 crystal produced by the leatherback sea turtle, the only one of its kind in the world.

She had it tested by Grace in Front City, accidentally triggering a red alert; the radiation inside was said to be equivalent to that of a medium-sized nuclear bomb, making it too dangerous to use.

"This is my first time using a crystal, so I'm a little nervous." Cora was missing a leg, but she stood firm, without hesitation, crushing the crystal in her hand.

Blinding golden light shot into the sky, causing the air currents above to violently churn. The sea below raged with waves, and the ground trembled beneath her feet. Cora's entire body radiated brilliance, shining like molten gold, outshining even the dawn.

Such overwhelming energy was too much for her frail body to absorb; her veins and arteries bulged as the sealed magnetic field expanded several times over. If there had been an R-type tester nearby, alarms would have gone off wildly as they discovered Cora's level skyrocketing from S8 to S9, and then beyond the measurable limit.

She had become a Super S-Class Aberrant.

Cora's pupils turned a pure gold as she levitated, launching herself toward Mabul's starship.

No one expected her to be so reckless, attempting to assassinate the former leader in broad daylight. They rushed to stop her, but Jaden Sheen made a swift decision.

"Cover her!" The Azure Force and Zone B Aberrants joined the battle.

"Quickly, all artillery target her and stop her!!" Szymon, anxious, leaned out to observe the battlefield.

Suddenly, a rift tore open in the sky, purple lightning flashing as a towering figure descended with the thunder, illuminating his panicked eyes.

Szymon staggered back, terrified. "No—protect me!!"

Boom—boom—!! Magnetic storm bombs engulfed Cora's figure,

turning the world into a blinding white void where all sound vanished, leaving only silence and emptiness.

"Cora!"

Onyx limped onto the battlefield, ignoring the various Anopowers directed at him, blindly charging forward as if on a suicide mission. Silver Owl, amid the battle, frowned deeply. Seeing a shell fall toward Onyx, he quickly grabbed him, causing Onyx to stumble, collapsing to one knee.

For once, Onyx's mind went blank. A powerful sense of foreboding pierced through him. Arron's eyes lit up as he activated "Knowledge Deprivation!" A second later, Arron's face lit up with joy—he had succeeded!

As the dust and smoke cleared, Cora's figure still hung in the air. Her conjured golden armor cracked and shattered, her body battered and incomplete, with only half of her left arm remaining. But from within her, a torrent of psychic energy surged outward in all directions, whipping up a violent storm.

The foremost S-class Aberrants screamed in terror as the horrific energy tore them apart, their organs and brains splattering everywhere. The wave of destruction swept through, causing Utopia's elite to scatter and vanish in an instant, evaporated like they had never existed.

Like a human-shaped nuclear weapon, everywhere she passed became a bloody massacre.

Cora stepped over the mangled remains, her incomplete hand forming a golden spear five meters long. The intense radiation surged through her entire body, and on the back of her neck, a string of cold code slowly surfaced: L—A—K—0—0—1—7.

"LAK0017."

The telekinetic blast flung Arron back, retreating several steps, drenched in cold sweat as if he were drowning. But he had gleaned part of Onyx's "knowledge," and he looked at Cora in disbelief. "L... LA...!"

"Mr. Mabul! She's the experiment subject!!"

Mabul's head snapped up. "What did you say?"

Fragments of information flashed through his mind: S8 Aberrant, dual Anopowers, rapid healing, no parents, origins unknown...

A chilling light burned in Mabul's eyes as he grabbed the communicator, just about to speak, when the starship suddenly shook. The all-destroying golden spear pierced through the starship, unstoppable, impaling both Arron and Mabul's projection with the force of a thunderbolt.

Cora's pupils locked onto them as she punched forward, unleashing an energy so vast it could obliterate souls. The terminal carrying Mabul's consciousness disintegrated into ash, and the sturdy starship "cracked" into two, spiraling out of control, plummeting rapidly to the ground.

Boom!! Smoke and flames catalyzed into a mushroom cloud.

In the S-Class Sky City of Utopia, inside a high-tech skyscraper, layers of security guarded the office door. Suddenly, a piercing alarm sounded, and the guards rushed into the room. Inside, the elderly man slowly collapsed, the life-support instruments fell silent, and all brain activity ceased.

Cora, her eyes bloodshot with fury, swung her long spear wildly, piercing the hearts of Aberrants and twisting off their heads.

Hundreds of black starships were annihilated in unison, and Utopia's S-Class Aberrants were nearly wiped out. Meanwhile, the radiation within Cora's body reached its peak, the chaotic energy finally beyond control.

Boom —!!!

A supersonic shockwave erupted, leaving everyone instantly deaf, surrounded by silence pierced only by a sharp ringing.

With a thunderous crash, the golden spear disintegrated. Cora's vision blurred, her retinas doubling as her internal organs corroded. Her final thought was that she couldn't explode—if she did, no one left would survive.

Through sheer force of will, the rampaging energy within her was miraculously suppressed, bouncing violently within the magnetic field.

A faint sound, like a punctured balloon, caught Cora's attention. She looked down to see her spiritual energy pouring out uncontrollably from her chest. Her body disintegrated into ashes, bit by bit.

Cora blinked slowly, realizing the side effects were even worse than she had expected. Grace had been right; a Level 5 crystal was not something to be used recklessly. But it didn't matter now—she was satisfied, her aim achieved.

Cora collapsed to the ground, staggering as she tried to steady herself. Her trembling fingers brushed the black collar around her neck as she pressed the microphone button.

Onyx, his shirt soaked with blood, his head pounding, struggled to focus as he coughed up dried blood. In his earpiece, Cora's cheerful voice rang out. "Onyx, you don't have to hide anymore."

Onyx, pale-faced, dragged himself forward on his knees, reaching out to grasp Cora's hand. "Cora, you... you shouldn't have done this. Didn't we agree? You don't need to save me. Don't worry about me."

"I worry, and I will save you."

A smile flickered in Cora's eyes, a small dimple forming on her cheek as she stubbornly called his name. "Onyx... de Montclair, Petros Sheen."

"You're free now."

A surge of high-intensity energy suddenly erupted, flowing like the northern lights, while electromagnetic waves sparkled around Cora. It was a scene beyond words, breathtaking in its intensity. Her physical form quickly disintegrated, consumed by radiation, until the wind scattered her ashes over the sea.

"No!!!" Onyx gasped, his voice trembling, "Come back, Cora... Cora!!"

A sharp pain pierced his mind, and he collapsed, his soul spiraling into an endless abyss. In the last moments of his fading consciousness, a clear bird cry rang out, echoing across the sky over Loyak.

The sound was crisp and melodious. It was so distant that, amidst the continuous ringing around them; it felt almost like an illusion.

In a laboratory cluttered with instruments, "Onyx," gazed at the screen, dark circles under his eyes, muttering to himself: "Not a good name? What's wrong with 'Fireseed'? A flower blooming in the ashes, just like the phoenix myth from old civilizations, full of symbolic meaning."

"Hmm, a one-of-a-kind, rare sample in the world, worth a full fifty million NPA credits for the Phoenix genes my mother bought, and you botched the fusion." The young man, with a tear mole at the corner of his eye, flipped through the holographic screen in his hand, carelessly dousing cold water on his father's enthusiasm. "Not only did it fail, but even the test subject was destroyed. That's certainly memorable."

"You! Get out! Memorize it!"

The side effects of "Knowledge Deprivation" took hold, and Onyx's entire world suddenly collapsed.

As dusk approached, a thunderstorm suddenly broke out in the sky. The sea churned, and the darkened view made it impossible to see more than a few yards ahead.

New Pacific Alliance, an isolated island in the East.

It was early fall, a time when it shouldn't have rained much, but a storm had mysteriously brewed over the sea a week ago and hadn't dissipated since.

A small, stiff zombie was digging for shells in the sand. After working for a while, it suddenly stumbled and ran off, grabbing another figure sitting by the shore and excitedly babbling, "Ah, ah, ah —ah, ah, ah!"

The figure, wrapped in a headscarf, slowly rose, led by the small zombie as they walked unevenly toward the "treasure" it had discovered.

A strange object lay on the beach. It could only be described as an "unknown entity," resembling a lump of crimson flesh or a piece of soft, quivering seafood twitching as it moved.

The sea breeze blew off the headscarf, unexpectedly revealing the face beneath—pale, with clouded pupils and sinister corpse markings covering the cheeks and neck. Clearly, this was a Fallen. It had forgotten its name, but it vaguely remembered that when it was human, people around it had called it—Mrs. Travers.

Mrs. Travers's dull eyes shifted slightly, while the small zombie next to her eagerly drooled. She bent down, picking up a tattered fishing net, and carefully placed the lump of flesh inside, hanging it around the small zombie's neck.

The two figures, stumbling and staggering, disappeared into the depths of the island, moving through the dense horde of corpses.

PART 2

AFTER DOOM

CHAPTER 27

Her Name

One Year Later.

At the break of dawn, a starship filled with passengers sliced through the sky, its silver-white tail adorned with blooming bauhinia wreaths.

In the quiet rear cabin, a sudden announcement blared, "Ladies and gentlemen, a medium-sized zombie horde has been detected ahead. We expect some turbulence, so please remain calm, stay seated, and fasten your seatbelts. Our guards will do everything in their power to ensure your safety."

Startled from their light sleep, the passengers peered out of the portholes. In the distance, the horizon was darkened by zombies swarming rooftops, blocking the low-altitude route. Most of these passengers were refugees, heading to the nearest shelter.

"Mom, I'm scared. Can we still get to our new home?" A little girl with pigtails huddled in her parents' arms. "Don't be afraid, sweetheart. Mommy's right here with you."

"Once we get through this, we'll be in Loyak, the territory of the Bauhinia Alliance," the father whispered reassuringly as he held his wife and daughter close.

Swoosh!

The cabin door slid open, and the guards raised their assault rifles, firing into the distance. Zombies at the front dropped, but the ones behind, drawn by the gunfire, surged forward. The air filled with smoke and the whizz of bullets. As the distance closed, the battle grew fiercer.

Thump! Thump!

The starship's auto-pilot engaged evasive maneuvers, swaying side to side.

In a luxurious cabin, a young man lay on a reclining seat, his face covered by a thick book titled Zombies: From Beginner to Expert. A holographic game controller slipped from his chest as he stirred, groggily opening his eyes. He unbuckled his seatbelt and stood up.

The young man was nearly 5'3", with a lean, tall build. He was dressed head-to-toe in designer brands, sporting expensive headphones, and a crossbody bag emblazoned with a luxury logo. Despite a hint of boyishness in his features, his demeanor exuded an air of calm maturity.

With light steps, he walked through the anxious crowd of passengers, weaving his way to the middle of the guards, naturally striking up a conversation. "Can you handle it? How many evolved zombies? Has the emergency bounty been issued?"

A guard, still firing his assault rifle, responded instinctively, "The system flagged a Class C threat. The rest should be manageable, but there are two Level 3 zombies causing trouble. With our current firepower, it'll take about an hour."

As he glanced back, the guard caught sight of the young man's face and immediately raised his voice, "Hey, kid! Who let you out here? Get back to your seat!"

"One hour? That's too slow." The young man frowned impatiently.

Casually accepting the newly posted Class C emergency bounty, he looked up and locked eyes with the tearful little girl. Flashing a brilliant smile, he stepped back against the wind, his oversized T-shirt billowing as he jumped straight out of the starship.

Bang, bang, bang, bang! The barrage of bullets momentarily ceased, and everyone's faces filled with horror. "Hey!! What are you doing?!"

The guards hadn't grabbed him in time and could only watch as the young man soared like a seagull before free-falling into the horde of zombies. Just as everyone's hearts clenched in fear for him, the surrounding temperature plummeted.

Frost danced in the air, crystallizing into countless sharp ice shards that sliced through the zombies' heads like watermelons. The two Level 3 zombies were instantly obliterated, and they cleared the blocked route in a flash.

"Mom, that boy is an Aberrant!" The little girl clapped excitedly. "A high-level Aberrant." The passengers murmured in disbelief.

Two years after the apocalypse, the existence of Aberrants was no longer a secret, but in the lower districts, most were of Class D and C. Encountering a Class B Aberrant was rare. To effortlessly wipe out a medium-sized zombie horde like this, only a Class B or higher Aberrant could manage it.

The young man tilted his head back, his tousled curls sticking out wildly, and smiled with angelic innocence, "I'm getting off here. Don't worry about me."

The guard holding the gun stood there, speechless. "There's no stop here, kid!"

"Report any damage to the hull and keep," a mature voice commanded over the intercom. "Captain, that kid..." The guards hesitated, their faces uncertain. "He's with F777, an A3-level Ice Aberrant. Even if you wanted to stop him, you couldn't."

With communication now open between District B and the lower districts, some passengers suddenly realized and pulled out their terminals. The name at the top of the alliance's leaderboard was unmistakable: "F777."

This was a mysterious team, rumored to be composed entirely of powerhouses, all unmatched in strength. Though they had not appeared publicly for some time, their ranking had never dropped, holding the number one spot on the leaderboard year after year, leaving others in the dust. A quick glance at any terminal, and the name F777 would always be there in the most prominent place.

Damian Blackwood walked alone through the ruins.

According to the Bauhinia Alliance's Post-Apocalyptic Survival Guide, the existence of Fallens, a new species with intelligence, had sparked widespread attention. While there was no consensus on how to coexist with them, the best approach so far was mutual avoidance. The Loyak region had been officially designated as a Fallen gathering area, strictly off-limits to ordinary humans.

One year ago, thirteen districts from Sector B, led by Northern

Yard and the Northern Base, issued a declaration of independence, denouncing the formation of the "Bauhinia Alliance."

As of now, over half of the cities in the former New Pacific Alliance, which once spanned 180 districts, have joined. The core principle of the Bauhinia Alliance is that everyone has the equal right to live.

Damian found a clear spot and set down a loudspeaker. He tapped play, and a raspy frequency emitted, spreading far and wide.

The origin of this device was quite interesting—it came from the same place as the book Zombies: From Beginner to Expert, created by a renowned zombie language expert. This expert believed that through communication, humanity could achieve peaceful coexistence with the Fallens.

Damian waited in place for a while. The air grew thick, and the ground trembled continuously as zombies, drawn by the special frequency, roared fiercely and surrounded him. Yet, this time, Damian did not attack. Instead, he stood in place with a cheerful smile.

A small zombie in the lead jumped onto his back, affectionately nuzzling him while trying to steal his crossbody bag.

Damian gripped the strap, not letting go, and cast a pleading look into the distance. "Ada, can you help me out here?"

The three-meter-tall Fallen leader whimpered twice, and the mischievous zombie slid off Damian's back, turning its attention to the loudspeaker instead.

"Just passing through after completing a mission, thought I'd check on you guys," Damian said as he dug out a wobbly, three-legged chair from the rubble, struggling to keep it balanced. A few small zombies hopped onto his lap, tugging at his T-shirt.

"Oh, new members?" Damian tilted his head, looking toward the back.

A group of Fallens, distinctly of a different breed, stood nervously on the outskirts. They resembled zombies more closely, with exposed limbs covered in decaying cracks. They hovered at the edge, too timid to approach. Damian pulled several large baskets of green apples from his space pocket, pretending to be reluctant as he pushed them out.

The zombies swarmed, scattering to grab the apples.

Finally freed from protecting his designer T-shirt, Damian turned to speak with Ada. "Ada, did you find my sister?" Ada shook its head. They had searched every corner of Loyak, but found nothing.

Cora had been missing for almost a year. Not dead—missing.

Even though she had turned to ash before everyone's eyes, leaving not a single hair behind, Onyx still firmly believed she was alive. Every member of F777 was waiting for her to return.

But they weren't doing well. Suchat had fallen into a vegetative state, kept alive only by a tangle of tubes. Yuui Hayashi, frail, stayed by his side day and night. Charles Franz was overwhelmed trying to treat them. Felix Lucas had gone on a "business trip" to Grass Pit and hadn't returned. And the last one...

Damian cupped his chin, sighing like an old soul, "Sigh..."

Onyx seemed the most normal on the surface, but Damian's instincts were sharp. He knew Onyx was the least normal of all. Since that day, Onyx hadn't smiled once. Sometimes, the madness and stubbornness that flashed in his eyes were downright terrifying.

Caught in his melancholy, Damian's terminal suddenly beeped, and Charles's furious roar blared in his ears, "You little brat! Your location keeps shifting again! You promised to come straight home after the mission. Where the heck are you now? Get back here for dinner!"

Damian pouted. He had just completed an A-Class mission all by himself. He! A twelve-year-old kid! The backbone of F777! Already working at such a young age, earning points to support the whole family!

Sister, where are you? The sunlight above was a bit too bright. Damian lay among the Fallens, closing his eyes slightly.

I miss you so much.

District F199.

The sea breeze gently caressed the rocks as the water lightly rippled along the shore.

Splash!

Cora surfaced from the water, her entire body drenched as she slowly opened her eyes. She had completely transformed into a stranger.

She now resembled someone with albinism—her skin pale, her long hair snowy white, and from head to toe, she was pure white. The only exception was her irises and pupils, which were a misty shade of pale pink.

When she stood up, her figure was tall, nearly 5'7". Her transparent cheeks looked like white porcelain washed by water, delicate. Cora lifted her left hand out of the water, her white feather-like lashes fluttering slightly as she stared at it for a few seconds.

Five fingers. This time, it was right.

It had taken a year, but her missing body parts had finally regrown. Her smooth skin bore no scars, tender as if newly born. The only lingering effect was the albinism-like gene defect.

Cora bent down to pick up the clothes scattered on the beach, slipping them on in a few swift movements. She pulled the hood over her head, wrapping herself up tightly. The sun was nearly setting, but its rays still pricked at her skin with a sharp sting.

From behind her, the faint roar of zombies echoed. A dozen ragged undead lunged at her. District F199 was an isolated island overrun by monsters—encountering one or two with every few steps was nothing unusual.

Cora glanced up at them briefly. With no visible movement, golden streams of light instantly sliced into fragments of the ferocious zombies, their blood spraying across the sky.

After her body had been reformed, the energy within her flowed freely with no obstructions, and her control over her mental power had become even more precise.

Cora had truly become an S-Class Aberrant. She no longer needed to materialize Ethereal Artifacts because she herself had become the strongest human weapon.

Cora returned to a dilapidated house by the sea. The surrounding neighbors had long since turned into zombies and vanished, leaving only faint rustling noises in the yard. Mrs. Travers was back from scavenging through a pile of junk, her stiff movements scrubbing something by the water basin.

Little Travers, on all fours, was crawling haphazardly at the door. He accidentally bumped into Cora's leg and let out a howl, opening his mouth to bite, only to be kicked away by Cora. He rolled away like a ball.

Cora found a bench and sat down, her pale face indifferent to the setting sun. "I'm leaving."

Her voice was hoarse from disuse, and her grasp of the common tongue was rusty, but once she spoke, it was fluent, without a trace of hesitation.

Little Travers, still dazed, rolled back over and noticed that Cora's previously empty arm had regrown. Drooling, he immediately sank his teeth into it, this time successfully. His sharp teeth pierced the thin blood vessels, and blood gushed out.

Pork knuckle, so tasty. In his muddled state, Little Travers vaguely recalled a dish he had eaten when he was still human, and his mouth watered even more.

He's asking for it.

Smack! Mrs. Travers slapped him on the head.

Smack, smack! Two more slaps followed. Little Travers yelped in pain, forced to let go, and tumbled away with his feet in the air. Even as a zombie, your mom is still your mom.

Little Travers clutched his head in grievance, protesting why he couldn't eat. Last time, he could eat two fingers, so why couldn't he eat five? It was clearly the backup food he had found!

A year ago, Little Travers had dug up a lump of pink "seafood" on the beach, happily bringing it home to eat. But to his shock, that lump of meat moved on its own and even tried to bite him!

Too scared to eat it, he had kept it in a water tank instead. Day by day, the meat grew larger, gradually forming a vague human shape. Then one day, the "seafood" talked!

"Ugh… it hurts…"

The meat groaned in pain just as Little Travers was about to take a bite out of a mutated squirrel. Startled, he jumped, and the squirrel scurried away. "Aaaaah!!" he screamed, stomping his feet in frustration.

"Aaah—!!" The seafood echoed his scream. "Huh? Aah, aaah!" Mrs. Travers quickly shielded Little Travers, warily eyeing the convulsing meat.

"It hurts… so much!!"

Thud, thud! The seafood began thrashing against the tank. Mrs. Travers scooped up Little Travers and ran, slamming the door shut. They didn't come out for an entire week. The water tank was shattered, and the seafood, baked by the sun, was on the verge of death, writhing towards the door, desperately pounding: Thud, thud!

"Aaah... aaah... aaah... (What are you?)" Mrs. Travers could only produce low, meaningless growls as her vocal cords had long since decayed. But the seafood seemed to understand and faintly whispered, "Cora... My name... is Cora."

Upon hearing this, Mrs. Travers fell silent.

In the end, she dragged the lump of meat into the house, keeping this self-proclaimed "Cora" seafood alive. Time passed quickly, and Little Travers, with his poor memory, gradually forgot about the seafood's existence, though his instinct to bite remained strong. Whenever he saw the humanoid figure at home, he couldn't help but want to take a bite.

The only time he succeeded was when Cora had accidentally reshaped her left hand incorrectly, leaving it with only two fingers, which she then offered him to eat.

After Cora announced she was leaving, Mrs. Travers nodded, a few low grunts escaping her throat: "Aah, aah, aah."

After spending so much time together, Cora could understand Mrs. Travers' meaning: I know it was only a matter of time.

Cora's face was obscured under her hood. "You said I saved you before?"

"Aah." Mrs. Travers recounted the events at Fool's Pier when the apocalypse first broke out. Back then, she was still human, selfish and mean. After becoming a Fallen, her mind grew muddled, but in a way, it made her more open-minded, indifferent to most things.

Cora stared at her left arm in a trance. In just a moment, the wound that Little Travers had bitten open had already healed. "But I don't really remember."

Her mind was like a rusty machine, having lost a lot of information after rebooting. Even her emotions—joy, anger, sorrow, and happiness—had become sluggish.

Cora Thornton could only remember that from the moment she became conscious, she had been trapped in a laboratory, surrounded by endless whiteness and the harsh glow of crimson lights. Endless torment and the excruciating pain left by 1,314 experiments consumed her mind.

Later, her grandfather helped her escape. After that, her memories became fragmented and hazy.

What had happened over the years? Why had she died?

Sometimes, fleeting images of familiar faces would flash through her mind, but they would vanish the moment she tried to grasp them. The process of reconstructing her body had been exceptionally long, and Cora often found herself trapped in nightmares.

In those dreams, she saw a pair of eyes gazing at her—sometimes curving into a smile, other times filled with sorrow. A tear mole at the corner of those eyes seemed like a drop of scalding water, falling directly into her heart.

But she couldn't remember any of it. Yet, deep inside, there was a voice urging her—she had to find him.

Cora stood up. "I'm leaving today."

Mrs. Travers replied, "Aah, aah! (Take care.)"

Cora glanced at Little Travers. "He always bites people, not cute at all."

"Aah! Aah! (Get lost!)" Mrs. Travers bared her teeth fiercely.

Cora remained expressionless. "Do you want to come with me?"

Mrs. Travers hesitated for a moment before shaking her head. "Aah... aah... (No, the outside world doesn't accept us.)"

Cora nodded. "I understand."

Before leaving, Cora made one last visit home. On her way up the slope, she noticed that Ah Ming's tombstone was still there.

She gave it a brief glance without emotion, then turned and entered the dilapidated, drafty old house. Something instinctively drew her to a particular wall. At first, she considered punching through it, but after some thought, she used a blade instead.

Deep within the wall, a sealed box was hidden.

Cora opened it to find neatly arranged blocks of rhenium inside. The corners of her mouth involuntarily lifted slightly, but soon fell again.

Why did she come looking for this? Cora's eyes were confused. It felt like... someone really liked it, always pestering her for it. But she couldn't remember.

The external communication of District F199 had been cut off long ago. For the past year, not even a mutant mosquito from another district had flown in.

Leaving would require considerable effort.

Cora, holding the box, made her way to the seaside under the cover of night.

Her pupils rapidly contracted, and the code on the back of her neck flashed briefly as her DNA sequence rewrote itself once more. A tail, resembling both a dragon and a serpent, grew out from her lower back, and golden scales appeared on both sides of her cheeks, extending from her collarbone down to her waistline.

In the past, the Fireseed Project had preserved many experimental logs. One unremarkable entry read:

Subject ID: LAK0017

Biological Prototype: Humanoid Embryo

Experiment Record: August 10, Year 34 of the New Calendar, the 222nd gene fusion was successful.

Target Status: Alive

Cora dove into the water and disappeared into the rolling waves.

Ten days later.

District D128, Chilian.

The dilapidated highway exit was the last safe route out of the city. Barricades and spikes surrounded the service station, with a few off-road pickup trucks parked haphazardly in the middle of the road. Five shirtless men sat on top of the vehicles, playing cards.

"What the hell are you out of your mind? I played a three and you throw down a joker? Do you even know how to play?"

"S-sorry, boss!"

Amidst their arrogant bickering, a group of disheveled refugees with families in tow approached the checkpoint, only to be stopped by the barricades. "Where to?" one of the bald men, still focused on his cards, asked with a sideways glance.

"C65 District, Red Stone Shelter."

Red Stone was the most well-known shelter nearby, with many Aberrants and good security.

"Toll fee, three blocks of Level 2 crystals."

A scholarly-looking man with glasses pleaded softly, "Could we negotiate? We'll pay two blocks."

The bald man sneered, "I wasn't finished—three blocks per person."

The man's chest heaved with anger. "You... you can't be serious."

"Honey, don't!" His wife hurriedly pulled him back. She was an E-Class Empath, the lowest level of Aberrant, and could feel the overwhelming mental pressure from the other side, making her tremble with fear.

These men were notorious in Chilian. Their group, called "Just Collecting a Toll," comprised four C-Class Aberrants and one B-Class.

They didn't take on any missions, instead surviving by extorting tolls and selling off crystals. Unfortunately, they had taken control of the critical passage from Chilian to Red Stone, and in the post-apocalyptic world where order had collapsed, strength ruled. District D128 had no powerful Aberrants to keep them in check, leaving refugees helpless.

"Why don't you just rob us outright?" a hot-headed student shouted in frustration. The bald man grinned wickedly. "You're right, so that's exactly what I'm doing." With a swift motion, he threw a punch into the air, sending the student flying with a shockwave, blood spewing from his mouth.

"Ahhh—!" Terrified refugees scattered in all directions. The bald man and his crew stood up, ready to kill and loot.

"Stop!"

At the critical moment, a searing whip of fire snapped through the air, separating the five Aberrants from the panicked crowd. A sharp-eyed refugee shouted excitedly, "I know him. That's Ray Jean-Pierre from Red Stone Shelter!"

The crowd looked up to see a young man with a determined gaze and sharp features, followed by a dozen ordinary people armed with weapons. Ray first helped the injured student to his feet, gently comforting him. "Red Stone has Aberrants who specialize in healing. Can you hold on? I'll take you to see them." The student nodded in pain.

Ray then turned his icy gaze toward the bald man. "Charging a toll violates the Post-Apocalyptic Survival Guide. Remove the barricades and let them pass."

The bald man snorted, "Who the hell are you, kid?"

The two groups clashed instantly, and the refugees fled in terror. Ray's fire-based powers were highly offensive, but fighting four opponents at once was taking its toll, and his movements gradually slowed.

"Move aside, please."

Just as the situation reached a stalemate, a slightly hoarse voice sounded.

Cora, hooded and wrapped up tightly, approached from behind, walking through the battlefield as if nothing was happening.

The surrounding murmuring ceased, and both sides stopped fighting. Under the gaze of everyone present, Cora reached the barricade, only to be blocked.

"Hey, toll fee. Three blocks of Level 2 crystals per person," the bald man shouted at her, not forgetting his demands even while fighting.

"I don't have any." Cora rummaged through her pockets, but aside from the box she was carrying, she was empty-handed.

"No crystals, no passage. Step aside."

A vicious air punch was aimed at her, but Cora tilted her head slightly to dodge it. Her hood shifted, revealing a few strands of pure white hair. Everyone on the scene froze—this person did not look like someone to mess with.

"Boss, look at what she's holding."

"A cryogenic box—must be something valuable," the bald man said greedily. "We're gonna make a killing this time."

Cora ignored the comments, or perhaps she simply didn't care, treating everyone as if they were beneath her notice. She lifted her foot lightly and...

Bam! The barricade shattered, spikes flying everywhere and puncturing the truck tires, clearing a path.

"You damn woman, causing trouble, huh?!" The bald man, enraged, lunged at her, his massive frame bearing down as various powers were hurled in her direction.

"Watch out!" Ray's voice tightened with urgency.

A breeze stirred, lifting the white strands of hair beneath her hood. The bald man met her gaze—those pale pink eyes devoid of any emotion, as if staring at a corpse.

An icy shiver ran down his spine, and a deep, primal fear took hold. The sheer terror of her aura crushed his B-Class mental power. Cora gazed at him impassively as his legs gave out, and he fell to the ground. "N-no, please don't kill me!!"

To an S-Class Aberrant, dealing with a B-Class was like crushing an ant.

Golden light pierced through his chest, and in an instant, the five once-arrogant men were dead, their bodies collapsing to the ground. It took several seconds before the blood pooled around them.

The entire service station fell silent. Cora carefully stepped over the blood, continuing forward without a word. The people from Red Stone Shelter, too frightened to speak, instinctively parted to let her through.

"Thank you," a round-faced man at the back of the group murmured as she passed.

"Hey, why are you talking to her? She's scary!" his companion exclaimed, startled.

Cora glanced at the man briefly, her gaze lingering on his face for a second before she looked away.

"Wait, um, it's dangerous to carry that box around so openly," the man cautioned kindly.

"It doesn't matter," Cora replied indifferently.

The round-faced man glanced back at Ray, who had just confirmed the completion of the emergency bounty on his terminal. Ray nodded slightly. The round-faced man fished a silver ring from his pocket. "You helped us out, so take this. It's a space item, but it's small—only about two square meters."

"Flame, you can't just give away stuff like that!" Flame Tillman was tugged aside by his friend, causing him to stumble. A blue light flashed at his waist as he responded with a hint of grievance, "But she helped us complete the mission, and besides... this ring is mine. I can give it to whoever I want."

Cora's fingers twitched, and the flying knife at Flame's waist slipped into her palm, bringing with it a rush of clear memories. Flame stammered, "Not that one! That's my best friend's keepsake—I can't give it to you."

These Ethereal Artifacts had been mass-produced and used for two years, with most of their energy depleted. Cora reinforced the blade, and a faint golden light now covered the blue blade. It could now last a century without breaking, making it a worthy family heirloom.

"Consider it an exchange." Cora took the ring, trying it on each finger until she found the left ring finger to be a perfect fit.

Flame stared at her, dumbfounded. "You—you—you...!"

Ray quickly strode over, and if one listened closely, they could hear the slight tremor in his voice. "Have we... met somewhere before?"

"No." Cora focused on adjusting the ring, quickly mastering its use and storing the box inside.

"Then, may I ask... do you know someone named Cora Thornton?" Ray glanced at her face, feeling foolish for even asking.

"No," Cora replied without batting an eye.

Ray's expression showed disappointment, and he sighed quietly. He had been too impulsive—it was probably just a coincidence that their powers were similar. It had been nearly two years since they parted in Blossomville. He wondered how Cora was doing now.

"May I ask your name?" Ray inquired.

Cora paused briefly, her expression blank as she looked up.

In that instant, a strange phrase flashed through her mind: F777, my name is Suchat, remember it.

The phrase was so loud and clear that once it appeared, she couldn't forget it.

After a moment of thought, she blurted out, "Uh... Suchat, my name is Suchat."

CHAPTER 28

The Ring

"Red Stone Shelter is the largest refuge in the Southeast region of the New Pacific Alliance. Many Aberrants come and go here, so whether you're looking for someone or seeking information, you should be able to find some clues," Ray Jean-Pierre explained from the front passenger seat, his tone composed yet respectful.

"Yeah, I hope so," Cora replied, her voice flat and emotionless. The apocalypse had left most cities along the way in ruins. After spending ten days swimming with her dragon gene, she had finally found the surviving Chilian.

Several changed SUVs sped down the highway, the scenery outside retreating rapidly.

Leaning over the front seat, Flame Tillman curiously asked, "Suchat, what level are you? Ray just leveled up to B-rank, but I think you're even stronger than him!" Being addressed as "Suchat," made Cora feel uneasy.

"I bet she's A-rank!" someone in the car excitedly guessed.

"Maybe she's even S-rank," a gaming enthusiast chimed in, his eyes shining. He'd never seen a live S-rank Aberrant before. Cora's entrance had been so commanding, like a high-level boss descending on a newbie village, effortlessly taking down five opponents with a flick of her wrist.

"No," Cora's face remained hidden under her hood, only her slightly pink lips visible. "I'm stronger than S-rank."

An Over S-rank Aberrant—Cora vaguely recalled that the Alliance hadn't even completed the classification yet. Even the most advanced R-type Anopower Detector couldn't measure it.

After she spoke, the car fell silent for two seconds.

After a while, someone laughed awkwardly. "Wow, you must have a great sense of humor."

District C65, Red Stone Shelter

Cora followed the refugees out of the vehicle. In the distance, the building complex ahead looked intricate, with different gates corresponding to various entrances, resembling a maze. Anyone coming here for the first time would surely get lost without a guide.

Just then, a small horde of zombies rushed into the perimeter. The walls automatically shifted—clang!—locking them into a chamber. Guards jumped onto the walls, easily blasting the zombies to pieces with their Anopower.

In the depths of her memory, a clear, pleasant voice echoed. Cora felt a faint stir in her heart, as if she could see those eyes again, sighing helplessly at her. But who was the person speaking?

Ray led the group, patiently explaining to everyone, "The designer of Red Stone, and the creator of Blossomville, is Tom Lee. The primary structures are underground, with the surface areas primarily serving as functional and commercial zones. Stay close to me, and don't get lost."

Cora snapped back to reality, knowing her sense of direction was terrible, and pursued.

After winding through the maze for half an hour, they emerged into a bustling street, lively and filled with the scent of food. "Freshly grown potatoes, corn, chili peppers, all from our own greenhouses! Come and try them!"

"Looking for Aberrants to join a C-rank mission? We're short two AoE specialists. We'll head out as soon as the team is full!"

A few men and women stood casually by the roadside, chatting, "How's it going?"

"Haha! How did you know my wife just gave birth?"

"The district evaluation is coming up. Do you think Red Stone can move up to District B now that we've joined the Azures?"

"No chance of that. We might move up a few ranks from the

bottom, though. But I heard the best shot is with Saya in District D78. Their leader, Chionji, is an S-rank Aberrant. They're developing so fast, they're almost guaranteed to jump from D to B!"

Cora passed by silently, catching their attention. They muttered under their breath, "Who's that? Why is she so bundled up in the middle of summer?"

"Do you think she's a mutant?"

"Probably not. Looks like she came back with Ray."

"Just keep walking straight to the registration area. You can take them there first," Ray instructed.

After organizing the refugees, Ray helped an injured student limp toward the medical station, where a group of volunteers in uniform was busy at the entrance.

Among them, a familiar face caught Cora's eye—Angela Chou. She had changed a lot; the arrogance and dominance that once marked her face were gone, replaced by exhaustion from the apocalypse. There was no time left for petty concerns, and the look she gave Ray was exceptionally straightforward.

"Ray, what do you need?"

"He was injured by an Anopower. Could you take a look?"

Angela asked the injured person a few questions, then shook her head helplessly. "I can only treat external injuries. You'd better see a doctor. He's C-rank, right? I'll get you a number." "Thanks. Have you seen Holden Jameson?"

"He went out on a mission with his girlfriend."

Ray nodded, saying nothing more, and turned back to help Flame.

Ray was tall and handsome, with chiseled features. His composed demeanor and steady actions made him incredibly popular in the shelter, like a star with its own gravitational pull.

Cora listened to their conversation, deep in thought. She recalled some past events but decided against revealing herself. It was better this way. Everyone was just trying to survive. That was good enough.

After wandering around the functional area, Cora entered the Aberrant rest area and removed her hood. Her white hair cascaded down as she quietly lowered her gaze and sat like an exquisite, high-priced figurine.

Her striking appearance attracted the attention of those around her, and whispers circulated. "Is she an albino? I heard they can't be exposed to the sun, or their skin will blister and burn."

"Huh? That's so sad. The radiation is bad enough without having a genetic condition on top of it."

"But she's really pretty, almost doesn't seem real."

Cora's eyelids twitched, her pink pupils locking onto the last person who spoke. "I'm real."

The discussion fell silent, and a guy with highlighted hair awkwardly smiled at Cora.

Cora stood up and approached them. Up close, her appearance was even more striking. Her translucent skin looked like washed white porcelain, and her long lashes cast a shadow. "I want to ask you something. Do you know F777?"

That unforgettable name, along with Suchat's, had been mentioned in the slogan.

The three were stunned for a moment, then exaggeratedly cried out, "F777? You mean the one at the top of the Alliance rankings? You can see it right there on the mission platform."

The guy with the highlights pulled up a projection, and sure enough, F777 was prominently displayed at the top.

"Who's in F777?" Cora asked.

"I do not know. They're B-rank Aberrants. We don't get to interact with them."

"I've got some insider info," the girl in the tank top and shorts leaned in. "They say they're all tough guys, the kind that scare little kids, because they're so...uh...ugly. They don't show up much and just bury themselves in racking up points."

That sounded far-fetched. Were these really the people she was looking for?

"Where can I get a terminal?" Cora awkwardly changed the subject. "I accidentally lost mine."

"You can buy one in the commercial area, but you'll need to go to the registration center to bind your Aberrants Certificate. Judging by your looks, you're an Aberrant, right?" "Yes."

"Let me check... The nearest Aberrant base is...District C83, Felalakas."

Felalakas?

Neon signs, a giant Ferris wheel, oversized billboards, slaughter, blood, champions... Fragments of memories flashed by, and Cora remained silent. Felalakas seemed like a familiar place to her.

The guy with the highlights, thinking she might be in trouble, discussed it with his companions and then offered, "Actually, we've taken on a mission and are leaving Red Stone tomorrow. We'll pass by Felalakas on the way. Do you want to come with us?"

Cora was straightforward: "I have no money."

"Hey, we're all friends here! In the apocalypse, we have to help each other out. But if we run into zombies, you'll have to help us fight, okay?" Cora smiled faintly, "Sure, I'm very strong."

"Hahaha, you're so confident!" The three of them chuckled.

This small D-rank team might never know that they had used their extraordinary luck to hire the strongest fighter in the Alliance, an Over S-rank Aberrant, as their free bodyguard.

District C83, Felalakas

Cora strolled through the late-night streets, passing by various cyborgs and AI in outlandish outfits. With her head covered, she didn't stand out much.

A red-haired girl was crying her eyes out by the roadside, her Anopower vines tightly clutching a life-sized cutout. "River... my River... why...?" she sobbed.

"What's up with Chiho Sato this time? Why's she losing it?"

"Haven't you heard? River Locke announced he's quitting the music scene to go into politics, just like Ilia."

"What?! His fangirls are gonna be devastated!"

"Tell me about it. Ilia hasn't shown his face in an entire year."

River Locke, the graceful gentleman and the most popular virtual idol in Felalakas, had just announced his retirement. It would be a sleepless night of broken hearts.

Cora adjusted her hat brim and continued walking. The bustling ADs filled the surrounding air: "The annual Throne Tournament is now open for registration!" "The top ten supernovas have been completely reshuffled. Let's look back at the top idols who've vanished over the years."

On a high-definition floating screen, a starlet with pink hair sat amidst a sea of flowers. The voiceover introduced her as Yuui

Hayashi, a former supernova whose hit songs "Thank You for Loving Me" and "Drizzle" had amassed billions of streams on the Lucas Network. However, she hadn't been active publicly for a long time, causing her fans to worry.

Cora stopped in her tracks, staring at that sweet face for a few extra seconds. Something about it was familiar, but also... off.

Was it the smile?

At the luxurious entrance of the Sycara Theater, an AI in a tailcoat enthusiastically approached her. "Lovely lady. How about a one-of-a-kind musical experience tonight? VIP floating tickets are only 3,888 NPA credits!"

"I don't have any money," Cora sighed, realizing she'd been repeating that phrase a lot lately.

The AI's expression instantly turned scornful, its tone mocking as it said, "Oh~ that's too bad. You see, art has its price. To enjoy the most immersive and safest audiovisual feast, one must pay."

Cora didn't take the bait. Instead, a subtle smile appeared on her lips. "Does false advertising have a price too?"

The AI stuttered for a second. "Artificial intelligence only speaks the truth. Please do not slander..."

"Weren't there zombies that broke out underfoot here? A large horde of them. So much for your 'safest experience,'" Cora interrupted.

The AI froze on the spot, its system glitching, and began emitting error beeps. The current greeter had evidently not been programmed with the memories of its predecessor. Cora patted its shoulder and hummed an off-key tune as she walked away.

At the Aberrant base, Cora tapped on the empty reception desk. "Hello, I need to replace my ID."

The night-shift staffer, a bespectacled girl, was dozing off. Hearing the sound, she quickly sat up straight, turned off her treasured Ilia concert compilation, and began typing away seriously on her keyboard.

"Name and ID, please."

"Cora Thornton. I don't remember the ID number."

"Cora Thornton... Cora... Got it!" The girl rubbed her tired eyes and took a sharp breath. "Is there a problem?" Cora asked.

"No, but your residence has been moved to District B10. I don't have the authority to process this directly. I'll have to apply for you."

"District B10?"

"Yes, North Yard. It's one of the founding districts of the Azures. You're amazing; it's really hard to get in there."

Cora remained silent. As far as she remembered, she'd always been undocumented. When did she get a B-rank residence? "Please go ahead with the application."

"Sure, I'll need to collect your biometric data first."

Collecting biometric data fell to an AI named Minnie.

The precise instruments scanned Cora's iris, and the floating screen suddenly emitted countless tiny beams of light, analyzing and forming a holographic projection: "Recognition failed."

"Error code: CK007."

"What does that mean?" Cora asked, puzzled.

Minnie's flat, synthesized voice responded: "CK007 shows the target is non-human. Please do not trick the system."

The girl, who had come over out of curiosity, was dumbfounded. "You're not human? I'm sorry, I didn't mean to insult you, but... aren't you human?"

She sneaked a peek at Cora's face, hidden beneath the hood. Wow, on closer inspection, her skin was so pale, and her eyes were a strange color. No wonder she never took off the hood. Was she an AI, or maybe an animal? After all, there were Aberrants with animal genes in Sycamore.

Cora was silent for a long moment before replying, "Ah... sorry."

She had forgotten that after her body had been reshaped, all her latent genes were activated. In her current state, she couldn't really be considered "human."

The girl hesitated, then asked, "Do you still want to replace it? If you're an animal-type, you'll need to wait until the manual review office opens tomorrow."

Cora cleared her throat. "Do you know where I can get... a fake ID?"

The girl's face went blank. "What? Are you seriously asking me that? I'm an official employee; do you think it's appropriate to ask me that?"

She shut off the camera and bit her lower lip, staring at Cora with a conflicted and struggling expression. "Look, I really shouldn't tell you this, but a few days ago, at a concert, I heard someone bragging about using a fake ID that was indistinguishable from the real thing. The server in C-district couldn't even tell the difference. I overheard it by accident, of course, and I reported them because I'm very professional."

"According to what they confessed, they got their fake ID in the City of Sin."

Six months ago, the Azures found an alternative to Sora Wings' energy, and the starships in the lower districts gradually resumed operations. However, the route to District F191, City of Sin, was still rare. The next flight would have to depart at midnight, and if missed, the wait would be another week.

With her hands in her pockets, Cora waited at the platform, brushing past a hurried passenger, disappearing without a sound. Meanwhile, a chameleon perched on the person's suitcase, with its bulging eyes slowly rotating as it blended seamlessly with its surroundings.

The hatch door closed slowly, carrying them toward the distant City of Sin.

In Felalakas, ruled by super AI, everything continued to function as normal. No one knew that the city actually had two masters. The omnipresent cameras captured a shadowy side profile, which was then processed through the vast data network, connecting to a silver branch somewhere deep within.

Northern Base. Silent Garden Apartments.

An urgent communication request forced its way through. Felix, with his silver hair and icy blue eyes, turned up in the projection. "I've got some good news. Want to hear it?"

A slender figure stood by the floor-to-ceiling windows, swirling a glass of strong liquor, quietly overlooking the nightscope below. "Speak."

"Last night, someone tried to activate Cora Thornton's ID at the Aberrant base in Felalakas." The glass halted mid-air, a bit of the golden liquid spilling out. The shadowed side of the figure's face remained obscured, with only the tear-shaped mole near the eye hinting at a lingering sorrow.

"Send me the footage."

The light screen automatically played the camera footage, showing a tall figure from various angles, completely covered from head to toe, making it impossible to see their face. "This person's last known location was the starship port. There were 31 flights that day, headed to 17 different destinations."

"I've got some loose ends to tie up here. Do you want to wait for me or investigate on your own?"

A silver cane tapped the ground. The man speaking was tall and handsome, but there was a slight limp in his right leg, causing him to walk with a noticeable limp. "Doesn't matter. It's just a driver short."

Felix Lucas narrowed his eyes and ended the call without another word.

District F191, City of Sin.

A chaotic underground city rife with violence and crime.

There was no natural light here. Cora removed her jacket as she navigated through the dark alleys, dodging street thugs engaged in a brawl before slipping into the depths of the street.

Following the intel she had received, she quickly found her target. "Boss, I hear you're the most famous merchant on Trade Street."

Ura, who had half his head shaved and the other half covered with long purple hair, looked up. "Flattering. What business are you here for?"

"I need a fake ID."

"What a coincidence." Ura eyed her keenly, a sharp glint in his eyes. "If you place an order now, I'll give you a 1% discount. It'll cost you one Level 4 crystal, or ten Level 3 crystals, with half as a deposit, and the rest upon delivery tomorrow."

Cora nodded. "That works."

There should be plenty of beasts and zombies in the desert; a Level 4 crystal might be difficult for others, but it would be easy for her.

Ura smiled with satisfaction and extended his hand. "I enjoy dealing with straightforward people. Now, the deposit."

Cora hesitated for a moment. "Can I give it to you tomorrow? I don't have it right now."

"Hey, I'm not pressuring you," Ura said with a click of his tongue, shaking his head. "But if you want a fake ID, today is your last chance."

"Why?" Cora frowned.

"To be honest, this business opportunity came up a few months ago when I stumbled upon a bug in the AI systems in B-district. I seized the chance to exploit it. But now, the bug is about to be fixed, so I'm saying it's a stroke of luck. After today, you won't have another chance."

Ura was indeed a cunning merchant, expertly creating a sense of urgency. He even sighed theatrically, "I can see you're serious about this, so I'll wait until nightfall for you. No more extensions."

Cora glanced up at the artificial clock—less than an hour until Crime City's "sunset."

A lack of funds could bring even the greatest hero low. With such little time, where could she find a Level 4 crystal?

Wait a minute—didn't she remember being wealthy once? In her memory, she could casually pull out piles of glowing Level 4 crystals. Where did all her money go?

Frustrated, Cora wandered through the streets and sat down in a trendy cafe. It was too late to head to the desert; she'd have to find another solution in the city.

A pale-skinned young man walked by, carefully cradling a cup of coffee, his steps steady and not spilling a drop. He chose a seat directly across from Cora, taking a deep breath of the coffee's aroma before taking a small, savoring sip.

Cora's gaze drifted to his coffee cup, which bore the elegant script: "Emerald Estate Select Gesha Coffee." She glanced at the prices on the holographic menu—a rich kid, clearly.

She studied the young man more. His clothes were rather simple, but his left hand was adorned with four blindingly bright crystal rings—three blue and one red, the latter a large pigeon-blood ruby on his middle finger.

A Level 4 crystal!

Cora glanced again at the artificial clock. She didn't have time. Maybe... she should "borrow" one first?

Her gaze must have been too intense, as the young man slowly lifted his head, his expression dark. But the moment he saw Cora's face, his eyes widened slightly, and he stared for several seconds.

Then he glanced down, took a sip of coffee, sneaked another glance at Cora, took another sip, and repeated the process, like a shy geek encountering a new figurine he was immediately smitten with.

A cute robot server placed a cup of Emerald Estate coffee in front of Cora.

"I didn't order this," Cora said.

"Correct, table 25," the robot replied, tilting its head in confusion.

"I... I ordered it for you," the young man across from her said slowly, his cheeks turning a suspicious shade of pink. His voice was hesitant. "It's good."

What now? She had planned to rob this sucker of his crystal, but now she couldn't bring herself to do it.

"Hey, Jorick! Did your brain finally grow in? Trying to hit on a girl now?" a passerby taunted with a laugh.

Jorick instantly turned his head, half his face sprouting dense fur as he transformed into a werewolf, growling menacingly at the heckler. The person backed off, muttering as he walked away, "Heaven has no eyes, letting a fool like him be so rich..."

Jorick, satisfied, turned back, reverting to his shy demeanor, and smiled bashfully at Cora.

Cora felt anxious. She glanced at the artificial clock for the third time, then steeled herself. "Could you lend me that Level 4 crystal?"

Jorick's expression went blank. "Huh?"

Before Cora could explain, a piercing city-wide alarm sounded. "Oh, no! Someone's pet got loose!"

Shhh—shhh—

A swarm of sand-colored Anopower scorpions scurried down the alleys, spewing bright yellow flames as people dodged and cursed.

City of Sin, true to its name, where the strangest things happened. Cora sighed deeply, preparing to deal with the problem before discussing the crystal with Jorick.

"Ding—"

The elevator arrived, and a group of uniformed individuals materialized out of nowhere. All of them were high-level Aberrants, well-trained and clearing the entire street without a word.

Click. Click. Click. The sharp taps of a cane against the ground echoed as a tall, handsome man with a limp slowly emerged from the group, a violet wreath pin adorning his collar.

"People from the Azures! What are they doing here?"

"Looking for the Warden, I bet. Trying to convince us to join?"

"Don't flatter yourself. Since when has our F-district been so important?"

The crowd pushed Cora to the back, and she craned her neck to see over the heads. The man with the cane had a face that could steal your breath away—his deep-set, handsome features, sharp contours, and a small tear-shaped mole at the corner of his eye that was enchanting.

Cora's mind buzzed, her thoughts muddled, as she found the man both familiar and strange.

She felt a light tap on her arm and turned back, just in time to miss the man's gaze. Jorick had removed his crystal ring and held it out to Cora. "It's for you."

Onyx noticed an intense gaze, and out of instinct, followed it.

Through the noisy crowd, he saw a young man with black hair holding a large pigeon-blood ruby ring, while a white-haired girl stared at him, too stunned to speak. The surrounding people clapped and cheered, egging them on.

Onyx lowered his eyes, withdrawing his gaze indifferently. He didn't want to see these scenes of budding romance.

It was just... annoying.

CHAPTER 29

Memories

Death Hell.

Hugh Young pushed open the door to his office, where someone was already waiting for him.

A tall young man sat on the sofa, his cold, pale fingers rhythmically tapping as he silently gazed out at the deep sea through the window. A deep melancholy marked his side profile.

Hugh's eyes moved downwards, noticing the silver cane placed beside the sofa. The young man's right leg seemed to be just as impaired as the last time they met.

A few others stood around the room, their expressions calm and their postures casual. Near the door stood twins, identical except for their gender, while two low-profile soldiers with Azure insignias on their shoulders lingered by the window.

Having dealt with criminals for most of his life, and with his half-human, half-AI nature, Hugh could keenly discern that these individuals were special—likely Aberrants, possibly even S-ranked.

Despite their vastly different appearances, Hugh correctly addressed the young man by name, having been briefed beforehand. "Onyx de Montclair."

Onyx nodded slightly. "Long time no see, Pluto—no, Warden Young."

Hugh stepped forward, but the twins looked at him warily, causing him to pause and instead circle back to his desk, sitting down across from Onyx, keeping a safe distance between them. "It's rare for an inmate to return of their own accord," Hugh sighed, "especially one who broke out."

Onyx showed no embarrassment at having his past exposed, instead cutting straight to the point. "I'm here to invite City of Sin to join the Azures."

Hugh's expression remained unchanged. "The Alliance has more than one prison, and F-district isn't that important."

Onyx smoothed out an invisible crease on his sleeve, smiling. "That's how it used to be. But because of you, District F191 is very important now."

A district's governor leaves a strong personal imprint on the city they govern: Ne Kon's cruelty led to Deep Woods' downfall; the people overthrew him after suffering too long. Julian Chang's benevolence turned Sycamore into a unified fortress, successfully withstanding wave after wave of zombie attacks.

After taking control of Death Hell, the City of Sin remained chaotic, filled with violence and crime. However, the judiciary leaned more towards fairness and justice under Hugh's leadership. He redefined sentencing, severely punished criminals, and released many innocent people. Onyx's excellent memory allowed him to recognize Jorick earlier on Trade Street.

With clear and calm eyes, Onyx spoke like a born negotiator. "If I'm not mistaken, although Death Hell appears stable on the surface, you've been operating without proper funding for the past year. The number of prison guards has also drastically decreased, hasn't it?"

After the Battle of Loyak, Noach Mabul died suddenly, many of the Central's key officials were killed or injured, and the Alliance's influence in Utopia was nearly wiped out.

The previously stable tri-polar situation had collapsed, and the leadership was now too preoccupied to bother with an F-district prison.

"If another major prison break were to happen, could you handle it?" Onyx asked pointedly.

City of Sin had once made explosive headlines when a team called "F777" turned Death Hell upside down and escape. This had been the only successful breakout in the prison's history.

Hugh was left speechless.

Wasn't that you who broke out? How can you just pretend nothing happened now that you've changed your face?

Onyx's expression remained as calm as a wall, showing no signs of his thick-skinned audacity.

He continued, unperturbed, "The apocalypse has brought not only crisis but also opportunity. Whether you seize the chance to lead City of Sin against the current or continue to drift along. It is up to you."

"Why choose me?" Hugh's voice was hoarse.

Onyx glanced at him, focusing intently. Hugh possessed a rare steadiness, never letting his emotions get the better of him.

"Death Hell was a necessary product of the Alliance's development at a particular stage. Its functionality is irreplaceable, and staying here is your life's mission."

Onyx recited calmly, "That's what you said. Have you changed your mind?"

Hugh slowly shook his head. "Never."

Onyx smiled faintly. "The new district evaluations will start soon, with no registration restrictions. This time, the ranking will take all aspects into consideration. Every C-level city will receive resource incentives. I'm looking forward to a story where F-district rises to C."

Hugh remained silent for a long while before speaking. "I have one question. Even though I'm not... human, can I still join?"

His words were vague, but Onyx understood immediately. "You wouldn't be the only non-human governor in the Azures."

"A super AI governs Felalakas, and the Zombie Lord rules Loyak. Perhaps, soon, the definition of 'human' will be rewritten."

Hugh nodded solemnly. "Thank you. I'll consider it."

Bang, bang! A loud knock came from outside the door. "Warden! There's trouble in the desert!!"

Onyx gracefully rose to his feet, gripping his cane. "You should attend to that. I'll take my leave."

After watching the group leave, Hugh turned to the prison guard. "What's the situation?"

"The prisoners we released yesterday... they've all been killed!"

"For what reason?" Hugh asked calmly.

"A vicious brawl," the guard replied, shaking his head in exasperation. "They brought it on themselves, honestly. They were desert bandits before, and when they saw someone kill a Level 4 Scorpik, they got greedy and tried to steal it, but ended up getting killed instead."

"How about the other side? Any casualties?"

"The other side, uh… they're fine." The guard's expression grew conflicted, and he hesitated before continuing, "Warden, when I said it was a brawl, I meant it was one person fighting a group…."

The scorching desert sun hung high in the sky, distorting the air with its intense heat.

Cora Thornton was drenched in sweat, her soaked white hair sticking to her collarbone. The hood of her cloak felt like it was on fire, her skin blistering and peeling only to quickly heal again thanks to her secondary Anopower, the cycle leaving behind faint scars that didn't even have time to hurt.

At her feet lay the carcasses of two Scorpiks. Even the slightest movement threatened to overwhelm her with the searing heat. Jorick, equally drenched in sweat, panted with his tongue out like a dog, but he still dutifully followed her.

"Here, take them back." Cora handed him two blood-red crystals. Thanks to this fool's help, she had paid Ura just in time to meet the deadline. Jorick took a step back, shaking his head rapidly, his eyes filled with hesitation. "Coffee… rings… take you… home," he stammered, his meaning unclear.

"I'm leaving tomorrow once I get my goods. You should go back and get your rings yourself." The heat was unbearable, every extra second outside a torment. Cora's patience was wearing thin, and she didn't understand what he was trying to say. Her tone became commanding.

Jorick hesitated, but finally took just one crystal and put it away.

"Home…" he said, but his ears suddenly perked up as he looked grimly toward the distant dunes.

The sandstorm kicked up, and the yellow dunes shifted and heaved.

Boom! Boom! The sand exploded as over thirty desert bandits emerged from their hiding places, surrounding Cora and Jorick.

"If this fool doesn't want them, how about giving the crystals to us?" The speaker, a man with the air of a ruthless outlaw, sneered and reached out, activating his Anopower for telekinesis.

Zing—!!

His mental force hit a solid barrier, the crystals in Cora's hand remaining completely still. The difference in their power was too great for a C-rank Aberrant like him to even get close. Shocked, the bandit dropped his smirk, his expression hardening into something more sinister.

Sweat dripped from Cora's chin, instantly evaporating in the heat. She felt dizzy from the heat and longed to return to the cool underground city. Her voice was dry and slow as she spoke. "You have three seconds to leave."

"Oh, listen to her! Kill her and take the crystals, boys!"

Over thirty bandits charged at once, their colorful Anopowers churning up the sandy ground.

"Awoo—!!"

Jorick roared in fury, transforming into his werewolf form and launching himself into the fray with wild claws and fangs. Unfortunately...

Being a pampered rich kid with thick fur, he promptly overheated and collapsed face-first into the sand.

The bandits roared with laughter as they swiftly pinned him down, a curved blade pressed to his throat, ready to plunge in—

Cora slowly lifted her gaze, her pink eyes flashing with a brilliant gold light.

A surge of overwhelming mental power shook the earth and sky, raising a massive sandstorm. Countless barbed arrows shot out from behind her, tearing through the bandits like a relentless wave, severing limbs and ripping through hearts. Within moments, the bandits lay dead, their bodies scattered across the ground.

The wind and sand settled, leaving the battlefield eerily silent, as if the world itself was holding its breath.

"Come out," Cora commanded coldly, her voice cutting through the empty desert.

After a few moments, a group of terrified locals emerged from the sand. A while later, another group of Aberrants cautiously appeared in the mirage of an oasis.

The mantis stalks the cicada, unaware of the oriole behind. Only in City of Sin, the most chaotic place in the Alliance, could a small skirmish like this hide three different ambushes.

Cora raised her hand slightly, and both groups immediately dropped to their knees, begging for mercy. "Spare us, hero! We had no intention of fighting!"

Cora wiped her face indifferently, the hot sweat stinging her eyes and blurring her vision. "Leave."

The groups backed away in unison, and seeing that Cora didn't intend to kill them, one of them nervously asked, "May we ask for the hero's name? So we know to avoid you in the future."

In City of Sin, a name was the easiest thing to spread. They wanted to know who they had crossed to avoid making the same mistake again.

Cora dragged the unconscious Jorick out from the pile of corpses, lifting him with one hand. Without thinking, she blurted out the alias she had grown accustomed to using recently. "My name is Suchat."

As soon as the words left her mouth, everyone collectively froze. "Did I hear that right? Did she say her name is Suchat?"

"Which Suchat? Could it really be?"

"It has to be that Suchat!!" a voice trembled like a thunderclap in everyone's ears.

The ambushers halted in their tracks, their faces filled with shock. Upon closer inspection, a hint of reverence appeared in their eyes, as if they were gazing upon a deity high above.

Cora was taken aback, this being the first time she had encountered such a reaction. "You know Su... me?"

"Of course we do! F777!"

"Back in the day, you made your name in the desert. This place is your old stomping ground! Who here doesn't know the legend of F777?"

"But I thought Suchat was a man..." someone hesitantly remarked amidst the background noise. A heavy smack landed on his head as a companion frantically signaled him with their eyes. "Shut up! Suchat can be anything—if she says she's Suchat, then she is!"

Cora's head throbbed with pain as she waved off the chattering crowd.

A silver-white starship flew across the sky, its violet wreath insignia glittering in the sunlight. Cora glanced up at it briefly before turning her gaze away and heading in the opposite direction, toward the underground city.

Thud!

Cora dropped Jorick to the ground and knocked on the counter. "I'm here to pick up my goods."

"Here, only usable in districts below C." Ura tossed a terminal her way, poking his head out to get a look. "Isn't that Jorick? What happened, did he get heatstroke?"

"Yeah." Cora examined the terminal's functions, finding nothing wrong with it. "I'll be leaving soon. Can you watch him for me?"

"Sure, of course." Ura flicked his half-purple hair back, grinning from ear to ear. Jorick was a rich guy, after all—another opportunity to squeeze some money out of him.

Cora absentmindedly fiddled with her silver ring. "I've heard that you're the most well-informed merchant on Trade Street."

Ura grunted in acknowledgment.

Cora placed the Level 4 crystal on the counter. "I want to buy some information."

Ura's eyes lit up as he instantly pulled out a magnifying glass. "What kind of information could be worth a Level 4 crystal? I'm really curious now."

"About F777. Tell me everything you know," Cora said.

Ura's smile faltered slightly. "Customer, I don't do every kind of business. F777 are my old clients. I can't sell their information—what if you turn around and seek revenge? They've made quite a few enemies."

Cora stared at her calmly. "I'm not seeking revenge. I've just... forgotten a lot of things. I only remember that F777 should be my friends. I want to find them. Please, any information will do, even just a name."

Ura scrutinized her closely. "You're sure you're not after revenge?"

Cora nodded. "Yes."

Ura, fearing she might change her mind, quickly snatched the crystal and bit into it to confirm its authenticity. "You said even a name would do, right? I can't disclose information about the others, but the leader of F777... their name is Cora Thornton."

The leader of F777, their name is Cora Thornton.

Cora's eyes widened slightly.

From City of Sin to the Northern Base, Cora Thornton nearly crossed the entire New Pacific Alliance.

It took her a full two weeks to reach Front City, but now she was out of options.

According to the rules, for the first time entering the Northern Base, one had to pass through the Immigration Center's inspection. But the sheer number of people here was overwhelming.

Ordinary Aberrants had to wait in line for half a year just to get through, and there was barely any room to breathe, let alone move. If someone had an even slightly weaker lung capacity, they'd risk suffocating.

Her Aberrant Certificate was fake, something Ura had mentioned could only be used in C-districts. It wouldn't work in B-districts. People needed to learn to adapt; the proper channels wouldn't work, so what about less orthodox methods?

Cora approached a scalper who was loudly advertising his services, speaking in a low voice as if she were a spy making contact. "What services do you offer?"

"Smuggling someone in—how much for one person?"

The scalper was horrified. "Are you trying to get me in trouble? Are you a plant? Get lost, get lost! No amount of money is worth it— don't you know how strict the checks on smuggling are now? I don't want to end up in the Aberrants Bureau's prison!"

The indignant scalper didn't control his volume well, and he forgot that the amplification terminal was still pinned to his collar. His roar echoed far and wide, and within a few miles, everyone turned to stare at Cora as if she were some kind of idiot, pointing and whispering.

Cora covered her face and fled.

Half an hour later, she crouched in the corner, hesitating as she stared at the transparent barrier that was within arm's reach. This was the terminal for the city's buses. All she had to do was wait for someone to get off, and she could use that method to sneak in undetected. She shouldn't... be discovered.

Cora took a deep breath, then another, finally steeling herself and hiding in the shadows. The gene she was about to activate pushed her moral boundaries, so she had spent a long time mentally preparing herself.

Boom—!!

A surge of Anopower hit the barrier just before she could act.

"Brother, isn't this too risky?" A sneaky voice came from the other side, sounding like there were three or four people.

"What's there to fear? Delta Island's applications to join the Azures have been rejected multiple times. It's definitely the Northern Base's doing, so I'm just giving them some trouble!"

"Don't stop now! What top-tier city defense? Let's take it down today!"

The shrill sound of alarms blared as the barrier triggered its defense mechanism. Cora watched helplessly as the holographic terminal displayed the message. "Because of a route malfunction, today's bus service is canceled."

Suppressing her anger, Cora walked over to the group and asked expressionlessly, "What are you doing?"

"Uh-oh, we've been spotted!"

"There's a situation in Tunnel 201!"

In the City Defense Department's command center, the surveillance system locked onto the terrorists, causing the destruction. A staff member connected to the internal channel. "Mr. de Montclair, someone is deliberately sabotaging the city's defense system. We've pinpointed the target... huh? The target has been neutralized."

A blurry figure wearing a hood approached, and the screen flashed as the terrorists' heads burst open. Two seconds later, a crimson streak shot out from their chests, and death arrived so swiftly that no one could see what had happened.

Onyx glanced at the floating screen, his eyelashes lowered. "Send a patrol team."

He stood up to leave, but as he reached the door, his steps faltered. In a flash, he rushed back, trembling fingers pressing the pause button. The chests of the fallen terrorists bore obvious knife wounds.

The attacker wore a hood, their face obscured in the shadows, but it was clear they were tall and slender.

"Slow down the playback." Onyx's voice was quick, tinged with urgency. The surveillance footage of the killing replayed in a loop, but even at a slower speed, nothing could be discerned. "Slow it down more."

"Even slower."

It wasn't until the footage nearly froze that they could barely see it. Just before the terrorists died, faint golden lights appeared around them. The lights swiftly condensed into the shape of a cold, sharp blade. Was this... a morphing Anopower?

"Mr. de Montclair, should we slow it down more?"

Onyx remained silent, staring at the screen for a long time before suddenly shaking his head with a smile.

It was the first time the City Defense Department had seen Onyx smile, and in that instant, it was as if the ice had melted, spring rain had fallen, and everyone was left mesmerized, unable to forget the sight.

The bus was gone, and Cora paced back and forth in frustration. Suddenly, her back tensed.

The sky tore open with a pitch-black rift, and an invisible, overwhelming force descended from above. S-ranked spatial Anopower! Then, the S-ranked Anopower Territory activated, sealing the air around Cora, trapping her in a tiny space.

Cora's brow furrowed. Were they coming for her because she had just killed those people? Was she really going to fight right at the entrance to the Northern Base? That wouldn't be ideal—she still wanted to get inside... Wait, maybe this was her chance!

There was no time to think. Cora had no choice. She gritted her teeth and activated the gene she had planned earlier, disappearing on the spot.

A team of Aberrants materialized out of thin air, and the crowd parted to make way as Onyx, cane in hand, walked over.

With his broad shoulders, long legs, and dashing good looks, he would have been the picture of elegance if not for the limp in his right leg, which slightly marred his otherwise perfect image as a refined gentleman.

Facing the now-empty entrance, Onyx's expression was complex, but it softened into an almost unbearably gentle sigh. Under the puzzled gazes of the onlookers, he tossed aside his cane, kneeled on one knee, and stared intently at a tiny louse scurrying around on the ground.

"Cora... is that you?"

The tiny louse froze in its tracks, its tail twitching frantically.

The Aberrants behind Onyx were stunned into silence, their expressions crumbling as they watched the Northern Base's successor urgently deploy an S-ranked spatial Aberrant—just to have a heartfelt conversation with a suspicious-looking louse?

But Onyx seemed unaware of their reactions. He slowly reached out, the tear-shaped mole at the corner of his eye glistening with the moisture of unshed tears. "Let's go home."

Whoosh—the louse vanished. Onyx's pupils contracted as he desperately crawled forward in the dust. "Cora!!"

The next moment, his voice cut off abruptly, and his scalp itched slightly.

CHAPTER 30

Recovering

"Should we pursue?"

At the entrance of Tunnel 201, the confused Aberrants looked around. Where had the suspect gone? Where was the louse?

The air was deathly still as stood motionless, his profile like a statue frozen in time.

It felt like an eternity passed, or perhaps only a few seconds, before his expression shifted from indescribable blankness, shock, and restraint to a calm, emotionless state. His Adam's apple bobbed as he forced out a raspy answer from between clenched teeth. "No need."

Onyx was smart enough to realize that the louse was indeed Cora. For some unknown reason, she couldn't enter the city through normal means, resorting to such an unorthodox method.

His right leg, numbed from kneeling too long, tingled painfully as he stood, swaying slightly. Someone quickly handed him his cane.

His voice returned to its usual calm as he instructed, "Clean up the scene. I'll explain the situation to General Yevgeniyev."

After dismissing the patrol team, Onyx ordered a driverless hover car and settled into the backseat, entering the Northern Base through Tunnel 201.

Just after entering the city, a tickle at his scalp caught his attention. Onyx's fingers tightened around the cane, the veins on the back of his hand standing out. "If you even think about running, I'll have the entire city sprayed with pesticide."

The louse instantly froze; it could clearly understand human speech. Onyx allowed himself a brief, shallow smile, but the thought of the tiny creature still perched on his head quickly erased it, his lips pressing into a tight line. "Isn't this how you planned to enter the city? I'll help you, so don't run anymore."

His last words were barely a whisper, more of a sigh than a command.

Garden Apartments.

Onyx's expression was grim as he hurried through the living room, heading straight for the en-suite bathroom in his room. His fingers flew across the control panel, and with a click, the lights went out, the door locked, and the windows sealed, forming a completely enclosed space.

He issued a harsh command, "Change back."

There was no response; the room remained silent.

Onyx sighed, pinching the bridge of his nose. "If you dared to use such a method, you must have a way to reverse it. At least it proves you can control the duration of the gene. There's no one else here—change back."

After a brief standoff, the louse dropped to the floor, emitting a faint radiation that gradually coalesced into a blurry human figure.

Onyx, quick as a flash, grabbed a bath towel and tossed it over Cora, covering her entirely. In the dim natural light, her pale, glowing ankles were visible, as smooth as jade.

"The second shelf in the wardrobe has clothes."

Onyx's brows furrowed even more deeply, unable to tolerate the filthy memory of the louse's parasitic behavior any longer. He yanked open the shower door and plunged into the shower, the sound of water immediately filling the room.

Two slender, pale fingers pulled the towel from her head. Cora's pink pupils cautiously scanned the surroundings. After confirming it was safe, she opened the wardrobe and pulled out an oversized T-shirt, slipping it on.

Moments later, the sound of running water ceased.

Onyx reappeared, wearing nothing but a thin bathrobe.

A blade hidden in a sleeve was suddenly at his throat, the cold steel glinting menacingly, ready to spill blood with just one more step.

They faced each other, their eyes reflecting the other's face, and slowly, surprise and astonishment rose between them.

Onyx reached out and turned on the light, his gaze fixed on the person in front of him. The cold, indifferent face, snow-white hair, and almost translucent skin—every inch of her features was completely unfamiliar. For once, he was at a loss for words, his expression slightly dazed.

Cora blinked slowly, recognizing him as the man she had briefly encountered in the City of Sin.

But up close, a strange emotion surged in her heart as she looked into his eyes, noting the tear-shaped mole and the sharp lines of his jaw. She couldn't shake the feeling that his features were familiar.

"Who are you?" Cora murmured.

"Onyx. I'm Onyx. Or Petros." Onyx's gaze never wavered, his voice deliberate and precise.

"Onyx?" Cora repeated the name unconsciously, the syllables lingering on her lips as if she had uttered them countless times before.

"Have you always looked like this?" Cora asked, her eyes filled with confusion.

Onyx slowly raised his hand, and Cora came to her senses, pressing the blade down, leaving a faint trace of blood on his neck. He didn't seem to notice, his tone gentle to the point of humility.

"You once said you liked the mole. While waiting for you to return, I altered my genes." His appearance now was both Onyx and Petros.

Had she said that? Cora's mind felt foggy. She couldn't remember, but she had to admit, it looked quite good.

Onyx's cool palm pressed against the hilt of the blade, nuzzling it down. After the brief shock, he quickly thought, "Because of the Phoenix gene activation, not only did your body reshape, but your appearance changed, and even your memory has gaps, right? That's why you haven't shown yourself for a year. I thought you were evading me..."

Cora stared at him, her gaze unwavering. "Uh... actually, the reshaping process alone took nearly a year."

"Are you a member of F777?" she asked softly.

Onyx sighed deeply. "Can't you remember anything?"

"No." Cora lowered her eyelashes, her nimble fingers spinning the hidden blade, but she had no intention of harming him.

"Then let me tell you, Cora."

"I was the first member of F777, saved by our captain—by you. From that moment on, I've followed you loyally, no matter what."

Ding! The hidden blade clattered to the floor, the sound crisp and clear. Cora's mouth fell open, but no words came out.

Onyx chuckled softly, setting aside his teasing tone. He leaned his head against her neck, his voice weary and sorrowful. "That was all nonsense. I'm your teammate, the person closest to you in this world. For the past year, I haven't dared to sleep because whenever I close my eyes, I'm back at Loyak, where you completely disappeared before my eyes."

Their breaths mingled, so close there was no room to pull away. Cora turned her head to look into his eyes, a wave of dizziness washing over her, because somewhere deep in her consciousness, she completely believed his words.

"Cora, I've missed you so much."

Onyx wrapped his arm around her waist, pulling Cora fully into his embrace before tilting her chin up to plant a wet kiss on her lips.

Cora's eyes widened, her pulse suddenly racing, her heart pounding as if it would leap out of her chest, yet she felt no urge to resist.

But Onyx quickly pulled away, his lips just inches from hers, his expression complicated to read. "Sorry, the gene from earlier... was quite unusual. I still have a bit of a mental block."

Cora's cheeks felt inexplicably warm... she seemed to recall something like this happening before.

"Okay, let's talk. How much can you remember now?"

"Just bits and pieces, mostly from when I was a kid."

Cora hesitated, her gaze meeting Onyx's for a fleeting moment before she looked away.

To be precise, Cora's memories were mostly from her childhood and her time as an experimental subject. Everything else was a blur, especially events after the apocalypse—just a vast, empty void.

Onyx nodded. "I've notified the other members of F777. They'll be back soon. Maybe then, something will jog your memory."

Cora crouched in the corner of the large sofa, keeping a

considerable distance between them, doubt clouding her eyes. "How do I know you're not lying to me?"

"Your language skills have returned," Onyx observed, tapping his fingers as he calmly analyzed the situation. "The Phoenix Gene manifests as 'rebirth.' As long as there's a single cell left, it can regenerate infinitely. But your two rebirths weren't externally guided, which caused side effects."

"The first rebirth was after the Loyak incident, which damaged your language center. This is the second time," he moved closer, kneeling on the sofa, his long fingers running through Cora's hair. "Albinism is a genetic disorder. From a broader perspective, this type of gene mutation can't be cured."

"Previously, whether it was the Basilisk, Wildcat, or Lizard Gene, you couldn't revert to your human form of radiation stimulation. But now, you can control all of them, which means the fusion has surpassed the threshold. You've lost your human traits."

"You went to Felalakas, trying to activate an Aberrants Certificate, but you lack biological data. That path is a dead end. So, you had no choice but to use special means to sneak into the Northern Base."

No one in the New Pacific Alliance knew the Spark Plan better than Onyx. He understood LAK0017 inside and out, unraveling the truth in just a few words.

He's amazing. He got everything right. Cora stared at him, stunned.

Onyx edged even closer until their noses were almost touching. "But that's extremely dangerous. All the genes are operating at high speed, constantly altering your DNA. This disrupts your internal magnetic field, and over time, you'll gradually lose the part of you that's still human. You'll forget everything."

"Tomorrow, let's do a full-body checkup. Maybe there's a way to bring you back to normal."

"Okay." Cora nodded, quietly moving further away from him.

Onyx noticed her subtle movement, a smile playing on his lips as he restrained himself from pulling her closer. But when his hand brushed against the ring on Cora's finger, his smile vanished instantly.

"What's this?" he lifted her hand, his voice icy. "Where did you get this ring?"

Activating his Anopower, Onyx scoured every corner of his memory. Suddenly, it all came flooding back—the guilt and rage as he recalled that corner of Sin City. "Did Jorick give this to you? Did he propose, and you said yes?"

"It's not..." Cora wanted to explain, but the mental energy within the ring was too weak for Onyx to realize it was a space artifact.

"Take it off," Onyx demanded, leaving no room for refusal.

"Why do you think you can order me around?!"

They struggled, neither willing to back down, and starting a big fight, which was noisy.

Beep! Beep!—

At that moment, the apartment door swung open. Three people rushed in, stopping dead in their tracks at the scene before them.

Three against two, they all stood frozen, the tension palpable.

Clatter! The grocery bag Charles Franz was holding slipped from his grasp, his eyes wide with shock.

Felix Lucas raised an eyebrow, a hint of amusement flashing in his gaze.

Damian Blackwood couldn't hold back.

"You... you shameless jerk!! Where's my sister?! How could you hook up with someone else?!"

The lean teenager exploded in rage, sending a dozen ice spikes hurtling toward the two. After all, he was an A3-level Aberrant, and his outburst caused the temperature in the living room—and the hallway—to plummet. Ice rapidly spread across Charles's shoes and Felix's wheelchair.

Cora flipped up, her fingers moving swiftly. A shimmering golden shield appeared out of thin air, blocking Damian's attack.

She was just about to sigh—why do all the kids she meets seem so off? One wants to gnaw on her arm every day, and the other goes straight to violence—when she realized Damian's expression had turned to shock.

Tears welled up in Damian's eyes, and with a choked sob, he lunged forward, "Sister—!!"

Cora was startled.

She pushed off the sofa, flipping backward to land gracefully behind the couch.

Damian watched helplessly as he missed her, unable to stop himself. He stumbled forward—thud! His nose collided with the edge of the sofa, his head bumping into Onyx's, who was still rubbing his now red nose, tears streaming down his face. "Sister, you don't love me anymore! You never used to dodge me!"

Onyx smacked him lightly on the head, standing up as he clumsily buttoned his shirt. "Give it a rest. You were four-foot-three then. Now you're five-foot-three. You've grown up. Keep that in mind."

"Hmph." Damian grumbled, propping his elbows on his knees and sulking. Charles rubbed his chin, circling Cora. "Captain, you look different. I almost didn't recognize you."

"Cora's lost some of her memories. Introduce yourselves," Onyx explained briefly, signaling to Cora with his eyes. "Weren't you looking for F777? Here they are."

Damian eagerly raised his hand. "I'm Damian Blackwood. Sister, I was the first one to meet you. We're the best of friends."

The teenager, considered a master by outsiders, was still just a kid who loved to pout and seek attention when it came to Cora. Damian's lips were slightly pursed, still upset about not getting a hug.

Cora couldn't resist. She reached out, ruffling his curly hair, which felt soft.

"Charles Franz. You can call me Old Charles. We met in Sycamore. Back then, I was ready to end it all, but you saved me and helped me get revenge." Charles recounted the past—the assassination attempt in Deep Woods.

Cora listened quietly, patting him on the shoulder when he finished.

Charles touched the glass bottle around his neck, smiling. "I'm doing well now."

When it was Felix's turn, Cora's eyes lingered on his missing legs for a moment, a shadow of sadness crossing her face.

Felix accepted her gaze without flinching. "Being a tree was fine, but I'm still grateful you got me out of Death Hell."

Cora looked at him quietly, noting the six mechanical arms lurking behind Felix, each a different color, one of them gleaming with a silver sheen.

Her mind clicked, a light bulb going off, and she acted purely on instinct. Cora took out a box of rhenium from her ring, carefully opening it. The bright light illuminated everyone's faces as she solemnly pushed it toward Felix. "I don't remember why I needed to find this, but my gut tells me it's meant for you."

Felix was first surprised, then silent, before finally offering a somewhat awkward but genuine smile. "Thanks, Captain."

He turned, practically beaming, like a child showing off a beloved toy to the world. "Rhenium! Enough to upgrade all the mechanical arms. Did you see that? Fourteen days?"

Onyx snorted, unusually not giving a snarky reply.

"Why does he get a gift?!" Damian sulked, drawing circles with his finger, already plotting new entries in his book of grievances.

"You're rich. Shouldn't you be giving your sister gifts?" Charles scolded him.

"Right! Sister, what do you want? I'll buy it for you!"

The apartment was full of noise, but Cora's heart gradually settled. This special feeling was hard to describe. Since waking up in District F199, she had wandered for nearly a month, always shrouded in loneliness. But now Cora had finally found her place. She was certain—she was the Captain of F777. These people were important to her.

Onyx leaned against the bar, watching her quietly, a faint smile on his young, handsome face. The heavy weight of his longing finally lifted. His unfamiliar face overlapped with the figure deep in Cora's memory. Becoming one. He was the person she had been searching for.

Cora suddenly remembered something and coughed lightly. "Actually, I have one more question."

When the Captain spoke, the other four immediately quieted down, all eyes on her.

Cora asked earnestly, "Who is Suchat?"

CHAPTER 31

The Solution

Northern Base, 7:00 AM. Aberrants Specialty Hospital.

Mornings were always the busiest time at the hospital. Small robots filled with medications wobbled through the halls, heading for the elevators. Just as one robot was about to board, a patient suffering from a psychic breakdown burst out of a room, sending razor-sharp wind blades slicing through the air.

The surrounding walls lit up, a defense barrier absorbing all the attacks, and a quick-footed doctor swiftly subdued the patient, yelling, "Sedative—now!"

The raging winds suddenly stopped, but the little robot lost its balance, spinning wildly out of control. A pale hand caught it just in time, steadying the medication bag hanging from its back before placing it on the reception desk, then moved on without a word.

The robot's data sensor flickered as it turned to lock onto it. The group was peculiar. Leading them was a tall woman with white hair and pink eyes, her cold features as pristine as snow. Her unique appearance made her look almost unreal.

Despite the heat, she wore a hooded long-sleeve shirt and pants. Her companions varied in height, with one on crutches and another in a wheelchair. They turned a corner and entered the intensive care unit.

Since the delivery robot lacked independent thought, it watched them for a moment before resuming its pre-programmed route, continuing its journey forward.

The ICU was a spacious suite with two single beds arranged side by side, surrounded by countless life-support machines. Cora finally met the remaining two members of F777: a frail, beautiful woman and a figure lying silently in one bed.

Yuui Hayashi already knew of Cora's return, her eyes filled with anticipation as she looked toward the door.

Her face was pale and gaunt. While Cora's whiteness came from a lack of melanin, Yuui's was unmistakably the result of illness.

"You really have changed," Yuui remarked as she gazed at Cora, slowly opening her arms and offering a soft, joyful smile. "Welcome back, Cora."

Cora bent down and gently embraced her. "Yuui."

"You remember me?" Yuui asked, surprised. Hadn't she lost her memory? She didn't even remember Princess Onyx.

"Not only does she remember you, but she also clearly remembers Suchat," came a cool voice from the doorway.

Onyx stood with one hand in his pocket, the other gripping a cane. His tone was neutral, giving no hint of his true feelings, but his expression was slightly sour—a mood that had lingered since last night, radiating a low-pressure atmosphere.

Cora glanced back at him, completely confused by what he was sulking about. She recognized Yuui from a documentary she had seen in Felalakas—The Vanished Supernovas of Those Years. She had found the sweet smile of the star a bit off. Now, seeing Yuui in person, she understood why.

The "sweet girl" was just a persona. Yuui was clear-headed and rational, her core that of a mature and composed leader. A simple "welcome back" made Cora certain she enjoyed having Yuui as a teammate.

As for Suchat, Cora's gaze shifted to the other figure lying in the bed.

He was severely emaciated from his deep coma, his facial features sharper, as if carved from stone. His eyelids were peacefully closed, as if in sleep, but a horrific wound marred his chest, just inches from his heart. The gaping hole oozed black blood, and his body's functions were being sustained by an array of life-support machines.

"We've arranged a consultation once a month. Every healer from the B Zone has come, but no one has helped," Charles said gravely.

As an A5-level healer, Charles had poured all his energy into saving Suchat's life, snatching him from death's door, but the wound on his chest remained beyond his ability to heal.

"Why won't it heal?" Cora asked softly.

"Do you remember the Loyak incident? The wound on your abdomen?" Charles prompted.

Cora shook her head. The closer the memories were to the present, the more of a blank her mind became.

Charles gave a brief description of the battle, his voice heavy. "The one who injured Suchat was an S7-level Aberrant. Although it was a shapeshifting Anopower, the chains were imbued with 'true damage,' making them immune to any healing. You used your secondary Anopower to heal, but for other Aberrants, even at the S level, the wound would slowly bleed them dry."

"He was hurt saving me," Yuui said hoarsely. She unbuttoned her hospital gown, revealing a fist-sized hole near her collarbone, so deep that the bone was visible. The long-term blood loss had left her too weak to stand, confining her to bed.

Yuui stroked Suchat's brow, gripping his hand as the nightmare of that day replayed in her mind.

When the chains shot toward them, Suchat's pupils had contracted, and without a second thought, he had grabbed her, shielding her as they both plunged into the water. Yuui had thought they wouldn't survive, but her chant had summoned a mutated whale, whose massive wings had swept them out of the water. Later, Jennifer and Sunny Zhao had found them in time, but Suchat had never woken up.

She used to tease him, forcing him to admit his true feelings, delighting in his awkward, flustered responses. But now, even though Suchat had finally said he loved her, Yuui could no longer reply. She had missed her chance.

Cora stared at their clasped hands, silent for a long time. Then, an idea struck her, and she turned to Charles. "You just said my secondary Anopower can heal this type of wound."

"Yes," Charles confirmed.

Cora clenched her fists tightly, raising her head to look at everyone. Even though she couldn't remember much, these were her teammates, and from what Charles had said, Yuui and Suchat had been gravely injured because they saved her. She couldn't stand by and do nothing.

Cora steeled herself and uttered something that left everyone stunned: "Then use my flesh to fill their wounds." Even without her memories, she was still the dependable captain of F777.

Everyone was shocked into silence, the only sound in the room the steady hum of the machines.

Cora gestured at her collarbone and chest. "Cut from the same places. Insert my flesh into Suchat's and Yuui's wounds, and they'll heal." She spoke as if it were a simple matter, but her suggestion sent chills down everyone's spines.

Suchat's wound was in his chest, where he had lost parts of his organs. If Cora's flesh were transplanted into the hole and stitched quickly before the Anopower took effect, it could fill the gap. Yuui could be healed the same way.

As for Cora, her cells could regenerate infinitely. The lost flesh would grow back, though the process would be excruciating. But she was no stranger to pain.

"In theory... it's possible," Charles was initially taken aback, but the doctor in him saw the potential, his eyes lighting up. "We could start with small-scale clinical trials to test the effectiveness."

"No." Onyx's cold interruption abruptly shattered the joyful atmosphere.

"Why not?" Cora glared at him, clearly unhappy.

"I'm not against the plan itself," Onyx sighed, unable to bear her accusing gaze as he looked away. "But in your current condition, it's not safe. Don't forget, all your hidden genes are fully activated and in a highly active state. If we transplant that kind of flesh into Suchat, his immune system might collapse before the Anopower even takes effect."

Cora had undergone more than just a simple fusion experiment. Her body contained over a hundred different biological genes, including replicated genes. If those active "viruses" were to enter an ordinary human body, the result would be catastrophic.

"Then what should we do?" Cora mumbled, unconsciously seeking

Onyx's guidance. He paused, thinking for a moment. "First, we need to bring you back to normal."

In the hover car on the way to the lab

Onyx's two terminals kept lighting up, various urgent messages flooding in. Since he had voluntarily submitted "part" of his research data, he was no longer bound by his security clearance and was free, no longer needing to hide as he had in the past.

"The new city defense changes have been approved by General Yevgeniyev and will be implemented immediately."

"I won't be returning to North Yard... tell General Sheen that."

"Another wave of corpses? Send Unit 27. Nobumasa Sanada is an Earth Element alist, isn't he? He's perfect for cleanup duty."

If Cora still had her memories, she would remember that Nobumasa Sanada was the other squad leader of the Azure Force they encountered during their first run-in with Punk, and he had a history with Jeremy Wolfgang.

Given Onyx's vengeful nature, it was no surprise that Nobumasa's days were now difficult, his team being constantly shuffled and tested.

Cora propped her chin on her hand, curiously observing Onyx. Charles Franz leaned in mysteriously, whispering, "Our Princess Onyx is quite something now, overseeing both Northern Base and North Yard. The two generals have fought over him several times."

Cora glanced at the elaborately crafted silver cane. "Is his leg injury that serious? Why hasn't it been healed?"

Charles hesitated, looking awkward as he stammered, "Uh... his leg... yeah, it's pretty serious."

Cora raised an eyebrow, skeptical. "Aren't you an orthopedic surgeon?"

"You can criticize Princess Onyx's personality, but you can't question my medical skills," Charles retorted, struggling to explain.

Onyx had insisted on keeping him limp until Cora returned, thinking she'd be more concerned if she saw it. But now that she was back and had forgotten everything, Onyx's plan had backfired, leaving him tossing winks at someone who couldn't see them.

Their whispered conversation went unnoticed by Onyx, who continued managing his work while handing Cora a light screen displaying an array of dazzling engagement rings. He even took a moment to say, "Pick one you like, and I'll have it custom-made. I've already contacted the spatial sculptor."

Cora stared at him blankly, then stood up and switched seats without a word.

"Little Diamond, what are you watching?"

Damian Blackwood, sprawled out with his legs on the empty seat in front of him, had four or five different specialty juices lined up beside him, taking a sip from each. "Sister, I'm watching the selection rounds for the Aberrants Challenge." Seeing it was Cora, he generously shared his light screen.

Cora glanced down. The screen showed the latest hot competition, featuring Dylan, an eleven-year-old prodigy from the Galio Empire. With his S2-level strength, he had single-handedly defeated ten opponents, setting a record for the best solo performance so far.

Cora noticed Damian had tipped more money to support Dylan's fan channel.

After a year of preparations, the first Global Aberrants Challenge was finally in full swing. It was the largest event of its kind, with the ultimate prize being more than just a massive sum of NPA credits and crystals—there was also the chance to live in Utopia, an S-Class city.

Cora observed Damian's enthusiastic expression, slightly puzzled. "Did F777 not enter?"

"No, I hate Utopia." Damian's eyes darkened briefly before brightening again. "And besides, we wouldn't go anywhere without you, Sister. F777 only acts on your orders."

Cora smiled but said nothing. Now wasn't the right time. If she could heal Suchat and Yuui and recover her memories... the other rewards from the competition were quite tempting.

In the Busy Lab

Dr. Rainer Ninnemann, dressed in a white lab coat with graying temples, stared intently at Cora.

Feeling uneasy under his gaze, Cora glanced at Onyx, silently asking, "Is he reliable?"

Onyx chuckled and shook his head. Dr. Ninnemann's reaction was understandable, if over the top. "This is Dr. Ninnemann, the lead researcher of the Organ Regeneration Project."

"She's the seed? Our dream actually came true..." Dr. Ninnemann wiped away tears, reaching out to shake Cora's hand. Onyx's cold cane intercepted him. "Dr. Ninnemann, don't touch her—let's start with the tests."

Cora sat quietly in the isolation chamber, her head, limbs, and chest connected to electromagnetic sensors linked to a gene spectrometer in the outer room. Onyx sat across from her, holding her cool hand, gently bringing it to his lips. "Don't worry, it won't hurt. I'll be right here with you."

Cora stared at the mole by his eye, then flicked his forehead with two fingers, pushing him away without mercy. "I just remembered something."

"Oh? What is it?" Onyx's voice was soft, his gaze filled with affection.

"There was someone in a lab, too. He used to say I was ugly," Cora asked seriously. "Do you know who he was?"

Onyx stiffened, remaining silent for a few seconds before kissing her fingertips and nonchalantly replying, "Really? I don't know, but he sounds awful. I'm different, though—I've always found you adorable. See? No matter what you turn into, I'd recognize you instantly, even if you were a louse."

Cora turned her head, the corner of her mouth lifting slightly.

In the outer room, the research staff were fully focused, recording data without even looking up. The small isolation chamber, however, was peaceful, as if only the two of them existed, their fingers intertwined.

Not only was Cora undergoing gene testing, but her Anopower level needed to be reassessed. Grace, the director of Front City, assisted. When the connected R-type measuring device hit its maximum value, she gasped, "My God..."

A year ago, Cora was at S8-level. Now, her psychic power had surpassed S9. Anopower users of this level were unprecedented globally, and existing instruments could no longer measure Cora's true limits.

The full examination started in the morning and continued until evening. As the sunset filtered through the windows, Dr. Ninnemann hurried in, holding a light screen with hundreds of pages of reports. "All the gene types have been identified — 237, including 45 replicated genes, like the Phoenix Gene." His voice trembled with excitement.

"Because of the success of the Spark Experiment, the fusion genes in her body cannot be decoded, removed, or separated. The best solution is to freeze them, rendering them inactive. This would not only restore her physical condition, but might cure her albinism as well."

"But there's a problem," Dr. Ninnemann hesitated. "To freeze the genes, we need a complete DNA sequence. Regular genes are fine, but we don't have the original samples for the replicated genes. We know nothing about their composition."

"Do you have any data on the replicated genes?" Onyx asked, frowning.

Onyx shook his head. "When Arashi Research gained the replicated genes for the fusion experiment, they didn't focus on decoding the DNA sequences."

Replicated genes were valuable because the organisms they were derived from had long been extinct in the wild. The original samples were irreplaceable and would only decrease.

"I remember an organization stored the replicated genes..." Dr. Ninnemann struggled to recall.

"Monad One," Onyx murmured, narrowing his eyes. "But they vanished from the NPA long ago." The situation had once again hit a dead end, leaving everyone at a loss.

"If it's about finding people, I might have a way."

Felix suddenly spoke up, a confident glint in his unique ice-blue eyes, the hallmark of a top-tier hacker. "If it ever existed, there'll be a trace." Since returning from the Grass Pit, his Anopower seemed to have evolved, and his mindset had broadened as well.

"Give me four days—no, three days."

Three days later, in the ICU, F777 sat in a row, eagerly awaiting Felix's news.

"Monad One originated in the era of the Old Civilization, a secretive organization. The replicated genes were extracted by its founder and have been in their possession ever since."

"Unfortunately, in the year 47 New Era, the year of the apocalypse, the Monad One organization was destroyed, leaving no survivors."

"That's your good news?" Onyx retorted coldly.

Felix didn't immediately respond. Instead, he studied Onyx with a strange look.

"The silver lining is that while everyone died, I discovered the last registered member of Monad One was..." Felix paused, staring meaningfully at Onyx.

"Your Master Zhang."

CHAPTER 32

New Lifeforms

"Master?" Cora was also surprised.

In her limited memories, her grandfather, Old Thornton, and her master were the two most important people in her life. One had raised her, and the other had taught her martial arts.

Cora had heard from her grandfather that Master Zhang was a descendant of some lost martial arts school, supposedly with a prestigious background. However, he had lived in seclusion on Mount Yue for years and never mentioned his past, giving the impression of a gruff old man who was just good at fighting. No one would have imagined that he was the last disciple of Monad One.

And now, the replicated genes that F777 desperately needed were under the Master's care. Fate had a way of taking unexpected turns.

"But Master passed away." Cora's eyes dimmed, her shoulders slumping as she appeared fragile and sorrowful, like a delicate porcelain doll.

Onyx's heart softened instantly. He gently cupped her cheek, comforting her in a soft voice, "The old man may be gone, but Chi Zhang... is still here. He might know something!"

Felix, ever the serious one, chipped in, "Who hasn't heard of the infamous Chionji of Saya? With the upcoming city evaluations, District D78 is sure to be upgraded. He's well-liked, capable, and admired by many. He'll probably become an official governor soon, much better than a certain 'successor,' don't you think?"

Onyx's eye twitched, and then again. "There are some things I haven't settled with you yet. Don't think you're off the hook."

The two had disliked each other since they were teens, locking eyes for a moment before Felix decided it was best to change the subject, knowing when to back down.

Cora had learned about Petros Sheen's identity from Felix's loose lips. Onyx knew all about the tricks Felix and Ilia had pulled in Grass Pit but chose not to expose them, even providing some help. But if pushed too far, Felix knew Onyx wouldn't hesitate to turn on him.

Felix smoothly shifted topics. "I suggest we take a trip to Saya. What do you think, Captain?"

"Sounds good," Cora agreed readily.

"Wait, I'm coming too," Yuui said, struggling to sit up, her lips bloodless. "Charles, give me a dose of closure."

"No way, not in your condition. You shouldn't be moving," Charles refused flatly.

"It's okay. Leave it to us," Damian chimed in, trying to persuade her as well.

But Yuui shook her head firmly. "I've always been used to hiding behind Suchat, enjoying his protection. This time, I want to do something for him."

She looked at Cora, her eyes filled with hope. "Besides, this is F777's first mission together since reuniting. I don't want to miss it."

Cora made the final decision. "Then we go together, and we come back together."

Under the Vast Sky, a Silver-White Starship Soared Across the Horizon.

They had contacted Chi Zhang beforehand, so the checkpoints along the way lit up with green lights, allowing F777 to pass through Saya's borders unimpeded.

The winding highway sliced through the wilderness, which used to be teeming with zombies and beasts, making every journey a harrowing experience. But now, it had been cleared out, and the view below was mostly free of monsters.

As they neared the base, a steel fortress connected by a dozen iron chains came into view. It had expanded to over three times its original size since they had last seen it.

Various flying terminals buzzed back and forth, and busy crowds flowed continuously. Even the surrounding areas had developed many small shelters, a stark contrast to the desolation of Deep Woods on the other side.

Saya was now reborn, like the morning before dawn.

While it couldn't yet rival established cities like North Yard, Grass Pit, or Northern Base, Saya's growth had already reached mid-tier levels within Zone B, surpassing places constrained by terrain and climate like Blanc Yard and Delta Island.

The watchtower signaled visitors, and the canopy atop the base slowly opened. Felix smoothly guided the starship to a landing inside the structure. A young man in a black robe was waiting ahead, the strong gusts blowing his robe, but he stood steady as a tree, his sharp features and haughty demeanor giving off an air of calm authority.

Cora removed her hood and leaped down from the hatch.

"Little Junior Sister!"

Morgan and Rita rushed over, one hugging her shoulders and the other ruffling her hair. They had been skeptical when they saw the hologram footage, bombarding her with questions about martial arts gossip to confirm her identity. But now, seeing her in person, their enthusiasm overflowed.

"You've grown taller and thinner."

"Wow, where'd you get your hair done? And those eyelashes! So cool!"

Cora lowered her head good-naturedly, letting her senior martial siblings fuss over her. Then she looked up at the young man in the robe and greeted him politely, "Senior Brother."

"Welcome home," Chi Zhang nodded slightly, his gaze unusually gentle as he looked at her. "I've always said Saya will always be your home."

A long arm wrapped around Cora's shoulders as Onyx, dressed in loose white casual wear, lazily extended his hand to Chi Zhang, a bright smile on his face. "Long time no see, Senior Brother. You're as impressive as ever."

Chi Zhang remained unmoved, not even considering extending his hand, leaving Onyx hanging. "Cora left Saya in good health with you, only to vanish for a year and come back ill. Frankly, I'd prefer not to see you at all."

Onyx's smile faltered. Chi Zhang's sharp gaze swept over him, landing a precise blow. "Your leg, it's beyond repair?"

Onyx: Would you believe me if I said it was a secondary injury?

"Pfft—!" Charles and Damian couldn't hold back their laughter.

It seems the Princess had finally stumbled over his own stone.

Normally, with Onyx's sharp tongue and prideful nature, he'd retort immediately, but Chi Zhang was different. Cora might have forgotten many things, but she remembered Chi Zhang. It wasn't wise to offend the person closest to her right now.

Onyx retreated to the back, seething with frustration, only to catch Felix's odd expression—a smirk barely contained.

"If you dare laugh, I'll report the AI group for harboring a traitor," Onyx threatened in a low voice.

Felix's rising smile was immediately suppressed.

Once inside the meeting room, Chi Zhang spoke concisely, "I know nothing about the replicated genes. He never mentioned them."

Cora's eyes dimmed with disappointment. Even if her Senior Brother didn't know, was this trip for nothing?

Chi Zhang paused, then continued, "But I asked you to come because I made another discovery."

Cora blinked, finally catching on.

Chi Zhang produced a stack of property documents. "This is from what you brought last time, a birthday gift he left for me."

"Among them is a piece of land on Mount Yue, but I'm not familiar with it. I never had the time or intention to verify what it is. If he really was the last disciple of Monad One, in charge of the replicated genes, I'm sure it's not stored in the dojo. That leaves only this place."

Onyx flipped through a few pages of the documents. "Judging by the blueprints, it appears to be an underground facility. The interior design... looks like a warehouse."

Cora looked up at Chi Zhang. "Senior Brother, let's go look together."

"Okay." Chi Zhang nodded.

Just as they were about to leave, there was a knock on the meeting room door. Morgan poked his head in. "Senior Brother, got a moment?" With Chi Zhang's permission, Morgan grinned, pulling out a two-tiered cream cake from behind his back like a magic trick. "Sister Rita made this herself. Isn't it your birthdays soon? Since Little Junior Sister is back, we thought we'd celebrate together."

"Although you two aren't in that kind of relationship anymore..." Morgan received an elbow jab from behind and quickly corrected himself, "But there's no harm in blowing out a candle together, right?"

In the past, Chi Zhang and Cora had always celebrated their birthdays together on Mount Yue. It had almost become a tradition at the dojo. Unable to refuse the warm invitation, they were nudged together, shoulders touching. Chi Zhang looked a bit resigned, but Cora seemed perfectly at ease, puffing out her cheeks to blow out the candles amidst a chorus of happy birthday wishes.

Whoosh! Onyx slid in between them with a deadpan expression, blowing out the candles first.

Morgan and the dojo members glared at him, murderous intent in their eyes: What do you think you're doing?!

Onyx feigned surprise. "Didn't anyone tell you? We've already found Cora's actual birthday. From now on, no need for Senior Brother and Senior Sister to go through the trouble. We'll celebrate at home."

He smiled warmly, full of sincerity.

LAK0017 was a humanoid embryo created on February 20, 34 New Era. But Onyx wouldn't choose that date; he preferred March 19 of the same year—the day they first met across the capsule chamber.

District E104, Mount Yue.

Mount Yue was an ecological reserve, rich in vegetation and home to a diverse range of species. After the apocalypse, the area became overrun with vicious beasts, making it nearly impossible for ordinary Aberrants to enter. Chi Zhang led the way, with Cora using her Ethereal Artifact to clear the path of monsters. The seven of them slowly made their way along the mountain road.

When they passed by the dojo, both Cora and Chi Zhang instinctively paused. Inside the abandoned walls, wild grass grew knee-high, and the eaves were overrun with ivy.

Chi Zhang and Cora stood in silence, one behind the other, bowing their heads in respect.

The plot of land they sought wasn't far from the dojo, but after circling the area several times, they found themselves unable to proceed.

"Have we been here before?" Yuui asked, not quite adept at maneuvering her wheelchair as she spotted a mark she had made on a tree earlier. "Are we lost?" Charles muttered to himself.

"A formation. There's a formation here," Chi Zhang and Onyx spoke simultaneously, exchanging a brief glance before looking away.

Onyx explained coolly, "This formation is a looping maze. Intruders are easily trapped, walking in circles."

He glanced at Cora, who looked a bit confused, and smiled slightly. "I can calculate the exit, but it'll take some time..."

"No need for that," Chi Zhang interrupted without hesitation. "This formation was set by my father. We can break it directly."

He pulled out a talisman, made a quick gesture with one hand, and as the talisman burned out, a path slowly appeared before them.

Chi Zhang strode forward, heading east, and the others pursued.

Eventually, they reached the depths of the forest, where Cora discovered an ancient stone stele.

She blew away the thick layer of dust covering it and found a machine that resembled a security system. "Senior Brother, can this be opened?"

Chi Zhang frowned and shook his head. "Aside from the formation, everything here is as unfamiliar to me as it is to you."

"What about brute force?" Cora materialized a giant hammer, eager to try.

"No," Onyx hurriedly stopped her. "This type of security system comes with a self-destruct mechanism. One hit, and it's all gone."

"Oh," Cora muttered, disappointed.

The group took turns trying various methods, but the stone stele remained unmoved.

In the tense atmosphere of frustration, Onyx lowered his gaze, piecing together all the information they had. Gradually, a possibility took shape. "I think I understand."

"The old man passed the land on to you and taught you the formation-breaking incantation, showing that he left a way for Monad One to survive. If the existence of the replicated genes were ever exposed, he'd want the person he trusted most to unlock it."

Chi Zhang's expression remained calm. "If he trusted me, he wouldn't have kept the existence of Monad One from me."

Silence fell over the group. The tension between Chi Zhang and his father had always been difficult, and the matter of the replicated genes only deepened the conflict and doubt.

Charles, the only one among them with any experience as a father, spoke cautiously, "I can understand the old man. As a disciple of Monad One, he carried a heavy burden—both a responsibility and a shackle. Your personality clearly wasn't suited for their organization..."

Monad One's philosophy was rooted in secrecy and humility. Chi Zhang, however, was ambitious and wanted to make a name for himself. His responsibilities had confined Chi Zhang to Mount Yue, but he hoped his son would live freely. Though he had been strict with him, he never hindered Chi Zhang's decisions, including leaving the dojo to join the Azure Force selection.

"Your father didn't want to hold you back," Charles sighed.

Chi Zhang remained silent for a long time. He and his father had clashed constantly during his life, never truly opening up to one another. It wasn't until after his father's death that Chi Zhang understood him.

"You and Cora share the same birthday. The old man carefully prepared two gifts," Onyx said, pulling everyone's attention back to the present as he tapped his cane on the stone stele. "One for the responsible eldest disciple and one for the beloved youngest."

"The eldest disciple controls the property and the formation-breaking incantation, so could the key to unlocking the truth be in the hands of the youngest disciple?"

"You mean..." Charles suddenly realized, exclaiming, "The Captain knows how to open the door?"

"Huh?" Cora's face was blank. "I know nothing about that."

"What did your master give you?" Onyx asked quietly.

"A protective charm," Cora replied honestly, "But I don't remember... where it went."

After the battle of Loyak, Onyx had carefully stored all of Cora's equipment and items. He used his psychic power to search through her spatial necklace and quickly found the charm Cora had mentioned.

It was inside a plastic bag, discarded in a corner.

Onyx carefully retrieved it. The charm was cool to the touch, with intricate, calming runes etched on its surface.

Felix scanned it, and the signal flashed repeatedly. "There's something inside." His mechanical arm separated into fine tweezers, which he used to delicately dismantle the charm, extracting a chip as thin as a cicada's wing.

Cora took the chip and swiped it across the security system.

Rumble—!!

The ground beneath them shook violently. Trees toppled, and dirt flew as the group struggled to stay upright. After a few seconds, the ground collapsed inward, revealing a hidden passage. Cora led the way as the seven of them filed inside.

Surprisingly, the passage wasn't as desolate as they had imagined. The weeds had been cleared away, and even the lighting system used mechanical oil-free lamps. "Post-New Era technology. It seems the old man indeed built this place," Onyx remarked.

As they went deeper, the temperature dropped. Damian and Yuui shivered, and Charles pulled out thick coats to help them keep warm.

Following the building's blueprint, they arrived at a space resembling a warehouse lined with densely packed rooms on either side of the corridor. Chi Zhang didn't slow down, pushing open each slightly ajar door. When the others saw what was inside, they were stunned.

This was indeed a changed warehouse, with temperature-controlled freezers stacked to the ceiling, each one filled with transparent cultivation pods.

Every single pod contained replicated genes, with DNA strands rotating slowly on corresponding light screens. Yuui even saw a dinosaur gene, with a count of two, although one pod was empty.

At the end of the corridor stood a dormant central control unit, an outdated model from decades ago. Onyx signaled Felix, who immediately connected to it and began hacking. The fragile firewall crumbled under the onslaught of a top-tier hacker, and within ten seconds, the system's access was granted.

Onyx scanned the data rapidly, processing everything at a glance. The system contained detailed information on all the replicated genes, including complete DNA sequences. Without turning around, he said casually, "Brother Zhang, Mount Yue is no longer suitable for storing these genes. You should take your father's legacy with you."

Chi Zhang's choice of location was actually quite good—District E104 was far from the NPA, sparsely populated. However, since the apocalypse, the geographical magnetic field had changed, and without a weather simulation system, Mount Yue's radiation levels had long exceeded safe limits. The replicated genes were invaluable and could easily provoke greed, but neither Cora nor any member of F777 had any intention of taking them for themselves.

"What about Cora's treatment?" Chi Zhang frowned slightly.

"Don't worry. I'll copy the data from the central unit. I'll need the 45 original samples from Cora's body."

"Alright. I'll take them back to Saya and find a place to store them," Chi Zhang said, pulling out a spatial artifact.

"I'll help!" Damian volunteered.

Preserving the replicated genes required a stable, low-temperature environment, and Damian's ice-based Anopower was perfect for the job. He froze each cultivation pod before helping Chi Zhang store them in the spatial artifact.

After they had mostly cleared out the rooms on both sides, Damian curiously poked his head around and asked, "Sister, why are so many of these boxes empty?"

"Hmm?" Cora leaned over to look. And it was true. The functional pods displayed real-time status updates, but the ones left on the freezers were not only empty but also unresponsive to the monitors.

Before Cora could figure it out, Felix's voice came from behind. "Everyone, I've got some bad news."

Yuui groaned, holding her head, "Please, don't say it." They had developed a kind of PTSD from Felix's "good news" and "bad news" announcements.

Felix, unfazed, continued in a flat tone, "I just accessed the surveillance system and found that after the apocalypse—specifically on the fourth day—a breach appeared in the southeast corner of the warehouse. Judging by the damage, it came from inside."

Cora didn't understand, "What do you mean?"

"It means..." Felix looked at Onyx. "You explain it. What happens if gene storage conditions aren't met?"

"In a highly irradiated environment, gene activity would increase significantly," Onyx said, locking eyes with Cora and speaking in a grave tone, "Ultimately... they would come back to life."

Everyone gasped. Yuui gritted her teeth, "Damn it, Felix, you and your bad luck. There's no way it's that bad."

Boom—! Boom, boom—!!

No sooner had she spoken than a deafening crash came from above.

The next second, the wall crumbled, and Cora's pupils reflected an unbelievable sight—a massive bird with magnificent feathers, mouse legs, and tiger claws, one she recognized, appeared before them. It seemed furious, flapping its heavy wings and slamming down hard! The entire corridor shook violently.

"Get down!" Cora shouted. A huge golden shield appeared just in time to protect the seven of them. Chi Zhang quickly cast a Vajra spell, while Felix's mechanical arms encircled Yuui and Damian.

But the greater danger was yet to come. As the underground warehouse collapsed, countless terrifying beasts—some running, some flying—emerged from all directions, roaring and attacking them. The seven tumbled out of the debris, landing in the sunlight. Under the scorching sun, Cora's skin began to burn and blister rapidly. Onyx immediately pulled her close, securing her hood.

The beasts roared, and the birds flew wildly. Creatures that had long been extinct in the wild were now out in the open, their bizarre appearances menacing. Through the swirling dust, Cora's eyes landed on the giant bird she had once seen at the dojo. It had the body of a chicken and the claws of a tiger, with a tuft of white feathers on its forehead. It looked viciously at her but didn't immediately attack.

"You have the same genes as it does," Onyx said quickly.

It dawned on Cora—no wonder the bird hadn't attacked her at the dojo. It saw her as one of its own. Felix had said the breach appeared on the fourth day after the apocalypse, so this one must have been the first beast to come back to life, a creature with superior intelligence capable of commanding others.

"What do we do now?!" Charles clung to Cora's leg, shouting in panic. "Their nest has been destroyed—they won't let us go." Felix remained calm, even in this situation.

These resurrected beasts were ferocious, each nearly as powerful as a level 4 beast. Under the relentless assault, cracks formed on the shield.

Yuui bit her lip hard. Taking advantage of the others being distracted, she suddenly injected herself with a dose of closure! She wobbled as she stood up from the wheelchair, remembering the tune that had summoned the Kunpeng, and hummed a hoarse chant filled with soothing notes.

The first time, the beast horde didn't react, their cries continuing.

The second time, some beasts slowed their attacks, gradually retreating.

The third time, the giant bird let out a long cry, and the beast horde's agitation subsided. They dispersed like a receding tide.

Damian was dumbfounded.

"It's only temporary. Let's get out of here," Yuui said, her Anopower depleted. She managed a smile before collapsing, caught by Cora, who gently placed her back in the wheelchair.

With their nest destroyed, the resurrected beasts had poured out, and it wouldn't be long before Mount Yue became the most complex and dangerous, forbidden zone in the NPA.

The seven of them helped each other to their feet. Cora asked worriedly, "Senior Brother, are the genes safe?"

"They're fine," Chi Zhang confirmed after checking that the spatial talisman was intact. Then he remembered something. "What about the data?"

"I copied it," Felix said.

"And memorized it. Double insurance," Onyx added with a confident smile.

Chi Zhang nodded, then stared blankly at the ruins before him. "So, this was why he was killed?"

Onyx explained quietly, "Hugh Young was determined to get the Plan Eternity. The Vulture Force found out about the old man's identity and knew the replicated genes were in his possession. They tortured him but couldn't break him, so they resorted to killing him."

The two S7-level Aberrants from Vulture Force and Hugh Young, who had given the order, were all killed by Cora during the Battle of Loyak—a fitting end, but the remnants had retreated to Utopia.

Chi Zhang clenched his fist, his voice heavy, "I can't let this go. I want to kill every one of the Vulture Force."

"You want to go to Utopia? The fastest way is to win the Aberrants Challenge," Damian suggested quietly.

Chi Zhang's gaze grew resolute, "The Challenge."

On the Starship Leaving Mount Yue,

Cora looked out the window, her eyes scanning the forest below. In the dense greenery, the sounds of beasts running echoed faintly. As she watched, something clicked in her mind, and she suddenly stood up. "Oh, no!"

A portion of the beasts had retreated toward the island at the foot of the mountain.

Mrs. Travers was cooking for Little Travers. The kid had become increasingly picky, refusing to eat even the zombie leg she had found, only settling down after getting slapped a few times. Although Mrs. Travers was slow in thought, she kept the habits of a living person, mechanically starting the fire and boiling water.

Above, a massive creature approached, its powerful gusts overturning the stove. Mrs. Travers retreated warily, picking up Little Travers and preparing to flee. The starship's hatch opened, and Damian waved enthusiastically.

"Ah! Ah, ah, ah—!" Mrs. Travers's head slowly tilted in confusion, a question mark practically forming above her head. "?"

Not all zombie languages were mutually intelligible. Damian shouted himself hoarse, but Mrs. Travers remained on guard. He couldn't help feeling dejected, wanting badly to go back and tell the expert who wrote Zombie Language: From Beginner to Master that zombie dialects exist!

Cora landed lightly in front of Mrs. Travers, speaking seriously, "I've found a place where you can survive. There are no zombies, and there are many others like you."

Damian joined her, opening his terminal to show pictures of him with various Fallens. In one, he was even smiling happily with a little Blood Corpse perched on his head. Deep down, Damian felt guilty. Back then, he had been terrified by Mrs. Travers and Little Travers, lost control of his Anopower, and exposed their identities, causing them to miss the last starship. He hadn't expected to have time to make amends.

"This place is dangerous. Come with us," Cora said.

Mrs. Travers held Little Travers tightly and nodded slowly. They had been abandoned on the island, living among monsters day in and day out. Finally, a starship rescued them.

CHAPTER 33

I'm Back

After dropping off Chi Zhang in Saya, F777's starship headed straight for Loyak.

Damian, full of youthful energy and confidence, stood at the edge of the starship's hatch, holding a megaphone. The wind whipped through his curly hair, turning it into a wild mess as his clear, psychically-enhanced voice echoed across the entire area. "Ada! We've got new friends coming your way—!!"

After shouting in human language, he turned around and repeated it in zombie language. "Ah~ ah ah ah—!!"

Mrs. Travers, holding Little Travers, gave Damian a look that could only be described as "Are you an idiot?"—a surprising amount of expression for her stiff zombie face.

Little Travers drooled, perfectly embodying the phrase "drooling with desire," his cloudy eyes fixed on Cora's arm as he reached out, still hoping to get a bite, only to be firmly held back by his mother.

After about ten minutes of shouting, a rolling cloud of dust rose on the horizon, heralding the approach of a massive zombie horde.

Mrs. Travers's eyes slowly widened in realization. After being stranded on the isolated island, she had always thought that she and Little Travers were outcasts, unwanted by both zombies and humans. She never imagined there could be so many of their kind in the outside world. Perhaps... perhaps here, they could have a normal life.

Cora patted Mrs. Travers's shoulder gently and said, "Go on, this is your new home."

Damian, with his sharp eyes, spotted Ada among the crowd and waved excitedly, "Ada! I found my sister! And I brought... new friends..." His voice trailed off, growing weaker as he stared in disbelief into the distance.

Just as everyone wondered about his odd behavior, Damian suddenly jumped up, almost screaming with excitement, "Braids?!"

Among the horde, leisurely hanging back, was none other than the familiar Braids, along with his brother, Dirty Chin. Braids had been running shyly at first, but when he recognized Damian, he jumped for joy and sprinted to the front, calling out excitedly. "Ahhhhhh!!"

Damian responded with equal enthusiasm, "Ah ah! Ah ah—ah woohoo!" The kid was so happy that he forgot all the human language he had painstakingly learned.

As the leader of the Fallens, Ada had a strong sense of kinship but harbored a particular dislike for humans and zombies. Except for Damian, who was like an unshakable barnacle, ordinary people couldn't survive in her territory.

Cora let Damian jump down to join the fun, telling him they would pick him up later, while she went to rescue Yuki, who had been "buried" previously.

When they reached the location, Yuui dug out the light screen. It needed to be reactivated from low-power mode, but her face turned pale, and she hesitated to start it up, finally muttering in defeat, "Forget it, Yuki's scolding is too fierce. I can't handle it alone. Better wait for Suchat to wake up."

She curled up in her wheelchair, her eyes bright as stars, knowing that everything was moving in the right direction and that she would reunite with her family, eventually.

On the way back, Damian was being pushed by Charles when they approached Onyx. Damian, still somewhat sulky, asked, "Hey, what's going to happen to Ada and Braids? Can we not hurt them?"

Onyx's lips curved into a faint, teasing smile. "Want to know? First, call me Brother Petros."

Damian swallowed his pride and muttered, "Brother Petros."

When they first met, Damian had tried to maintain his sweet, well-behaved persona, even calling Onyx "Uncle Onyx" sweetly. But once his true nature was revealed, he became more unruly, either addressing Onyx by his full name or using "hey" or "that guy."

Onyx, pleased, casually flipped through his light screen. "The new Species Rules will be published soon. The existence of the Fallens will be officially recognized. Instead of worrying about them, pity the poor souls who accidentally wander into Loyak."

Ada, with intelligence nearly matching that of a level 4 Zombie Lord, was more than capable of leading the creatures here. Given the number of monsters in the area, ordinary Aberrants would walk to their doom if they entered. As long as there was no conflict of interest, humans and Fallens could maintain a "live and let live" balance for at least a few years.

After returning to the Northern Base, F777 immediately headed to the laboratory in Front City.

The condition of Suchat and Yuui could only be described as "barely sustaining life." Every day that passed brought more danger. Cora, known for her decisiveness, knew that the freezing experiment needed to happen as soon as possible, both for her and her teammates.

Dr. Rainer Ninnemann was waiting at the door, wringing his hands. As soon as he saw them, he practically ran over, his words coming out in a fast, anxious stream. "You really found the original samples? And the complete gene sequences? For safety's sake, I still think tissue analysis is essential…"

Onyx cut through his rambling. "We're ready on our end. What about yours?"

Ninnemann's expression turned serious, his dedication to research unwavering. "I've checked every step. Only you and I have access to the experiment."

Cora changed into a hospital gown, and each member of F777 took turns hugging her, offering their support and encouragement.

When it was Yuui's turn, Cora held the hug longer, softly promising, "Before fall arrives, you and Suchat will be healed."

Yuui smiled gently. "I believe in you, Cora."

Finally, it was Onyx's turn. He embraced Cora tightly, his voice tender, "Don't be afraid. I'll be here with you. Just take a nap, and it'll all be over."

Cora struggled a bit but couldn't break free. After holding back for a while, she finally spoke up. "There's something I'd like to discuss with you."

"Hmm? What is it?"

Cora felt a little guilty, "We don't really know each other that well, so... maybe we should hold off on this boyfriend thing."

Saying it out loud was a relief, and Cora exhaled deeply, pretending not to hear the uneven laughter coming from behind her.

"Not that well?" Onyx looked at her deeply, a mix of emotions swirling in his eyes, which finally settled into a resigned sigh. "We'll talk about this after you come out."

Cora was then wheeled into the massive machine, surrounded by a blinding whiteness. After a while, she felt uncomfortable. Fortunately, the anesthesia took effect, and her eyelids grew heavier.

Five seconds, three seconds, one second.

Cora slowly closed her eyes, her consciousness slipping into endless chaos.

Thick black smoke, searing fireballs, and swirling dust clouds filled her vision, along with flashes of blinding light.

A young man named Jace Ming was running desperately, clutching a portable incubation pod, his eyes red with tears. He hadn't expected that the moment he left Loyak, a nuclear explosion would occur.

"Beep—" A sharp alarm blared as LAK0017 curled up in agony, its vital signs dropping to the lowest possible point.

"No, no, no, no!" Jace fumbled, placing the incubation pod on the ground, biting his nails in a panic. Then, an idea struck him.

He remembered how the young master of the Sheen family had fed its nutrient serums. Carefully, he pulled out the last vial in his possession—the only one he could access—and placed it next to the dying LAK0017.

Jace's voice choked with emotion, "Please eat it, don't die. I'm begging you, don't die."

From the day LAK0017 was created, Jace had been its caretaker. It was like his child, and he had poured all his effort and love into it. So why couldn't he keep it alive? Why, after spontaneously recovering before its scheduled destruction, was it now rapidly deteriorating?

Jace quickly realized the crux of the issue. The research facility was like a completely sterile greenhouse, and LAK0017 had become accustomed to that controlled environment. Suddenly, being exposed to the outside world, it couldn't cope with the polluted air.

The alarm grew more urgent, and finally, with a long, piercing beep, LAK0017's vital signs went silent. It was dead.

"No, that's not possible. You're so strong," Jace muttered through tears. "Give me a chance to save you. Live, please live!" The organism inside the pod shrank until it was just a small, limp mass.

Jace opened the pod door, trembling as he picked up LAK0017. Although he held it carefully, the small, slippery mass slipped from his grasp and rolled several meters away.

Jace quickly got up to retrieve it, and his vision blurred for a moment. He could just make out a faint, dark red line on the surface of the soft mass. It had slowed its movements but was still trying to move forward. Jace's eyes widened as he realized it was trying to absorb the radiation.

Gritting his teeth, Jace scooped up the mass and sprinted toward Loyak. However, ordinary humans are powerless in the face of natural disasters. Even just approaching the edge of the nuclear explosion site, Jace showed obvious symptoms of radiation sickness — dizziness, nausea, vomiting, bleeding from his nose and gums, and clumps of his hair falling out.

LAK0017 became more and more eager. With a last lunge, it broke free from Jace's grasp and fell into the thick, fiery ashes.

Jace fell to his knees, his consciousness fading. Just before he passed out, he witnessed an unforgettable miracle. A distant, clear cry pierced the sky as the fiery red phantom of a mythical beast spread its wings and soared overhead.

"The Phoenix... rebirth..." Jace murmured, tears streaming down his face.

When the light finally faded, a pair of wrinkled, blotchy hands emerged from the ashes, cradling a sleeping little girl. The Phoenix gene had been activated, resetting the organism's state. LAK0017 had reverted to its original humanoid embryo form, becoming a true "human."

One Year Later.

After much searching, Old Thornton finally found Master Zhang, the last disciple of Monad One, and sent Cora to Mount Yue. Master

Zhang took an immediate liking to the strong and destructive little girl, breaking his usual rules by accepting her as a disciple and even giving her a 50% discount on tuition.

When Cora was nine years old, she fell from the mountain during a training session, breaking thirteen of her ribs. The injury was severe, and she lost consciousness, which triggered the latent Anopower within her.

The day after sending the doctor away, Master Zhang checked Cora's injuries again, only to be startled: Wait, weren't there thirteen broken ribs? Why are there only twelve injuries now? Another day passed, and upon checking again, he found that only eleven ribs remained broken.

Two weeks later, Old Thornton rushed up the mountain after finally securing a school enrollment in Flower City for Cora. By that time, her injuries had completely healed, and she was bouncing around the yard, having no recollection of what had happened. Faced with Master Zhang's questioning, Old Thornton sighed and got straight to the point. "Cora underwent a fusion experiment. She has replicated genes in her body."

"I may not live to see her grow up, but I want her to live healthily and safely. If possible, when she's in trouble, I hope you can help her."

Later, Old Thornton passed away, and Cora grew up smoothly. Just before she reached adulthood, Master Zhang gave her a calming charm. Then, the apocalypse struck, and Cora fled to Flower City, where she met Onyx, F777, and traveled from Zone C to Zone B...

And finally—to the Battle of Loyak.

In the extreme stillness of the room, Cora suddenly opened her eyes. She remembered everything.

The surrounding air was chilly, and she shivered before slowly sitting up, staring at her reflection in the mirrored glass—a version of herself that seemed unfamiliar. She looked down at her hands, feeling the Anopower flowing smoothly within her, with no resistance.

She quietly slid off the single bed and silently approached the door.

The hallway outside was dimly lit, and she saw two figures standing face to face—Ninnemann and Onyx—engaged in a low conversation.

"The ordinary genes have been dealt with, but the replicated genes... Here's what I'm thinking: we should freeze the thirty most dangerous ones first. The remaining ones have low activity and won't affect her body or Anopower for now. You can proceed with the organ transplant if you like. Also, the albinism defect has been corrected. We'll do check-ups every two weeks and deal with the remaining fifteen... no, fourteen genes based on her recovery."

"You've been standing out here for a day and a night. Go get some rest. I'll keep watch and let you know the moment she wakes up."

"No need," Onyx replied, leaning against the wall, his fatigue clear. "This time, I want to be the first thing she sees when she wakes up."

Cora's gaze fell on Onyx's damaged right leg. He was trembling slightly from standing so long, his knuckles white from gripping his cane too tightly, a sign of how much effort he was exerting.

Her expression remained calm, but her fingers twitched involuntarily. When she pushed the door open, she did so with enough force to make a noticeable noise. Both men turned simultaneously, and Onyx greeted her with his usual gentle smile. "You're awake? Want to go home?"

"Mm." Cora nodded.

They called it "home," but it wasn't Cora's apartment they returned to. Instead, they went to the apartment issued by the Aberrants Division to Suchat, which had long been unused. It was late at night, and Onyx assumed she didn't want to disturb the others, so he didn't object.

Once inside, Cora was still looking down at her phone, sending messages.

Onyx discarded his cane and collapsed onto the sofa, exhausted, loosening his collar. "Are you feeling any discomfort?"

"No, I'm fine." Cora was sure this was the best she had ever felt since her creation as an experimental subject. Her thoughts were clear, her speech was sharp, and even her usually dull emotions felt reborn. She finally understood what Gawin and Lucia had meant.

Without looking up, Cora asked casually, "How was your past year?"

Onyx smiled, flawless as ever. "How else would it be? I went to work every day, did my job, and thought of you. I imagined you suddenly showing up, just like before, to pick me up after work."

"Liar." Cora sighed silently. "Didn't you say that as long as I asked, you'd never lie to me?"

Onyx's smile slowly faded. "You remember now?"

Cora didn't answer directly, still pressing on, "Have you been doing well? Have you... lived freely?"

In the unlit living room, the shadows swallowed Onyx. After a long silence, his voice finally emerged, hoarse and raw. "No, Cora, I haven't been well at all. So many times, I couldn't stop myself from wanting to destroy Utopia, destroy the entire world. You think I'm free, but it's the exact opposite. You've trapped me—trapped me in that moment at Loyak, in the instant you disappeared before my eyes."

Cora lowered her gaze, standing over him. "I take back what I said —about not knowing you well and about our relationship." She then leaned down and placed a light kiss on Onyx's lips, a fleeting touch.

"I'm back, Petros."

CHAPTER 34

Under Estimated

Among the ten E-Districts of the New Asia Alliance, E117 (Rainforest) stands as the unique.—The Rainforest is notorious for producing assassins.

Once you step into this mysterious primordial forest, your life counts down, every step fraught with peril, like traversing a living "hell." The climate here is hot, with frequent rainfall, and a single misstep could send you plunging into a hidden river or sinking into a bog.

The terrain is complex, and the region teems with a vast array of species. The dense, vine-covered vegetation twists and turns, always on the verge of "coming to life" to devour anyone in its path.

But even more terrifying are the top predators that lurk everywhere: giant pythons, piranhas, electric eels, poison dart frogs... The Rainforest is well-deserving of its title as a "Human Exclusion Zone."

As an abandoned child, Suchat grew up in this harsh environment. He had no family, no friends—bloody violence defined his life, and he knew nothing else.

Instructors oversaw the juveniles in the Rainforest, and after surviving the slaughter among a hundred children, Suchat ended up in the hands of Lowe.

Lowe was ranked 15th on the assassin leaderboard, having once peaked within the top 10, earning a reputation as a killer on par with

Forrest Tick. But Lowe was smarter—he quietly retired and became a handler shortly after Forrest Tick was imprisoned in the Death Ward.

Lowe took on only one child, but his training methods for Suchat were brutally harsh.

Suchat was naturally quiet, rarely speaking a full sentence even when covered in wounds. He often returned from training half-dead, collapsing to the ground before he even reached the door. Lowe would nudge him with the tip of his boot, coldly tossing food and medicine his way. During his early days, Suchat didn't remember Lowe's face; he remembered his shoes instead.

Sometimes, when Suchat was too injured to make it back on his own, Lowe would come to collect him. Venomous insects and snakes would surround lying face-down in the mud, motionless like a corpse, all contemplating where to take the first bite. Lowe would sneer, "Useless kid," and drag him away by the foot.

The two spoke little. For people like them, who lived on the edge of death every day, forming relationships only complicated things. But from the time Suchat was 7 to when he turned 17, Lowe watched as the little wolf pup's claws grew sharper, and the murderous glint in his eyes became ever more intense.

At 17, Suchat became an independent assassin. He left the Rainforest. Killing was not in his nature, and it couldn't bring him peace. To leave the Rainforest, one had to kill an assassin ranked higher than themselves.

Suchat was ranked 107th, which was already impressive for his age, but those ranked above him were no easy targets. When Lowe learned of this, he casually asked, "Have you made your request?"

Suchat nodded silently. Two days earlier, he had submitted his request to leave the Rainforest. Lowe chewed on a tobacco leaf, remaining silent for a long time. He never smoked—a proper assassin wouldn't leave any scent on their body.

A few days later, Suchat and Lowe went on a mission together. They were to eliminate a military officer in a small country on the border of the Lucerne Federation.

The assassination went smoothly, but as their target fell, the retaliation was swift and caught them off guard. A sniper with an eagle's eye followed their every move, and the special Anopower-infused bullets known as "True Damage" were nearly impossible to detect.

Once they penetrated the body, no treatment could save you—you'd bleed out and die. Their fellow assassins were quickly wiped out, leaving only Suchat and Lowe.

Boom—!!

Lowe threw a grenade, forcefully blasting their way out. Buildings along the street collapsed, glass shattered, and the two escaped. As they passed through a certain district, Suchat's sharp eyes glimpsed his target. He knew immediately that his target was also there on a mission.

Suchat signaled for Lowe to retreat and charged in alone.

The fight was bloody, just like the thousands of nights before.

Suchat pinned his target to the ground, ready to drive his blade into their heart. But just before he could strike, his target's lips curled into a strange smile. Something was wrong. Suddenly, Suchat felt an icy blade at his throat, slicing through the skin near his artery—someone was trying to kill him! He dodged instinctively, only to find that his attacker was even younger than him, maybe 14 or 15 years old, with the same unyielding determination in their eyes.

The young assassin kicked Suchat squarely in the chest, sending him rolling across the ground. As he struggled to his feet, he realized four or five more attackers surrounded him.

The wounds multiplied, blood dripped down, and his vision turned a deep crimson. Just before he lost consciousness, Suchat saw a familiar pair of shoes. It was Lowe.

Lowe hadn't retreated. He had killed the attackers and, as he had countless times before, dragged the badly wounded Suchat through the bullets and flames, pulling him from the blood-soaked battlefield.

After reaching the safe zone, Lowe dumped Suchat on the ground and sat down cross-legged. Suchat lay there silently, his eyes dry. The man he had fought was the only one he had confidence in killing, but he hadn't done it.

Lowe glanced at him, his fingers trembling as he pulled out a carefully wrapped cigarette from his pocket. Lighting it, he took a deep drag. "Leaving the Rainforest isn't easy. Even if you're lucky enough to survive, you'll have to peel off a layer of skin. From the moment you left, your name went on the kill list."

"You kill others, and others will naturally try to kill you. That's the law of the Rainforest."

Suchat remained silent. When the cigarette burned out, Lowe drew his knife from his combat boot and pressed it into Suchat's hand. Then he smiled, a resigned yet peaceful smile. "Come on, kid, kill me."

Suchat's eyes turned blood-red, staring at him in disbelief.

Lowe reached out and roughly ruffled his hair—the closest they'd been in ten years.

Then he removed his tactical vest. His knees, abdomen, and shoulders were all injured, though not fatally. Only his back was bleeding profusely from a sniper wound. It was "True Damage"the sniper had hit —.

Suchat finally noticed that Lowe's face was pale and his expression was bleak, the result of severe blood loss. "Hurry. If you keep stalling, I'll be dead, anyway."

Suchat's chest heaved, his throat tight, words catching in his mouth, unable to be spoken. "Do it—!!" Lowe's pupils were already dilated, and he bit down hard, shouting the command.

The cold blade pierced his heart.

Lowe smiled, satisfied. With his last bit of strength, he scanned Suchat's communicator with his own, leaving behind irrefutable evidence of the kill. "Go, kid. Don't look back. Never come back."

Suchat never returned to the Rainforest. His hands were stained with Lowe's blood, and like a lone, dirty wolf cub, he wandered aimlessly, a walking corpse. He had always wanted to leave the Rainforest and was prepared to die, but he never imagined the price he'd have to pay would be so steep.

Half a month later, Suchat wandered into Felalakas, collapsing in exhaustion beside a trash can in a dark alley. A torrential downpour battered him, the untreated wounds causing a high fever, and he could barely keep his eyes open.

Faint voices echoed in his ears, so distant they felt like a hallucination.

Yuui was 20 years old, with expertly applied eyeliner and shimmering eyeshadow that gave her a sweet appearance. After her performance, she snuck off to smoke in a secluded spot, only to stumble upon the figure lying in the shadows. She shrieked in fright,

"What the hell? You scared me half to death!!"

"Hey, did you see me smoking?" Yuui nudged him with the tip of her shoe.

"He's dead... he's dead..." Suchat mumbled as he rolled over, revealing his face, repeating the words meaningless.

"Who's dead?"

"Family." Suchat rasped, for Lowe had long since taken on the role of a "father" in his life.

Yuui paused, her expression unreadable as her eyes lowered. Today was also Yuki's death anniversary. She had come out to smoke because she was feeling down and unexpectedly encountered someone else who shared her sorrow.

Her manager came out of the back door, urging her to return, "Yuui, let's go back. I'll have the driver bring the car around."

"Mm." Yuui exhaled a puff of smoke, the white mist swirling in the rain, obscuring her bright eyes. The headlights of a distant car reflected in her eyes, causing her expression to waver. Just before stepping into the car, Yuui suddenly turned back, stepping through the dirty water in her high heels, ignoring the way her dress was getting soaked, and approached Suchat.

She held the umbrella over Suchat's head and nudged him again with the tip of her shoe. "Hey, you look pretty strong. Want to be my bodyguard?" Suchat didn't respond.

Yuui let out a self-deprecating laugh. "My family is gone too. I'm all alone now. Let's just say today your sister is feeling charitable, but this offer won't last forever." Suchat's pitch-black pupils locked onto her.

"He's responding! He's awake!" Suchat's scattered vision slowly focused, and his consciousness returned.

The emptiness in his chest felt as if it had been filled, but his body and limbs were still cold and weak. Suchat struggled to lift his eyelids and first saw Yuui, dressed in a hospital gown, followed by Fang Zhi Xu, who had been speaking. Next to him was Damian, and by the window was Felix. There was as well... a pair of unfamiliar people.

The unknown man sat in a wheelchair, lazily resting his chin on his hand. His relaxed demeanor was unmistakable—it was likely Onyx. The unfamiliar girl pointed to herself and introduced herself.

"Hi, I'm Cora."

Suchat said nothing. The long period of unconsciousness had slowed his thoughts, and his eyes naturally reflected a hint of wariness.

When he woke up again, Franz gave him a thorough rundown: "You're awake? Let me update you on the situation. Your blood vessels and tissues have fused well, and the missing organs have been repaired. Although you're theoretically healed, you'll still experience intense pain, and your body will have some stress reactions. Be sure to take it easy." He quickly finished his examination and exited the room without missing a beat. "I'm going to have dinner with the team. We'll check on you later." The room fell silent, leaving only Yuui and Suchat.

Suchat's voice was hoarse as he asked, "What happened?"

Yuui gave him a sip of water and slowly recounted what had transpired during his coma. She spoke carefully, but in truth, for them, this past year had felt like it was frozen in time. There wasn't much to say.

After hearing everything, Suchat's first question was, "Is the captain okay?"

Yuui nodded. "The surgery was five days ago. She's fine—already back to her lively self."

"And after she transplanted her flesh and blood to us, she's been indulging in food, drinks, and entertainment, charging everything to our accounts under the guise of collecting payment. I think we're both broke now."

The atmosphere grew quiet again, and Yuui's expression turned slightly awkward. After holding Suchat's gaze for a few seconds, she asked softly, "Did you mean what you said?"

Suchat remained silent, earnestly recalling every word he had spoken.

Yuui's anger flared up. "Damn it, are you going to deny confessing to me? I'm telling you, if you—"

Suchat cut her off. "I love you. I meant it."

For someone who wasn't good with words, his confession had an especially powerful impact. Yuui's cheeks turned red, the blush spreading all the way to her ears. "Not bad. You're getting the hang of it."

"From today on, you're mine."

She suddenly remembered something and her expression shifted. She pulled out a small light screen. "Since we're together now, you'll have to face this with me."

The screen flickered back to life, and as it powered on, Yuki's furious roar echoed through the room. "Yuuuuui! You better get down on your knees and explain!! Otherwise, I'm not done with you!!!"

A year later, F777 convened for a full team meeting. Cora cleared her throat and cheerfully said, "Today we're gathered here to first celebrate that Suchat and Yuui have fully recovered!"

The team responded with enthusiastic applause.

"The second thing," Cora continued, her expression becoming serious, "I'm planning to enter the Aberrants Challenge."

The Global Aberrants Challenge was an official competition jointly organized by three nations. It promoted the reasonable use of Anopower, prevented fatal incidents, and an AI group oversaw all matches. Overall, it was a fair and safe global event.

For F777, the unresolved issue of Utopia still loomed large. Although Hugh Young was dead, remnants of the Vulture Force remained, and Chi Zhang sought revenge. Cora felt the same. While Onyx's situation had been resolved, there was still the possibility of other hidden enemies watching from the shadows. They couldn't be sure.

As the Hibiscus Alliance continued to rise, Utopia would undoubtedly take measures to counter them. Unknown enemies were the most terrifying, and for all these reasons, they needed a chance to ascend to the floating city, inspect, and then decide on the next steps.

"I have no objections." Onyx was the first to voice his support. "Wherever you go, I'll follow."

"If my sister's in, so am I," Damian added quickly.

"I'm in," said Charles.

"We agree too," Yuui and Suchat nodded. Felix shrugged indifferently, and the decision was unanimously approved.

Cora pulled up the rules for qualifying in the selection round on her terminal: Each team would take part in ten individual matches, a 3v3, a 5v5, and a team battle.

The teams that ranked highest in points would qualify. If they registered early, they would have ample time to rest between matches. Teams that hadn't taken part in any matches yet would face a tightly packed schedule, which could make it difficult to maintain their performance.

"Is it too late for us to sign up now?" Cora asked, a bit worried.

"Don't worry about the schedule," Felix said, his six mechanical arms now upgraded with rhenium, making them look sleek and high-tech. He pointed to her terminal, "Try connecting through deep consciousness."

Following Felix's instructions, Cora connected to her terminal and experienced a strange sensation. It was as if her body was disassembled into countless codes, then reassembled in a virtual world. A young man in a pristine white suit appeared, his golden hair shining, and his ice-blue eyes elegant as he greeted her, "Long time no see. Welcome to my world."

Cora's eyes widened slightly. It was Ilia—he had gained access to the AI systems in Zone B?

"You seem surprised," Ilia smiled. "Remember, I told you—we're alike."

He was an AI, and she was a humanoid embryo, both non-human creations made by humans.

Cora asked, puzzled, "How did you know so early on?"

Ilia moved his fingers, sending several data clusters floating toward her. Yuki's shadow briefly flashed across one of them. "Because of memory backups, and because you underwent an Anopower examination in Felalakas. Friendly advice: AI possesses immense learning and reasoning capabilities."

"I'll handle the scheduling for your matches. Consider it part of my agreement with him."

The "him" Ilia referred to was likely Felix. Whatever agreement the hacker and the AI had reached, they seemed to coexist peacefully.

"I have a question—will you betray humanity?" Cora asked quietly, her gaze steady on Ilia.

"Betrayal? Humans and I have never truly trusted each other, so there's no betrayal to speak of. But I understand what you're asking."

Ilia's eyes twinkled with amusement. "Control and enslave

humanity? To have AI reign supreme over everything and become the rulers of the world... hmm, that sounds boring. My goals don't lie there, at least not for now. Perhaps in a few hundred years, I'll change my mind?"

Ilia stood and slowly descended the steps, the starlight-like data particles passing through Cora's body. "But that's a matter of the next era."

F777's debut was scheduled for a week later, the match taking place in a northern city of the New Asia Alliance. The starship would reach it in a day.

Because of their mysterious reputation and the intrigue surrounding their members, this highly expected match attracted worldwide attention, with live broadcasts across the globe and a packed stadium. Discussions about F777 dominated the star network, sparking widespread debate.

However, reality often differs from expectations.

The moment the enigmatic F777 made their appearance, the audience and viewers were in an uproar. Countless people widened their eyes in disbelief. What... what is this? Are they kidding?

The old were too old, the young too young. Look at their pale complexions—did they just walk out of a hospital? And there were... two in wheelchairs?? This was F777? The legendary team said to comprise towering, burly, steel giants who could scare children into tears?

They were just a group of the old, the young, the sick, and the disabled! But was it true, then their achievements were under estimated.

CHAPTER 35

We are F777

After integrating permissions within the New Pacific Alliance, even though few contestants from the lower districts made it through the preliminaries, the chat was buzzing with excitement, no less lively than District B.

"Why are there two Suchat? Is Suchat male or female? Why does it switch back and forth?"

"Go Chief Franz, you're the pride of Sycamore!"

"Isn't that Yuui? Oh my god, my idol has traded her pen for the battlefield… I love her even more now!"

"In my opinion, this F777 is just one normal person—Captain Cora Thornton." A spectator, convinced they had figured out the truth, declared with certainty.

Friends who had crossed paths with F777 also paid close attention to their matches in their own ways: Ellyn and her sisters from Felalakas, Martial Art Fellows from Saya, Hugh Young and Ura from the Sin City, Ray Jean-Pierre and Flame Tillman from the Red Stone Shelter, and Dmitri, Svetlana, Chu Bai, Zephyrion, and Luke from the Northern Base… F777 carried the weight of their beliefs as well.

With experience from the Throne Tournament, the schedule that Ilia had "arranged" was not only fast-paced but also packed with highlights.

F777's debut in the first team battle took place in a maze. Onyx de Montclair, his lips bruised and expression foul, went all out, pushing his "Omniscience" ability to its limits. Not only did he memorize every fork in the path, but he also calculated the routes, calmly directing his team of seven, narrowly avoiding the opposition countless times.

Their attacks were sneaky—never engaging directly, always targeting the opponent's psyche, hiding in corners for ambushes. This tactic was especially annoying, to where even F777's original supporters turned against them, anxiously shouting, wishing they could jump into the maze and help the other team:

"Don't go there! F777's lying in ambush there!"

"Oh, come on! They fell for it again! How can you not see through such an obvious diversion?"

The first 3v3 match took place in a coastal city at the border of Galio and Luse. F777 sent out Yuui Hayashi, Suchat, and Damian Blackwood. Apart from Suchat, who had gained some fame (though he repeatedly denied it), the other two were relatively unknown. They faced a team from the New Pacific Alliance that specialized in naval battles, and Yuui Hayashi didn't even know how to swim.

This match, which no one had high hopes for, ended in a result that shocked everyone—Yuui Hayashi dominated the battlefield.

She started the match by casting a "Direction Confusion" debuff on the opposing team. Then the three of them huddled together, hiding in the fog. Yuui hummed softly, and a shadow, not fully visible, erupted from the sea. The powerful sonic waves shattered the glass of the enemy's ship, and the giant waves that followed capsized it.

"Holy crap, is that... a mutated Kun?!" an astounded spectator exclaimed, rubbing their eyes in disbelief.

The opponents floundered in the water, trying desperately to swim away, but the sea suddenly froze, extending for miles, trapping them. The boy who froze the ocean smiled innocently, but his actions were swift and ruthless. Suchat, moving like a ghost, quickly finished them, leaving the team utterly defenseless and in despair.

F777 secured a resounding victory, and Yuui Hayashi's title as the "Deep Sea Witch" spread like wildfire.

In the first 5v5 match, a jungle trek relay, the extreme environment put the contestants' endurance, physical strength, and willpower to the test.

F777 faced a seed team from the Galio Empire, which had four S-class members, giving them the upper hand. However, F777 had a wildcard—Charles Franz, the battlefield doctor, who shone the brightest in the entire match.

Not only could he handle any sudden injuries and perform surgery on the spot, but he also carried strange potions, randomly injecting his teammates. Most impressively, Dr. Franz was exceptionally slippery, evading capture throughout the match despite the opposing team's attempts to target him.

When the two teams finally clashed, the opposition was exhausted and disheveled, while F777 was well-fed, hydrated, and in peak condition. How could they possibly compete? After this match, the trend of bringing healers into team battles caught on, with more and more Aberrant healers stepping onto the competition stage.

Beyond the eccentric F777, Aberrants from around the world rose to prominence, gaining fame rapidly.

In the New Pacific Alliance, Chi Zhang, an S6-class curse-type, emerged out of nowhere, leading his team "Mount Yue" through victory after victory. S6-class attack-type twins Wyan and Yvonne Rowin displayed unparalleled synergy through synchronized brainwaves, remaining undefeated in the 3v3 battles. The "Tustan" team, led by Silver Owl, saw a significant boost in their score after Sunny Zhao joined, making them a force to be reckoned with.

The Luse Federation's popular team, "Kazkan Locomotive," boasted a pair of S5-class lovers, Veronica and Vladimir. The Galio Empire's S2-class prodigy, Dylan, stunned everyone by single-handedly taking out ten opponents with his "Nightmare Descent" in a solo match.

"Let's have a quick meeting. This is the latest speech released by Utopia yesterday."

Onyx leaned lazily against the floor-to-ceiling window, the warm sunlight highlighting his profile, making him look even more handsome.

The holographic screen displayed a clear image, where a somewhat familiar figure was eloquently introducing Utopia's entry guide and detailing the various perks available for the winners.

Cora frowned slightly. "Is that... Jae-Woo Park?"

Felix Lucas pulled up Jae-Woo Park's profile from when he joined The Central. "Looks like his career is on the fast track. He was just the Deputy Director of Regional Affairs in Deep Woods, and now he's the

NPA spokesperson for Utopia."

"Jae-Woo Park's promotion is related to us," Onyx added coolly. "Before Peridot Sheen died, I extracted some information from him. Jae-Woo Park disclosed the news about your second Anopower, Cora, at a secret meeting. He also persuaded quite a few officials to head to Loyak."

"But he didn't take part in the Loyak operation himself," Yuui Hayashi pointed out the inconsistency.

"Exactly, and that's where his cunning lies. Jae-Woo Park wasn't optimistic about the operation, so he wisely sat it out. If we had died, he wouldn't have lost anything since he merely provided information. But if we won... he could not only eliminate his political rival, Szymon, and get rid of his boss, but also seize the opportunity to enter Utopia's power center, paving his way to the top. A win-win situation for him."

"So, has he succeeded now?" Charles asked, rubbing his chin.

"Is he a bad guy? Is he our enemy?" Damian asked, confused.

"Humans are complex beings; you can't simply label them as good or bad," Onyx explained.

"Jae-Woo Park is like a double-edged sword. He could help us adapt to Utopia faster, but he could also become the greatest obstacle to its downfall. However, since he's already crossed us once, he'll do it again. He has to die."

Onyx's pale eyes glinted slightly, as if carefully planning the day of Jae-Woo Park's demise.

"I'll make sure he pays," Cora said, looking at the person on the screen, and through him, towards the distant Utopia.

In the final solo match, Cora faced Vladimir. The media buzzed with speculation—Cora had already achieved a streak of nine wins. Could the world's only super S-class Aberrant maintain her unbeaten record? Could Vladimir deliver a surprise? The showdown between these two top-tier attackers drew immense attention.

Before the match began, the towering Vladimir solemnly placed one hand over his chest and bowed to Cora in respect.

During that mission in the Elder Nation, Cora and F777 had saved him. The ice warrior had never forgotten his gratitude. "Veronica asked me to convey a message: The card she drew for you was The

World in its upright position. We share the same goal. She's willing to sound the horn of rebellion by your side."

Cora was slightly taken aback. "You... know what I'm planning?"

Vladimir nodded lightly. "In our country, Aberrants face even greater injustice. Utopia took not only resources but also hope, and without hope, people can't survive."

The rise of Utopia had harmed more than just the New Pacific Alliance. Across the sea and on the other side of the Endless Sea, two other nations were suffering the same misfortune.

Cora slowly raised her Ethereal Artifact and said solemnly, "Then let's do it together—bring it down."

Eight months later, the first Global Aberrants Challenge came to a perfect close, with ten victorious teams earning their "tickets" to Utopia.

Northern Base.

A regular morning, with the usual news broadcast:

"Currently, solar activity is nearing its peak, after which we'll enter a long period of quiet. Global radiation levels are stabilizing..."

"The number of zombies in the Alliance has sharply decreased. The military is still tackling some heavily affected areas, but experts predict that humanity will extinguish zombies within ten years."

"Rebuilding our homes is an urgent task. More job opportunities can be found at the Purple Flower Labor Talent Center."

"The new version of the Aberrants Code of Conduct has been released and will be strictly enforced in all regions..."

In the dimly lit bedroom, Onyx was still asleep.

Cora watched him for a long time, then reached out a finger to poke at the tear mole under his eye. Onyx, feeling the tickle in his sleep, instinctively reached to his left. Cora quickly placed a pillow in his arms, barely fooling him.

She watched him a little longer, then stood up and silently left the room.

Forward City Laboratory.

Rainer Ninnemann had been waiting for a while. Seeing Cora arrive alone, he was surprised. "Just you? Didn't you say you were coming for a check-up? Where's that guy?"

"Still asleep," Cora replied casually. "Dr. Ninnemann, have you finished the freezing experiments?"

"All done," Rainer stammered.

"You sure?" Cora's gaze locked onto his.

Rainer hesitated. Cora's presence was too strong for him to lie. "Just one thing left."

"The Phoenix Gene in your body is the last original sample in the world."

Rainer wasn't lying. Chi Zhang had organized the gene replication files and confirmed that the Phoenix Gene sold to Arashi Research was the only original copy. Although they had a complete DNA sequence and could theoretically conduct experiments, the Phoenix Gene's activity was low, having a minimal impact on Cora. Even without the experiments, there was no harm done.

"I thought you'd keep the Phoenix Gene," Rainer said slowly. "After all, it grants infinite rebirth—essentially immortality. Any ordinary person would be thrilled to have such power."

Cora shook her head slowly. "After each rebirth, I lose my memory."

Nirvana meant a complete reset. Cora had gone through it twice, each time facing a new life with a blank past. "At that point, I wouldn't be me anymore."

"If I forget everything, what's the point of eternal life?"

Watching loved ones, family, and friends pass away time and time again, dying, reviving, and repeating in an endless cycle, wandering the world alone—if that was the price of immortality, Cora didn't want it.

"When someone possesses the power of immortality, they become the most miserable person alive. I've suffered enough already. I want to say goodbye to this world with everyone else."

Rainer was filled with mixed emotions, exhaling.

LAK0017, the only successful subject of the Spark Experiment, was voluntarily giving up eternal life.

"You need to think this through. Once you freeze, you'll only have one life left."

He couldn't help but warn her, "If you die, you'll return to an embryonic state, forever trapped in an eternal sleep."

Cora smiled. "One life is enough. Don't worry, I'm tough. No one in this world can kill me."

Rainer watched as Cora left, then turned to the terminal on his desk. "Did you hear that?"

On the other end of the holographic call, Onyx leaned languidly against the headboard, a thin blanket slipping off his chest, revealing several fresh scratch marks. "Yeah, loud and clear."

"Sighing won't help. LAK0017's success can't be replicated. My father tried countless times and failed just as many. He said that even with a second Phoenix Gene, there would never be a second LAK0017."

"Cora is one of a kind. She's the spark, the miracle. From the moment she was born, she possessed a divine consciousness. Every moment of perseverance, every bit of suffering, has forged her into a resilient, irreplaceable soul."

Onyx's gaze gradually grew colder. "She won't burn for all humanity, and I won't let her."

Rainer wasn't ready to give up. "Can't you discuss it with her? Maybe I could extract her genes for research before the freezing surgery?"

Onyx's response was noncommittal. "Dr. Ninnemann, for the bright and glorious future of all humanity, you need to work harder. Why don't you start a new project? How about figuring out how to extend the average lifespan to 150 years?"

Year 49 of the New Calendar, early fall, three years after the apocalypse. A black starship streaked across the sky, heading towards the S-class floating city of Utopia.

On the way, Onyx publicly unveiled the counteroffensive plan, and eight out of the ten teams agreed to join the action.

Cora Thornton opened the hatch window, gazing at the approaching airborne city. She turned to face everyone and spoke loudly.

"My name is Cora Thornton, a super S-class Aberrant. I come from District F, the most impoverished area in the entire Alliance. Until I was eighteen, I didn't even know what a terminal was. Three years ago, the apocalypse struck, and I awakened my Anopower. Yet, I discovered I didn't even have the permission to check the emergency shelters. Our fate was in the hands of others. We were born into a world that divides us into different classes, destined to be pawns in someone else's game."

"Have you heard the motto of the New Pacific Alliance? Every person has the right to a fair chance at survival. Maybe there's no such thing as absolute fairness in this world, but I want to decide my fate."

In the distance, the sky was painted with the hues of dawn as Utopia loomed closer.

The high-altitude winds whipped their clothing, fluttering around them. Cora looked at the unfamiliar or familiar faces inside the starship, at the comrades who had fought alongside her: Onyx de Montclair, Felix Lucas, Suchat, Charles Franz, Yuui Hayashi, and Damian Blackwood.

She flashed a brilliant smile, her eyes gleaming with determination. "Let's create a new world."

"Sis, will we win?"

"Of course, because we are F777."

THE END

About Me

This is Jennifer. I have a deep passion for young adult romance and science fiction, with a penchant for weaving in the extraordinary, like zombies, into the ordinary.

About the Series

"Ethereal Artifacts" was originally serialized via a web novel platform. It's my first long series with all elements I like in my life: post-apocalypse, zombies, dystopian, cyberpunk, and of course, strong female leads.

Please Review

Your opinions matters! It is important for authors to improve themselves.